"WHERE ARE YOU TAKING ME? TO THE GALLOWS?" SHE ASKED.

"You need to stop talking that way. I've never met anyone so ready to die," the dragon complained.

"I am always ready to die. At any time."

He stopped. "Why?"

"Why what?"

A female who had dark hair and eyes like the fool before her stepped in. "I'll let them know you're bringing her." Then she ran off laughing.

The dragon gave a short snarl before facing Elina. "Why do you *want* to die?"

"I have no desire to die."

"Then why do you seem so ready for it?"

"To die with honor. If you cannot avoid death, then you must die with honor. Do you not plan to die with honor, dragon?"

"No," he said plainly, dark eyes staring at her. "I plan to fight death all the way, dragging those trying to kill me along for the ride."

"I would agree with you, dragon . . . except I am guilty of trying to kill your queen."

"But you didn't do a very good job. Perhaps if you were better at it, I'd feel more inclined to take your head myself. But at this point, it would feel like stepping on a squirrel. Annoying. Sad. And a little messy."

D0980574

More Dragon Kin novels from G.A. Aiken

DRAGON ACTUALLY

ABOUT A DRAGON

WHAT A DRAGON SHOULD KNOW

LAST DRAGON STANDING

THE DRAGON WHO LOVED ME

HOW TO DRIVE A DRAGON CRAZY

A TALE OF TWO DRAGONS (eBook novella)

Published by Kensington Publishing Corporation

LIGHT
MY FIRE

G.A. AIKEN

WITHDRAWN

ZEBRA BOOKS
KENSINGTON PUBLISHING CORP.
http://www.kensingtonbooks.com

ZEBRA BOOKS are published by

Kensington Publishing Corp.
119 West 40th Street
New York, NY 10018

Copyright © 2014 by G.A. Aiken

All rights reserved. No part of this book may be reproduced in any form or by any means without the prior written consent of the Publisher, excepting brief quotes used in reviews.

If you purchased this book without a cover you should be aware that this book is stolen property. It was reported as "unsold and destroyed" to the Publisher and neither the Author nor the Publisher has received any payment for this "stripped book."

All Kensington titles, imprints and distributed lines are available at special quantity discounts for bulk purchases for sales promotion, premiums, fund-raising, educational or institutional use.

Special book excerpts or customized printings can also be created to fit specific needs. For details, write or phone the office of the Kensington Special Sales Manager. Attn.: Special Sales Department. Kensington Publishing Corp., 119 West 40th Street, New York, NY 10018. Phone: 1-800-221-2647.

Zebra and the Z logo Reg. U.S. Pat. & TM Off.

First Printing: December 2014
ISBN-13: 978-1-4201-3159-8
ISBN-10: 1-4201-3159-1

First Electronic Edition: December 2014
eISBN-13: 978-1-4201-3160-4
eISBN-10: 1-4201-3160-5

10 9 8 7 6 5 4 3 2 1

Printed in the United States of America

For you, Ma

Chapter One

Elina Shestakova of the Black Bear Riders of the Midnight Mountains of Despair in the Far Reaches of the Steppes of the Outerplains—or just Elina for those who are lazy—carefully made her way up the mountain toward her destiny.

It was, of course, not a destiny she wanted for herself. This had not been her plan for her life. But she didn't have a choice, did she? The leader of her tribe, Glebovicha, had ordered her to take on this task. Glebovicha had said it was to help Elina get a reputation she could be proud of among their tribe. Even, perhaps, all the Tribes of the Steppes that were under the rule of the Anne Atli herself. But Elina had no delusions about any of this.

Her life was over no matter which choice she made, so she might as well string this pathetic existence out as long as she could manage. And who knew? Perhaps the end would be quicker and much less painful than if she'd told Glebovicha to go to hell with her ridiculous task.

So Elina continued to climb that mountain. Devenallt Mountain, it was called. Deep in the heart of Southland territory. Said to be the mountain home of the Southland dragons' feared queen.

It was a big, imposing place, but Elina had been taught to climb bigger mountains from the time she could stand. Her people, the Daughters of the Steppes, or as others called them, Terrors of the Outerplains, were a war-loving people. At one time, the Steppes had been broken into random territories of always-fighting marauders. It had been a nasty way to live, and the females of those tribes had ended up on the worst end of it all, often ripped from one tribe to another, forced to leave their children and families behind so they could be the concubines of some male they didn't know.

Then, four, maybe five, thousand years ago, a female warrior named Anne Atli had been born. The first Captain of the Riders, she'd had a way with horses, and she'd possessed skills with weaponry that put her above all others. She eventually took all the power, destroying any who challenged her. And she did it again and again until finally, she united the tribes under her banner and turned the attention of the warriors from each other, to those who attacked the Steppes to raid and plunder.

Since then, the Daughters of the Steppes had ruled the land and the Anne Atli, Mother of the Steppes Riders, ruled them all. It was a title and name that was not given to the next in line by birth, but to the one willing to take it for her own and keep it while still honoring the woman who had begun it all.

Of course, Elina was not willing to take anything. She'd never be willing. She had no interest in ruling the Steppes. She had no interest in being a warrior. But each of the tribes under Anne Atli's banner still cared about its individual reputation, and "having you around, doing nothing," Glebovicha had told Elina, made the rest of their tribe look weak. Something Elina doubted considering Glebovicha's personal reputation. She was a feared tribal leader, and Elina was one of many in the tribe. But Glebovicha hated her. Violently, it seemed. So she'd sent Elina off to challenge and kill the one they called the White Dragon Queen.

So here Elina was now . . . climbing a mountain very like the big ones that surrounded the Steppes. Those, it was said, had dragons in them, too, but Elina had never met one. In truth, she'd be happy never to meet a dragon. She could have gone her entire life having never met a dragon and been quite happy about it.

That was no longer an option, though. So she climbed. And she kept climbing. For days. Even setting up a tent against the mountainside at night so she could sleep. Thankfully, she did not turn in her sleep. That would have been . . . unfortunate.

On the fifth day, Elina finally reached the top of Devenallt Mountain. She pulled herself up over the final rock face and stayed on her knees, taking in deep breaths as she thanked whatever horse god might be listening.

It was bright out. Midday. So that big, dark shadow that slowly covered her was a bit . . . off-putting. She hoped it was a cloud. A big, nightmarish cloud that foretold a horrible storm. But she knew . . . she knew it was no cloud that covered her.

Shoulders sagging, she looked behind her.

It was big. So very big. And black like the diamonds from the Steppes dwarf mines. All of it black. Its scales. Its talons. Its eyes. Its long mane. All except its fangs. They were quite white . . . brilliantly so.

They stared at each other for what felt like forever. Then, it finally spoke. Spoke like a man.

"What are you doing here?" it asked.

Elina tried not to show her surprise. She'd been raised to believe that all dragons were nothing better than animals. Like a jungle cat or a bear. Just bigger and able to breathe fire—so definitely to be avoided. But this one wasn't some mindless animal. He spoke the common language with a Southland lilt. She'd met quite a few Southlanders as she'd traveled through the territories of these decadent and lazy people. Yes, he spoke just like the human male South-landers.

Elina slowly got to her feet and faced the dragon.

"I've come to kill the White Dragon Queen," Elina announced, struggling to speak in a language that was not her own.

The dragon blinked, a few times. "Really?" he finally asked.

"Really."

"Huh," he said after a few seconds, then slowly turned and began to walk away as silently as he'd come. Elina was surprised. Perhaps the Dragon Queen's subjects weren't as loyal as her people thought. Perhaps they wanted this queen dead. Well, it didn't really matter to Elina. She had a task to die trying to do. Not a positive thought but, sadly, an accurate one.

So Elina secured her traveling pack on her shoulders and picked up her spear. And that was when the dragon's long black tail suddenly whipped out and wrapped itself around her waist, pinning her arms to her body.

Shocked, Elina didn't even yell, didn't fight, though the spear was still clutched in her hand. And the dragon walked on with Elina securely tucked into his tail . . . and he was humming.

She had to admit, she found the humming annoying.

Celyn the Charming of the Cadwaladr Clan loved his job! As far as he was concerned, he had the best job in the queendom.

Though he'd admit, his siblings mocked him. While they went off to battle, spending months in muck and killing every bloody thing, every bloody day, Celyn was one of Her Majesty's Personal Guards. He trained every day just like his siblings. Lived the life of a military dragon just like his siblings. And he killed when necessary—unlike his siblings, who killed whenever they felt like it.

And yet few of them took Celyn seriously because he wasn't face-first in the blood and brains of a battle. But he didn't need to be. Because he had the best job ever!

He glanced back at the human female he had trapped with his tail. He hadn't seen a human who looked like her before. Such interesting features. Long, white-blond hair that reached down her back and framed an oval face. Pale skin covered razor-sharp cheekbones beneath bright, *bright* blue eyes that were narrow like a house cat's. Full pink lips and a cleft chin rounded out that face. She was definitely someone Celyn would take the time to chat up if he'd met her at the local pub. But he hadn't. Instead, she'd been at the top of Devenallt Mountain. The *queen's* mountain.

Devenallt Mountain was the seat of power of the Southland Dragon Queen, Rhiannon the White, and the only humans who came here were ones who were invited by Her Majesty or were brought here to be eaten. A practice they'd stopped when the queen's offspring—and Celyn's royal cousins—began mating with humans. To the queen, it seemed tacky to eat the brethren of those her children loved. Celyn, however, didn't have a preference. He was just as happy with a good cow, and there was always more meat on those bones anyway.

Still, having a human show up and openly admit she was there to kill the queen . . . that was unusual. But Celyn liked unusual.

Celyn had known the woman was climbing the mountains for days. All the guards had. It was their job to protect the queen, and that meant knowing who was in the queen's territory at all times. Yet after she hadn't fallen to her death the first day, all the guards had wanted to see how far the human would get. They had bets going. Celyn had been certain, though, that she'd make it as soon as he'd watched her set up that tent against the mountainside and spend her first night there—so they'd left her alone . . . and waited. He had been on duty when she'd reached the top, so he'd confronted her first. Softly. No need to blast her with flames or unleash a roar of rage to make her piss herself. He left that sort of thing to his siblings. Celyn preferred a gentler approach.

Yet he'd never expected her to *admit* that she was here to kill his queen. Again, his siblings would have killed her right then. But Celyn knew his queen. She was his aunt-by-mating and they amused each other. She loved to be entertained.

And he was very certain this woman was going to be the best entertainment his queen got today.

The White Dragon Queen sat on her stone throne, her massive head resting on the talons of her left claw, the elbow of her forearm resting against the arm of the stone throne she sat upon. One talon on her right claw tapped against the other arm of the throne. Her excessively long tail snaked around the back of the throne to the front, where the tip tapped against the stone floor in time with the talon on her right claw.

Studying Elina, the queen finally asked, "Could you . . . repeat that?"

Elina blew out a breath and gripped her spear a little tighter. The spear the black dragon had allowed her to keep. She'd thought he was being foolish until she'd seen the size of the Dragon Queen . . . and all the other dragons standing around her court . . . staring. Gods, Elina had never seen beings so big before—or known there were so many.

"I am here to . . ." She cleared her throat. ". . . take your life, queen of the dragons, and bring your head back to my noble people."

The white dragoness nodded slowly. "Aye. That's what I *thought* you said."

A deadly silence followed, and Elina prepared herself to meet with her ancestors on the other side. But then one of the old dragons standing behind the queen suddenly snorted. And once he snorted, the rest of the dragons burst into hysterical laughter, while the Dragon Queen waved at the old dragon behind her.

"Elder Clesek!" she said around her incessant giggles.

"I'm sorry, my queen. I just . . . I can't . . ." He burst into further laughter and the rest of the Queen's Court laughed with him.

Elina glanced behind her, but the black dragon who'd brought her in was gone. After a whispered conversation with the queen, he'd deserted Elina. Not that she blamed him. Perhaps he didn't want to view her messy death.

"My dearest girl," the queen said around the others' laughter, "who hates you so much that they'd send you here . . . to face *me*?"

"It is a quest of honor."

"One you thought of yourself?" she asked. And when Elina did not answer, the queen nodded. "If you'd thought of all this yourself, it would have been bloody stupid. But for someone to send you to me? It's just cruel. Someone clearly wants you dead."

Elina sighed. "This I know."

"Then why did you come here? Why did you not run? Start a new life somewhere else?"

"I am Daughter of Steppes," she replied, automatically knowing she wasn't getting the Southlander language quite right. They seemed to use too many words; it was hard to remember all that needed to be there.

"I do not run," Elina went on. "If I am to meet my death at your claw, then I will meet my death."

"Daughter of the Steppes? You are from the Outerplains?"

"I am."

"The Rider tribes that raid the valley territories of the

Northlands, Quintilian Provinces, and Annaig Valley. Your people are greatly feared. Tell me, little human, what is your name?"

"I am Elina Shestakova of the Black Bear Tribe of the Midnight Mountains of Despair in the Far Reaches of the Steppes of the Outerplains."

The queen blinked several times before she asked, "That entire thing is your *name*?"

"It was one I was given at birth."

"Kind of cursed coming and going, weren't you, sweetness?"

The old dragon leaned forward and said, "My lady, perhaps we should end this quickly rather than drawing it out unnecessarily, now that we know the truth of her situation."

The queen looked at the dragon. "Whatever do you mean?"

"It seems cruel to toy with her."

The queen frowned, shocking Elina with her ability to show emotion despite all those scales. The queen looked over her court, her expression now confused. Finally, she exclaimed, "Wait . . . do you all think I plan to eat her?"

The old dragon behind the queen gave the smallest of shrugs. "Don't you?"

"No! I don't do that anymore. It seems unacceptable . . . with the grandchildren and all. Besides . . . look at the poor thing." And they all did. The size of the dragons was harrowing enough, but really it was the expressions of pity that had Elina's stomach curdling in horror. It shouldn't, though. She often received that same expression from other tribe members.

"You poor, poor thing," the queen said again.

The black dragon who'd brought Elina here suddenly returned, barely glancing at her as he passed. It was the same way Elina glanced at a mouse that ran past her in the woods outside the tribes' territories.

"My queen," the black dragon began, his voice low, "you wanted me to let you know when Lord Bercelak was nearing the mountain."

"Yes, yes. We'll have to get her someplace safe."

The black dragon glanced again at Elina and back at the queen. "Someplace safe?"

"Aye. And we must keep this information away from Bercelak."

The black dragon shook his head. "No."

"I am your queen."

"Yes. But you adore me. Your Bercelak . . . not so much. And he hits."

"Oh, honestly! Are you afraid of your own uncle?"

"Yes! I am. Hence the whining in my voice."

"Take her, Celyn. Someplace safe."

"Auntie—"

"Don't auntie me, Celyn the Charming! And how did you even get that name? You clearly don't deserve it!"

"You gave it to me."

"That was obviously a mistake on my part."

"You never make mistakes, my queen. You told me that yourself."

Slowly, the queen looked over at the black dragon and, in return, he slowly grinned, flashing a number of exceptionally large fangs. The largest fangs Elina had ever had the misfortune of seeing.

"Take her," the queen ordered, "someplace safe. And do it before I am forced to get my ass off this throne so that I can throttle you *to death!*"

The black dragon gave a small bow. "As you command, my queen."

"Oh, stop it, Celyn."

She heard the black dragon chuckle, his big body slowly turning. He studied Elina a moment, then walked off. After he passed, Elina looked down in time to see his tail circling her waist.

"Not—" was all she managed to get out before his tail lifted her up and carried her out of a side exit to the chamber. As they moved, Elina could hear the queen call out, "Bercelak, my love! I'm so glad you're home!"

"Why," another low voice demanded from the queen's throne room, "do you all look guilty? What are you hiding from me, Rhiannon?"

Celyn landed outside Garbhán Isle, the seat of power of the *human* Southland queen. He dropped the female he held in his tail and shifted to human. He glanced back at the woman and warned, "Don't try to run away."

"Run away?" she repeated in that thick Outerplains accent. "Run away to where, dragon? You cannot outrun failure. Disappointment. Misery. So why even try?"

Celyn, reaching for a set of clothes that was left outside the city for the many dragons coming and going, paused for a moment, again glancing back at the human female. "You're a fun, perky girl, aren't you?" he joked.

She shrugged. "I am known as annoyingly cheery among my tribe. A curse I cannot escape."

Unwilling to even think too much on that bit of information, Celyn quickly pulled on chain-mail leggings, a chain-mail shirt, and leather boots. Once dressed, he took the spear from the woman's hand and tossed it on the pile of other weapons. Then he grabbed hold of the woman's arm and led her past the city gates. The guards nodded at him and he nodded back.

"So," she suddenly asked, "will my execution be long and painful or quick and brutal?"

"If the queen had wanted you executed, she would have done it herself. You live because of her good graces."

"She is not what I expected," the woman admitted.

"What did you expect?"

The woman shrugged. "A slobbering beast of lizard that deserved to die a thousand deaths. Instead . . . she was quite pleasant."

Celyn grunted. "So sorry we disappointed you."

She patted the hand holding her. "Not your fault."

Celyn stopped walking and faced her. He was about to explain to her how insulting she was being when something about her struck him and he guessed, "You didn't want to do this . . . did you?"

She quickly looked away from his question before finally saying, "Does that matter? I was given task and I failed task. I failed tribe. Do your worst to me."

Rolling his eyes, "Lady Misery, get off the pyre. . . . We need the wood."

"What do you mean?" she asked as they headed down the street.

"It means stop feeling sorry for yourself. Clearly someone sent you here to die. That should make you angry. *I'd* be angry."

"First, dragon, I do not feel sorry for myself. I failed and if I must die for that failure—so be it. That is the way of things. And second," she continued, getting testy, "do not act like you are better than us." He thought she meant dragons versus humans, but no. That wasn't what she meant. "You are lazy, decadent Southlanders, living off the poor as only imperialist scum can do. And," she went on, pointing a finger, "I know you think I am weak because I am woman. But I am Daughter of Steppes. Not some needy, useless Southland female begging for man to take care of her. I can at least say I am stronger than *that*."

Celyn laughed. "Aye. That's *definitely* the problem. South-land females are *so* very weak. All I know are weak females. Oh, how they disgust me! The weak Southland females."

"What I thought," she sniffed.

The black dragon pulled her into the city jail. Her people didn't have "jails" or prisons. It didn't make sense to keep someone around or alive once tribe law was broken. So they never did. But the Southlanders were big believers in prisons . . . and dungeons.

Elina felt confident that prison was preferable to a dungeon. She didn't like the idea of being placed in an underground cage. It would be too much like being buried alive.

The dragon stopped in front of a poorly made wooden desk. The large man behind it got to his stubby legs, the keys at his side clanking.

"My lord," the man said, nodding at the dragon.

"Constable. I need to stow this woman here."

"Here?" He glanced around. "Is she guilty of some-thing?"

"Besides wearing on my nerves . . . yes. But you will not mention her presence to anyone. Especially Lord Fearghus or Briec. Understand?"

"Well . . . ?"

"*Understand?*"

"Aye."

"Good. You'll keep her here and you'll keep her safe. I'm sure you understand what I mean."

"Yes. Of course, my lord."

"Good." He placed his hand against Elina's back and shoved her toward the constable. "Someone," he muttered to Elina, "will be around to move you at some point."

Elina turned to ask when that might be, but only managed to catch a glimpse of the dragon and his long, black hair disappearing out the door. And she had the uneasy feeling she'd never see him again.

"This way, miss," the constable said kindly.

With a sigh, Elina followed the constable until they reached a cell. He unlocked the door and Elina stepped inside.

It wasn't much of a cell, with only a small bed, a desk, a weak-looking chair, and a chamber pot. But there was a window with bars, and the room appeared mostly vermin-free. And since Elina normally lived in a tent with eight of her sisters . . . this was actually better than what she was used to.

Sitting on the bed, Elina looked up at the constable, nodded. "Thank you."

"Of course." He glanced around. "Is there anything you may need? Something to read, perhaps?"

"That would be nice."

"All right. And you just let me know if there's something else."

He walked out, closing the door, but only until it just touched the frame. He didn't close it all the way. Maybe he was hoping Elina would make a run for it. But a run for where? Back to the mountains of the Outerplains so her tribe could look upon her in disgust and disappointment? Since she'd been seeing that expression for most of her life from most of her tribe except one sister, Kachka, it would be kind of nice to have a break from it for a little while. Besides . . . how long before these Southlanders sent her on her way? Not long, she was sure.

So Elina settled on her bunk, her back against the wall, and she thought about taking a nap.

Chapter Two

Season of the Goddess 195,202

They rode up to our blessed temple at midday. Led by the City Guard, the pair rode on two enormous war horses. Even if they were not riding into battle, those horses were desperately needed. Especially for the male. I'd heard he was not human, but a dragon in its human form. It showed. He was so huge! Then again, so was this woman. Not as large as the male but large. Muscular. Maybe even a little, dare I say . . . manly?

I watched as the group of six walked up the many stairs to our main doors. The dragon was pale as any Northman. So very white with actual blue hair. The woman with him was clearly a descendant of our Desert Lands, but she still didn't seem to belong here.

They reached the top step and the City Guard commander gave a small bow. "Good day to you, Sister. We're here to see Elder Elisa."

"Elder Elisa is unavailable, but Elder Haldane is waiting for you inside," *I said.*

The warrior woman rolled light brown eyes and without even looking, the dragon growled at her, "Stop it."

"It's not like they didn't know we were coming to see Rhian," *she snapped back.*

"Stop. It."

The City Guard smirked behind her helmet with the nose guard. *"Please, lead the way, Sister."*

So I did. And quickly! I did not want this warrior woman any more upset than she already was.

Dressed as any hardened warrior in chain mail from head to foot, weapons of all kinds attached to the belt around her waist and across her back, she was clearly not a person one should challenge.

Luckily, Elder Haldane waited for us not too far in. I was so relieved to see her! But I could tell by the look on her face she was in one of her less-than-cooperative moods. I wanted to shake her. *"Just give them what they want!"* I wanted to scream.

We stopped in front of Elder Haldane, but before I could properly introduce everyone, the warrior woman threw her arms open and exclaimed, "Grandmother!" Then she hugged Elder Haldane! Hugged her! And I knew she was doing it on purpose. Simply to irritate the one woman who could turn the pair into the bears they both resembled.

"Get off me!" Elder Haldane finally snapped, pushing the warrior woman away.

"You've missed me, haven't you?" the woman taunted, grinning. Oh, goddess, she was clearly enjoying her little *"joke"* on Elder Haldane. Nearly as much as Haldane was not enjoying this joke.

"They are here to see Sister Rhianwen," I quickly explained, hoping to keep this all as civil as possible.

"Perhaps another time," Elder Haldane said, sounding bored and put-upon. *"We're quite busy here with the winter solstice coming up. I'm sure you understand."*

But as I watched, the warrior woman's face slowly stopped smiling and such a dark look came over her that I, along with everyone else, knew she did not in any way understand. Nor was she about to start understanding.

The male saw all that right away, quickly stepping

between Elder Haldane and the warrior woman, his gaze focused on Haldane.

"We understand you're busy, my lady," he said in a shockingly low voice, his silver eyes suggesting a much more caring soul than his companion. "But it's been such a long time since we've seen my niece. Just a few minutes and then we can arrange another, better time for a proper meeting. You do understand, don't you?"

Elder Haldane sucked her tongue against her teeth in that way she has and, dear goddess, I thought it would get ugly there, but no . . .

Thankfully Elder Haldane was swayed by the dragon's soft words and with a curt, "Oh, come along then," she led the way to Sister Rhianwen's room.

I ran up ahead to open the door myself. As one of Elder Haldane's assistants, it's been the only job she will give me at the moment. And, yes, I'm still trying hard not to be insulted by that.

I arrived at Sister Rhianwen's room first and knocked on the door. "Sister Rhianwen?" I called out. "You have visitors."

I didn't wait for an answer, but instead opened the door and held it. That's when I saw that poor Sister Rhianwen. . . . She was . . . she was being dragged! That's the only way I can describe it. Dragged from this world into another. An arm coming out of some portal had hold of her wrist and was pulling Sister Rhianwen into it!

"Elder Haldane!" I screamed and the small group rushed to the door in time to see poor Sister Rhianwen turn toward them.

"Izzy!" Sister Rhianwen called out, her face filled with shock. "Gods, Izzy! Don't tell Mum!"

"Rhi!" the warrior woman bellowed, pushing past everyone and charging into the room. "Rhi!"

She reached for Sister Rhianwen, but after a good pull and one more yelled, "Just don't tell Mum!" the mysterious arm yanked my coven sister out of this world and into some other.

The warrior woman tried to follow, but the portal slammed shut before she could reach it, leaving her standing there, her back and shoulders heaving from her exertions. She'd only gone a few feet into the room, but it was like she'd run miles.

Elder Haldane, never one I would turn to for comfort, simply folded her arms across her chest and asked with great annoyance, "You couldn't have moved a little faster, you useless girl?"

It was not a good or smart thing to say.

The warrior woman looked over her shoulder at Haldane and before I could take a breath, she was suddenly right in front of her, big hand reaching for Haldane's throat. But the dragon was so very fast for such a large beast, he caught hold of the warrior woman by the waist and dragged her back.

"Izzy, no!"

"I should have killed her years ago. I should kill her now!"

"You can try," *Haldane said.* "And I remember quite well that my magicks cannot hurt you." *She pointed at the dragon.* "But I can hurt him. I can tear the scales from his back and make my own armor."

At Haldane's words, the warrior woman exploded, nearly getting away from the dragon who held her. I knew he was strong even in his human body, but gods. This woman. Her strength was . . . terrifying.

"I will kill everyone here!" *the warrior bellowed, shaking me to my very soul.* "I will bring the walls of your temple down and pick my teeth with your bones!"

I cannot lie. I was so terrified, I couldn't move. I couldn't scream. Although I quickly realized it wouldn't have helped. None of my sisters was going to step in, and Elder Sister Elisa—the strongest amongst us—was out for the day.

Gods, I felt so very alone.

The dragon pulled the warrior woman farther back into the room and turned her to face him. He said something to her, but I could not hear it. But whatever he said seemed to calm her. For the moment.

Then he closed his eyes and I knew that he was using his mind to talk to someone. But I was not powerful enough—or brave enough—to find out who that might be. It only took a few seconds; then he opened his eyes and said, "We have to go."

"Go?" the warrior woman asked.

"Aye. Trust me."

Calmer now, the warrior woman nodded and faced them. I tried to shrink as far back into the wall as I could, praying she wouldn't even see me.

She didn't. Her gaze was focused solely on Elder Sister Haldane. The warrior woman walked toward her and had just passed when Elder Haldane rolled her eyes and made the softest sound. As if she'd clicked her tongue against her teeth. I always heard a louder version of that when I did something to disappoint her. But this time, it was so faint, I didn't think anyone could hear it.

But the warrior woman did hear it and her fist slammed into the side of Elder Sister Haldane's face with such speed and force that I could only gasp. The Elder Sister went down hard, landing on the floor so that her nose was broken in the process. Just as her cheek and jaw were shattered by that big fist.

Then, making her own sound of disappointment with her tongue against her teeth, the warrior woman sauntered out. The dragon began to follow, but briefly stopped to nod at me and mutter, "Sorry about that."

I just nodded back. What else could I do? Except wait until it was safe and then spend the next hour with my fellow sisters trying to wake up Elder Sister Haldane. . . .

Chapter Three

Annwyl the Bloody, queen of Southland territories, rode into Baron Pyrs's courtyard, stopping in front of the big stone steps that led into the castle where the meeting was to take place.

"Are you sure you should be doing this?" her general commander, Brastias, gently asked.

Annwyl patted her horse's neck. "I'm going to meet Baron Pyrs, not get into a pit fight."

"Are we really sure about that?"

Annwyl gritted her teeth, her lip curling. She knew what Brastias was really saying to her. "Do you really think that *you*, of all people in the universe, can handle this without removing someone's head? You? *Really?*"

It was a tone that Annwyl had been hearing for quite a long time. A very long time. In years, she was nearly . . . ? Gods. Fifty? Maybe more. She'd lost track. Not because she'd become so doddering that it had all been lost in her head, but because she'd stop caring. When she looked in the mirror, she still saw a woman of less than thirty winters. Not because she was blind to her aging, but because of a gift from Rhiannon the White. A gift that would—should she not die in battle or from an assassin's blade to the back—allow her to age much more slowly than other humans, the way dragons do. So that she and her black dragon mate, Fearghus, could grow old together.

Although Fearghus often suggested that Annwyl "played

with death far too much" to keep him company for another six or seven hundred years.

But what did Fearghus expect her to do? She was queen of the Southlands. A title that Annwyl did not take lightly. Her people meant far too much to her, which was why, for the last few years, Annwyl had been trying so hard not to be as . . . what was the word her battle lord often used? Oh, yes. Ridiculous! Dangerously ridiculous. Stupidly ridiculous.

It was no secret Annwyl had a bit of a temper. During war times, when she was busy protecting her children, Annwyl knew she could be a tad . . . touchy. But her battle lord and steward, Dagmar Reinholdt, Beast of the Northlands, had made a very good point. If she were to continue to protect her children—now off in different regions of the world, learning important skills so that one day they'd be ready to lead in Annwyl's stead—she would have to learn to be a "proper" royal.

A "proper" queen.

Not some screaming, mad noble bent on destroying everyone and everything that even looked at her wrong. But a nice, normal noble that people didn't automatically fear and despise.

A change Annwyl was finding hard to make, not because she didn't want to, but because so many didn't seem to believe in her. Even her own general commander.

Yet, instead of snapping at Brastias that he should "fuck off" before she slapped him off his horse, she took a breath, waited ten seconds, and calmly replied, "I can handle it."

Brastias shrugged. "All right."

No. She didn't hear a lot of faith in that reply. Not a lot of faith at all. But she wouldn't slap him off his horse, no matter how much she truly wanted to.

And gods . . . did she want to.

"You lot wait here," she ordered him and her personal guard.

"Are you sure you shouldn't wait for Briec and Gwenvael to arrive?" one of her guards asked. "They shouldn't be too long."

Why should she do that? She could handle this. Why was everyone questioning her?

"I said—" Annwyl stopped. *Calm and easy,* she told herself. *Calm and bloody easy.*

"It'll be fine." Annwyl dismounted the large horse that had been specifically chosen by her mate for the beast's calm manner in battle and ease around dragons.

Annwyl climbed the steps two at a time and walked into the large hall. The four men standing by one of the tables immediately stopped speaking and turned to face her.

She forced a closed-mouth smile. "My lords."

"My lie—" Baron Thomas stopped, tried again. "My Quee . . . uh . . ." He glanced at the other royals. "My . . . lady?"

Annwyl shook her head. "They're all fine," she lied. She hated all the bowing and scraping that came with being a ruler, and they all knew it, but part of being queen, according to Dagmar, was "sucking up" the royal titles that were thrown one's way.

Annwyl was trying hard to suck it up.

"We appreciate your taking the time, my lady. We all know there is much occupying you in the kingdom."

"True, but I can't neglect the lords who help protect my lands."

Annwyl winced a bit. Did those words sound as false to their ears as they did to her own?

She reached to scratch her head but knew that would mean her hair would fall in her eyes and, as she'd been told many times by Dagmar and her dragon sister-by-mating Keita, that just made her "look like a mad cow."

But having her hand just linger by her head like that

looked strange, she was sure, so she carefully smoothed down her hair to either side of her head so that the part stayed clear and her hair appeared shiny and straight. Not messy and insane.

"Now . . . what can I help you with, Baron Pyrs?"

"Queen Annwyl," a female voice said from behind her.

Annwyl's hand instantly reached for her sword as she turned just her torso to get a look at who stood behind her.

"My lady, please!" Baron Pyrs begged as he ran around to stand between Annwyl and the woman behind her. "You are not in danger. I swear on my name. This is just a casual meeting."

Annwyl's hand shook as it rested against the hilt of one of the blades strapped to her back. It did not shake from fear, but the overwhelming desire to remove the sword from its scabbard and kill everyone in the room.

But Annwyl heard Dagmar's voice in her head. She'd been hearing it for years now, telling her the same thing. *I'm sure that, with some practice, you can stop killing people who simply annoy you. Come now, let's give it that royal tutor try, shall we?*

Then Annwyl thought about Brastias and her personal guard standing outside. She knew they were waiting for her to start a massacre they'd have to clean up or explain to the two dragons headed her way at this very moment.

She could already see Gwenvael's smirk and hear Briec's put-upon sigh. She could hear it all.

They all expected her to fail.

Again, Annwyl let out a breath, carefully lowered her hand, and turned to squarely face the woman behind her.

"Priestess Abertha."

Or, as Annwyl liked to call her, "Priestess Fucking Abertha."

She hailed from the Annaig Valley, a small but powerful valley territory tucked behind the Conchobar Mountains of the Outerplains, which reached as far inland as the Quintilian

Provinces. The city of Levenez was its seat of power and its ruler was Duke Roland Salebiri.

To be honest, Annwyl had never paid much attention to the Salebiri family. For almost three decades, she'd been focused on troubles from the horse riders of the Western Mountains, who ran a still-thriving slave trade, and the senate of the Quintilian Provinces. So some little territory caught between the raiding Steppes Riders of the Outerplains and the outskirts of the Provinces had been the least of her worries.

Until Salebiri had found what would bring him true power. The worship of a god. Not several gods, but just one. Salebiri ruled from that religious power, demanding loyalty not to his land or his people but to one demanding god.

Chramnesind. The Sightless One, he was called, because he lacked eyes or something.

Annwyl didn't know or care. She hated the gods, pretty much all of them. But more than gods, she hated humans who did horrible things while proclaiming themselves holy and righteous because of their gods.

Yet of all the holy sycophants she'd had to deal with the last few years, Annwyl loathed most of all Priestess Abertha, the sister of Duke Salebiri and the biggest hypocrite Annwyl had ever had the displeasure of meeting.

The priestess smiled that falsely warm smile. "You remember me, don't you, Queen Annwyl?"

"Of course I remember you," Annwyl said, forcing her own smile. "You're beautiful." And Priestess Abertha truly was with her lean figure, waist-length golden-blond hair, and startling green eyes.

She was also the diseased cunt who'd preached from her ever-more-powerful pulpit that Annwyl's twins "should have been drowned at birth to appease our good and wondrous lord."

"So what brings you to my territories?" Annwyl asked.

"Baron Pyrs thought it would be good for us to meet under better circumstances than last time."

Now Annwyl worked very hard *not* to smile—as much as she might want to. It had been years. Her son had gone off to train with the Brotherhood of the Far Mountains on the other side of the Quintilian Provinces. Her daughter had gone to the Ice Lands to train with the Kyvich warrior witches. And her niece, Rhianwen, had gone off with her own blood kin to the Desert Lands to train with the Nolwenn witches.

A meeting of local rulers from the west, north, and south had been arranged, and all had been going relatively well until, during a grand feast, Abertha's younger brother, Thomas, pointed a damning finger at Dagmar and called her a seething whore of corruption. Why? Because he'd seen her kiss her mate, Gwenvael the Handsome, a known dragon. Gwenvael had been in his human form at the time, but Thomas Salebiri had not cared.

Dagmar had been unimpressed with all the theatrics, and Gwenvael had been amused. Annwyl, however, had taken the loudmouth fuck's head. Right there in the Great Hall of her home.

It had not gone over well with the other royals. Her current alliances still held, but barely.

And that's when Dagmar had begun explaining to Annwyl, "You just can't do that, you mad bitch. No matter how much I love you, *you can't do that!*"

It had been the last head Annwyl had taken outside of battle or a trial. So it was a fond memory . . . for Annwyl.

"That sounds . . . promising," Annwyl lied. "What is it you wish to speak to me about?"

"The peace of our two nations."

Nations? Really?

Annwyl could already see the first problem. That the Salebiris believed they ruled a nation rather than a good-sized valley stuck between practically impassable mountains and a land of vicious raiders. But Annwyl would play this out like a proper queen, no matter how much it physically hurt not to start punching people.

"Ahh, I see. That does sound like an excellent discussion. But one that should be pursued under more . . . amiable conditions. Don't you think?"

"Amiable conditions? What's wrong with right here and right now?"

"To be quite blunt, treaties and alliances and truces are not what I do. I ensure they are maintained, but I don't really draft the contracts and put them into play. I leave that to my steward, Dagmar Reinholdt, and Queen Rhiannon's Royal Peacemaker, Bram the Merciful. If you want to be ensured of peace for your lands, Priestess, they would both need to be involved in any discussions between us."

"Really? The Beast of Reinholdt and some dragon's lackey? They tell you what to think?"

"No. But they do let me know whose head to put outside my castle walls for all the world to see . . . and enjoy until the flesh *rots* away." Annwyl smiled. "You remember what that looks like . . . don't you, Priestess?"

"My ladies," Baron Thomas quickly intervened, stepping between them as Abertha's Annaig Valley guards grew tense, their gazes hardening on Annwyl. "Please."

"It's all right, Baron." The priestess patted the man's arm. "We're just two ladies talking."

"Are we?" Annwyl asked.

"Oh, yes. There's just so much for us to discuss," she said pleasantly, as if they were having tea and scones. "For instance, your vile offspring, the Abominations, who will bring the True Darkness to this world. The Defiled Ones, such as yourself, who have lain with dragons like unholy whores and then birthed the spawn of such matings. All of that will have to be dealt with. Between us. Between friends."

As Baron Pyrs, his face now a grey-white, slowly backed away from the pair, the other barons edged closer and closer to a side door. They hoped to make a mad escape.

Annwyl could see them all through the red haze that now surrounded her.

For a long moment, Annwyl didn't move. She couldn't breathe. But she forced herself—*literally* forced herself—not to move. Not to react. Not right away.

And that moment of doing nothing allowed her to notice that Abertha's guards had not moved. They did not rush to their royal's side, ready to defend her with their lives. And yet they were clearly waiting for Annwyl to do *something*.

Then it hit her. Like a slap to the face. This woman wanted Annwyl to cleave her head from her shoulders. She wanted Annwyl to unleash the wrath that Annwyl had become so famous for. They all knew what would take place if that happened. If Annwyl suddenly snapped and destroyed the bitch standing in front of her. And her guards. And the barons. Maybe even the poor servants who rushed in to help Baron Pyrs. They'd all fall to Annwyl's swords, like so many before them. And after that . . . the word would travel like lightning throughout the lands: "Mad Queen Annwyl killed a defenseless priestess and her own royals!" all the traveling bards would sing.

This wasn't about a truce or an alliance or even a chance to avenge her brother's death.

No. Abertha was here for one reason and one reason only: to become a martyr to her god's cause, most likely advancing it a thousandfold.

And if that happened, it would be no one's fault but Annwyl's.

Knowing the bitch was trying to use Annwyl's well-honed rage for her own ends did nothing but piss Annwyl off more. But it also brought out what Annwyl's father used to call her "petty, hateful side." Then he would add, "You're the only cow I know willing to cut off her own nose, just to spite her own gods-damn face."

And he was right. Annwyl didn't like being pushed. If she was pushed one way, she was likely to go another . . . just out of spite.

So she held on to that spite like a lifeline and *calmly* said, "We're done here, Priestess Abertha."

"My lady, please," Baron Pyrs begged.

Annwyl, unsure how long she would be able to hold her temper in check, waved the baron off as she walked toward the front doors, but she stopped short when four of Abertha's guards, in bright white surcoats with the rune of their god emblazoned in the color of blood, stepped in front of her—keeping her from the exit.

"Move," Annwyl ordered softly. She didn't dare scream that order. If she started screaming, she wouldn't stop until everyone in the room was dead.

"We insist you stay, Queen Annwyl," the priestess said from behind Annwyl, that warm note still in her voice. "We're not done talking, you and I."

Finally, Annwyl's smile was real. Because now she had something to focus on. Something . . . disposable.

"Yes," Annwyl replied, already feeling the relief in her muscles and brain. "I guess you are *insisting*."

The winds rose up around them and Brastias looked to the skies to see two of his brothers-by-mating drop to the ground.

He walked away from his men and closer to Briec the Mighty and Gwenvael the Handsome.

"Brothers," he greeted.

"I thought we told you not to call us that," Gwenvael

reminded him, tossing his overly long, golden locks off his face. The gold dragon had been forced to cut that hair to his shoulders in the last war, and since then, he'd let it become quite the unruly mane.

"What is wrong with that female?" snapped Briec, the perpetually complaining silver dragon. "Fearghus leaves for one bloody day, and she does something stupid. Is her whole purpose in life simply to irritate *me*?"

"Yes," both Gwenvael and Brastias said together.

"Quiet," he spit between his fangs. "Both of you."

"Where is she, Brastias?" Gwenvael asked.

"She's inside with Baron Pyrs."

"Alone?"

"She's still my queen, Briec. If she orders me and the guards to stay outside—"

"You ignore her! Why is that so hard for you weak humans to understand?"

Brastias looked to Gwenvael, and the Gold smirked. "That wasn't rhetorical. He actually expects you to answer that question."

"Well." Briec sighed dramatically, the entire world apparently on his silver shoulders . . . or at least he seemed to think so. "I guess we have to go in there and get her."

Without shifting to human, Briec stomped across the courtyard toward the front castle doors. But as he reached the steps, two swords rammed through the hard wood, blood streaking down both blades so that some of it hit Briec in the face.

Brastias winced, but Gwenvael just laughed.

"That can't be good," Gwenvael joked.

Briec looked over his shoulder at Brastias. "*Do you see?*" he bellowed, his claw wiping the blood from his eyes. "Do you understand *now* why I say the things I say?"

"Because you're a mean bastard?" Brastias asked, which made Gwenvael laugh more. Something Briec didn't appreciate in the least. But before he could swipe at Brastias with his tail—as he'd done more than once since Brastias had committed his life and love to Briec's sister, Morfyd—the front doors opened and Annwyl walked out.

Drenched in blood—she'd always been a messy fighter—and carrying four heads by the hair, Annwyl came down the steps toward her horse. She walked under Briec like he wasn't even there, easily maneuvering around his tail.

"What have you done now, ridiculous female?" the silver dragon snapped at her.

"Not what you think." She gave a short whistle and her big horse lowered himself so that Annwyl could get onto his back without releasing her new heads.

Once in her saddle, her horse stood and Annwyl took hold of the reins in her free hand. Without another word, she turned her horse around and headed out.

Brastias motioned to her guards and they immediately followed after their queen. Not that she needed them to keep her safe. Her barely contained rage should do that until she got back to Garbhán Isle.

"Well, well," Gwenvael said, his gaze on the castle steps. "The lovely Priestess Abertha."

Brastias swung around to see that Gwenvael was correct. The lovely—and infinitely cruel—Abertha stood on the steps of Baron Pyrs's castle, her white robes pristine, the suns shining down on her head, casting her in a glow that brilliantly hid her true evil nature.

But, at least she was alive. Alive! Shocking, to be honest. Brastias had always thought if Annwyl had the chance, Abertha would be the first person she would kill. Ten years ago, it wouldn't have even been a question. But it seemed that Dagmar Reinholdt's work with the queen had been effective.

As he looked past the priestess, the only bodies Brastias saw were of her guards. A "misunderstanding" that could easily be explained away, unlike the death of an important and "innocent" priestess.

"My dear lady," Gwenvael noted, smirking, "you seem . . . disappointed. Did Queen Annwyl not give you what you crave?"

Abertha tried to smile, but all she could manage was a small grunt as her lips sort of turned up in the corners. It was not attractive.

Briec, seeing Abertha alive, turned away from her without speaking, but he swung his tail out and, instinctively, the priestess dropped to the ground before the sharpened tip could slash her face or toss her slim human body into the unforgiving stone walls.

"I'm going home," Briec said, shaking out his wings. "I suggest you do the same, Brastias."

Brastias agreed. It was never a good idea to linger after Annwyl had one of her "moments" as Morfyd liked to call them.

He mounted his steed and briefly watched Priestess Abertha get to her feet. As she did, Baron Pyrs ran down the steps toward Brastias. Now that Annwyl and the dragon brothers were gone, the baron wasn't afraid to venture from the safety of his castle walls.

"My Lord Brastias—" he began.

"I am no lord, Baron Pyrs. Merely a humble general of Queen Annwyl's armies."

"Yes, but—"

"And if you see me again, it'll most likely be to tear down the walls of your fine home, stone by bloody stone."

Brastias turned his horse to ride away, but the baron quickly moved to stand beside him.

"Brastias, wait—"

"It's not me you need to be talking to, my lord. I'm a soldier. I bring war, I don't stop it. If you want to beg for the safety of your family after this foolishness, then you'd best get in touch with Lady Dagmar. She is the one you need to plead your case to. She's the one who will keep you alive. Do we understand each other?"

Pyrs let out a breath, nodded. "We do."

Not needing to hear anything else, Brastias headed back to his home and his mate.

Chapter Four

A door slammed somewhere deep in the castle and Celyn put his claws over the back of his head and prayed for death. Another door slammed, followed by raised voices and more door slamming.

When death did not come—the bastard!—Celyn rolled to his back and opened his eyes to look around. For a few moments, he had no idea where he was. He looked at his claws and realized they were hands. Lifted his head a bit and realized he was in his human form, dressed, and on a bed.

Letting out a breath, he slowly lowered his head back to the pillow and moved just his eyes to look around.

A castle. He was in a castle.

Celyn raised himself up on his elbows, but then he had to stop because he was afraid he'd end up tossing whatever was in his stomach all over the room.

This was his fault. His fault. He knew better than to go drinking with his sister.

Foolish dragon.

The door to the room he was in slammed open, and he gasped at the pain that sound caused in every part of him.

"We need to get out of here," his sister told him.

Branwen the Awful was Celyn's younger sister, but with only two decades between them, they were considered almost twins by dragon standards. Plus, they looked a lot alike with their black hair, black eyes, and square jaws like their mother's. But Brannie was more Cadwaladr than Celyn. She drank like their kin, fought random beings like their kin, and loved war like their kin. Understanding Celyn's happiness at being a member of the Queen's Personal Guard eluded her.

"What's wrong?" Celyn asked as he slowly placed his feet on the floor and his poor, throbbing head in his hands. *No more drinking. Ever*, he promised himself for the millionth time.

"Annwyl killed some guards or something, and no one is very happy about it. And Fearghus isn't here."

"Dammit." Their cousin Fearghus had a way of controlling his mate that no one else had. Especially important when she began killing things because she got in a bit of a mood. "Who did she kill?"

"Not sure. But Dagmar was sent for."

Dagmar Reinholdt. The Northlander who'd become steward to Queen Annwyl and Battle Lord to Garbhán Isle although the human female had never lifted a sword or axe once in her life. A good thing since she had no skill with weapons. But what she did have was a potent skill with war strategy and a bone-deep love of plotting.

"You're right," Celyn agreed. "We need to go." Unless, of course, they wanted to get caught in the middle of one of Annwyl's misadventures, which he did not.

Forcing himself to stand, Celyn asked, "Did you bring me here last night?"

"I did. You were too drunk to shift back. I was afraid you'd accidentally wipe out the town."

Once standing, Celyn swayed, but a steadying hand on the bed's headboard kept him from falling to the floor.

"You never could handle your liquor, brother."

"Shut. Up."

"Because I, as always, speak truth?"

"No. Because your voice is typically loud and grating." He rubbed his brow. "Why do I ever let you talk me into going drinking with you?"

"Because I'm your sister and you adore me?"

"*No.*"

Brannie laughed. "Come, brother. Before we get trapped by one of our kinsdragons' stupidity."

His sister was right. More times than he cared to think about, Celyn had ended up in the middle of his royal cousins' problems and dramas. And, as a Cadwaladr, he was obligated to help in any way he could. Because a Cadwaladr always protected family. Even when family was a bunch of bratty royals who seemed to find reasons to argue with *everyone.*

Celyn took a few tentative steps, stopped, and asked his sister, "I am dressed, right?" Because he honestly couldn't remember.

"You are. You passed out in your clothes last night and sadly I didn't have time to take them off so that when I sent the maids in to clean the room, they could find your naked ass waving at them and scream in human terror. You know how I love that."

Celyn glared at his sister. "What is wrong with you?"

Brannie shrugged. "Nothing. Why?"

Celyn went to the bedroom door and eased it open, peeking into the hallway.

"Well?" his sister whispered.

"It's clear. Let's move."

Together, the siblings rushed down the hallway, down one set of steps to the second-floor hallway, and another set of stairs toward the Great Hall.

Celyn worried he'd start vomiting, but he was determined to do that only once he was outside and far away from whatever drama was about to erupt among his royal cousins.

But as he and Brannie cut between two long dining tables, Celyn was hit in the face with a . . . well . . . a human head, forcing him to stop.

Celyn stared down at the head he now held in his hands.

"Quick hands," his sister noted.

"Not quick enough *not* to get hit in the face with a human head."

Before Celyn could toss the head away and make a run for it, Annwyl the Bloody stormed into the Great Hall. Briec, in his human form, wearing only leggings and boots, stalked right behind her.

"I fail to understand," Briec snarled at Annwyl, "how one woman could do so many stupid things at one time."

"I don't owe you, Briec the Annoying, any explanation whatsoever about the decisions *I* make about *my* kingdom." She walked over to Celyn and snatched the head from his hands so that she could add it to the others she held. "And stop throwing my heads." She lifted them so they were right under Briec's nose. "I'm putting these on spikes outside the walls."

"Because you want to declare to the *world* that you make stupid decisions?"

"Are you under some delusion that you rule here, dragon? Because you don't." She turned in a circle, shaking the heads and spraying blood as she yelled, "*I answer to no man and no dragon! And I definitely don't answer to you!*"

Celyn had just managed to clear the blood from his eyes when Briec slapped the heads from Annwyl's hand, knocking them into Celyn's defenseless face.

That was also when the slap fight broke out between the pair.

Disgusted, Celyn pushed his way between them and shoved them apart.

"Stop it! Both of you! You're acting like hatchlings!"

"She started it!"

"He started it!"

"*Shut up!*"

Both royals stepped back and glared at Celyn.

"Who do you think you're speaking to, Low Born?" Briec demanded of Celyn.

"I am *queen*," Annwyl spit at Celyn.

"And I am a Dragon Prince," Briec added.

"And *I* am one of the chosen of Her Majesty, Dragon Queen of these lands! Which makes me more important than *either* of you!" Celyn placed his hand to his forehead. "Oh. The pain." He dropped back into a chair and Brannie rushed to his side. "My head hurts so, sister."

"What have you two done to my poor brother?" Brannie demanded while petting Celyn's head. "You bastards! Do you care for no one but yourselves?"

Briec shrugged. "I don't know about this ridiculous woman, but I don't care."

Fearghus the Destroyer, first-born son to Queen Rhiannon and future Dragon King of the Southlands unless he could find another sucker to take such an oxen-shit job— *Maybe I can talk Morfyd into being the next queen . . . no. She's not that stupid*—landed in the courtyard and shifted to human.

"Brother! Good day to you!"

Fearghus let out a long sigh and turned to face his younger sibling. "Gwenvael."

"You're missing a fight."

"I don't care."

"Between Annwyl and Briec."

At his brother's words, Fearghus glanced off.

"What's that look for?" Gwenvael asked.

"I'm trying to figure out if Mum will forgive Annwyl for taking Briec's head."

"She might, but Talaith and the girls never will."

"True," Fearghus sighed. "And I do like Talaith and my nieces."

Fearghus caught the clothes that Gwenvael tossed to him and put them on. As the brothers headed toward the stairs of the Great Hall, the ground shook beneath their feet as their mother and father landed in the courtyard.

"By the power of the most unholy of gods, this party's getting better!" Gwenvael happily cheered.

"Stop it," Fearghus told him, but he wasn't exactly surprised. Gwenvael loved to stir shit and had been doing so since he'd hatched from his egg and managed to start a fight between their parents. Fearghus still didn't know how Gwenvael had managed it since he'd been too young to speak . . . but he had.

Rhiannon tossed her white hair off her face and greeted them. "My handsome sons!"

"Mum," they both replied.

Their mother shifted to human and, with arms wide open, walked toward them.

"Clothes!" their father barked. "Clothes, female!"

Rhiannon stopped, her arms dropping to her sides. "These tedious humans with their insecurities. Who has time for all this?"

Bercelak threw a burgundy velvet robe around his mate's shoulders. "Five bloody seconds. It takes all of five bloody seconds to cover yourself."

After putting her arms through the sleeves, she knotted a belt around her waist to hold the robe closed and impatiently waited while her mate tugged on black leggings and boots.

"Why are you here, Mum?" Fearghus asked.

"Éibhear called to me. Said to meet him and Izzy here. They should be along shortly."

"What's happened now?"

"Nothing any of you have to worry about. Good gods, what is that?"

"What is what?"

"That giant, phallic-looking building." She pointed at the tower Annwyl had been having built for quite a few weeks now. The stonemason was hurrying to finish his project before the harsh snowstorms of the winter season began to hit.

"That is Annwyl's tower."

"Tower? What does she need a tower for? Does she plan to torture a lot of people?" Rhiannon frowned. "Gods, she plans to torture a lot of people."

"Mum," Fearghus said. "You left your mountain fortress for a reason. Why not just tell me rather than giving me a lot of horse shit. What is it?"

She stroked her hand against Fearghus's cheek. "Always so smart. You make me so very proud."

"That doesn't answer my question."

"I know." She grinned and walked around him. "I know."

Boots on, their father stood beside Gwenvael. "Why are we just standing here?" he demanded.

Fearghus frowned. "We were waiting for you."

With a grunt, the dragon pushed past his sons, but before Fearghus could throttle the mean bastard, Rhiannon caught one of Fearghus's arms and Gwenvael caught the other.

"Why is he always such a rude bastard?" Fearghus growled.

"Only to you lot," Rhiannon reminded him, patting his arm. "He adores *me*."

Celyn and Brannie neared the open front doors of the Great Hall while the arguing between Briec and Annwyl continued.

The siblings had only this one chance to escape and they knew it. But just as they reached their last step to freedom, they were suddenly blocked by the Dragon Queen and more of their royal cousins.

"Brannie! Darling!" Rhiannon called out happily, her arms opening wide to grab Brannie in a smothering hold.

Celyn eased past his queen, more than ready to leave his sister to fend for herself as she would have done to him if their positions were reversed, but a large hand gripped him around the throat and pushed him back.

"Cousin!" Gwenvael falsely cheered. "How wonderful to see you! It's been . . . days. At least."

Celyn pushed against his cousin's chest, but tried his best to hide his desperation from his queen and uncle.

"Come!" Gwenvael continued. "Join us!"

"Let me go, you bastard!" Celyn snarled softly at his older cousin.

"No, no! You're family! You must join us!" Gwenvael's voice lowered to a mean whisper. "I insist."

It had been years—bloody years!—since Gwenvael had warned a very young Celyn not to go near his adopted niece, Iseabail the Dangerous. A warning Celyn had promptly ignored. And a few years later, when it had come out that Celyn and Izzy had become lovers, Gwenvael had made it his business to torment his cousin. Celyn didn't know why. Chasing after unrelated, beautiful females was something Gwenvael had always done himself before he'd mated with Dagmar. And, according to Annwyl, Gwenvael had definitely at least tried with her before Fearghus had properly Claimed Annwyl as his.

Surprisingly, though, Gwenvael was shockingly sly about his small bouts of revenge. Never making a big deal of it, or involving his brothers. It was as if he wanted to hide the fact that something so minor bothered him so much. He was considered the jovial one of the royal siblings, after all.

But none of that changed the fact that the golden-haired

bastard was currently making Celyn's throbbing head that much worse.

Gwenvael reached out and grabbed Celyn's shoulder, spun him around, and shoved him forward.

"Mum!" the bastard cheered. "Look who's here to escort you home once you're ready to go? Our wonderful cousin Celyn!"

With her arm tight around Brannie's shoulders, her grin appearing as plotting and unholy as her son's, the queen said, "Wonderful! And dear, sweet Brannie can stay, too! I simply *adore* family time!"

Gwenvael's arm looped around Celyn's neck and his chin rested on Celyn's shoulder. "So do I, Mummy. So do I!"

Chapter Five

Éibhear the Contemptible shifted to human and quickly pulled on leggings. He had to drag on his boots while following an angry, stalking Izzy. The only thing keeping her from completely outpacing him was that she wasn't running and he had longer legs.

"Izzy, wait!" he yelled after her, even though he knew she wouldn't listen. Not when she was *this* pissed off. "Iseabail!"

But it was no use.

Éibhear got the last boot on and ran after his mate. He'd just cleared the last step when he saw Izzy, in front of everyone, walk boldly up to Rhiannon, point an accusing finger, and say, "What have you done—?"

"My lovely granddaughter!" Rhiannon exclaimed, cutting off the rest of Izzy's words. Then she grabbed Izzy about the neck and yanked her into her body, hugging her tight. So tight, Éibhear was sure Izzy couldn't breathe; her arms desperately flew out from her body, trying to push Rhiannon away.

"Oh, my dearest girl. How I've missed you! It's been what?" Rhiannon asked. "Days? Weeks? Since I've seen you last?"

Éibhear ran over to extricate his mate from his mother, but then, suddenly, his idiot cousin Celyn was between him and his goal.

"Move," Éibhear snapped at him.

Celyn the Charming—yeah, right, bloody "charming" all right—gave a bit of a smile before turning to Éibhear's brothers and asking, "Aren't you all glad to see your little brother returned to the safety of your collective bosom?"

"Not really."

"I hadn't thought about it."

"Who?"

Éibhear was about to move Celyn himself since the black dragon couldn't seem to get out of his way with any speed, when Éibhear stopped, and faced his brothers. "Wait . . . what? You don't care I'm home?" he asked his brothers. "To the big, fat, disgusting warmth of your collective bosoms?"

"Yes, because we definitely want the Mì-runach in our home," Briec said on a bored sigh.

Éibhear's lip curled a bit. He was aware of how his brothers felt about the Mì-runach. They were considered vile, vicious bastards who took orders from no one but their queen and killed only those no one else would go near. They had also been the only group of Dragonwarriors willing to take Éibhear on as one of their own. His time with them had made him a better dragon and definitely a more worthy soldier. But the reputation of the Mì-runach seemed to mean more to his brothers than what they'd done for the youngest of their siblings.

Typical!

"Now, now, you lot," Gwenvael unhelpfully cut in. "Let's not blame the boy for being worthless and irritating. Let's blame our father. It's his fault poor little Éibhear is like this. Sad. Pathetic. With bones tied in his strangely colored hair as if he were still on the cold, barbarian mountains of the Northlands."

"Strangely colored hair? Our grandfather was a Blue," Éibhear reminded them.

"His was more of a hearty navy blue that sparkled in the moonlight. Yours is a flat, boring blue. Kind of like yourself."

Suddenly Fearghus focused on them all as if he'd never seen them before and snapped, "Who are we talking about?"

That was when Éibhear threw the first punch. . . .

"In here," Annwyl said as she led Rhiannon, Dagmar, and Talaith, into the library, the sounds of the brothers' fighting fading as she closed the door behind them. "They never come in here."

"Nicely handled, dear Celyn," Rhiannon told her nephew who, along with his younger sister, had followed them here. Celyn had always been one of her best guards, knowing exactly what she needed without Rhiannon ever having to say a word.

"You're welcome. But I think you should let Izzy go now. She might be passing out."

"Hmmm?" Rhiannon glanced down at her adopted granddaughter and saw that the warrior had slumped in her arms. "Oh, dear!"

She dropped the girl and Izzy fell into her mother's arms.

"I wish you wouldn't do that," Talaith chastised while she and Morfyd worked to awaken the girl.

"She was about to open that large mouth she inherited from you and I was trying to stop her." Rhiannon pointed at her nephew. "Celyn, be a dear and you and Brannie there block the door."

"Really?" he asked with an annoyed sound in his voice. "You want *me* watching the door. Like one of Dagmar's dogs?" He pointed at the large beast that always shadowed the Northlander. Her name was Adda and she was the size of a miniature horse. "Look. She's already standing there. Can't she do it?"

"For the love of . . . you two just guard the bloody door!"

By the time the siblings locked the door and stood in front of it, Izzy was awake and slowly getting to her feet.

Rhiannon started to order Ghleanna's offspring to the *other* side of the door to keep out her sons, but she realized she didn't have much time. At some point, her sons would realize that the rest of them had snuck away. So she had to make this quick.

Izzy, again, pointed a damning finger. "Gran, you tried to kill me!"

"Now, dear," Rhiannon said with a smile, "we both know that if I'd actually *tried* to kill you, you'd be nothing but ash and a lovely memory by now."

Like one of the lesser Queen's Guard, Celyn and his sister were forced to stand in front of the library door to keep out Rhiannon's spoiled sons.

It hadn't been hard to start that fight among the lot of them. They used to get into fights almost all the time until Éibhear came along and calmed everyone down. Then the big bastard had hit puberty and he'd gone from ending

fights to starting them. But deep down, he was still that
sensitive blue dragon everyone adored—and Celyn was not
ashamed to say that he used that weakness to manipulate all
the queen's sons whenever necessary.

Of course, helping Rhiannon with her sons didn't usually
end in this kind of indignity. He hoped it was worth all this
and not just some ridiculous issue that could as easily have
been worked out with everyone involved.

"This must be old hat for you," his sister mocked in a
whisper. "Standing around, guarding the queen's doors."

"Would you shut up? I'm trying to be nosy."

"What the hells is going on?" Talaith demanded of
Rhiannon and Izzy.

With light brown eyes still glaring at Rhiannon, Izzy
said, "That bitch Haldane lost Rhianwen."

"What the battle-fuck do you mean, she *lost* Rhi? How
do you lose a grown woman? *How do you lose my daughter?*" Talaith exploded, most likely ready to run all the way
back to the Desert Lands just to choke her own mother to
death. Talaith had never been close to the witch Haldane
from what Celyn had heard. Then again there was "not
close" and "I will kill you as soon as see you." Celyn was
pretty sure the way Talaith felt about her mother was the
latter.

"Haldane lost no one," Rhiannon said.

"I was there, Gran," Izzy shot back, getting stronger by
the second now that she could breathe again. "Something
opened some magickal door and pulled Rhianwen from this
world into another."

Without a word, Talaith headed for the exit. Gods, Celyn
didn't look forward to this. Talaith was a scrappy fighter,
and she could do a lot of damage before Celyn got control
of her.

Thankfully, though, Rhiannon simply reached out and
grabbed Talaith by her long, curly hair, yanking her back.

"What are you doing?" Talaith snarled, trying to fight her way out of Rhiannon's sturdy grip.

"There is no point in going after your mother. No point involving the Nolwenns at all. This has nothing to do with them. They've served their purpose."

Dagmar's lips briefly pursed before she asked, "What's going on, Rhiannon?"

After pushing Talaith back and releasing her, Rhiannon looked at each of the women standing before her. Talaith. Iseabail. Dagmar. Annwyl.

Celyn was sure it had never occurred to the powerful Dragon Queen that these humans would become an important part of her life. At one time, the queen thought of humans as nothing more than wily food that could make a boring dinner that much more interesting as they begged for their lives.

Yet all that had changed a few decades ago when Fearghus had rescued a dying Annwyl the Bloody. At the time she'd merely been a rebel leader, battling against her sadistic brother after the death of their Southland-ruling father. Fearghus, with the help of his sister, Morfyd the White, had nursed Annwyl back to health and, pretty quickly, he'd fallen in love with her. And once a dragon falls in love, there is no turning back. There is no flying away to find someone new. Someone dragon.

Rhiannon could have handled her eldest son's situation like most royal dragon parents would have. Ordering him never to see the human again, having Annwyl killed so he couldn't, or allowing Fearghus to take Annwyl as his lover while forcing him to choose a royal She-dragon as his mate. A She-dragon who would have his offspring so that the line of the House of Gwalchmai fab Gwyar would live on.

But, to everyone's surprise, Rhiannon the White had

done none of those things. Not once had she told her son, the heir to her throne, that he had to choose someone else. That he could never rule if he were to make a human female his mate. Instead, she'd accepted Annwyl the Bloody. Accepted her whole-heartedly. And, in return, Annwyl wore her love for Fearghus the Destroyer on her shield, her armor, and her body. When Fearghus had Claimed Annwyl, he'd branded her forearms with his mark—and, rumor had it, her inner thighs, but Celyn had thankfully not seen any of that.

In all the years Celyn had known the human queen, she'd never once hid who she was and who—or what—her mate was. If anyone was brave enough to express disgust at her choosing a dragon, Annwyl allowed that person his or her opinion.

And if someone went beyond merely having an opinion . . . ?

Annwyl took their head.

"There's something I haven't told any of you about Rhianwen and the twins," Rhiannon said to the women.

"Gods help us," Talaith gasped. "They're all dead."

Rhiannon briefly stared at the Desert Land beauty before asking, "Why would I not tell you *that*?"

"Because you knew it would destroy us?"

"Even then, Talaith, I'd still tell all of you if something had happened to my grandchildren. And no, you ridiculous female, they're not dead. They're on the move."

"The move to where?" Dagmar asked.

When Rhiannon didn't answer, Talaith threw her hands into the air. "*You don't know where they're going?*"

"Not specifically, and don't get snappy with me, Lady Hysteria!"

"Everyone stop." Annwyl stepped back to one of the tables. She pushed the books covering it aside and sat down.

She rested her elbows on her legs and clasped her hands between her knees.

Celyn guessed that this was what Dagmar had been calling "the new and less insane Annwyl." The Annwyl who took a moment to breathe and think before reacting with the full force of her mighty will.

"Where are my children, Rhiannon?" the human queen quietly asked.

"I don't know."

"Where are they going?"

"I don't know."

"Who are they going to?"

"I don't know."

Talaith crossed her arms over her chest. "Well, when you put it like that . . ."

"I know they're safe," Rhiannon insisted.

"How could you possibly know that?"

"Because they told me they are and I trust them."

"Trust them?" Talaith briefly closed her eyes and shook her head. "Why the hells would you do that?"

"Because they're *my* grandchildren. That's why."

"You don't want us to tell Fearghus and Briec," Dagmar guessed.

"We can't. They simply won't understand."

"And Bercelak?"

"I don't hide anything from my Bercelak."

Celyn laughed at that, and Rhiannon glared at him.

He cleared his throat, nodded. "Sorry, my queen."

When Rhiannon returned her focus to her sons' mates, Celyn looked at his sister and they silently laughed.

"He has complete faith in his granddaughters on this," Rhiannon told the women. "And he'll follow my lead."

Annwyl sat up a bit. "He has faith in his grand*daughters*? What about his grand*son*?"

"The one he keeps accidentally calling Gwenvael? I don't think there's hope there, dear. I'd let it go."

"Éibhear knows," Izzy reminded them.

"He won't say a word," Rhiannon immediately replied. "He contacted me as soon as he saw Rhi escape through that portal, and I told him then to keep his mouth shut."

"Escape?" Dagmar asked.

"I'm sorry, what was that, dear?"

"You said as soon as he saw Rhi *escape* through that portal. She was escaping the Nolwenns? Is that what you're telling us? Are they *all* escaping?"

"You ask too many questions," the queen accused Dagmar.

"No. I'm certain I ask just the right amount."

"What is happening, Rhiannon?" Talaith snapped.

"All you need to know is that the children—of their own free will—are on the move to a safer place."

"Safer place? Safer than here?" Annwyl asked.

"Much safer. They'll be hidden until they're ready."

"Ready for what?"

"Only the gods can answer that, and I am no god. Besides, we have more important things to do."

"What things?"

Celyn stumbled forward when the door he rested against was shoved, the wood pulled from the hinges. He looked at his sister and together, they rammed their bodies backward, shoving the door closed again.

"Ow! You rude bastards!" Gwenvael yelped from the other side.

Rhiannon pointed a finger at the human women. "Not a word," she whispered to them. "We'll talk more later."

Rhiannon nodded at Celyn. "Let them in."

Celyn and his sister stepped back, and Celyn removed

the now-damaged door and set it aside. Fearghus, Briec, Gwenvael, Éibhear, and their father, Bercelak, walked in.

"What's going on?" Fearghus demanded.

Rhiannon opened her mouth to make up some lie that Fearghus would never believe in an eon, but Annwyl cut her off by giving a casual shrug and stating, "I took a few heads this morning, and Dagmar is being completely irrational about it."

"Yes," Dagmar said drily. "Because I'm known for being *so* irrational when you do something so incredibly stupid."

"See?" Briec said, triumphant. "Even the devious human knows what you did was stupid."

"My sweet Dagmar is not devious," Gwenvael happily corrected. "She's conniving and cold-blooded in a way that I adore like the suns."

Dagmar grinned. "Thank you for that, my love."

"You're so very welcome, my sweet."

Fearghus walked past his brother and, as he did, he grabbed him by his ridiculously long hair and threw him backward, sending him flying through the now permanently open doorway.

"You heartless bastard!"

Fearghus brushed the back of his hand against Annwyl's cheek. "Want to tell me what happened?"

"The meeting with Baron Pyrs was a setup. Priestess Abertha was there, waiting to *talk* to me as she put it. But really, all she wanted to do was piss me off so much that I cut her nasty little head from her nasty little body."

"But you didn't?"

Annwyl held Fearghus's left hand in her own, her fingers tracing the scars and veins on the back. "I knew that's what she wanted. You know how I hate giving anyone what they want."

"She wanted you to kill her?" Bercelak asked.

"She wanted to be a martyr to her god. I kill her and everyone turns on me. I wasn't going to give her that. And I only killed her soldiers because they wouldn't let me leave."

Dagmar patted Annwyl's shoulder. "That's very good, Annwyl. You handled that situation well."

Eyes narrowed, Annwyl snarled, "I'm not one of your dogs, Dagmar."

"I never said you were."

"Then stop treating me like you're about to toss me a bone!"

"That's enough!" Rhiannon clapped her hands together. "Stop it. Both of you. We're not going to start turning on each other now. After everything we've been through."

Gwenvael, who'd picked himself up and come back in the room, opened his mouth to speak, but Rhiannon immediately raised a warning finger. "And not one gods-damn word from you. Not one."

Celyn's cousin closed his mouth and stepped behind Brannie, as if she'd ever bother protecting the big idiot from his own mother.

"Now," Rhiannon went on, "all of this with Abertha and that family of hers is a clear sign that they're coming after this kingdom. Not with sword and soldier, but with their god. Although I'm sure sword and soldier are soon to follow. But are we going to wait for that? Are we going to wait to see what they do next? Or are we going to start planning now? So that we're ready?"

Fearghus eyed his mother, a small smirk on his lips. "What are you planning, Mum?"

Rhiannon grinned. "I'm so glad you asked! I've come up with something brilliant!" She clapped her hands together. "But I need a map. A big one."

Chapter Six

Celyn thought he could make a run for it when the discussion was moved to the war room, Morfyd and Brastias now included in the discussion, but Bercelak shoved Celyn and Brannie inside with the rest of them, "You two should probably hear this."

Gods, Celyn couldn't get out of this. And he kept trying! It wasn't like he wasn't trying!

"I had the most brilliant idea today," Rhiannon announced as she unrolled one of the large maps on the big desk at the front of the room. "I've been thinking about alliances a lot lately."

"Perhaps my father should be here for this," Celyn suggested.

"He's already on his way, but let's get started now."

"I can see if he's arrived," Celyn said, turning toward the door. But his uncle caught him by the front of his chainmail shirt and spun him back around. "Stay."

After he was back in position, staring at a stupid map, his sister leaned over and whispered, "Sit, doggie. Good boy," which prompted Celyn to snarl and hit her with a small fireball right in her human face.

"Bastard!" she yelped before punching him in the arm. Celyn punched her back.

But before things could get out of hand, Bercelak growled, "Leave off and listen! Both of you!"

"Thank you, my love," Rhiannon said before turning

back to the map. "Now as Annwyl's little visit with Priestess Abertha has taught us, the real danger these days is coming from Annaig Valley and that Duke Salebiri. His territory is protected by the Western Mountains and Quintilian Provinces on one side and the Outerplains on the other. Now here"—she pointed at the map—"on the eastern side of the Conchobar Mountains, we have complete access to this portion of the Outerplains so that we can come and go into the Northlands. But on the western side of those mountains, we are not allowed access due to tribal rule, which leaves Salebiri and Annaig Valley relatively safe from an attack from our human armies."

"The only way into Annaig Valley from the Southlands is through the pass that cuts through Conchobar Mountains." Annwyl shook her head. "The pass is too small to get an army through with any speed, which would allow Salebiri's men to pick us off one by one as we reach the end."

"Yes, I see that. And, of course, we could send my Dragonwarriors to attack by going over the mountains except that the Outerplains dragons control all the mountains in that region. And they'll protect those mountains from us no matter what, which might cut down on a good number of my troops reaching Annaig Valley successfully. Something I'd like to avoid doing, if we can."

"We can pass over the Western Mountains, which is next to Annaig Valley on the left," Fearghus suggested.

"Except that Gaius Domitus is still battling his kin for complete control over the Quintilian Provinces. If we go over those mountains, we may have only to deal with the Rebel King and his troops or we may have to deal with one of his idiot cousins. Don't get me wrong," Rhiannon quickly added, "I'm not ruling that out as an option. But I'd like to have something a little more in our favor. Especially since we'll still have the same problem with the Western Mountains that we have with the Conchobar: tribal horsemen. Only the Western Mountain horsemen really and truly hate Annwyl."

"They burn an effigy of you every new season to celebrate the end of the dark nights," Briec pointed out, which got a little smile from Annwyl.

"Then what are you suggesting?" Dagmar asked.

Rhiannon again pointed at the map. "There are two passes through those mountains. One goes directly into Annaig Valley and the other goes into the Outerplains—"

"And right into tribal territory. Again, Rhiannon, that second pass is just as narrow as the first and—"

"We need an alliance with those tribes."

Annwyl shook her head. "No."

"Why not?"

"They're slavers. You know my feeling on slavers."

"The Riders of the Western Mountains are slavers. I'm talking about the Riders of the Outerplains. The Daughters of the Steppes. And they don't sell slaves."

"But they do raid and destroy towns and cities that won't pay them their 'taxes' as they like to call it," Fearghus reminded her. "Mum, they're a nightmare."

"And they hate us," Annwyl added. "All of us. Not just me. They think Southlanders are worthless and corrupt. They won't have anything to do with us."

"Yes, but—"

"My father tried to arrange an alliance with their leaders and they sent his emissary back, riding on his horse, but when he got close we realized that not only was he dead, but his body had been cut into three distinct pieces." Annwyl shook her head. "How they got his body to stay up on that horse until it reached my father, I've never figured out. And I've tried."

"Yes, yes, I know all that. But then when I was thinking about it today, I remembered that the Steppes Riders had recently sent one of their own to kill me!"

The best part of that statement, Celyn realized, was how

happy and proud Rhiannon looked when she said it. Her obliviousness was what made Celyn's job so very wonderful.

"Wait . . . what? *What?*" Bercelak sputtered. "What are you saying to me?"

"Oh, don't get so upset, Bercelak."

"Someone was sent to kill you and no one told me? *Me?*"

"Perhaps no one told you because you get kind of hysterical?" Gwenvael asked. But when his father turned those black eyes on him, the gold dragon picked up Brannie and held her in front of his body like a shield.

"Really?" Brannie asked her cousin. "I mean . . . *really?*"

"Gwenvael, put her down," Rhiannon ordered. "And Bercelak, stop huffing and puffing. It was not a big issue at all."

"How could it not be? They sent someone here to kill you."

"Not really. The poor thing was kind of sad and pathetic. I just couldn't have her executed. She broke my heart."

Her cold, dead heart, Brannie joked inside Celyn's head, forcing him to bite his tongue so he didn't laugh out loud. It was a gift dragons had. The ability to talk to siblings or a parent using only their minds. It was a gift that Celyn often appreciated. More than once he'd called his kin to his side when he'd needed them most.

"I don't care how pathetic and sad she was," Bercelak snapped back at his mate. "She should have been executed."

"Oh, Bercelak, clearly that's what her tribe leader was trying to do. She sent the girl here, alone, to kill me. Not just any dragon. But *me*. And as someone who was left at your doorstep by my own mother in the hopes that you'd kill me, I feel for her."

"Fine. We'll feel for her as we string her up and—"

"No. That is not what we're going to do. Instead, we're going to use her. To send our message to the head of all the tribes in the Outerplains."

"Wait." Annwyl scratched her neck. "You want the person

they sent here to die at your hand to go back and negotiate an alliance for us?"

"Aye."

"How is that a good idea?"

"The one who wanted the girl dead was the head of her particular tribe."

"Which tribe?" Annwyl asked.

"No idea. She said it in her name, but, my gods, that name was so long there's no way I could be bothered to remember it all."

"Well, that's good."

"But," Rhiannon went on, ignoring Annwyl's sarcastic tone, "we don't want her to negotiate anything with some tribe leader. We want her to negotiate with the head of *all* the Outerplains tribes. They have a name for her, I just don't remember what it is. . . ."

"Anne Atli," Celyn stated. Then he blinked, wondering how he knew that.

"That sounds right." She smiled at Celyn. "Your parents should be joining us any second so we can now get Bram's perspective on this."

"Oh, goody for us," Bercelak complained.

Brannie, always protective of their father, started to march across the room to say something to their uncle, but Celyn caught her by the back of her shirt and yanked her to his side.

"Not now," he warned her.

Rhiannon clapped her hands together. "They're here!" She motioned to Celyn. "Let them in, dear boy."

Celyn stepped away from the door and opened it, but there was no one standing there. Surprised—Rhiannon usually got that sort of thing right—he stepped out into the hallway and turned, coming face-to-face with his father.

Startled, they both jumped back, then laughed.

"Sorry, Da," Celyn said, hugging his father.

"It's all right." His father's return hug was warm and loving. Just like the dragon himself.

Against Celyn's ear, Bram the Merciful asked, "How bad is it?"

"Not too bad. One of Rhiannon's crazy schemes. Shouldn't take long to talk her out of it."

"Good. Good."

He stepped back and then Celyn's mother hugged him.

"Hello, Mum."

"My sweet hatchling. Is everything all right?" She leaned back, peered into his face. "You don't look well."

"Went drinking with Brannie last night. I'm still recovering."

"I thought you knew better."

"So did I."

With a wave of his hand, Celyn invited his parents into the war room. Once he closed the door, he turned to find Rhiannon throwing her arms open and moving toward his father with the intent of hugging the poor dragon. Something that Bercelak, after all these years, still hated.

But Bram was not alone. Ghleanna stepped in front of him, blocking the queen from getting near him.

Rhiannon pulled back her arms from her sister-by-mating. Celyn understood why, though. No point in hugging Ghleanna since it wouldn't make her mate jealous. "Sister. How pleasant to see you. As always."

"Rhiannon." Celyn cringed at the way his mother bit out that one word. It was like a curse. Honestly, several centuries and these two still insisted on bickering like a pair of fight dogs over the same bone. The poor bone being Celyn's father. "Is there something you want? Besides hugging my mate, I mean."

"I can hug whoever I want in *my* kingdom. So perhaps you should move."

"Perhaps you should make me, queenie."

Maybe we should do something, Brannie suggested in Celyn's head.

No need. We have our secret weapon.

What secret weapon?

"I don't have time for this ridiculousness," Dagmar cut in before the fight between the two She-dragons could become physical. "So let's move this along, shall we?"

When the Dragon Queen stared at her, Dagmar pointed out the window toward the suns. "It's getting late. . . . I have things to do, my good lady."

"I think you might be getting a bit big for your leggings, Miss—"

"Don't believe me?" Dagmar cut in. She dug into one of the hidden pockets of her dress and pulled out a piece of parchment. "Let me read my daily list to you."

"Don't bother." Rhiannon immediately stepped away from Ghleanna. Nothing the She-dragon hated more than hearing Dagmar's daily chores.

Smirking a bit, Dagmar slipped the parchment back into her dress. Amazing how just a little paperwork seemed to make every dragon nearly wet him- or herself at even the tiny suggestion of such boredom.

And Dagmar wasn't ashamed to admit . . . she used that fear to every advantage she could wring from it.

While Celyn stared mindlessly at a spot on the stone floor of the war room, Rhiannon quickly went through her plan again for Bram and Ghleanna. When she was done, Bram gave a small shrug.

"It's not a horrible idea. But until we talk to this Rider, we can't count on her to do anything for us."

"The idiot has a point, Rhiannon," Bercelak said as

Bram caught the back of his mate's chain-mail shirt to prevent her from throttling her brother, while Celyn caught the back of his sister's chain-mail shirt to prevent her from throttling their uncle. "We need to talk to this . . . person. Where is she?"

"Oh . . . I don't know."

Bercelak began rubbing his temples with the tips of his fingers and softly growling.

"Oh, stop it, Bercelak."

"How do you not keep track of someone who was sent here to kill you? How is that possible?"

"*I* don't know where she is. I'm the queen," she reminded him. "I don't need to know. But I know who does know where she is."

"And who would that be?"

That's when Rhiannon suddenly pointed at Celyn.

And Celyn immediately looked behind him to see if someone was standing back there.

When he saw no one, he faced the queen and pointed at himself. "*I* know?"

"Of course you know. I told you to take her someplace safe."

"You did?"

"You knew about this?" Bercelak asked Celyn.

Celyn blinked and calmly asked, "Knew about what?"

"The girl," his queen said.

"What girl?"

"The girl I asked you to keep safe."

Celyn scratched his chin. "The girl you asked me to keep safe . . ."

The queen sighed. "You don't remember, do you?"

"Not even a little."

Bercelak started to stalk toward Celyn, but Ghleanna quickly grabbed his arm, halting him.

"The girl who came to kill Rhiannon?" his mother prompted. "And she wasn't very good at it?"

"Ohhhh! *That* girl."

"Aye!" the queen cheered. "That girl!"

"Some bitch comes to kill your queen," Bercelak snarled, Ghleanna still holding him away from Celyn. "And you did *nothing*?" He ended on a bellow.

"I followed my queen's orders." Celyn repeated the creed of the Queen's Personal Guard. A creed that had been rewritten by Bercelak himself when Rhiannon came into power. "My duty is to follow her orders and no one else's. For I am—"

"*Shut up!*" Bercelak roared.

"Oh, stop it, Bercelak!" Rhiannon snapped. "We have no time for this." The queen smiled at Celyn. "Now, dear boy, where did you put that pale little girl? In that cute pub in town?" She snapped her fingers. "Or that lovely house by the river?"

"Uh . . ." Everyone was staring at Celyn again, so he had no option but to admit the truth. "Well . . . since she did try to kill you, my queen—"

"Gods, Celyn!" Rhiannon gasped. "Tell me you didn't kill her!"

"No, no! You ordered me to keep her safe. So that's what I did."

Gwenvael snorted, easily spotting the hole in that story in seconds. He was so much smarter than any of his siblings gave him credit for. "And what exactly did keeping her safe entail, *cousin*?"

Celyn cleared his throat. "I . . . uh . . . I put her in the Garbhán Isle . . . jail."

Rhiannon's eyes grew wide as Annwyl and Talaith gasped in horror, Dagmar groaned and rolled her eyes, and Gwenvael laughed outright. The prissy bastard.

"You put that woman in jail?" Rhiannon yelled.

"She tried to kill you!"

"Oh, come on! She didn't try very hard!"

"That's not the point! Auntie Rhiannon—"

"Don't you dare!" she snapped. "I gave you strict orders. And as my guard—"

"You gave me *vague* orders. 'Keep her safe.' That's what I did. Because behind bars . . . where was she going?"

Dagmar lifted her hand and silenced everyone. Honestly, Celyn wanted to know, who really ruled the Southlands?

"It may not be that bad," Dagmar said calmly. She focused on Celyn. "How many days since you put her in jail?"

"Uh . . . eight or nine . . ." Celyn cleared his throat. ". . . months ago."

"*Months?*" Izzy roared. "You left a human female alone in a jail for *months?*"

"She tried to kill my queen!" he reasoned.

Rhiannon dramatically threw up her arms. "She's probably been raped to death by now!"

"Rhiannon!" Talaith snapped.

"Don't blame me, little girl. It's your human males with no self-control. They see a pussy and they just have to fuck it!"

"Mum!"

"Oh, pipe down, Morfyd."

"I'll go get her," Celyn stated, trying to keep everyone calm. "I'll go get her."

"Don't you mean get what's left of her, cousin?" Gwenvael asked.

Finally sick to death of the prissy royal, Celyn started to stalk across the room to cut his tongue out, but Brannie grabbed him by the hair and led him through the doorway and out into the hall.

"We'll be right back," she said before closing the door.

"I hate him," Celyn snarled. "I hate him. I hate him. I hate him."

"Be grateful he's just a cousin and not one of our brothers."

"If he was one of our brothers, he'd be scale-less, bald, and alone."

"Let's just go, brother," she said, pushing him toward the exit.

As they walked, Brannie chastised, "I can't believe you left some human female alone in a jail run by human men."

Celyn winced at his sister's words. "None of this is my fault!"

"How is this not your fault?"

"It simply slipped my mind. I have a lot of things to worry about and some female who attempted to kill my queen was not exactly top of my list. And I don't need to hear this from you, sister."

"If she's dead or damaged—"

Celyn halted in the middle of the courtyard they were now in and faced his sister. "Please stop."

Brannie blinked and gazed up at him, her smile fading. "Gods, Celyn . . . you feel terrible about this."

"Wouldn't you? I mean"—Celyn rubbed his once-again-throbbing forehead—"she tried to kill my queen. But I did mean to go back for her. I just . . . I forgot."

Brannie placed her hand on Celyn's shoulder. "Brother, you can't blame yourself for this. She was an assassin."

"Not a very good one."

"That doesn't change anything," Brannie said on a laugh.

"Still, if anything has happened to her at the hands of those humans . . ."

Brannie took his arm. "Come on."

"Where to?"

"Where do you think? To get your sad little assassin." She tugged his arm. "Don't walk, brother! Run!"

And they did. All the way to the jail.

Chapter Seven

Branwen the Awful—a name she was immensely proud of because her own mother had given it to her after a particularly brutal battle—pulled open the jail door and walked inside, her brother behind her. The building wasn't very large, but Annwyl kept control of crime with the fear of her wrath. Those who went beyond some mild stealing, ended up executed faster than they could imagine.

Well-lit and relatively clean, this jail didn't stink of death and pain like many others Brannie had been to over the years. There were no guards at the front. And no one was manning the wood desk.

With her hand on the hilt of her sword, Brannie slowly and carefully made her way down the hall toward the cells. She didn't bother to turn to see if her brother followed suit. Battle readiness was trained into each Cadwaladr offspring from hatching. Being close in age, Brannie and Celyn had been trained together by their older siblings, cousins, and mother, while their father, however, had patiently taught them how to read and write.

Brannie held up her hand to halt her brother and tilted her head to the side to hear a little better. But she needn't have bothered. A burst of raucous male laughter had Brannie charging down a hall filled with cells. She turned a corner and quickly stopped, holding out her arm to again halt her brother.

At least ten well-armed guards stood outside the doorway of the last cell at the end of the hall. They had their backs to Brannie and Celyn, busy being entertained by whatever nightmare was going on inside that room.

She silently indicated to her brother how many men she saw and that they were all armed. They both eased their weapons from their scabbards and moved down the hallway toward the laughter.

Brannie locked on to the one who would be her first victim. He wasn't the biggest, but she could tell from the way he stood, he was the best trained among them.

Holding her blade in both hands, she raised it high near her shoulder and centered her body so that when she was ready, she could charge with ease. But before she could take that next step, her brother caught her shoulder, his fingers briefly gripping and releasing. Together, the pair walked up behind all those guards. Brannie went up on her toes to look over the tallest of the human males; her brother didn't have to bother.

Is that her? she mouthed to her brother. And Celyn nodded.

Brannie blinked and looked again.

Pale-skinned with bright blue eyes and long, pale-blond hair that reached down her back, she wore a shirt and leggings made from deerskin, and fur boots. The woman had one leg pulled up onto the chair she sat upon and one arm wrapped around her calf. The other hand held a mug of ale as she regaled the men who were supposed to be guarding her.

"Another," one of the men begged.

"All right," she said. "One more from before the time of the first Anne Atli. The story of Olezka Tyushnyakov."

"How do you pronounce these names?" one of the men laughingly asked.

"He was very big man," she said in what Brannie knew to be a very thick Outerplains accent. "Arms like chest of oxen. Legs like stumps of trees. And strong. He could take sword made of hardest steel and break it between his giant hands. Many said he had no heart, he had no soul. But he did. All men do. But Olezka did have weakness."

"Women?" one called out.

"Ale?" called out another.

"Too obvious." She leaned in, glancing around as if she was about to tell them a deep, dark secret—and the men leaned in with her. She had their absolute attention and it wasn't simply because she was a woman. "Kittens."

The men reared back. "Kittens?"

"Kittens. Little, fluffy kittens. He adored them. Had hundreds, all around his hut. He had many wives, but they all hated him because of the damn kittens. So much fluffy fur. Impossible to clean."

"Well . . . what happened?" one of the men pushed.

"He went out hunting one day and when Olezka Tyushnyakov returned, he found his children crying, some of his wives dead . . . but what made him truly angry? His kittens were dead."

The men, these guards, gasped in horror. Brannie looked at her brother, but all he could do was shrug.

"So what did he do?" a guard asked.

"He knew who had done this to him."

"Who?"

"His brother." More gasps. "And because it was someone who had once been close to him, his rage . . . it could not . . . *would* not be contained. He exploded and laid waste to an entire region. He left no one alive. Not man. Not woman. Not even child. They all burned." She raised one finger. "All except his brother . . . he wanted the man to see just what he had wrought. And the kittens." Her head tilted a bit as she let this last part sink in. "He protected *all* the remaining kittens."

Brannie bit her lip to stop from laughing out loud, and

Celyn's eyes rolled so far back into his head, she feared they would stay that way forever.

Slipping his weapon into his scabbard, Celyn waved his sister back and stepped forward, clearing his throat. Glaring, all the guards faced him, separating a bit when they saw the size of her brother.

He gave his most charming smile as he stood outside that cell.

"Hello," he said, his voice lower than she'd heard it in a long while. "Remember me, little human?"

And, apparently, the storyteller did remember Brannie's brother, based on the way that pewter mug the human had been drinking from spun out of the cell and slammed right into Celyn the Charming's forehead.

Celyn gripped his forehead, which now throbbed ten thousand times more than it had less than a minute before. The hysterical giggling of his sister not helping matters one bit.

"*What the hell—?*" he roared.

"You!" the evil wench accused. "Dragon! Left me here to die!"

"Vicious harpy of hell—"

"Left me to rot. In this cell!" She got to her feet, kicking her chair behind her. "And now you return. For what this return? To see my suffering? To relish in it?"

"What suffering?" Celyn demanded. "From the width of your hips, you look like you've been eating quite well!"

She pointed a finger. "Are you calling me fat?"

"I'm calling you healthy, as in not starving. As in not suffering, you whiny cow!"

She walked out of her cell and into the hallway, not one of the guards attempting to stop her. Celyn had the feeling she'd had free rein in this place since he'd left her here.

In fact—he glanced into her cell—someone had decorated

her room so that it was warm and friendly. Almost inviting. There was even a tapestry tacked to the wall. A tapestry! In a jail cell!

What the hell had been going on here? Had she bewitched all these weak-minded human males? His sister was right—nothing was easier to manipulate than human males. They were bloody pathetic!

"What do you want, useless dragon?" the woman demanded. "Why do you come here after all this time?"

"My queen has requested your presence, Rider."

"To execute me?"

"No."

"Why not?"

Perhaps Celyn had drunk so much the night before, he'd lost his mind. It had been known to happen. Especially to the uninitiated who'd taken a few sips of his grandfather's ale.

But when he looked at his sister, her eyes were wide and her hand was over her mouth to keep from laughing out loud—and he didn't think he was imagining that part.

"Could we just go please?" he asked the woman. Nearly begged.

"So you can continue my shame?"

Deciding not to engage this crazy female one second longer, Celyn simply stretched out his arm and pointed toward the exit.

"Wait," one of the guards said, a catch in his voice. "You're leaving us?"

"I must go, comrade," the Outerplains female explained sadly. "I have been ordered to leave by this cruel, worthless dragon."

"I let you live, didn't I?"

"I do not speak to you!" she growled back at him.

"Will we ever see you again?" another guard asked.

And at that point Brannie walked off, unable to take a second more of this.

"If not in this life, comrade, then in the next."

"No," Celyn said, grabbing the back of the woman's shirt. "I won't listen to another word." He began walking, dragging her with him. "I refuse to. I absolutely *refuse*."

The dragon rudely pulled Elina out of her home for the last eight months and into the bright sunlight of the town square.

The sunlight didn't actually bother her. She'd been allowed to come and go as she'd pleased since being tossed into the jail. She'd soon become friendly with the townspeople, earning a little money at the local stables.

"Where are you taking me? To the gallows?" she asked.

"You need to stop talking that way. I've never met anyone so ready to die," the dragon complained.

"I am always ready to die. At any time."

He stopped. "Why?"

"Why what?"

A female who had dark hair and eyes like the fool before her stepped in. "I'll let them know you're bringing her." Then she ran off laughing.

The dragon gave a short snarl before facing Elina. "Why do you *want* to die?"

"I have no desire to die."

"Then why do you seem so ready for it?"

"To die with honor. If you cannot avoid death, then you must die with honor. Do you not plan to die with honor, dragon?"

"No," he said plainly, dark eyes staring at her. "I plan to fight death all the way, dragging those trying to kill me along for the ride."

"I would agree with you, dragon . . . except I am guilty of trying to kill your queen."

"But you didn't do a very good job. Perhaps if you were better at it, I'd feel more inclined to take your head myself.

But at this point, it would feel like stepping on a squirrel. Annoying. Sad. And a little messy."

Elina assumed that to a dragon she must seem like a small animal, but still . . . she didn't appreciate being called one.

Pulling her arm away, Elina glanced around the town and nodded east. "Isn't there a gallows that way?" she asked, walking off in that direction.

The dragon cut in front of her and, after a very long sigh, he leaned down and lifted Elina up, placing her on his shoulder.

As he stalked away from the gallows, he muttered something under his breath, but Elina couldn't quite make it out.

Strong, cool fingers pressed against his temples, making soft circles before slipping into his hair.

Éibhear the Contemptible relaxed into his mate, enjoying how Izzy's chain mail pressed against his back while she stood there rubbing his head.

They were all waiting. Still in the war room, everyone quietly chatted amongst themselves.

"You know," Izzy said softly, her words for him alone, "you no longer have to be so bitchy to your cousin."

"I didn't say a word to him."

"You don't realize, but your silence speaks volumes. You don't think Celyn notices that? And when you do deign to say something to him, you're definitely bitchy."

Éibhear smirked. "I wouldn't call it bitchy. I just call it terse and unpleasant."

"It's been years, Éibhear. Years. It's time to let it go."

"We buried our issues ages ago."

"But you still do not speak to one another."

"Not true. When he sees me, he says, 'Hello.' And I always reply, 'Cousin.'"

Izzy returned to his lap, her arms slipping around his neck. "I want you two to be friends again."

"Izzy . . . we were never that close. He, like everyone else in the family, always thought I was an idiot."

"What makes you think that?"

"Because they said . . . 'Éibhear . . . you're an idiot.'"

"I don't see how you can be so close to Brannie but so cold to her brother."

"Brannie and I are close because of you. And she stopped calling me idiot after I threw her into that jungle pit with the hungry crocodile."

Izzy laughed, but stopped abruptly when the war room door opened and Brannie walked in. "Celyn will be here in a minute," she announced to the room before rushing over to Izzy's side and pulling up a chair next to her.

She sat and stared at Izzy, her lips a thin line because she clearly had something to tell her.

"What?" Izzy whispered.

"You have to experience it for yourself, cousin."

"Tell me," she ordered, leaning forward and wiggling her bum around on Éibhear's lap . . . something that he greatly enjoyed. "I must know, you cow!"

Éibhear often had to remind himself that in battle these two were an unbelievable team, bringing blood, death, and pain to all who challenged them. But when not in battle . . . they were absolutely ridiculous.

The door opened again, this time kicked in by a stern-faced Celyn. He stalked into the room with a pert-assed bundle tossed over his shoulder.

Without a word, he lifted the woman off and placed her on the floor in front of the big wooden table with all the maps.

Izzy glanced at Éibhear, both of them—he guessed—sharing the same thought. *She looks awfully healthy for a woman who has been trapped in the city jails for the last eight months.*

"There you are!" Rhiannon said, getting to her feet and towering over the woman. "Oh, hello, my dear."

The woman, so very pale, dropped to one knee in front of Éibhear's mother.

"My lady. I regret what I have tried to do," she said, her accent as strange as her eyes. But Éibhear hadn't met any Riders from the Steppes of the Outerplains before. He knew they had their own languages and laws, but what those languages and laws were, he had no idea. "But I implore you to take my head quickly and with no remorse. It is the least I deserve."

Rhiannon studied the woman for a long moment before looking at her nephew-by-mating. "What the bloody hells did you tell this female, Celyn?"

"I haven't told her anything," Celyn growled as he walked toward the back of the room and an empty seat. "But apparently she lives for death . . . or something."

"That is *not* what I said," the Rider snapped at Celyn. "Do you even attempt to listen, dragon?"

"Not when all I hear is insanity."

"Insanity? Why? Because I have honor?"

"Squirrel!" Celyn yelled before dropping into the chair and crossing his arms over his chest.

Izzy looked at Éibhear, but when he only shrugged, she sighed in exasperation and looked at Brannie. And Éibhear knew at the moment . . . he no longer existed for his mate. Why? Because there was entertainment afoot that involved the torment of a family member and, eventually, juicy gossip.

Shaking her head, Rhiannon leaned down and placed her hands on the woman's shoulders. "Please, dear. Get up. Get up."

While glaring at Celyn, the woman got to her feet.

"My dear girl," Rhiannon said sweetly, capturing the

woman's attention, "I have no intention of executing you. If that's what you fear."

"I do not fear, Queen Rhiannon. Simply expect."

"*Squirrel!*"

Those pale blue eyes locked on Celyn again. "Quiet."

The queen glared at her "very favorite personal guard!"—as she insisted on calling Éibhear's cousin—and slipped her arms around the woman's shoulders. "You have nothing to worry about here, my dear. All that happened before is in the past. Now, I'd like to introduce you to someone."

She led the Rider around the enormous table and over to Annwyl. "This, my dear," Rhiannon announced, "is Annwyl."

The human blinked. "Annwyl? *The* Annwyl?"

Every dragon and human in the room winced at that, knowing how sensitive Annwyl the Bloody was about her reputation and her name. Yet it was a well-deserved reputation. At one time, she would have killed a man—or anything really—as soon as look at him, though Annwyl always had a reason. Always. But with the help of Dagmar, things had mostly changed. Mostly.

Shame there were so few who understood that.

"You are Annwyl?" the woman asked again.

Annwyl sighed, her face a sad, resigned mask, as she replied, "Aye. I'm Annwyl. *The* Annwyl."

"You are the Southland queen who earned the respect of the decadent and lazy Southland male. That is not easy thing to do."

"Well . . . thank you." Annwyl gave a very small smile. "That's nice."

The woman nodded. "Your blood-soaked hands and heartless willingness to kill all those who dare invade your territory bring *some* respect from the Mighty Daughters of the Steppes. Although the imperialist, decadent life you and your royals lead on the backs of your defenseless peasants still disgusts most of my people greatly."

Izzy cringed, Brannie dropped her head into her hands, and everyone else fell silent, except Gwenvael who snorted a laugh. Of course that got him a hard slap to the back of the head from their father.

"Isn't that nice," Annwyl practically snarled between clenched teeth.

"It is," Rhiannon quickly cut in. "Very nice. Especially because we need a little favor from you . . . uh . . . what was your name again, dear?"

"Elina Shestakova of the Black Bear Riders of the Midnight Mountains of Despair in the Far Reaches of the Steppes of the Outerplains."

"Ah, yes. *That* name."

"Do you actually ride bears?" Gwenvael felt the need to ask.

"The old ones say that our ancestors rode the black bear. But now we only ride the horse. They are easy to manage and do not have the big claws."

"Do you have a shorter name we can use?" Fearghus asked.

"No," she stated flatly, but when everyone simply stared, she added, "I joke."

Talaith scratched her nose. "Funny."

"Since you are not kin or part of my tribe, you may call me Elina Shestakova, Daughter of—"

"Elina then," Rhiannon quickly cut in. "That's such a nice name. Isn't that nice, everyone?"

There were barely muttered agreements.

"Now, dear Elina, as I said, we need you to do us a small favor and all will be forgiven regarding that nasty business of you trying to kill me."

"What is it you need?"

"We need you to arrange a meeting with the leader of all your tribes."

"You want to meet with the Anne Atli?"

"Is she the one who rules all the tribes of the Steppes?"

"Yes. Anne Atli rules all the tribes. It not only is her title but also was the name of the first female Captain of the Horseriders, and it is the name taken by every female leader who has come after her."

"Then, yes, that's who we want to meet with."

"I am unable to promise I can arrange such a meeting. I will have to go through the leader of my tribe, Glebovicha. But I will do all I can."

"Is Glebovicha the one who sent you here?" Celyn asked.

The Rider took a moment to answer. "Perhaps."

"So," Celyn barked, "the woman who sent you here to die is the woman you need to go through to get to the tribes' leader?"

"*Why are you talking to me?*" she suddenly bellowed.

"*Because I'm fascinated by your willingness to die!*"

"Enough!" Rhiannon ordered. She stopped, took a breath. "Will you do this for me, Elina?"

"I will. Of course."

"Excellent!" the queen cheered, wrapping her arms around the woman's shoulders and hugging her tight. "Such a . . . dear . . . sweet . . . girl!" she added between sniffs of the top of the human's head. "And tasty-smelling."

"*Mum!*" Morfyd instantly chastised.

"What?" Rhiannon pushed the woman away. "She . . . just smells nice, is all. I wasn't planning to eat her or anything. As I've been told many times . . . that's still wrong."

* * *

Now, his sister said inside Celyn's poor, abused head, *this is where Rhiannon says that someone has to take the poor little pale waif home.*

Ah, yes. The downside of his siblings being able to communicate with him with their mind—that one's siblings could talk whenever they wanted. Like now. About ridiculous bullshit.

I'm not taking her anywhere. She's beyond irritating.

Of course you're not taking her anywhere.

That hadn't been what he'd expected his sister to say.

What do you mean?

I mean our parents are not about to allow you to go anywhere.

Our parents? I'm not a seventy-year-old hatchling, Brannie. I can go where I like.

Uh-huh. Sure you can.

Confused by the entire conversation, Celyn heard the queen state, "You'll sleep here tonight in a proper bed, and get started tomorrow. We'll make sure you have food and a fresh horse for your trip."

"I have horse. I get own food."

Celyn rolled his eyes.

"What?" the woman demanded, immediately catching his annoyed expression. "What is that look?"

"You won't take food? You're going to starve instead?"

"The forests are filled with food. I hunt."

"As well as you assassinate? Because you might starve."

"Celyn," his mother said softly. "Let it go."

"Fine. I'll let it go."

"Wait," Rhiannon said, raising her index finger. "Celyn has a good point."

"I can hunt my own food. I do not need *his* help," the Rider sneered at Celyn.

"Clearly you need someone's help."

The woman made a noise, and Celyn snapped back, "Did you just hiss at me, female?"

"Stop it," Rhiannon cut in. "Both of you. *I* am queen here—"

Fearghus suddenly cleared his throat and gestured to Annwyl with a tilt of his head, so Rhiannon amended her statement to, "I am the most important queen here—"

"Mum, that's not what I—"

"—and I think it's necessary for you, dear Elina, to have someone to ensure your safety. And I think that should be—"

"Bercelak," Ghleanna suddenly cut in. "Bercelak should escort her."

Celyn's uncle stared at his sister until she elbowed him in the ribs.

"Oh. Right. I guess I should do it."

Celyn heard Brannie chuckle inside his head. *Told ya*.

Elina didn't know what was going on. Nor did she care. She suddenly had something important to do! Someone was trusting her to do something that could change . . . everything.

The Tribes of the Steppes didn't have alliances. They didn't have truces. Instead, they took payment to not attack the territories closest to them. Those who didn't pay risked an onslaught beyond comprehension. Of a seemingly never-ending army of Riders raining terror and pain and blood down upon their heads.

Most paid.

An alliance would be a good thing. A change in the right direction. Elina's people weren't barbarians. They weren't demons in human form. They were merely herders who had grown tired of being trampled upon by the armies of big cities and royal landowners. So although battalions of Queen Annwyl's army had been allowed through the Outer-plains closest to the Eastern Coast, they weren't allowed past the Conchobar Mountains into tribe lands. But an alliance with Annwyl the Bloody . . . ?

Of course, the problem wasn't the Anne Atli, was it? It would be Glebovicha. She would not be happy about the "weakest of my tribe" talking to Anne Atli. Only with special permission from tribal leaders did one get to speak to Anne Atli about tribal business. Glebovicha would not like that.

Yet in this task . . . in this task Elina would not fail. She could and *would* do this. Not only for her honor but for her people.

Even if it meant being forced to spend more time than was acceptable with that idiot dragon.

She'd prefer the cranky man who kept growling. He clearly didn't want to go with her, but . . . wait. Was he a dragon, too?

Elina looked closely at the man. Like the annoying dragon, he had dark eyes, black hair that reached past his massive shoulders, and a strong square jaw. Then again, so did the short-haired woman sitting next to him.

Exactly how many dragons were here? And how did they manage to walk around as human? As dragon, they were so gigantic, she didn't understand how they could get all that bulk stuffed into these considerably smaller human bodies.

"I have another task for my dear mate," the Dragon Queen told the short-haired woman. "So Celyn can take her."

"*No*," the short-haired woman snapped back. "He can't. He must protect you." She smiled, but it was so forced that Elina instinctively leaned away. "That's his most important job," she finished between a smile that involved clenched teeth.

The queen's arm slipped around Elina's shoulder, pulling her closer. Her smile was there, but as false as the other female's. "Perhaps you forget who I am, Low Born," the queen said in a cheery voice. "I am the queen. I rule. And if

I want one of my personal guards to do a task, he will do that task. Do we understand each other?"

The female stared at the queen for several long moments until her fist suddenly came down on the empty seat beside her, decimating it in the process. She was up and near the queen when another male went around the big desk and cut between the two females.

"No, Ghleanna. No, no, no, no, no, *no*."

He placed his hands on her shoulders and held her back.

Looking over the man's shoulder, the female pointed a damning finger at the queen. "You may rule these lands, Rhiannon the White, but you *do not* rule my family!"

"Everything belongs to me. *Everything!*"

"That is enough!" The idiot dragon stood up. "Enough." He looked at the short-haired female. "Mum"—*Oh, that's his mother*—"I'm an adult. She's my queen. I follow *her* orders. Not yours." He looked at Queen Rhiannon and nodded his head. "And I will be happy to escort her . . ." He gestured at Elina with a flip of his hand. ". . . to wherever."

"My name you do not know," Elina accused.

"It's impossibly long! What do you want from me?"

"Respect! But I do not think you understand word, worthless one!"

"Keep in mind, She of the Impossibly Long Name, that I am your protection. You might want to be nice to me."

"Nice to dragon who forgets woman he takes to prison?"

"Would you let that go?"

"No! I will never let that go!"

"Fine! Suit yourself! *And would you stop laughing!*" he bellowed at the younger dark-haired female who also looked just like him. God, how many of these dragons who could become human were there?

The younger female, who hadn't been laughing, merely smiling, shrugged at Elina. And when the dragon turned away, she pointed at her head and mouthed, *He's crazy.*

Yes. Elina, sadly, could see that.

Chapter Eight

Elina watched the people or dragons or whatever they were walk out of the room. No one said anything to her. She seemed to cease to exist once the rude dragon had agreed to travel with her.

Deciding it was probably best to get moving now rather than wait a day, Elina turned toward the door . . . only to find the rude bastard standing between her and the exit.

"What now?" she demanded, glaring up at him. Good thing her people were tall, because these dragons when human . . .

"We're not leaving tonight," he told her. Ordered her, really.

"Will we not?"

"We will leave in the morning. Be ready to go at daybreak."

"And what do I do until then?"

"Manage to stay alive? That would be great."

Without another word, he walked out.

Elina stared at the open doorway. It had been a long time since she'd disliked someone so much. Especially a male. Like most Daughters of the Steppes, she'd been taught that men served three purposes—breeding, child rearing, and trash removal. She needed no one's protection. She'd gotten here alive, hadn't she?

But she had to remember that the dragon was not her problem or priority. She had a task she needed to accomplish and she'd committed to that. And it was a task she would truly enjoy doing, unlike the task that had brought her here.

Confident that she could tolerate the dragon until she reached her homelands, Elina headed to the doorway.

She stepped into the hall but took a quick step back when two females suddenly moved in front of her. Both wore chain mail and had weapons hanging from belts around their waists and strapped to their backs. Many in Elina's tribe would love for her to look this much like a warrior and be able to back up that battle-ready appearance. But she really had no desire to be a warmonger. It simply was not in her blood.

The one with short black hair and black eyes, who seemed to be the sister of the rude dragon, smiled at Elina. "Hi."

Elina gave a typical Rider greeting. "Hope death finds you well today."

"Um . . . okay." She cleared her throat. "I'm Branwen. This is Izzy."

"Elina Shestakova of the Black Bear Riders of the—"

"Yes, yes. We got that. Earlier. Your . . . extensive name."

"Have you come to kill me?" Elina asked.

"Uh . . . no."

"Then move."

They did, and Elina stepped between them and began walking. She studied the castle as she walked. There were beautiful tapestries on the walls. Some depicting battles. She stopped to look closely at one and realized the two females were still behind her.

She faced them and asked, "Do you fear I still plan to kill your Dragon Queen?"

"Surprisingly, no," the one called Branwen replied.

"So you follow because you find me attractive? Sadly, for you," she went on honestly, "I do not desire females. But there are many in my tribe who do. I can introduce you. You can become one of their many wives."

"What? No."

"There is no shame. Many of our tribes are made up of only females. They do not like men. They do not like cocks. They only like the pussy."

"No, no, no," Branwen quickly corrected. "We like the cocks."

The brown-skinned woman, Izzy, suddenly turned to her comrade. "What are you doing?"

"I don't know. But she's completely freaking me out! I think it was that greeting. Who says hello like that?"

"If death does not find you well," Elina explained, "he will take you. So we hope he finds you well."

Izzy nodded. "See? That is quite logical."

"You have eyes like bastard dragon," Elina noted about Branwen. "And you were with him earlier at jail. Do you share mother? Or do all your dragon people who are not royal look alike?"

"We share mother."

"Now you're starting to talk like her?" Izzy asked.

"I can't help it! The way she talks is oddly entrancing." She took a breath. "He's my brother."

"I pity your soul. He is bastard. And deserves painful death. You, however, seem very nice. I am glad to know you." She nodded at Izzy. "And you, too, dark-skinned female with big shoulders. You remind me of bear I once hunted during snowstorm. I use his pelt now on my hut floor."

Since the females did nothing but stare at her, Elina turned and went in search of food.

Celyn caught up with his parents in the Great Hall. "Mind telling me what that was about?"

"You have a job *here*, Celyn," his mother said in her most "I'm a general and you're not" tone.

"I'd believe that, Mum, if Brannie wasn't busy telling me

in my head that you two wouldn't let me go because you consider me weak. Do you consider me weak?"

"Of course not!" Ghleanna tapped her mate's arm. "Tell him, Bram. Tell him we don't consider him weak."

"Ow, Ghleanna," Bram whined, rubbing his poor arm.

"Tell him."

"Because gods forbid a Cadwaladr be considered weak."

"Yes," mother and son said together.

"No one considers you weak, Celyn," Bram said. "You have to know that."

"Then what's going on?" He stepped closer. "Brannie called me Fal. Am I Fal in this?"

Fal was Celyn's older brother and one of the most useless dragons in the Cadwaladr Clan. He'd been sent to the Desert Land borders to guard the salt mines. Only the most worthless or corrupt troops were sent to the salt mines. And it was too horrifying a thought that Celyn might be considered a Fal.

He was not a Fal!

"First off," Ghleanna snapped, "don't talk about your brother that way. Fal has many . . . talents."

"Do you pause like that when you talk of me?"

"Of course not!"

"Son," Bram said, his hand resting on Celyn's shoulder. "We have complete and utter faith in you."

"Then why don't you want me to escort that girl? It's one of the things Cadwaladrs are called on to do all the time."

"And we're sure you'll do it very well."

Celyn reared back, horrified.

"What?" Bram asked, panicked. "What did I say?"

"That's what you said to Fal before Uncle Bercelak had him shipped off to the salt mines."

"Oh." Bram glanced at Ghleanna. "Did I?"

Disgusted, Celyn turned and stalked off. He now, officially, had the worst headache of all time!

* * *

Dagmar, her dog Adda by her side, searched the library until she tracked down her nephew Frederik. She wanted to fill him in on all the latest. Not because she needed him to do anything, but because he was always a good source of rational thought in this insane household filled with a mad queen, her dragon consort, and the dragon consort's entire bloody family.

Frederik had been left on Queen Annwyl's doorstep by Dagmar's older—and idiotic—brothers some ten years ago. It was something done by many a Northman when faced with a boy he didn't know what to do with.

And, at first, Dagmar had found the boy's presence the highest inconvenience. As Battle Lord to Queen Annwyl and Steward of Garbhán Isle, Dagmar had little time for boys who seemed tragically . . . stupid.

Yet she'd been as wrong about Frederik as her own people had been wrong about her simply because she was a woman. Frederik had not been stupid. Cursed with as poor eyesight as herself? Yes. Stupid? Oh, very far from it. In fact, he'd been much smarter than she'd been because he'd successfully hidden his keen mind from his kinsmen, forcing them to send him away rather than deal with his supposed uselessness.

But Frederik had become quite useful to Dagmar once he'd gotten some spectacles to help with his close-in sight and was given the freedom to be who he was. He was a thinker, that one. He had a talent that was nothing but a curse in the harsh Northlands, but worthy of praise in the gentler south. A smart, quick-thinking plotter. But he was never cruel. Never heartless. Simply bright and cunning.

Just like his aunt.

Unlike Dagmar, however, Frederik did manage to find the hidden warrior within. It hadn't been easy for him. Not like it was for her other nephews, who many believed had been shot from the womb with small warhammers at the ready. Frederik had had to work much harder to get as far as he had, but—as always—he'd been very smart. He didn't ask any of Gwenvael's brothers for battle training. Instead, he'd approached Bercelak the Great. A bold and risky move that had impressed *everyone.*

Because of his bravery, many dragons and humans came to Frederik about sensitive issues that they hoped he'd bring directly to her. It should have bothered Dagmar, but it didn't. There was something about knowing that dragons feared her the way many humans did that had a rather heady effect.

Especially considering where her life had started. As a "girl child" of the great Reinholdt. True, girls were revered in the Northlands because they were so rare, but they were also protected to the point of smothering. It wasn't until Dagmar came to the Southlands that she'd found her home, where she could happily be her true manipulative, plotting, conniving self. And she'd found a dragon who was the perfect match for her.

Although, Dagmar had to admit that as things had changed so drastically between them over the last few years, she'd thought Gwenvael's feelings for her would change too. But she'd forgotten he was not a human male. He was a dragon and dragons were different. Difficult, but different.

She was grateful, though, because she still loved the devious bastard. With all her hard heart. Important since the last ten years they'd been forced to need each other more than they'd ever thought possible.

Dagmar turned a corner in the expansive library that Éibhear and Frederik had organized together and that Frederik now meticulously maintained, and she stopped as she neared a large table covered in books and scrolls.

Frederik, always sensing when Dagmar was nearby, lifted his head from his work. He had the Reinholdt eyes. Grey and cold . . . just like her own. He smiled at her, a warm and loving smile that disappeared as soon as that ball of parchment hit her in the forehead.

She sighed and glared at the offender, desperately trying to ignore all those giggles. "Does someone want to miss supper yet again?"

"You'd starve us?"

"Yes. Yes, I would."

Small feet landed on the table, small balled fists were placed on small hips. "I'll tell my father that you *dare* starve his precious offspring."

Dagmar pointed a finger at her eldest daughter, Arlais. "You would think you'd be grateful."

"Grateful for what exactly?"

"That I didn't smother you at birth. A situation that can change at any moment."

"Auntie Dagmar!" Frederik admonished, even while he laughed.

"She started it!"

"*You're* the adult."

"*She's* the demon spawn."

"Auntie Dagmar!"

Dagmar's saving grace came up behind her. As beautiful as his father but as cold and devious as his mother, her eldest child and only son looked over his six sisters.

"All of you, out," the boy said calmly, a thick book tucked under his arm, cold grey eyes locked on the eldest girl.

"We don't take orders from *you*," Arlais snapped.

A silent battle raged between grey eyes and gold until Dagmar's daughter snarled, "All right, fine!"

She jumped off the table and motioned to her younger

sisters. "You lot, come on." She walked toward the door but stopped next to Dagmar. "Perhaps you should keep in mind that while you may be the daughter of a warlord, *I* am the daughter of a prince."

Dagmar slowly looked at her child. "And perhaps you should keep in mind that I am the one woman not afraid to send your insolent ass to a nunnery."

Arlais sniffed, her haughtiness resting on her shoulders like a mantle. "My father would never allow that to happen. And when *I* rule, you'll suffer my wrath!" And with that, the spoiled little bitch marched out the door, her golden-headed younger sisters happily following.

Once they were gone, her son turned to her.

"What?" Dagmar demanded, but already knowing what he was going to say.

"You'll have to learn to handle them on your own eventually, Mum."

"When they're older and less annoying—"

"They are, tragically, just like my father. So they'll never be *less* annoying."

"Unnvar, your father does love you."

"Perhaps, but I don't see how that knowledge helps me in any way."

Dagmar shrugged. "My father's love kept me going for thirty years before I escaped the Northlands. I hope the same for you."

"You do know, Mum, that my father is your only true weakness?"

"I know." She sighed. "I've learned to live with that flaw . . . just as you'll have to."

With a sad, forlorn sigh, Var nodded his head and walked away.

Frederik cleared his throat. "Are we really sure he's—"

"Yes, Frederik. He's ten."

"If you say so."

* * *

Annoyed and more than a little angry, Celyn returned to the room he'd been in before and dropped face-first onto the bed.

What had he gotten himself into? Trying to prove something to his parents, he'd bargained himself into a right shitty situation with that female. He'd passed her on the way to his room. She'd been studying some silver chalices and he wondered if she planned to steal them. The Riders were known thieves. He doubted she was much better.

Which was worse? he wondered. Being so unappreciated by his own parents or being forced to deal with that harpy all the way to the Steppes of the Outerplains?

He didn't know.

Honestly, how could any female, dragon or human, be as annoying as that woman? There were dragons who lived in the Steppes who were said in legend to be annoying, but they weren't friendly or organized and wanted to be left alone, so other dragons did. That meant Celyn didn't know exactly how annoying they might be, but he refused to believe even the Steppes dragons could be as annoying as this one human female.

Celyn rolled to his back and stared up at the ceiling.

All right. So he'd forgotten her. Not his best moment, he'd admit. But she had been sent to assassinate his queen. How could she be so haughty about it all when she'd come here to do something that would normally get her head bitten off?

In fact, he'd saved her life. Because if Uncle Bercelak had gotten his cruel claws on her, he would have torn her to pieces for such an affront. But it had been *Celyn* who spirited her away in time.

Yet did he get any credit for that? A bit of appreciation from the death-ready female? No! The squirrel simply nattered at him. The way real squirrels nattered at Dagmar's dogs from the safety of the trees.

Natter, natter, natter.

And now? Now he would be stuck with her for *days*. Listening to her complain about his life while wishing for her own death.

The bedroom door opened, and his sister and Izzy walked in.

"Oh," Branwen gushed, "she is *fabulous!*"

Celyn lifted himself up on his elbows. "Why is this happening to me? I'm a lovely, *lovely* dragon. Everyone adores me. Human. Dragon. Centaur. Even those little things in the forests . . . with the ears . . . and the little fluffy tails?"

"Rabbits?"

"Aye! Rabbits. They love me, too."

His sister smirked. "Only because you don't eat them. Because you equate dragons eating rabbits with humans eating rats. . . . It's beneath you."

Celyn glared at his sister. "They still *love me.*"

Izzy perched herself on the footboard of the bed, long arms wrapped around even longer legs. "It may not be that bad."

"She threw a pint at my head."

"Nailed him, too," Brannie unnecessarily added.

"She was upset," Izzy reasoned. "Women do not like to be forgotten about. It insults us."

"She wasn't *my* bloody responsibility."

"She is now," Brannie muttered, but when Celyn glared at her, she quickly turned her eyes to the ceiling.

"I only did this because my parents think I'm Fal."

"No, they do not! Who told you such a despicable thing?" Izzy turned to Brannie. "Why would you tell your brother such a despicable thing?"

With a roll of her eyes, Brannie admitted, "Mum and Da don't think of you as Fal. He's a failure at life all on his own."

"But they clearly didn't want me to go. Why?"

Brannie shrugged. "You talk too much."

"What?"

"You ask too many questions. 'Why are we doing this? Where are we going now? Is all this armor really necessary? Why do you insist on yelling at me? Do all humans smell like you?' It's bloody endless."

"I'm curious is all. Is there something wrong with that?"

"Yes. When you constantly ask questions."

"It's not like I ask them during battle."

"No. But you do ask them constantly every other time." Brannie gave another shrug. "I think Mum and Da were worried you'd end up getting killed by the troop leaders. Or you'd cause a war. But Uncle Bercelak refused to have your talents wasted. So you were assigned to Rhiannon's protection guard."

"Wait. Are you telling me that's it? That was their big problem?"

"Aye. They don't want you to go anywhere because you're good at protecting Rhiannon and she doesn't get violently annoyed by your constant chattiness. Unlike every soldier in our battalions."

"Are you telling me that I've attached myself to that Rider female because of *this*?"

"Looks like it!" Brannie's head flew back from the pillow Celyn winged at her. "What was that for?"

"I'm now trapped with this vile little female because of you!"

Brannie giggled. "Yeah. I know."

The bedroom door opened again and Éibhear's giant bulk filled the open space, completely blocking out the light from the hallway.

Silver eyes searched the room before he said, "Oh . . . you're in here, Izzy."

"I am," Izzy said. "Why don't you join us? We're just chatting."

In answer, Éibhear grunted. Like a bull. Reminding Celyn they still weren't very close.

Many years ago, Celyn's relationship with Izzy had come between Celyn and Éibhear. But Celyn's logic at the time had been if the blue idiot was going to pass up his chance at a woman like Iseabail the Dangerous, that was his bad decision. Why Éibhear insisted on blaming Celyn for his own shitty decision-making skills, Celyn would never know.

Celyn had actually loved Izzy at that time. But it had been a young love. Both of them just figuring out what they would want from their mates one day; and something Celyn refused to ever regret no matter how much Izzy's adoptive kin made their own blood cousin suffer for it.

Besides, from their temporary passion had grown a great friendship. One that meant more to him than he'd ever thought it would.

And yet . . . Celyn wasn't above using his past with Izzy to get what he wanted *now*. And what he wanted now was to get that ridiculous female out of his life. For good. Without worrying about listening to that speech from Bercelak about "making commitments and sticking with them."

"You know what's going on here, don't you, Éibhear?" Celyn asked his cousin.

The *giant* dragon—gods! Éibhear was so bloody *huge* as human—locked those silver eyes on Celyn. "What's going on?" he grumbled.

"Yeah," Izzy asked, confused, "what's going on?"

"I'm trying to get Izzy back, you know? It won't take much. I was the best she ever had."

"What the battle-fuck are you doing?" Brannie demanded, her eyes wide in panic. Izzy didn't look much better, both of them clearly remembering the beating Celyn had received all those years ago when Éibhear had found out that Celyn had been sleeping with Izzy.

Unable to face his own feelings about Izzy, Éibhear had

lashed out. And it was, honestly, the worst beating Celyn had ever taken. But he knew if he'd survived that—which he obviously had—he could survive bloody anything because his cousin had wanted him dead that day. And, as a Cadwaladr, Éibhear would have been allowed to kill Celyn because it had been a "proper challenge." Among their clan, "proper challenges" were allowed and expected. And if one of their kin died because of it . . . oh, well. That was just the way of things.

Éibhear studied Celyn for a long moment, his eyes narrowing, his entire, big body tense and ready to attack. But then, one side of his mouth lifted. It was almost a smile.

"Forget it," Éibhear said, and Celyn pushed himself off the bed.

"Come on," Celyn implored. "Be a lad!"

"Not on your life! You're stuck with that morbid little bitch. She's your problem now."

"Izzy's still in love with me. She's never loved you. She's just using you to get me jealous."

Éibhear threw back his big head and laughed. "That pale bitch is better revenge, cousin, than beating the shit out of you was that first time. And watching her make you miserable will bring me such joy." He scratched Celyn's head as if he were a small child. "Absolute joy."

"You're a bastard."

"Good luck on your trip to the Outerplains. Best bring something warm. I hear those Steppes are surprisingly chilly." Laughing, Éibhear walked out.

"You bastard! Ow!" Celyn covered the spot on the back of his head where Brannie slapped him and faced his sister. "What was that for?"

"Have you gone mad?" Brannie demanded. "He's a bloody Mì-runach!" she reminded him. And Brannie had a point. The Mì-runach were feared for a good reason.

But none of that mattered when Celyn was desperate.

"He could have torn you apart in seconds," Brannie went on.

"But he didn't even try, did he?" Celyn sadly complained.

"Are you really so desperate over one human girl that you'd actually goad Éibhear the *Contemptible* into a fight you couldn't possibly win just so you could be too wounded to leave?" Izzy asked, shaking her head in disgust.

"I suffered a beating before," Celyn reminded her. "For our love."

Izzy rolled her eyes and walked away while Brannie sneered, "You are pathetic."

A nice woman who'd been cutting up a pig in the kitchen had been kind enough to get Elina a bowl of stew and a few loaves of freshly baked bread, then lead her to the enormous dining room. The woman had called it the Great Hall and sat Elina down at one of two long tables in it.

Once alone, Elina dived into her meal. The food was hot and good and fresh. Her people often lived on dried supplies, especially during the winter storm months.

Even better, as Elina reached the bottom of her bowl, it was whisked away and another full bowl of hot stew quickly replaced it. Elina looked up into a smiling woman's face.

"If you need anything else, m'lady, you just let me know. Name's Jenna."

Elina nodded her thanks and went back to her food.

So . . . this was the "decadent" Southland lifestyle she'd always heard about from the Elders in her tribe. Stories of the materialistic ways of the Southland royals, who let their people starve while they lived in luxury, were repeated among her people, who shared everything. Life on the Steppes was hard but rewarding. There were no luxuries. There were no servants to bring hot food without one asking for it.

Elina had to admit . . . she could easily get used to this life. But the tribes' Elders always reminded everyone about how seductive the Southlander's awful lives were.

Of course, with stew like this . . . how awful could it really be?

"Mind if I join you?"

Elina finally lifted her head from her second bowl of stew and looked into the face of the handsome man who'd stepped between the queen and the dark-haired female nearly an hour ago. Now he stood before her alone, his silver hair reaching past his broad shoulders while warm blue eyes patiently waited for her answer.

"Are you dragon?" she asked.

He blinked. "Does it matter?"

"No."

He seemed to be waiting for her to say something else, but when Elina didn't—what else was there to say?—he pulled out the chair next to her and sat down.

A servant suddenly appeared and placed a plate of fruit, cheese, and bread in front of him. Another servant brought a chalice and a crystal pitcher of water. The man poured himself a glass of water, smiling as he glanced at Elina.

"Decadent, isn't it?" he asked.

"Very."

"Does it offend you?"

"No. But I enjoy looking down on others and judging them for things that are none of my concern."

The man laughed. "Good to know." He placed the pitcher aside and took a sip. "Your name—"

"Elina Shestakova of the Black Bear Riders of the Midnight Mountains of Despair in the Far Reaches of the Steppes of the Outerplains."

"Yes. Well, Elina Shestakova of the Black Bear Riders of the Midnight Mountains of Despair in the Far Reaches of the Steppes of the Outerplains," he repeated back to her perfectly, "mind if I call you Elina as Queen Rhiannon suggested?"

"No. Days are long on the Steppes, so there is time for saying names. But things in the Southlands . . . they move faster, it seems."

"Not really. We just have much less patience. My name, by the way, is Bram the Merciful."

Elina sighed in envy. "Such a deliciously simple name." She studied him. "Why Merciful?"

"It's a nice way of saying I'm not much of a fighter."

"Nor am I. But my comrades just call me weak and pathetic. As children, they would spit on me. But last boy who did that I pushed into pit fire . . . so no one does that to me anymore."

"I'm sure they don't."

"What did your people do to you, Bram the Merciful?"

He shrugged. "Send me out to negotiate treaties and alliances."

"So cruel."

He leaned in a bit and whispered, "I actually like it, but I make sure to complain a lot."

"That is good. You make them think you hate it and then they make you do it more. Very smart."

"Thank you. So you came to the decadent Southlands to kill our queen?" he asked between bites of bread and cheese.

"I did. I failed. I am pathetic."

"Except, Elina, it didn't sound like you tried very hard. And clearly you're not lazy. You made the trip here, by yourself. So perhaps you just felt killing the queen was . . . wrong?"

"I am not warrior. I kill to eat. I kill in defense. But the Dragon Queen . . . she had done nothing to me. To my people. Why kill her? Other than her head would look nice outside Glebovicha's hut."

"There is no shame in not wanting to kill for no reason."

"There is shame in failure."

"You can't fail at what you didn't even try."

"Perhaps."

"But this new task you do plan to do?"

Elina nodded. "I made commitment to Dragon Queen."

"Excuse me, Elina, but didn't you make the commitment to *slay* the Dragon Queen as well?"

"I was not given option. I was told to do. No one asked me anything." Elina winced. She didn't mean to sound so bitter. "Do not worry, I plan to do whatever is necessary to assist the Dragon Queen and Annwyl the Bloody. They did not kill me when they had every right. For that alone I must give my all."

Bram the Merciful nodded, his lips curved in a soft smile. "And my son will be by your side to help you as much as possible."

"Your son?" Elina eyed the man. "The dolt?"

Bram chuckled. "Aye. The dolt."

"That is impossible. You are . . . smart. Wise. And you would never forget woman you left in prison."

"Don't think too poorly of my son. He is smarter than he realizes, and he doesn't know how to deal with that."

"Would he prefer stupid?"

"Not at all. It's just a little complicated to explain to those who do not understand the ways of the Cadwaladr Clan."

Elina jerked back a bit, a piece of bread still gripped in her hand, but nearly forgotten. "The Cadwaladr Clan?"

"You've heard of them?"

"Who has not? They are vile, brutal monsters reared to kill from birth." Elina nodded. "The tribes respect them greatly."

The male smiled. "Of course they do."

"They are dragons?" Elina shook her head. "That we did not know."

"Does it lessen your respect?"

"No. Just explains things."

Elina went back to her food, the sudden screaming behind her startling Bram the Merciful but not Elina. She was used to such screaming on the Steppes.

"Gods," Bram muttered under his breath. "I keep forgetting about their presence." Then he jumped again when "*Daaaaddddy!*" was screeched, the sound tearing through the stone walls.

With a sigh, the dragon looked over his shoulder at the little girl standing in the doorway at the back of the hall. "Hello, little Arlais."

"Great-Uncle Bram. Where is my father?"

"I don't—"

"What's happened?" the astoundingly beautiful golden-haired man called Gwenvael demanded, his long legs bringing him quickly into the Great Hall. Elina had noticed him earlier. So pretty. He would be in much demand among the tribes' best warriors.

The little girl leaped onto the table with ease and crossed her arms over her chest.

"I want that woman executed," the child announced.

Gwenvael stopped walking, rolled his eyes. "She's your *mother*, Arlais."

"Not by choice. She is a Low Born human who orders *me* around."

"Arlais, my darling—"

"She is the daughter of a warlord, but *I* am the daughter of a prince. I outrank her . . . in many ways. In beauty, talent, and a rare grace that comes with being royal born."

"Awwww. I've taught you so well." He placed his hands over his chest. "It warms my hard dragon heart to see so much annoying and painful arrogance at such a young age." He shrugged. "But you cannot have your mother executed."

She stamped her little foot. "That is unfair!"

"But you already knew that life was unfair and cruel, so none of this should surprise you."

The little girl gave an angry roar that shook the weapons

tacked to the walls. "When I rule this kingdom—and I *will* rule this kingdom, Daddy—"

"You'll have to get past your cousin Talwyn first and she'll skin you alive before she gives you anything," he said in singsong to his daughter.

"—you will *all* bow down before me in fear and—oooh," she suddenly said. "Shiny." She reached down to pick up something off the table but was quickly tackled from behind by smaller versions of herself. She hit the table hard while those five versions pummeled her. Even the smallest and youngest, barely a toddler, got in several good punches to the child's head before they all jumped up and yelled, "Destruction-ho!" Then they scrambled off the table, charged past Gwenvael—who, Elina guessed, was also a dragon—and out the door. The toddler was the slowest, so she stopped to hug the large dragon's human leg.

"Love you, Daddy!"

He stroked the toddler's golden head. "Of course you do. Because you are wise."

Laughing, she fled out the door and by now a boy and a tall, well-built, attractive young man, with round pieces of wire-held glass perched low on his nose, was helping the battered child off the table.

"Go upstairs and clean yourself, Arlais," the boy ordered.

"I already told you I don't take orders from *you*, mummy's boy," she snapped.

The boy didn't respond. He simply stared at her with cold grey eyes until the girl threw up her hands. "Fine!"

She stormed off, and Gwenvael, now standing near Elina, murmured with pride, "The boy has eyes just like his mum."

"And her intelligence, thankfully," Bram muttered.

"Not everyone can be as smart as me, dear Uncle Bram." Gwenvael's smile never seemed to fade. It, like the male's handsomeness, seemed to go on and on. Endlessly. Elina didn't know if she found that annoying or enrapturing. "Although I don't know how my daughter can think she'll take over any kingdom when she can't seem to focus on one thing at a—oooh." He reached down and picked something up off the ground. "Look! A gold coin." He blinked. Glanced off. "What was I talking about?"

"Focus," Bram said.

"Ahhh, yes. Focus." He was silent for another moment. "What about focus?"

The boy who'd helped the girl up now moved toward them, but when he was close, Gwenvael suddenly opened his arms wide.

"Son—"

The boy immediately stopped and held both hands up as if to ward the dragon off, his head slightly turned away. "No," he said flatly.

"But—"

"*No.* We discussed this. You promised my mother."

"But I'm your father—"

"Not by my choice."

"—and I love you."

"Not as much as you love yourself."

"Can you blame me?" Gwenvael demanded. "I am perfection."

The boy focused on Elina's table mate. "Uncle Bram . . . ?"

"I'll talk to your mother, Var. But you know I can't promise anything."

"Talk to your mother about what?" Gwenvael asked, finally lowering his arms. He began to slip the coin into a pouch tied to his sword belt, but stopped and focused on Elina. "I'm sorry. Do you need this because of your impoverished state?"

"*Gwenvael,*" Bram chastised

"*Father,*" the boy chastised.

"What?" the golden-haired one asked Bram and the boy. "It was a fair question. She's one of the poor barbarian hordes of the Steppes. This meal is probably the first she's had in years."

"Elina," Bram said, "I am *so* sorry."

Elina shrugged. "He is decadent, imperialist Southlander dog. He could not survive in our beautiful but harsh lands. But such pretty face as his would be made use of by many of our warriors."

"Wait," Gwenvael asked, still grinning at her. "What did she mean by that?"

"Guess," the boy told him before training those shrewd slate-grey eyes on her. After a moment, he said in her native tongue, "May death find you well this day, beautiful lady."

Shocked to hear a lazy Southlander speak in any language but his own, Elina grinned and replied, "And may death find you very well, young lord."

"I had heard one of the mighty Daughters of the Steppes was in our lands, but I had no idea it would be one so beautiful."

"As smooth as worn stone you are. Did you learn that from your father?"

"You can't be serious."

"Where did you learn my tongue?"

"I study many languages. Yours is harder than most and I am still . . ." He struggled for a moment. ". . . learn cow."

Elina smirked. "Learn*ing*. You are still learn*ing*. Cows have little to do with it." She shook her head. "But you are very good. I am impressed." Which was something Elina rarely was.

"Thank you." He gave a small bow. "I am Unnvar, son of Dagmar Reinholdt, also known as the Beast of Reinholdt—"

Elina smiled and said, "I always knew the Beast was not a man. Only a woman can strike that kind of fear."

"—Grandson to Northland warlord The Reinholdt, and Dragon-Human Prince of the House of Gwalchmai fab Gwyar."

"In all that barbarian banter," the golden one said, "I did not hear *my* name."

"And you won't," the boy flatly replied before turning

back to his uncle and returning to his Southland tongue. "Talk to my mother as you promised, Uncle Bram. My patience"—he glanced at Gwenvael—"wanes."

With a smirk, Bram nodded. "Understood."

"Thank you, Uncle Bram. Lady Rider." Sidling around Gwenvael to avoid another hug attempt, Elina guessed, the boy walked out.

Gwenvael focused on Bram. "You going to tell me what's going on?" he asked.

"No."

The golden one raised his arms as if he were about to argue the point, but they fell limply at his sides.

"I know I should care more but . . . eh." Then he walked off, leaving the Great Hall.

The other male, who wore those pieces of glass, dropped several books onto the table before sitting across from Elina and Bram. He was a very handsome boy. A Northlander by the look of him. Broad of shoulder, thick of neck, pale of skin; but he appeared smarter than most Northlanders. Much smarter.

"What do you think, Frederik?" Bram asked him.

"About?"

"About whether your aunt will allow me to take over Var's education?"

"I don't know. Var is her saving grace. But he wasn't blessed with her patience. Especially where Gwenvael is concerned."

"And my nephew takes so much patience," Bram sighed.

Elina pointed at the younger man. "Are you dragon, too?"

"No."

"Your aunt? Is she dragon?"

"No."

"But the golden one . . . ?"

"Very dragon."

Elina took a breath. "So the rumors are true. Dragons and humans . . . they can create the baby."

"As my aunt has shown in true Northlander style . . . they can create many of the baby."

"The Abominations grow in number then?"

Panicked, the two males looked around desperately, eyes wide. When they saw no one, they focused back on Elina and leaned in.

"You shouldn't use that word," Bram quickly, but quietly, explained. "It's not a good idea."

"Both queens take it personally," the younger male added.

"Do not see why. There is no shame to being scourge of gods."

Bram waved his hands. "No, no, no. No scourge. No abominations. These are not good words to use when discussing the offspring of dragons and humans."

"Words. You Southlanders worry so much about words."

"You don't worry about words?"

"I love words, but I know they are just . . . noise. To ignore truth that sits in our face. Like angry cat about to claw."

Bram glanced at Frederik. "Well . . . I have nothing pressing to run to at this moment. So please, Elina Shestakova . . . tell us about this truth."

Shrugging . . . that's exactly what Elina did.

Chapter Nine

Gisa held the flower bud in her hand and focused all her inner magicks toward getting the flower to bloom. It had taken her teacher five minutes to make the bloom happen. . . . Gisa had been staring at this bloom for near on an hour.

She hated this. She'd rather be in battle training. She was good at battle training. Good at battle, which was important for the Kyvich witches. They were warrior witches. They didn't do one or the other, but both.

Sadly, even though Gisa had the warrior part down, she was still struggling with the witch part.

Then again, as she glanced around at the other students, she discovered she wasn't the only one struggling.

"You got it yet?" Fia whispered.

"Nah. You?"

"Nope. Think we'll really need to make flowers bloom during a battle?" she asked.

"Doubt it," Gisa whispered back.

"And yet," their teacher suddenly announced, "once you learn to control nature, you can use it to your advantage during a battle with sword-wielding soldiers."

Gisa and Fia glanced at each other. Their teacher had her back to them and was a good fifty feet away. How had she heard them?

She looked at them over her shoulder. "So even if it bores you, work on it."

Gisa went back to the flower she held, again trying her best to get it to bloom when Fia tapped her ribs with her elbow. When Gisa looked at her, Fia gestured with her chin.

She saw Princess Talwyn of the Southland kingdoms standing a few feet away from the group of Kyvich, her arms crossed over her ample chest, her long hair in warrior braids, her powerful legs braced apart, her attention seemingly far from what was going on right in front of her.

Princess Talwyn was an anomaly among the Kyvich. First off, she was a royal. The Ice Lands had warlords, but not a lot of princes. None that lived long anyway. She had also *not* been taken from her family at birth. All Gisa knew was the Kyvich. She'd been taken from her mother's home near the Western Mountains when she was barely three months old. Some of her Kyvich sisters had been taken earlier than that, others no later than five or six years old. But the royal hadn't come to the Kyvich until she was ten winters and eight. She involved herself in all training, battle and magicks, and yet she never seemed part of the Kyvich. She never seemed like one of them.

Their teacher turned, suddenly noticing that Talwyn wasn't paying her the least bit of attention.

"Princess Talwyn . . . care to join us?"

Without turning around, Talwyn replied, "No."

Gritting her teeth, the teacher picked up a flower bud and held it out to the princess. "Perhaps you can at least attempt the spell and—"

Before their teacher could finish her sentence, Talwyn—her back still turned—waved her hand once in the air and the bud in the teacher's hand bloomed into a beautiful, healthy flower.

Shocked, the teacher stepped back, the flower still in her hand, still blooming. Then the stem began to grow, extending, wrapping around the teacher's fingers and palm. Their teacher finally dropped the flower, but the stem was now attached to her hand and steadily winding its way around her arm and up toward her shoulder.

"I have to go," Talwyn announced to no one. Of course, none of them were actually shocked. They'd never really thought she'd be spending the next thousand years living among the Kyvich until she died in battle and was honored the Old Way.

What did surprise everyone was when she looked over her shoulder at Gisa and Fia and asked, "Want to come with me?"

Gisa and Fia glanced at each other, then looked behind them to see if she was talking to someone else.

"Oy. You two. In or out?" the royal pushed, not really sounding like a royal.

"You don't even know our names," Fia said.

"Isn't that something I can learn . . . eventually?"

Frowning, Gisa and Fia kept staring at Talwyn until they heard a scream.

Gisa watched in horror as the stem from that small flower—now nearly the size of a ten-year-old tree trunk—covered most of their teacher's body, dragging her to the ground. The other students were trying to help, desperately cutting at it with their swords and daggers or trying to pull it off with their hands.

"Come on," Talwyn said with a toss of her head. She walked off, assuming, it seemed, that Gisa and Fia would follow.

"We're not going, are we?" Fia asked.

"I . . ." Gisa shook her head. "I feel a pull," she finally admitted. "As if somehow our lives are with her rather than here."

"Perhaps she cast a spell to *make* us feel that way."

"Perhaps." Gisa studied Fia. "Do *you* feel she cast a spell?"

"No."

Again, they glanced at their teacher. She was now pinned to the ground, the stem digging into the soil around her, trying to drag her down with it.

That was power. Gisa knew that much. Power and strength poured off Princess Talwyn like sweat.

"She's hated," Fia noted.

"That's true."

"Which means wherever she goes, battle and mayhem are sure to follow."

"Excellent point."

Together they jumped up and followed after the royal. As they ran, they could still hear their teacher and the other Kyvich struggling with whatever Talwyn had cursed them with.

They caught up with Talwyn quickly, finding her standing and waiting by her horse. A breed of horse given to her by the Kyvich. The only horned horses with burning red eyes that any of them knew about other than undead demon animals from one of the hells.

Standing beside Talwyn's horse was the dog Talwyn had been given by the Kyvich as a puppy. The dog was another horned beast that would charge into battle beside the Kyvich witch that had trained it from nine weeks old. Every Kyvich received a horse and dog when she turned sixteen.

But before Gisa could think too much about the horse and dog she'd be leaving behind by going with Talwyn, she saw that both her horse and dog and Fia's were also there—waiting for them. The blankets they used on their horses instead of saddles already rested across their backs along with packed travel bags.

"We don't have much time," Talwyn said as she mounted her horse. "That flower won't distract the Elders long and then they'll be coming after me."

"How did you know we'd agree to come with you?" Gisa asked.

The royal shrugged. "I just knew."

Then, without another word, she turned her horse and charged off.

Confused and wary, Gisa and Fia stood their ground another minute or so until they saw that the stem from that damn flower was now spreading throughout the forest like wild vines. They could hear the calls from the other Kyvich, as they hurried to stop whatever magicks Talwyn had unleashed.

"Well?" Fia pushed.

With a deep breath, Gisa walked to her horse and mounted him. Fia did the same and, together, they set off after Princess Talwyn.

It would be hours before they both realized that they had no idea where the hells they were going.

Chapter Ten

Celyn woke up with his headache gone and feeling much less cranky. Yawning, he sat up, scratched his scalp, and looked out the window. The suns had gone down and his stomach was clearly telling him it was time for evening meal.

Throwing his legs over the side of the bed, Celyn stood and stretched. Now that he'd had some sleep, things weren't looking nearly as awful as they had a few hours earlier. He was grateful for that, too. He hated when he felt nothing but angry. He left snarling and snapping at all times of the day to his uncle Bercelak and royal cousins, Briec and Fearghus. He didn't understand being angry all the time. What was the purpose? What did it accomplish except to give him stomach acid and make everyone avoid him?

Pulling his black hair back and tying it with a leather thong, Celyn went down the stairs. By the time he reached the second floor, he could hear raised voices. He couldn't make out what was being said, but he could tell there was yelling involved.

As he reached the final set of steps that led into the Great Hall, he stopped and stared at the long dining table. That's where all the yelling was coming from.

Well, yelling might be the wrong word. Yelling suggested anger, and Celyn saw no anger. Instead, he saw . . . passion. A passionate discussion that involved very loud talking.

Fascinated, he continued down the stairs and over to the

table and found himself a seat beside Gwenvael, who was also watching.

As soon as Celyn was seated, one of the servants placed a bowl of hot stew in front of him, followed by a large plate of ribs and a platter filled with bread. He didn't eat at Annwyl's castle often, but when he did . . . the servants clearly knew how to feed dragons in human form.

Something that Celyn appreciated.

"So what's going on?" Celyn asked his cousin between spoonfuls of stew.

"Well, when we started to come in for dinner, we found your father, Frederik, the Outerplains female, and Annwyl chatting . . . but by the time we all sat down to dinner, the chatting had turned into a lively debate."

Celyn studied the Rider. With her elbows on the table, she sat between Annwyl and Celyn's father, tearing pieces from a crusty loaf of bread, and shoving those pieces into her mouth while she stared blankly across the room.

"She looks miserable," Celyn observed to his cousin.

"Who?"

"The Rider."

"You mean Elina Shestakova of . . . whatever, whatever, whatever?" Gwenvael snorted. "She's not miserable. She's in whatever an Outerplains barbarian considers heaven."

Celyn had no idea what Gwenvael meant until Elina snorted at something Briec said and cut in drily with, "You hoard like angry squirrel, Briec the Mighty. Keeping all riches for yourself and sharing with none."

"Why should I share with anyone?" Briec demanded, sounding more haughty than usual. "My hoard is *my* hoard."

"But you stole that hoard," Annwyl reminded Briec, her legs tucked under her on her chair, her torso stretched over the table, elbows against wood, hands clasped.

"I don't understand your point."

"How is it yours? You didn't earn it."

"I *did* earn it. I stalked those caravans, had to fight off their protection, tear apart the carriages to get at the treasure, and then transport that treasure back to my cave. That took a lot of work, and often the only thing I got out of it was a warm meal that screamed for mercy."

Talaith, sitting next to Briec, slowly brought her hands to her head and began to rub the temples.

"Bah," the Rider exclaimed, dismissing Briec's words with a hand swiped through the air. It was so amusing to see someone other than Talaith taunt Briec so brazenly that Celyn and Gwenvael glanced at each other and grinned.

"You brag and brag, Briec the Mighty. But who among you *has not* killed an enemy while he begs for mercy, laughing as he dies in pain and torment?"

For some unfathomable reason, Dagmar Reinholdt raised her hand at that, which got her bewildered stares from everyone in the room.

"She said who here has *not* killed an enemy. . . . She didn't say anything about *having* your enemies killed, now did she?" Dagmar announced, her tone smug.

"Our people," the Rider went on, "share what we have with our other tribesmen. Those who have less, get some from others. Then we all have equal."

"No." Briec shook his head. "I don't like that idea. What's mine is mine."

"Would you not share with your brothers?"

"No," all the brothers replied.

"You are very pretty." Elina stared. "But very sad." She gestured with her bread. "All we have is each other. Without that, we are nothing."

"I am a dragon. I don't need anyone else."

Talaith threw up her hands. "Thank you *very* much!"

"I'm not talking about you, so there's no reason to get hysterical."

"Hysterical?"

"She's going to kill you in your sleep," Fearghus noted when Talaith glared at Briec. "And I wouldn't blame her."

"So," Celyn cut in, "your people share everything?"

The Rider did not turn to look at him so much as her bright blue eyes simply cut his way. Kind of like when a wolf sensed Celyn was near . . . and knew that Celyn was hungry.

"We share our food. Our clothing. Anything to keep everyone healthy . . . and strong. You cannot have defenses when some of your people starve and others are dying from diseases simple to fix."

"What are," Morfyd suddenly asked, "your people's feelings on dragons . . . and the dragon-human offspring?"

"You mean Abominations?"

Eyes widened, bodies tensed, hurried words spouted, and Fearghus readied himself to tackle his mate and take her to the ground in seconds. The panic among Celyn's kin was palpable. But then, Annwyl raised her hands to quiet down everyone who felt the need to say, in some form or another, "I'm sure she didn't mean it *that* way, Annwyl!"

"Wait, wait," Annwyl ordered calmly. "Don't everyone panic." Leaning forward a bit more than she already was, Annwyl asked the Rider, "What does that mean to *you*?"

"Abomination?" The Rider shrugged, bit off a hunk of bread, chewed, then finally answered, "It means the off-spring of dragons and humans are unholy mixes of death and evil, born to destroy the world as we know it."

Huh, Celyn thought to himself, *maybe I won't have to go to the Outerplains tomorrow, but I may have to bury a body. . . .*

Annwyl raised one forefinger, holding Fearghus at bay, since, based on the black smoke pouring from his nostrils . . . he was not happy about anything the Rider had said and would now happily allow his mate to cut off the woman's head.

Not that Elina Shestakova noticed any of that. She was still chewing . . . and staring at the wall behind Dagmar's head.

"But," the woman continued on, "change is good. Without

change comes age and death. We, as a species, cannot have that. We need new blood. Even if it is dragon blood, which according to our Elders is the most evil of all blood. But I am not sure I believe that after meeting Bram the Merciful. Would have still believed that if I had only met the dolt."

Annwyl leaned back, smiling. "See? You *really* have to wait for her to finish her thought."

Elina lifted a puppy off the floor. She liked dogs. They were like small horses you could not ride.

"Your paws are huge," she told the pup, their noses touching. "Like big shovels. Maybe you *will* be horse one day."

"Dagmar breeds those dogs for battle." The Dolt sat down beside her. The other members of the household had finished eating and were now off in different corners of the Great Hall, chatting or wandering outside to enjoy the night. "Do you like dogs?" he asked.

"You want to eat him," Elina accused.

"No." He patted his stomach. "I'm full."

"What do you want, dragon?" she asked, already annoyed by him. She just wanted to play with the puppy. To spend one night enjoying the decadence of these Southlanders. Without guilt. Without worry. Without feeling like a failure to her people.

"We got off on the wrong claw."

"Wrong claw?"

"I'm sorry I left you—"

"To die?"

He barely stopped himself from rolling his eyes. Rude bastard. "I didn't leave you to die. If I wanted to do that, I could have left you staked out on top of Devenallt Mountain. Eventually someone would have gotten a little hungry." He let out a breath. "We've got a rather long trip ahead of us, and I think we should start over."

"There is no starting over. It is what it is." She stood up, the puppy in her arms. "We tolerate each other because I owe your queen for her kindness to me. I'll put up with you because of her. But that is all. We will not be friends. We will not get along. We may have sex, but it will be cold and impersonal. Just something to pass time during long nights. So do not come to me with your wrong claws. I have no use for your wrong claws."

Feeling that they now understood each other, Elina cuddled the sleeping puppy closer and followed a servant up to a room. A room she would not have to share with anyone.

So decadent!

Celyn didn't know how long he had been sitting there, staring at the wall.

"What happened?" Brannie asked as she sat down next to him. Izzy sat on the table, her long legs hanging over the edge. And Éibhear sat between him and Izzy.

"I'm not really sure," Celyn admitted.

"What did she say?" Éibhear asked.

"She basically said . . . she does not like me. We would not be friends. And if we had sex, it would be only because she was bored. Long nights and all."

"The suns are setting earlier," Éibhear noted.

Celyn gazed at his cousin, but he had nothing to say to him. Because as book smart as the blue dragon was, as battle-ready . . . he could be kind of stupid.

"Are you going to be okay doing this?" Brannie asked.

"Sure."

"Maybe Brannie and I should come with you?" Izzy offered.

"Why not me?" Éibhear asked.

"That's a good idea," Brannie snorted. "Bringing a berserker Mì-runach along for a goodwill trip. Maybe you could decimate a few of the tribes to show them how much we care."

Éibhear glared at his cousin. "Or you could have just said it wasn't necessary for me to come."

"Could have." Brannie shrugged. "Didn't."

"You know what we need?" Izzy cut in before a fight could break out. "Information."

Izzy looked over her shoulder at the back hallway and made a soft whistling sound between her teeth. Frederik, walking along with his head in a book and one of Dagmar's dogs at his side, stopped and glanced over. He pointed at himself, seemingly surprised by the sudden attention, and Izzy rolled her eyes. "Yes, you."

"Oh." He closed the book and walked over to the table. "What is it?"

"We need information."

"About?"

"The people of the Steppes. We can't just send our dear Celyn out there alone with no information."

"Well, we can—" Éibhear began, but Izzy cut him off by placing her hand over his face.

"Have anything for us, dear Frederik?"

"Not really. I just started doing some research since the decision was made to make an alliance with the Daughters of the Steppes. But," he quickly added, "I do know someone who can help us. I'll be right back."

As he quickly walked away, the dog dutifully following, Izzy and Brannie leaned over a bit to get a better look at the young man from behind.

"He's filling out quite nice, yeah, Iz?"

"Very promising."

"You are aware I'm sitting right here?" Éibhear snapped.

"I'm just looking," Izzy shot back. "Not licking."

"Besides," both females said together, "he's Frederik."

Celyn shook his head. "Éibhear and I don't know what that means."

Izzy patted Celyn's shoulder. "That's because you're not female."

"I'm not sure that's a good enough excuse."

Before the discussion could continue, Frederik returned, but he was carrying a stone-faced Unnvar by the shoulders.

Izzy frowned in concern when Frederik stood the young boy on a chair.

"Shouldn't he be in bed?"

"I don't sleep," the boy replied. "Not much. Too much to learn."

"If you're not tired, why did you need to be carried out here like a statue?"

"Because when I asked him to come talk to you," Frederik replied, "he said he didn't have time for ridiculous conversations with his ridiculous kin about ridiculous issues. Not when he had a kingdom to help his mother manage." When they all just stared, Frederik added, "Aunt Dagmar assures me he's only ten . . . but I still question."

"What is it?" Var pushed. "I have things to do and all of you are wasting my time."

"Oookay," Izzy said before asking. "What can you tell us about the people of the Steppes?"

Celyn and the others patiently waited for an answer . . . and they kept waiting.

Finally, Brannie snapped, "Are you going to answer us?"

"You actually expect information for free?"

Celyn leaned toward Éibhear and muttered, "I see that his mother has taught him well."

"Here." Izzy reached across the table and pulled a plate of pastries left over from the dinner close to the group. "Tell us and you get a treat."

"Because now I'm a pet?"

Celyn exchanged wide-eyed glances with his sister. When they were only ten winters, they used to bet their older siblings that they could be the first to tear down their father's castle by ramming their heads into the stone walls. They would eventually have to stop, though, when their father finally complained about the "gods-damn noise." Of course they were both ten winters at different times, with Celyn being older, but according to their mother, all her off-spring went through the same "destroying your father's home with your head" phase at ten winters.

It seemed, however, that little Var wasn't much like his Cadwaladr kin.

"Then what do you want?" Izzy snapped.

Not waiting for a reply, Éibhear took a coin pouch from his sword belt and removed a gold piece from it, holding it up for the boy to see. "If you answer our questions, I'll give you this nice, shiny—"

Sighing, Var crouched down and snatched the coin purse from his uncle. He hefted it in his hand and nodded. "This should do. Now what was it you wanted to know?"

Celyn laughed but stopped when Éibhear coldly eyed him.

"The Steppes, tiny boy," Izzy snarled.

"Ahhh, yes. Fascinating people. They are called the Daughters of the Steppes and they rule most of the Outer-plains from the Conchobar Mountains to the Quintilian Provinces."

"Wait," Éibhear interrupted. "I thought the Outerplains cut through the Northland and Annaig Valley territories."

"They do. But the Daughters of the Steppes' territories go far past both until they reach around to the end of the Annaig Valley territories and slam right into the Quintilian Provinces."

Izzy and Brannie chuckled and said together, "Reach around."

"What's their culture like?" Celyn asked.

"They are matriarchal. Women rule the Steppes and the women rule the men who live on the Steppes. When the first Anne Atli tore power from the original marauders, most of the men were killed. So when they go on raids, they often steal the older boys and young men."

"They take slaves?" Brannie asked. "Annwyl's *not* going to like that one damn bit."

"Except the Riders do not consider their spoils of war slaves because once the boys are old enough, they take them as husbands."

"Husbands?"

"The stronger and more mighty the warrior, the more husbands she can have. And some of them have many husbands."

"Wait, does *this* Rider have many husbands?" Celyn asked.

"Awww, jealous?" Éibhear joked.

"No. I just don't like to be used. I do have my boundaries."

Brannie patted his knee. "Of course you do, brother."

"Elina Shestakova of the Black Bear Riders of the Midnight Mountains of—"

"Do not repeat that entire name, Unnvar," Celyn snapped.

"Anyway," the boy went on, "she told me at dinner tonight that she has no husbands. No offspring. Until she proves to her tribe leader her worthiness, she will not be able to have a husband. Although she's chosen not to at this time, she can have as many offspring as she wants since the Daughters do not believe in controlling a woman's right to breed—"

"You mean they just control the men by forcing them into marriage?"

"Basically," the boy replied with a shrug. "I'll admit, it's not what I would call a perfect system. But it has worked for the Riders for at least five thousand years. I doubt they'll be willing to change just to accommodate Auntie Annwyl's sense of right and wrong. Especially when they have little respect for Southland ideals in general. They consider us vapid wastrels unworthy of attention."

"Why haven't they tried to raid Southland towns?" Celyn asked, completely fascinated by all this. When he returned, he'd have to spend more time with Dagmar's oldest offspring. He was a veritable font of interesting knowledge! Celyn could ask him questions for days! Of course, he'd need to make sure he had enough coin to get the answers.

"Luck. Our luck, I mean. The Conchobar Mountains separate their territory from ours, making it risky to move all their tribes through the narrow passes that cut through the mountain terrain. Since the entire tribes go along on raids, it would be easy to rain arrows down upon them, wiping out most of them in the process. Plus, the Southland royals who live between Annaig Valley and the Conchobar Mountains are more than willing to pay hefty sums of gold to keep the Riders from their door. That being said, of course, Annwyl would do well to either create an alliance between our two nations or at least not poke the bear, as they say. Thankfully, there's always been enough to keep the Riders on their side of the Conchobar Mountains and away from us. But I'd hate for that to change because Annwyl suddenly decides to consider their husbands as slaves she will need to save. Please keep that in mind, cousin Celyn, when you accompany Elina Shestakova back to her territories."

There was silence in the Great Hall as they all gazed at the boy in wonder. After a few seconds, Frederik leaned forward and stated, "Once again, I've asked, and according to his mother, he really, truly is only ten years old." Then he gave a small shrug. "But I still have my doubts."

Chapter Eleven

Elina woke up before the suns rose and was dressed and heading down the stairs into the Great Hall just as the servants began their daily chores. She started toward the Great Hall doors but stopped and turned, walking through the back double doors.

As she walked down the hall, she saw Queen Annwyl. The Southlander royal wore only her leggings and boots and had her breasts bound. She'd found a low-hanging rafter and was using her arms to pull her body up again and again, her legs bent at the knees and crossed at the ankles.

Elina marveled at the power of those muscles.

"Oy!" a voice yelled down the hallway. "Your royal majesty! Your training partner is about to set himself on fire waitin' for yer arse!"

"Shut it!" the royal yelled back.

Annwyl released her grip and dropped to the ground. She moved her shoulders until her back cracked, then turned to pick up her shirt and the two short swords next to it. That's when she saw Elina.

"Everything all right?" she asked.

"You sure you are queen?"

"I'm sure I'm Annwyl." She pulled her sleeveless chainmail shirt over her head. "The rest I just take as it comes."

"You seem like leader. But you do not seem like queen."

Annwyl frowned at that, but she took a moment before

she finally asked, "Do you mean with robes and a crown and a throne . . . ?"

"And your royal sycophants bowing and scraping and begging for attention while they let your people, the ones who work the land, starve."

"Royal sycophants?" she laughed. "Royals don't come to me unless they have to. They find me . . . off-putting. And a little terrifying. And I let them find me that way, so I don't have to talk to them unless necessary." Annwyl stepped closer. "I took the throne from my brother because he abused his people. I took his head because he abused me. I'm not here to let others lead, Elina. I'm here to protect my people. And that's what I do as best I can."

Although the queen, with all the scars that spoke of hard battles, had stepped close to her, Elina didn't feel threatened. She didn't know why. Annwyl the Bloody was kind of terrifying-looking. She had scars on her face and chest and brands on her arms.

Elina took her forearms and turned them so she could see the brands clearly. They were dragons burned into the flesh. A testament, she guessed, to Annwyl's commitment to the dragon Fearghus.

This woman, queen or not, hid nothing. From her people. From Elina. From the gods. She was exactly what she was and no crown or throne would ever change that. Elina knew this. In her bones, she knew this.

Elina took a breath, released Annwyl's wrists. "I will return to my people, Annwyl the Bloody. I will talk to the Anne Atli. I will tell her there are no lazy, greedy Southlanders here."

Annwyl laughed and walked off down the hall, tossing over her shoulder, "I guess you won't be telling her about the dragons then, huh?"

"No," Elina muttered to herself after a little snort. "Probably not."

She headed back to the Great Hall, stopping as she walked through the open double doors.

"You ready?"

Elina looked over at the black-haired dragon who spoke to her. He leaned back against one of the open doors, one leg bent at the knee, the foot braced against the wood.

"Do I not look ready?"

"Maybe the fur and spear are part of your nightclothes. And where did you get that spear anyway?"

"From that wall."

"So you just stole it?"

"It is not like anyone had use for it."

Elina headed toward the Great Hall front doors. "Come along, Dolt. I wish to see the mighty Steppes of my people."

"Aye. Because multiple little hills are just so fascinating."

Elina stopped and turned, her nose now only an inch or two from his chest. "Know that even your voice irritates me. But I made commitment to your queen and Queen Annwyl."

"All right—"

"But do not push, Dolt."

He smirked and she wanted so badly to slap the expression off his face. "Or what?" he asked. "You'll try to sneak up on me, get caught, and end up *not* killing me?"

"Life and the land between here and the Steppes are filled with unfortunate accidents."

"And you'd be sad if something happened to me?"

"No." Elina threw her hands into the air, forcing the dragon back a few steps to avoid getting hit, and bellowed, "*I would welcome your demise like the rising of the suns!*" She rammed her forefinger into his chest, her voice low again. "But I am trying to do right thing by your queens and by my people. So do not piss me off."

"I can't promise that," Celyn told her with what seemed like honesty. "But I do promise not to *try* to piss you off."

* * *

Celyn led Elina to the stables and to the stallion his mother often used when she went into battle as human. The horse was from a line of large beasts bred specifically for their size, strength, speed, and ability not to become completely terrified at the mere scent of nearby dragons.

He'd asked his mother the evening before if he could take her horse and, since she was sticking around for a bit, she'd said yes. She was also able to provide him with human-ready clothes, weapons, and equipment since Celyn rarely traveled far from his queen's side. Unlike his sister, who fought so often with Annwyl's human army that she now commanded her own human battalion.

Holding onto the reins, Celyn led the horse out of the stables until he stood in front of Elina.

"Ready?" he asked.

She'd been focusing on a shop across the square, so she turned to look at him and her eyes blinked wide.

"What is that?" she asked.

Surprised—he had always heard about the Outerplains people's love of horses—Celyn replied, "He's a . . . horse."

"He is mountain that runs on four legs. Why do you need something so . . . ridiculous?"

"He's not ridiculous. He's bred to carry dragons in human form into battle. They're fast. Smart. And loyal."

"How fast can he be with so much of him?"

She walked around the horse, examining him closely, her lips curling in deep disapproval.

"He is like moose with long legs," she finally said. "You should be eating him, not riding him. Do you ride cow, too?" she suddenly demanded.

Celyn was about to answer, then realized it was a stupid question.

"Can we just go?"

"We can try. If you get your travel-cow to move."

Celyn bit back an annoyed sigh and moved off, bringing his "travel-cow" with him.

As they walked past the gates, Celyn saw his father and sister Brannie coming toward them in human form, both enjoying treats from the baker in town. True, they could get the same quality of treats from Annwyl's castle baker, but going into town and chatting with the locals was how Celyn's father made sure to always have access to the latest gossip. While Dagmar used coin and, when necessary, extortion to get the information she needed, Bram the Merciful had always used his pleasant disposition.

"So you're off?" Bram asked once he was near enough to Celyn and Elina that there was no need to shout.

"Aye." Grinning, Celyn carefully wiped away the cream his father had on his chin.

Bram laughed. "Thank you. And, Celyn, remember. No need to always be so curious."

Confused by that comment, Celyn said, "I thought curiosity was a good thing."

"Not for you."

"I never saw it as an issue."

"I know, but trust me. You don't go to many territories outside of the Southlands, and curiosity—"

"Or just being plain nosy," Brannie said around a mouthful of cream and pastry.

"—is not welcome everywhere. Understand?"

"No," Celyn admitted since he'd never understood why a few questions irritated so many so quickly. Especially his Cadwaladr kin. They really hated his questions, but Celyn had no idea why. How could one hate questions? You couldn't get to the bottom of things without asking questions.

And Celyn loved questions.

"I don't understand," he went on to his father. "But I'll do as you say for this trip."

"That's all I ask, my dearest son."

Elina, who'd been standing silently beside father and

son, finally announced, "I still do not see it. How can such a dolt be the son of such a fine dragon? She," Elina went on, pointing at a startled Brannie, "has her father's wit and intelligence. But you . . ." She gave a sad shake of her head. "I see nothing but thick skull and dazed, stupid eyes. Like your travel-cow."

Celyn looked at his father, but the old bastard was too busy grinning to give any sympathy to his poor son, who would be trapped with this female for days and days.

"It was good to meet you, Bram the Merciful," Elina said, her hand reaching up to land on Bram's shoulder. "I hope death finds you well for many more centuries."

"Safe travels to you, Elina Shestakova of the Black Bear Riders of the Midnight Mountains of Despair in the Far Reaches of the Steppes of the Outerplains."

Celyn glanced at his wide-eyed sister before asking his father, "How do you remember that ridiculously long name?"

Before Bram could respond, Elina pointed at Bram and snapped, "Brilliant." Pointed at Celyn. "Dolt. Do math!"

With what some might call a cordial smile—of course, Celyn wasn't one of those beings—Elina walked down the road.

"I love her," Brannie sighed. "Like the suns and good ale."

"Do you have no concern for your own brother?" Celyn demanded of his sister.

"Because you are a pathetic puppy, sheltered by our parents in a sad job that makes you feel like you're in charge when you're not?"

"No. Because I've got to put up with"—he gestured at Elina's retreating form with a weak wave of his hand—"*that* until I can dump her on her people."

"Don't be so hard on her," Bram warned around his own laughter. "Life on the Steppes is not for the faint of heart.

I'm sure she's been through much more than any of us can imagine."

"And you did forget about her," Brannie needlessly reminded him. "Females of all species take that sort of thing quite badly. I'd have cut your head off meself if you'd done that to me. And I'm your sister."

"Thank you for that."

"Travel safe," his father told him. "And remember that you do this for our queen and for Annwyl. So be your most charming."

"That should be easy for you since it is your name," his sister teased sweetly, which was why he shoved the rest of her cream-filled treat, and not his fist, into her face.

While Brannie cursed the day Celyn was hatched, Celyn walked quickly to catch up with Elina, bringing his mother's horse with him.

Elina had turned off the road and was now cutting through the woods. She stopped a few times, her blue-eyed gaze looking far off before she started walking again. He had no idea where she was going, so he asked.

"Where are we going?"

"Are you not aware of our travel plans?"

"This is not the road to take. In fact, we're going in the opposite direction. Are you planning to take a roundabout way to your people? One I'm not aware of?"

"Can you not be patient? Wait until things unfold?"

"I could. But I'd be more patient if I knew where we were going right *now*. Can't you give me a hint? A tiny idea? Just a—"

Elina stopped and spun on him so fast, Celyn immediately closed his mouth.

"Why do you keep talking?" she asked.

"I'm just asking questions."

"Do not."

"But if you gave me complete answers to my first questions, I wouldn't need to ask follow-ups."

"You are still *talking*."

"You still haven't answered my questions."

Growling a little, she stalked off and Celyn followed. He went along for about five minutes in silence until he asked, "Is there a reason I need to be quiet?"

"Yes."

"Well, if you told me that reason I could easily be quiet. But when you don't tell me anything, then all I can do is—"

"Quiet, Dolt."

"There's no need to get that nasty tone. I'm merely trying to—"

The female abruptly stopped again, faced Celyn, went up on her toes, and stretched her arm out so she could silence Celyn by slapping her hand over his mouth. "*Quiet*," she whispered.

When she seemed sure that he wouldn't speak again, she slowly lowered her hand. With her eyes fixed on a spot somewhere in the forest, she silently walked backward until she reached an old tree. There she crouched down and began digging through a mass of dead leaves. That's when she pulled out a curved composite bow and a quiver of arrows.

She had her bow nocked and was getting to her full height when Celyn heard a roar and turned in time to see a flash of fangs and claws coming right at him.

Elina loosed her arrow, her aim—as always—true. But when it hit the big jungle cat in the chest, right in the heart, both arrow and cat were engulfed in flames.

Rage moved through her veins as she faced the idiot dragon who'd nearly set the surrounding woods on fire.

He was grinning at her. Grinning like the dolt he was.

"Why," she tried her best to ask calmly, "did you do that?"

"To protect you from one of the famous Southland cats. Trust me. They may not be incredibly big, but I've seen them tear the faces off humans before they can even pull their sword."

"I was not using sword. I used bow."

"Aye. You did. And you're a surprisingly good shot. I don't know why you didn't have your bow with you when you came up Devenallt Mountain. That could have worked nicely on either queen."

"Are you now telling me *how* to kill your queen?" Elina snapped.

He frowned. "Oh . . . I think I was. But logic-wise—"

"Shut up!"

"Why are you yelling at me? I just saved you from a disfigured face."

"I'm yelling because that cat was mine!"

"They're not good to eat. Trust me . . . I've tried. *Not* a delicacy."

"Not for food, you fool! For Glebovicha. We do not have cats like these on the Steppes. I bring one with me, perhaps I can absolve shame of not killing your queen."

"Oh." He nodded. "*Now* I understand. And if you'd just told me that at the—"

"Shut up!"

"Still yelling at me." He shook his head as if it all confused him so. Perhaps it did. He was a dolt, after all. "And who is Glebovicha again?"

"She is head of my tribe and the one who sent me here. The one I need to go through in order to get time with Anne Atli."

"Again, if you'd told me all that in the beginning—"

"Och!" Elina roared, unwilling to listen to another moment of the dragon's incessant babbling!

Elina secured her bow to her back and grabbed her

quiver of arrows. Then, without even looking at the dragon, she walked on until she reached a clearing with a large herd of wild horses.

"Are you going to break a wild horse?" the dragon asked.

"I cannot believe you are *still* talking."

"I didn't know I had to stop."

Shaking her head, Elina called over the horse she'd ridden from her homeland. And, as soon as it stopped in front of her, she heard the dragon behind her—laughing.

"What?" she asked him.

"You call *that* a horse?" he asked around his laughter. "I wouldn't even eat that, it's so small. It's barely a snack."

"This is a Steppes horse. Its speed, power, and endurance unparalleled. Do not let size fool you, Dolt. You do not have to be big to be strong. To be feared."

"But it helps."

"Your shoulders may be wide, but your mind is very small. Like peanut."

"You don't even know me yet."

"I have seen enough." She moved over to where she'd buried the rest of her things.

After a few minutes, she unearthed her saddle and travel bag, and brought them over to the horse.

"What is its name?" the dragon asked.

"I do not know. He has not told me."

"He hasn't told. . . . You speak to animals?"

"No. That is why he has not told me."

The dragon frowned, his eyes briefly gazing at the sky. Finally, he asked, "Why didn't you just name him yourself?"

"He is not mine to name. He belongs to the land and the people of the Steppes belong to the land—so we are kin in our hearts. We cannot survive without the land or the horse. We do not own the horse. It allows us to use it. We do not own the land, the gods merely allow us to use it for our survival. Do you understand?"

"I do." He nodded. "But—"

"No," Elina cut in, her voice practically begging. "No more questions. Decades could pass with your questions before we get on road."

"I know. I know. It's just—"

"No." She placed her hand against his chest. "*No.*"

"Can I ask you questions later? Like during a break for food?"

He sounded so hopeful. Did the other dragons not speak to him? Was his curiosity as painful to them as it was to her?

Elina didn't know. But she did know that her weakness sickened her when she replied, "Yes. I can answer questions then."

His grin was very wide. He didn't seem smug so much as simply excited at the prospect of asking even more questions.

By the horse gods, what had she gotten herself into?

Chapter Twelve

They rode for bloody *hours*. Celyn hadn't thought any human could go so long without taking any breaks, but he'd been wrong.

Elina kept her horse moving at a brisk pace, not stopping to eat or drink. Instead, she had food in convenient pockets sewn into her deerskin leggings. She had a canister of water tied to the pommel of her saddle, which she sipped from throughout the day.

It wasn't until Celyn was sure his horse was about to toss him off that he insisted on stopping near a stream.

Elina led her horse to the stream before slipping off the animal's back and disappearing into some nearby trees. When she returned about ten minutes later, adjusting her leggings and swatting at some annoying flies, she barely looked at him.

"How are you holding up?" Celyn asked, sitting down on the ground.

"What?"

Assuming she didn't understand him, he repeated his question. "How are you holding up?"

"Holding up?"

"Aye. We've been riding hard all day."

"Do I look weak to you? As if I cannot handle a simple ride?"

"This is a simple ride? Then why is my ass killing me?"

"You need to ride more."

"I'm a dragon. . . . I normally fly everywhere I need to go."

"And your wings do not get tired?"

"No."

She stared at him with that disappointed expression she always seemed to wear before saying, "It must be nice to fly."

"Is that sarcasm?"

"No. If I could fly, I would live in tree. Stare down at everyone . . . quietly hating them all."

Afraid he'd laugh or say something to insult her, Celyn instead handed Elina dried beef from the small bag he had tied to his sword belt. She nodded her thanks and sat down. Her horse nuzzled the back of her head, and Elina reached up, stroking the animal's muzzle.

"So," she suddenly said, "your family does not trust you to do anything but look pretty and stand near queen?"

Celyn nearly choked on the beef he'd just eaten. "What?" he snapped around his sputtering.

"Is it not true?"

"It's *not* true."

"Then why so many cautions from Bram the Merciful? He looked ready to come with us, or to replace you entirely with ten-year-old boy who cannot stand his golden-haired father."

"My father—my *parents*—respect the work I do."

"The work you do? You mean looking pretty? Because you are very pretty when human."

"I don't just look pretty. I have a sacred, honored duty to protect our queen."

"She is nearly size of mountain she lives in when she is dragon. I doubt Queen Rhiannon needs anyone's protection. Least of all from pretty but chatty dragon."

"It's an honor to serve the Dragon Queen. One I was awarded after cutting my fangs in battle as dragon *and* human."

"I notice you did not get any scars on your pretty face. Even Annwyl the Bloody has scars on face."

"Because at one time she used to be so busy destroying everything around her, it never occurred to her to protect her face. But I, personally, prefer having my face in one piece and my brain still in my skull."

"I do not know why you get so angry. There is no shame for male to have pretty face. It is better for you. Warrior female will notice you and make you one of her husbands one day."

"What?"

"No warrior wants to come home to hut full of ugly husbands. Yes, a few ugly ones who can hunt, protect children and weaker, older tribesmen, and make sure everything runs smoothly. But the rest should be pretty. So a warrior is glad to be home after day of hacking and killing."

"You can stop talking now."

"You said you want to chat."

"Not anymore!"

She shrugged. "Fine. No need to bellow."

Elina had a wonderful ten minutes of silence before the dragon couldn't stand it anymore.

"So how many husbands *can* a woman have?"

"One," she sighed out, deciding not to try to silence him again. "Unless she brings in much gold and cattle from raids. Then she can have as many husbands as she likes."

"I see."

"Anne Atli has fifty-four husbands."

The dragon slowly turned his head toward her, eyes wide. "That sounds like a lot."

"She does not seem to mind."

"But you don't have a husband yet?"

Elina shook her head, her gaze focused on the stream. "No. I have nothing to entice a man. No raids. No bounty on my head. No one fears me." She looked him in the eyes. "As far as the tribes are concerned, I am nothing."

"But you're cute."

"I am . . . cute?"

"Aye. Cute. In the Southlands, cute can get you a baron and a full staff."

Elina didn't bother to hide her disgust. "That is appalling."

"It works for some."

"Even Annwyl?"

"Annwyl?" The dragon shook his head. "Gods, no. She gained her power by taking her brother's head. He deserved it, though. He was a right bastard. Eventually Rhiannon would have had him killed. She loathed his father, so she wasn't going to go through another reign like that."

"Rhiannon cares much for the humans then?"

"She doesn't like anyone tormenting her cattle. It makes the meat tough." When Elina only stared at him, the dragon said, "Just kidding."

"No. You do not kid."

"No," he admitted. "I don't. But Rhiannon has come a long way," he went on quickly. "Now she wants to protect *all* her kin, including the human ones. And especially her grand-offspring."

"Which is why I will help her."

"It won't be easy for you, though, will it?"

Elina thought a moment. She didn't trust or even like this dragon, but she should be honest with him. In case things didn't work out.

"No. Getting past Glebovicha is one thing. Even if I do that, I will still need to convince the Anne Atli that an alliance with the decadent Southlanders is worth her time. That will be very hard. She, too, has no respect for the Southland people."

"What if we have proof?"

"Proof? What kind of proof?"

"Look," he said, turning his human body so he was facing her directly, his knees brushing against her leg as he moved. "We could help each other here."

"Help each other? What do you need help with?"

"I am *not* Fal. I will never *be* Fal."

Elina frowned. "Who is this Fal?"

"He's my brother. A lazy, worthless, idiotic dragon . . . I love him dearly."

"Yes. That I can see. So very clearly."

Ignoring her sarcasm, the dragon went on, "But I need to prove to my parents that I am not some pathetic dragon that needs to be hidden away. I have bigger goals than that."

"What goals?"

He stared at her for such a long moment that she thought it was some big secret he was afraid to tell. Until he admitted, "I'm working on that."

Elina cringed and asked, "What do you propose, Dolt?"

"When you came here, you avoided populated areas, didn't you? Cities, towns, anywhere with people?"

Elina nodded. "Considering what I was tasked to do, it seemed logical not to make my presence known."

"Well, I think on our journey back, we should travel through as many towns as we can."

"Why?"

"Gather information, proof, that the spread of the Chramnesind cults out of Annaig Valley is real—and dangerous."

"What makes you think that the Anne Atli will care about some worthless religion that worships only one god?"

"Because like a plague, this cult is spreading beyond Annaig Valley borders, even beyond species. Already there's unrest coming from the Northlands and Quintilian Provinces from both human and dragon."

"The Provinces are known for fights between the cults of their territories. And the Northlands are filled with weak males and sad, useless females, begging for some god to save them rather than saving themselves."

"I think we know different Northlanders. You know, to be honest, I'm surprised the Northland warlords didn't try to capture your females. They have fewer than they need in that country."

"We tried to help them with that. We used to take their men when we could. But they put up such a fight. . . . Things often ended badly."

"I see." He cleared his throat. "Anyway, I've always believed it's easier to get people to cooperate when you back up your argument with facts. If we have actual evidence to present to your Anne Atli . . . it may change everything."

"And how will that help you?"

"I have no idea, but I'm willing to give it a chance."

"To prove your worth to your people?"

"More like to my parents . . . my siblings . . . and my uncle Bercelak."

That was a need Elina understood more than this dragon could ever know. So she agreed.

"Excellent!" The dragon grinned. "Now, first . . . we need to get you some new clothes."

Elina looked down at what she was wearing. Leggings, shirt, and boots made of animal skin and fur. She didn't understand the problem. "New clothes? What for new clothes?"

"We can't blend into Southland cities with you looking like . . ."

"Like what?" she pushed when he did nothing but open and close his mouth for a few seconds.

"Like an outsider." He seemed pleased by his moment of verbal brilliance. "If we want these humans to be honest about things going on, we'll need to look like we belong."

"And you look like you belong?"

"As human, I do. Thankfully I wasn't cursed with blue or green hair, like many of my cousins. Nor am I freakishly tall or wide like my cousin Éibhear, who also has blue hair." The dragon briefly glanced off. "Gods, how does he function as human?" Before Elina could tell him she had no intention of answering such a ridiculous question, he went on. "Anyway, I may be tall and well-built, but I fit in quite nicely among the humans. Something the Cadwaladrs have been very good at for generations."

"I do not care," Elina told him.

"What?"

"I do not care. You talk and talk, and I do not care."

"But you asked."

"And you could have said, 'Yes, I belong.' But you ramble. So much talking!"

"Are you done?"

"Are *you*?"

They both glared at each other until the dragon said, "Fine. I will work on not rambling if you allow me to dress you more like a Southlander."

"That I agree to."

"Then we have a deal?"

"Yes. We have deal."

He held out his hand and Elina punched it. The dragon recoiled, holding his hand close to his chest.

"Ow! What was that for?"

"Agreeing to our deal."

"That involves punching?"

"Of course," she lied, hiding her smile until he stood. Then she giggled, unable to help herself.

The dragon glared down at her. "What?"

Elina shook her head. "Nothing."

He didn't look like he believed her, but he simply said, "Then let's get started."

Gwenvael did what he did every night around this time. Tucked his five youngest girls into their beds.

Although they could each have their own rooms, they stayed together. Only their eldest sister insisted on her own room, which was a good thing since she could be bitchy when she first woke up.

As ordered, Gwenvael "flew" each of his daughters into her bed. Each girl screeching until she hit the mattress. It drove the rest of the family crazy, which was why they all did it. These five were, much to his siblings' horror, small, female versions of Gwenvael.

Plotting, ridiculous, and beautiful, his five youngest daughters brought absolute joy to Gwenvael's life because they enjoyed the tormenting of others so much. And they were all so eager to learn his many techniques!

All his wonderful little girls.

He tucked in his little Seva last. She was the eldest of Gwenvael's Five—as they'd been named by his uncle Addolgar. It was also Addolgar who had named Unnvar "Dagmar's Little Sneak" and Arlais "The Snobby Brat." They all felt that last one was not very original, but in Addolgar's defense, at the time he'd been gripping the ankle Arlais had kicked while Arlais referred to him as "blood, perhaps, but you are still a Low Born!"

"Daddy?"

"Yes, my little tormentor?"

"Mommy is sad. You should talk to her."

"She is? She seemed fine at dinner."

"She lies, Daddy. I thought we all knew that."

"We do. But she lies to protect us."

"She doesn't want you to know she's sad. She sees sad as a weakness."

Gwenvael sat on the bed next to his daughter and brushed her golden hair off her forehead. It was finally growing back after he'd found her shaved bald a few weeks ago. Arlais had not reacted well when she'd discovered that Seva and the others had made it rain . . . inside her bedroom. For hours. Until everything Arlais valued had been ruined. Gwenvael's Five could also set fires, control lightning, and create enough wind to blow people out of any room they chose. And since his daughters never used their skills against him, Gwenvael found it all highly entertaining.

But shaving off his child's beautiful, golden hair? Unacceptable!

"So why is your mother sad?"

Seva pursed her lips and looked up at Gwenvael with an expression that had clearly been inherited from his Dagmar.

"The boy?" he asked.

"Of course."

"How can he not love it here? I love my uncle Bram, but he's not exactly fun. It's just him and books . . . and reading. So much bloody reading."

"Var likes to read. He likes quiet. He doesn't much like you."

"But I'm darling."

Seva placed her small hand on Gwenvael's forearm. "We all know that, Daddy. And we love you just as you are. But Var . . . he might kill you while you sleep. Although I'm sure he'd feel badly about it . . . eventually."

Gwenvael doubted that, but it didn't matter. "She doesn't want to let him go, does she?"

Seva shook her head. "She loves us all, but Var and Mum understand each other the way you understand the five of us. She doesn't want to let that go."

"I see." He leaned down and kissed Seva's forehead. "I'll talk to your mum. And thanks for the heads-up."

"Of course."

Gwenvael stood and walked over to the fireplace and the dying fire within. He unleashed some fresh flame to warm it up again and added wood to keep it going for a bit. Then he blew out the candles that lit the rest of the room and walked to the door. There he stopped and looked back at his daughters.

"We're all close, yeah?" he asked.

"Yes, Daddy," his girls replied.

"And your mum has Var."

"Yes, Daddy."

"Then who is my Arlais close to? I don't want her to feel alone."

"Keita," they all replied together.

"Oh. You're probably right."

"All Auntie Keita and Uncle Ragnar have are those ridiculous male offspring," Seva explained. "They'll only ever have males. Arlais will be like Auntie Keita's own daughter."

"Hmm." Gwenvael reached for the door handle, remembering growing up with Keita and her way with herbs and turning them into poisons.

"Well," he said to his girls, "just remember . . . never eat or drink anything that Arlais gives you, and I'll make sure the kitchen staff lets us know if she's ever lurking around . . . touching the food." He opened the door. "I'm sure we'll all be fine."

"Don't worry, Daddy," Seva promised around a yawn. "We'll warn you if she decides to kill us all. Then we'll get her first."

And her sisters agreed with a "Destruction-ho!" Their favorite chant.

Gwenvael walked into the hall and closed the door. "They're so cute," he gushed.

Chapter Thirteen

Elina walked into the center of the store and stood in front of the Dolt. He sat in a chair and studied her. Her hands kept clenching and unclenching. They did that because she so desperately wanted to punch him.

When they'd gotten up that morning, he'd told her that they'd be getting her clothes to help her "blend." To be honest, she assumed they'd steal some freshly cleaned clothes that someone had hung out to dry. Instead, he'd taken her into a nearby town where he knew the proprietress of a clothing store. Most of the clothes were made to order, but she had some clothes at the ready in different sizes.

Which was why Elina was now standing in the middle of this ridiculous store in a full-length white silk dress.

The dragon, one foot resting on his thigh, his large body somehow comfortable in that chair, made a circle motion with his forefinger. "Turn around."

"No."

"I need to see the back. You have fuller hips than I originally thought and we don't want you looking too wide from behind."

Elina's hands curled into fists again . . . and stayed that way.

"I will not wear this *ridiculous* garment!"

"You look lovely . . , from the front. I just want to check the—"

"Shut up!"

"Here we are," the shopgirl trilled as she walked up to Elina and placed on her head a large white hat decorated in feathers.

The shopgirl stepped back. "Ohhhh," she breathed. "That's lovely. What do you think, Celyn?"

He shrugged his shoulders. "Lovely."

"That is *it*!" Elina exploded, unable to stand another second. "I will not do this anymore!" She slapped the hat off her head and stomped on it several times before kicking it so that it hit the dragon right in the face. "I will not wear these ridiculous Southlander clothes! You are a reckless, corrupt, immoral race that are not worthy of my help or the help of my people!"

She clawed at the dress. "Get this off me!" she ordered while storming back to the changing room. "*Get this off me!*"

* * *

Celyn watched the Rider stalk to the changing room at the back of the store. Lolly tried to run after her, but she was silently laughing so hard, she could barely stand, while Celyn, with his arms around his stomach, was bent over at the waist, tears streaming down his face as he desperately attempted to hold in his laughter.

Lolly playfully slapped at his head. "Stop it!" she whispered. "Stop it!"

Lolly was right. He really should stop it. But Elina made it simply too easy for him. It had been downhill for Elina ever since he'd had Lolly put the woman in something called petticoats. Yet uphill for Celyn. Because her rage entertained him more than he thought anything could.

When Celyn finally caught his breath, he told Lolly, "Put her in what I picked out."

Gasping, Lolly nodded and headed toward the changing rooms.

"And I'll pay for whatever she's ripped up or set on fire."

That made Lolly laugh harder as she stumbled away.

Celyn stood and walked to the front door of Lolly's shop. He stepped outside and relaxed his back against the wood post where the store's sign hung.

This was a small town, but it had a wonderful blacksmith. He made strong human armor and the Cadwaladrs provided him and his blacksmith son and daughters with much business. It was why Celyn knew the town so well. He'd often come here with Brannie, his mum, and Izzy, but since he never needed as much human armor as they did, he'd spent most of his time chatting up the locals. Found out lots of things when talking to people. Once he'd even found out about a plot to assassinate Annwyl. He'd immediately let Fearghus know, but the future king of the Southland dragons had said nothing to Annwyl, although he'd informed all of her guards. Celyn had been a bit confused about that. He felt it was something she *needed* to know. But he had quickly figured out just how much Fearghus simply enjoyed watching his human mate personally tear the skin from her enemies.

Aye, they were an interesting couple, Fearghus and Annwyl.

When Celyn had first met the human queen, he hadn't understood what had lured his older cousin. For a human, she wasn't exactly plain, but clearly keeping up her looks wasn't a high priority either. She wore nothing to entice and until recently her hair had always seemed to need a good brushing. But as Celyn came to know her, he understood more. Annwyl was blunt, strong, smarter than she seemed, and loyal. Gods, so very loyal. Annwyl would stop at nothing to keep those she loved safe. Absolutely nothing.

Such loyalty made her a monarch feared by those who did not understand her. And her love of a dragon whose mark she wore boldly not only on her armor, but on her body, did nothing but put people off. Then Annwyl had had the twins, and the fear of many humans had doubled. For eons it had been impossible for dragons and humans to produce offspring. Yes, they could mate when a dragon took human form, but nothing had ever come of it except mutual enjoyment or general disappointment. But all that had changed with Annwyl and Fearghus. Now there were many offspring of dragon-human couplings, and those who hated and feared these offspring referred to them as the Abominations.

Seemed a bit unfair, but as usual, Celyn could see both sides of the matter.

He could understand the fear of humans and dragons alike. The offspring of dragon-human couplings were uniquely powerful. They looked like humans for the most part, but they had powers that were never exactly the same from one offspring to another.

That was where the fear came from, Celyn believed. The not knowing. Not knowing what these offspring could do. Even they didn't know. At least not right away.

So Celyn did understand the fear, but not the hatred. He didn't understand dragons who hated humans. Or humans who hated dragons. Or anyone who hated someone for being brought into this world without any say in the matter.

Then again, no one ever asked his opinion on anything. Except Rhiannon. But he always felt she did that simply to irritate Bercelak. She enjoyed irritating Bercelak.

"Lord Celyn?"

Celyn snorted. "Lolly, you of all beings know I am no lord." He turned and walked back into the store. "If anything I'm as far from . . ."

Celyn stopped. Nodded at what he saw. "Perfect."

"If you already had this, Dolt," asked the Rider, standing beside a grinning Lolly, "then why must I put on other clothes?"

"To amuse me."

"I loathe you more and more every day."

Lolly quickly covered her mouth, turned her face away.

"Aye, I can tell," Celyn agreed.

He walked around Elina. Aye. These clothes were perfect. Black leggings, a blue cotton shirt, and black leather boots that went over her knees. He had no need to pass her off as some grand lady, simply as a traveler. But he still wanted to make sure she could move on her horse and, more importantly, use her bow unobstructed by the sometimes-ridiculous clothes of humans.

"That fur and leather cape I picked out should do it, Lolly."

Lolly put the cape around Elina's shoulders. She fussed

with it a bit before she was satisfied, stepping back beside Celyn and smiling. "You look wonderful," she gushed.

Elina stared at the two of them, her mouth slightly open, her eyes drawn down in a distinct expression of disgust.

"I do not understand you people," Elina finally admitted.

"That's all right," Celyn said. "I'm here to lead the way."

"I would be better off with your travel-cow leading the way."

"No need to get nasty." Celyn took the bundle of extra clothes he'd chosen for Elina from Lolly, then kissed the shopgirl on the cheek. "As always, Lolly, thank you for your help."

"Of course."

Celyn gestured to the still open front door. "Ready?" he asked Elina.

"I have been ready for hour. You waste my time."

"You need to learn to relax."

"Shut up."

Celyn managed to wait until Elina brushed past him before he grinned. And that's when Lolly grabbed hold of his arm.

"Lolly?" Celyn prompted when she said nothing.

"Be careful on your travels, Celyn." She glanced at the door as if she expected to see someone listening to their conversation. "Things are different out there."

"What brought this on?"

"The questions you were asking me earlier . . . I'm fine with those questions. We've known each other a long time. But there are some . . ." She again glanced at the front door. "Just be careful. I always enjoy your company, dear Celyn."

"And I yours." He leaned down and kissed her cheek again. "And thank you, old friend."

* * *

Elina hated her new clothes, but only because she liked them so much. She couldn't remember the last time she'd had clothes that she hadn't sewn herself from animals she'd hunted down on her own, or clothes that hadn't been handed down to her by her older sisters.

Torn between wanting to tear the clothes off and wanting *never* to take them off, Elina began walking toward the big gates at the entrance to the town.

The dragon easily caught up to her with his long legs. "That's strange," he said softly.

Elina stopped immediately. "If you have problem with these clothes, Dolt, you should not have bought them for me."

The dragon frowned, his head tipping to the side. "What are you talking about? There's nothing wrong with your clothes."

"Then what was strange?"

"Lolly suddenly warning me about not asking too many questions while we're traveling through the cities and towns on our route."

Elina folded her arms over her chest. "By death, how much do you talk that even the shopgirls need to warn you to stop?"

The dragon glared at her. "I don't talk *that* much, but I do ask questions. I listen to gossip."

"If you need to believe that . . ."

"Are you done?"

"At the moment."

"Anyway, I think we'll need to be even more careful than I first thought."

Elina started walking again, already bored by this conversation. "I am always careful."

With two steps, the dragon was again by her side. "Even while welcoming your old friend death?"

"If you fear death, it will only come for you sooner. Why fear what is inevitable?"

"Every word you speak," he announced, swinging his arm out, "like a ray of suns-shine!"

"At least I keep my words short, meaningful, and to point. Shopgirls do not tell me I need to keep quiet."

"She did not tell me to keep quiet. Stop twisting this!"

"I twist nothing. I simply note."

"Well, stop noting, and do me a favor."

Elina stopped again and faced the dragon. "What favor?"

He glanced off, his lip curling in disgust. It lasted for several seconds before he finally said, "Just . . . if you notice I'm talking too much or someone seems particularly interested in what I'm asking about, let me know. That's all. Just . . . have my back."

"Have . . . back?"

"Have *my* back. Simply make sure that I don't put me foot in it."

"Foot?"

He rolled his eyes. "Gods, you're literal. I mean make sure I don't talk us into a bad situation."

"Oh. Step on dick."

His eyes widened. "Pardon?"

"When men do stupid thing . . . we say they step on dick."

"That would imply an impressively sized dick."

Elina smirked. "Rider women already took the balls, which makes the dick of men look that much longer."

The dragon briefly closed his eyes, and he smiled. "Do you say *that* to the men of your tribes?"

She reached up to his wide shoulder and patted it. "We sew it on our pillows."

Chuckling, Elina walked off, the dragon eventually catching up with her once more.

Chapter Fourteen

Brother Magnus, as he was known at the monastery of the Brotherhood of the Far Mountains, barely stifled a yawn of absolute and utter boredom. He hated this place. Always had. But he'd been dropped at the doorstep of the Brotherhood when he was barely two, and here was where he'd stayed.

It could have been worse, though. He could have been sold as slave labor to a farmer or a mine. At least with the Brotherhood, Magnus always had a full belly and a roof over his head. But at twenty-nine winters, he was beyond bored and it didn't seem that anything would ever change that.

Magnus yawned again and wasn't able to catch it in time. From across the study room, the Elder Brother glared at him, and with a nod, Magnus got up and walked out into the hallway. Perhaps some fresh air would help wake him up a bit . . . but he doubted it.

As he headed toward his cell, he heard a door open and watched one of the brothers slip out of a cell and head down the hall toward the back stairs.

Although the cowl of his robe hid his face, Magnus knew that brother. He should know him. He was closer to that brother than anyone else at the monastery.

Prince Talan of the Southlands, firstborn son of Queen Annwyl and Prince Fearghus, twin brother to Princess

Talwyn and first cousin to Princess Rhianwen, and what Magnus liked to call "The Consummate Obtainer of Pussy."

Glancing around and seeing that the halls were barren except for the pair of them, Magnus chased after Talan, catching up with him as the royal made it to the back stairs.

"Talan?"

Talan stopped, his eyes briefly closing, but when he turned and saw Magnus standing there, he let out a relieved breath. "Oh, Magnus. It's you."

Magnus noted the bag slung over Talan's shoulder. "Are you heading into town?"

Usually when they snuck out of the monastery together and headed into town for ale, food, and women, they left later, when it was easy to blend into the dark and shadows. But as bored as Magnus was today, he was willing to risk a lashing or two for leaving the grounds during the day. *If* they were caught. A big if. Over the years, Magnus and Talan had become very good at not being caught.

But Talan didn't answer Magnus right away. Instead, he stared at him for a long moment, a frown on his face. Strange, since Talan rarely frowned. He was usually too busy smirking and mocking the other brothers under his breath to ever look serious . . . about anything.

Finally, after what felt like hours, Talan said, "I'm leaving, old friend."

"Leaving?"

"I have to. My time here is up."

It was strange how Magnus somehow knew, deep inside, that Talan was never meant to spend his entire life here with the Brotherhood. Talan played along. Practiced all the rituals. Studied diligently. Pretended to respect the Elder Brothers enough to keep from receiving any punishments or beatings. But Magnus knew his friend was not meant for this life. And not because he was a royal either. There was just something about Prince Talan of the Southlands that spoke of more important things than life in a monastery.

"I will miss you, though," Talan admitted.

"But I'm coming with you."

Magnus really hadn't known those words were going to come out of his mouth until they did, but he knew as soon as he said them . . . he meant every one. He couldn't stay with the Brotherhood. He couldn't spend his life like this. He wasn't meant to.

"I can't ask you to—"

"You're not asking. I'm telling. . . . I'm coming with you. We're going together."

Talan studied him a moment longer before he nodded. "You have two minutes to get what you—"

But Magnus didn't wait for Talan to finish. He simply went back to his cell and grabbed his travel bag, his short sword, a few daggers, and whatever coin he had, and pulled his fur cloak over his monk robes. It took him less than a minute. That's what his life at the monastery amounted to . . . less than a minute to pack up and leave forever.

He returned to Talan's side and together they moved quietly but quickly down the back stairs and out the monastery's back door. They headed through the forest that surrounded the property until they reached the grazing land where they kept the animals they used for food. They were near the stone wall that surrounded the monastery and was covered in protective powerful magicks when Talan suddenly veered off and carefully approached one of the massive bulls.

"Talan?"

Talan didn't answer but silently waved Magnus off.

The bull watched Talan's approach but didn't run or attack. The monks had taught them how to handle animals, from small to large, no matter the temperament.

Once Talan stood by the bull, he drew his short sword, caught one of the bull's horns and slammed the blade up into its neck.

The bull let out a cry of pain before dropping to the

ground, its blood pouring out onto the snow-covered ground.

Talan knelt by the animal and placed his hand on its head. He prayed over the animal for a minute, stood, and then performed the same action again on two more bulls.

It seemed excessive to Magnus, performing sacrifices at this moment, but perhaps Talan was hoping to bless their journey.

Talan returned to Magnus's side, wiping his blood-covered hands on his robes.

"You sure about this?" Talan asked Magnus. "You come with me past this stone wall . . . and there will be no turning back, my friend."

"Then, gods, Talan, what are we waiting for?"

Talan grinned and they walked the rest of the way to the wall. Bending at the knees, Magnus launched himself to the top and over, Talan right by his side. One of the many skills their brothers had taught them over the years.

They landed and stood tall. Talan glanced at him and Magnus nodded. Then they faced the five men who'd clearly been waiting for them on the other side and stopped short. In one second, Magnus felt his bright and brilliant dream of leaving this place forever slip away. A dream, he knew, that would haunt him for the rest of his days.

"Father Robert," Talan greeted. "Brother Oliver. Brother—"

"Where are you going, dear boy?" Father Robert asked. His voice soft and comforting but, as Magnus knew, his will made of iron.

"I have someplace to be, Father Robert."

"That's not possible, Brother Talan. You know that." Father Robert gave a small smile. "Now you will come back with us. We have a place for you. Both of you. A place for you always."

"You can't force him to stay," Magnus argued, even though he knew he, himself, was doomed to stay. Doomed because he was no one's prince, no royal's child. He was no one.

"We can and we will," Father Robert lashed back. "Don't make us."

Magnus took a step to protect his only friend, his anger getting the better of him, but Talan quickly caught his arm and pulled him back to his side. Eyes locked on the monks, Talan reached into the pocket of his robes and quickly salted the earth in a circle around them.

The monks immediately backed up, their eyes desperately searching, while Father Robert pointed an accusing finger at Talan.

"What have you done, Abomination?"

"And there it is," Talan announced. "The truth. How you think about me. *All* of me."

Magnus jerked at the sound of something crashing into the wall behind them.

"You are an abomination against the gods," Father Robert roared over the increasing sounds of crashing coming from the other side of that damn wall. "A demon of the earth. You do not deserve to live!"

"My mother would disagree with you. She adores me. I'm her little boy."

"She is the bitch that spawned you. It is her sin that brought the Abominations to us."

"Or yours, Father. Perhaps the sins of this world were so great that you brought us to you. And now you must pay for your sins. With blood."

The wall burst outward, forcing Magnus to duck as chunks of stone flew. When he was able to look again, three bulls stood in the opening, eyes bright red, wounds still open so that he was able to see bone and sinew, their blood still oozing out of their big bodies.

Massive heads and horns turned toward Talan. With an easy gesture, the royal pointed at the five monks. "Kill them all."

The bulls' heads twisted in the other direction, and the

monks stumbled back, raising their hands and quickly calling on protective forces to do battle.

The bulls charged and Talan ran. "Come on!" he called back to Magnus.

Taking off after his friend, Magnus glanced back to see that one bull was down, but the other two had already impaled one monk and stomped another into the ground.

Deciding not to look back again—it was too much—Magnus caught up with Talan, the two running toward a main road about three leagues away.

"You can raise the dead," Magnus noted stupidly, unsure what else to say as they continued to run.

"I can raise *some* dead. Animals, mostly. Still a bit to go before I'll be able to raise more complicated creatures."

Magnus knew Talan meant humans and dragons. Creatures with souls and brains.

"Does that bother you?" Talan asked him after a few moments of nothing but their breathing and their booted feet running over snow-covered land.

"No," Magnus answered, a little surprised by that. "It doesn't. Just don't do it to me."

"You're already alive. . . . Why would I raise you?"

"I mean if I die."

"What if I'm still in a fight and need you to back me up? Can I raise you then?"

Magnus stopped and Talan did as well. They faced each other.

"All right. You can do it then. But don't let me hang around, pieces of me dropping off, body beginning to spoil."

"I'll have to wait then, won't I?"

"What are you talking about?"

"I've learned how to raise some dead . . . but not to actually put a time limit on how long they can be around."

Magnus gestured with a thumb over his shoulders. "What about those bulls?"

"They could drop suddenly and turn to dust."

"And if they don't drop suddenly?"

"Then our dear brothers will have to chop them to bits, bury them in consecrated ground, and salt the earth around their graves."

"You sure that'll work?"

Talan frowned a bit, his gaze moving in the direction they'd just left. After a moment, he shrugged. "I'm sure it'll be fine."

With that, Talan charged off toward the main road. Magnus took one look back, briefly chewed his lip. He could still hear screaming and the sounds of magicks being used to combat the undead beasts.

Whether to go back to what he knew, or go forward . . . into the unknown?

"I'm sure," Talan yelled at him, "the other Brothers will come to help at some point!"

Briefly closing his eyes, Magnus muttered, "He's probably right."

Then Magnus headed after his friend—and into the unknown.

Chapter Fifteen

At the edge of another town, Celyn and Elina dismounted their horses and slowly entered, slipping into the flow of foot traffic, so they looked like all the other travelers coming through.

This wasn't the first town they'd been to since leaving Lolly's shop, but it was the first one they'd decided to walk through. They had simply ridden through the others, Celyn feeling those towns were a little too close to Lolly's shop for his comfort. And since they hadn't seen anything very interesting anyway, it had seemed fine to just keep on riding.

But the town of River Road was a good distance from Lolly's place and it was large enough that Celyn felt sure they'd be able to find out more here than in any of the smaller towns.

"Are you hungry?" he asked Elina.

"I could eat." Then she turned and started to walk away.

"Where are you going?"

"I saw hearty-looking sheep at pasture a league away. I will go kill one."

"No, no." Celyn shook his head. "I was suggesting we go eat at a local inn or tavern."

Elina frowned. "You mean have others make food for us?"

"Aye. Won't that be nice?"

"What if they put poison in our food?"

Celyn smiled, but even he knew that it was mocking. "What a happy place you come from, Elina Shestakova of the excessively and ridiculously long name. A land filled with such joy!"

"Because we do not expect others to cook for us, you mock?"

"Do your warriors cook for themselves?"

"Why should they?" she snapped back. "They protect the Steppes of the Outerplains and have husbands to do it for them. So, should they not have—"

"Everything?"

Her eyes narrowed the tiniest bit. "We all share with each other. It is the way of our life. It is how we survive."

"And that's great. Fabulous. Really. But while you're in *my* world, we can have others cook for us and there is no shame. I know I don't feel shame."

"You snatch up cows while they graze and eat them whole, even though they offer you no challenge. I doubt you feel shame for anything."

"Shame is something dragons simply don't understand. And why should we? We know dragons are superior to all other beings. And that's just fine with us. Now . . . can we go eat?"

"Anything else, handsome?"

Elina looked up at the barmaid who'd been serving them since they'd walked into the place. Although the dragon was friendly with everyone and most were friendly right back, it was the women who paid him the most attention. Then again, it wasn't exactly surprising. He was extremely pretty. He'd have many suitors if he spent time among the Steppes Tribes. As she'd said before, Rider women liked to have at least a few pretty husbands.

"Another bowl of stew for me. More bread. Another ale." He finally looked at Elina. "You want more?"

"More?" She glanced down at her third bowl of stew. Like the Steppes wolves, her people gorged when they had ample food because there was a good chance supplies would be scarce the next day. Plus, with so much traveling, they needed to make sure they ate enough to keep up their strength. Getting too skinny on the Plains simply led to a quick death and sobbing relatives.

But even so, she still didn't feel the need to eat as much in one sitting as this dragon, who, Elina knew, would eat again in a few hours.

"No. I am fine."

"You sure? Another ale?"

"Water."

"And a pitcher of water for my friend."

"Of course. I'll be right back."

The barmaid walked off, not even looking in Elina's

direction. Elina often received the same treatment from her own people, but she guessed it was for very different reasons.

Once they were alone again, the dragon focused on Elina and asked, "So what about your family?"

The stew Elina was about to eat hovered on its spoon, right outside her mouth. She stared at the dragon. She did not understand him. He was supposed to be chatting up the locals. Not pestering her with all his bloody questions.

"What?"

"Your family."

"What about them?"

"Are you close to them? Do they like being part of the Steppes Tribes? Do you look like your mother or your father? Does your mother have many husbands? Do you even know who your father is? And what about—"

"Stop." She dropped the spoon back into the bowl of stew. "By all death, please stop." Elina relaxed into her chair and gazed at the dragon. "Your mouth is like panicked horse. It just keeps running."

"I'm curious." He pointed at her with the last piece of bread left until the barmaid brought more. "And you said I could ask you questions during breaks. This is a break."

"But you ask too many questions."

"You didn't put a limit on how many questions I could ask."

"Why do you need to know?"

He shrugged and repeated, "I'm curious."

"I am surprised your curiosity has not helped you meet death much sooner."

"You'd think," he said with a smile. "I suppose it must be my majestic charm." He grinned and she glowered. It seemed to be their way these days.

Elina raised her forefinger. "You can ask me *one* question about my kin."

"Just one?" When she glowered more, he quickly said, "All right. All right. No need to get vicious."

The dragon thought a moment, then asked, "How many siblings do you have?"

Why he was asking her that, Elina had no idea. That question hadn't been among the ones he'd just asked, and she couldn't see how the answer would be very interesting to anyone. But if that's what he wanted to know . . .

"Twenty-four."

"Are you close to any of them?"

"A-aah." She raised her forefinger again. "One question. *One!*"

"This is a *continuation* of the one question. It's not a new question. Simply a clarification of the original question."

"A clarifi—" Elina briefly closed her eyes and shook her head. She did not and would never understand this dragon. "I am close to one. A sister."

"Out of twenty-four?"

Elina must have glowered again because the dragon quickly raised his hands as if to ward her off. "Not a judgment. Just another follow-up question."

"My sister Kachka," she said before he could delve any further, "accepts me just as I am. With all my many flaws."

The dragon studied her for a moment, then asked, "What flaws?"

Elina quickly looked at the dragon, expecting to see that mocking expression of his. But, instead, all she saw was pure confusion. As if he had no idea what she was talking about.

She had to admit, it was a nice feeling. But she knew that his confusion would not last. Her flaws, like everything else about Elina, were out there for the world to see. . . .

* * *

After purchasing four extra loaves of the wonderful bread served at the inn and stuffing them in his travel bag, Celyn stood. "You ready?" he asked Elina.

Her reply was to stand and walk away from him. Celyn watched her for a few moments before he followed, stopping by the barmaid to place several gold pieces, including a fat tip, into her palm. He smiled at her and she blushed back, her eyes glancing toward the inn stairs that led to the bedrooms. It was a clear invitation, but Celyn didn't bother to say yes or no. He simply winked at her and walked out.

Celyn quickly caught up to Elina as she moved toward the bridge that would take them back to the main road. He threw his arm around her shoulders and deftly steered her around to one of the shops in the main square. He stopped to point at something in the window as if that had been his plan all along.

"Why do you touch me?" Elina asked.

"Because we're not leaving yet," he said quietly, stepping closer to the shop glass, "but I didn't want to make a big thing of it."

"So you touch me."

"Stop complaining. It's not like I tried to fuck you right here."

With a meaningless nod, he moved off from the window, bringing Elina with him. Now they were going in the opposite direction.

"Where exactly are we going?"

"To Temple Row."

"What is that?"

"A row of temples."

"Smart-ass."

"No, no. Just answering your question. There's no other way to explain it."

"Then tell me *why* are we going to row of temples?"

"Because that's all they were talking about at the inn. Didn't you hear?"

"I could not hear much over your constant chewing. You feed like bear."

"I was hungry."

Elina stopped, forcing Celyn to stop with her. "You really heard about this in pub?"

"Yes. Isn't that why we were there?"

"But between chewing . . . you were talking. Or asking me questions to make me talk. And you responded to my answers as if you were listening."

"I was listening. I find your life *fascinating.*"

"Shut up." Her bright blue eyes narrowed on his face. "You really listened to others while talking to me?"

Celyn shrugged and admitted. "It's a skill. My mother can cleave off a dragon's head by bringing two swords together simultaneously. We all have our talents."

"Your mother did seem like cold, unfeeling viper determined to destroy world. . . . I like that in woman."

Celyn was about to remind Elina that his mother was not "woman" but then, after glancing around, he decided it was in his best interest not to say anything about that. Instead, he led her down several streets until they reached Temple Row.

That's where they both stopped, at the very beginning of the street, and stared.

"Horses of Ramsfor," Elina swore beside him.

Celyn didn't know who Ramsfor was, but he had to agree with Elina. He might not have traveled as far and wide as some of his kin, but Celyn knew the Southlands quite well. And he'd never seen such a thing before.

Whispering, Elina noted, "It is like giant cock pointed straight at the heavens."

She was right. The Cult of Chramnesind had taken a relatively small piece of land between two temples that had been in those spots for decades and shoved in a building that . . . well . . . that resembled a giant cock. With balls.

It was set back from the street a bit so that it had a little more room for the "balls," two rounded buildings attached to either side of the tower. And the tower that stood in the middle traveled straight up and seemed to go on forever. It was taller than he would be as dragon. Gods, the damn thing was taller than Éibhear as dragon! And that alone was shocking.

The entire building overwhelmed everything else on the street, making the other temples seem puny and weak in comparison.

Something Celyn was sure had been done on purpose.

Elina walked toward the building, taking Celyn's hand and pulling him behind her. But the closer they got, the more unsettled he felt.

Unlike his royal cousins, Celyn didn't have definite feelings about any gods. They served their purpose, they sometimes helped, and perhaps if he were more magically inclined, he'd happily turn to them for assistance during spells or whatever. But, in all honesty, he could take or leave the gods. Just like most dragons. So going into temples had never bothered him before.

Until now. Until this very moment.

Celyn tried to stop but Elina yanked him along.

Gods, she's strong.

They reached the front doors and a pretty priestess, her hair cut so short that it barely covered her skull, smiled at them.

"Blessings, lady. Sir." She stepped to the side and gestured with her hand. "Please . . . join us."

Elina walked inside and forced Celyn to follow. The smell of some foreign incense hit him first. And it hit him like a stone wall.

He stumbled a bit and the Rider glanced back at him, her head cocking to the side. She suddenly reminded him of a dog and he laughed.

With a shake of her head, she continued on.

As Celyn walked, he studied the people here. They were on their knees, some with arms outstretched; others with hands clasped. But all were praying to their god. To Chramnesind.

Who suddenly didn't seem that bad a chap to Celyn. So Chramnesind thought the offspring of dragons and humans were wrong. Maybe they were. Maybe Celyn's cousins *shouldn't* be here. Maybe *Celyn* shouldn't be here. And what about the world? Should the world be here?

Should any of them?

"Dolt. Are you listening to me?"

Celyn blinked, pulled from his absolutely *amazing* thoughts. "Aye?"

"What is wrong with you?"

"Nothing. You know . . . you're very pretty."

"What?"

"Not in the conventional sense. You're not Talaith pretty. But she's astounding. Briec lucked out with her. Though she argues *everything* with him . . . but I think he likes that. But you are pretty. And a beautiful soul. We should get naked," he announced, now walking forward, "lay ourselves on that altar, and fuck for the blessings of the gods!"

He faced Elina, grinned. "What say you, Death Worshipper?"

Elina grabbed Celyn's balls and twisted until she had him on his knees, his loud grunts of pain catching everyone's attention.

"I will tell you once, Dolt. You will snap out of whatever is happening to you right now or I will tear these off and wear them around neck like ornament."

"Is everything all right here?" some fool in white robes asked as he came near.

Elina glanced around and noticed that there were several men moving in. Close. Too close.

It was one of the first things that Daughters of the Steppes were taught: never let a group of men get too close. In a lot of ways, they were like wild beast packs and when they got too close to a lone woman, they attacked. That's why it was so important to keep control of them and make sure they weren't allowed to congregate in large groups.

Because they couldn't be trusted.

"Get up, Dolt. Now."

She released Celyn's balls and he got to his feet. Reaching under his cape, she grabbed his chain-mail shirt and pulled him through the praying sheep on the ground. As she cut through them, she kicked a few, stepped on others, and forced Celyn to do the same.

It woke some of them out of their stupor and they shot up, confused and lost, stumbling into the way of the men trying to grab Elina and Celyn. They only slowed those priests for a few seconds, but the distraction gave Elina enough time to run through one of the doors that led into another part of the building. She slammed the door shut and threw the bolt closed.

She grabbed Celyn's hand and started down toward the hallway, but more priests came from that direction while banging came from the door behind them.

"They will get through that in no time, Dolt."

"Don't worry, pretty little lady." He patted her head. "I will help you."

He turned toward the wall, took in a big breath, and then unleashed . . . a big breath.

"Huh," Celyn said when he saw that nothing had happened to the wall. "Isn't that funny?"

"Not really."

A large hand clamped down on Elina's shoulder and she immediately slapped it off.

In response, the priest backhanded her across the face. "Insolent fema—"

His words ended when flames drowned them out, and Elina flew back from the fire as Celyn shoved her out of the way.

The priest's screams filled the long hallway and Elina rushed behind Celyn and pushed him down the hall until they reached a large window.

A priest followed behind her and when he was close, she grabbed him by his robes, spun them both around until she had some momentum, and rammed him into the thick glass. The glass didn't break, but it shattered a bit. So Elina pulled the priest back and rammed him again, breaking the glass into pieces.

She dropped the priest's body, kicked out the shards of glass that could cut them, and forced Celyn through. She quickly followed, took his hand, and started running.

Celyn didn't know how long they ran . . . or when they reached their horses . . . or how he got on his horse and started riding . . . or how long they rode.

He just knew he had to stop, dismount, go off to the side of the road, and throw up everything he'd eaten in the last twenty-four hours.

The vomiting seemed to go on for hours, but he couldn't have stopped it even if he'd wanted to.

When, finally, he could think again, Elina was there with a pigskin of water.

"Here. Drink."

He was so dehydrated now, he finished it all.

"What the hells . . . what the hells happened?"

"You do not smoke, do you?"

"Only from my nostrils. And only when I'm annoyed."

Elina gave a short laugh. "Not that kind of smoke.

Before the Daughters of Steppes ride into battle, we take plants from land, dry them, shred them, and then smoke."

"Why?"

"It makes one feel invincible. And most of the Daughters usually are. I smoked little because I usually stayed back with the old people and the children. But Glebovicha used to force me to attend the ritual anyway . . . to stand by and watch. So that I was well aware that I was not worthy to be among the warriors." She shrugged. "I have been around so much smoke that none affects me now."

"I'm sorry."

"For what?"

"I'm not quite sure. But I really feel like I should say I'm sorry."

Elina shook her head. "For this, you should not apologize. This had nothing to do with you and everything to do with these cult people."

"This is bad," Celyn said, forcing himself to stand. "Worse than we thought. I mean, the building alone . . ."

"It's like they want all priests and disciples of the other gods to know they are bigger and better."

"We can't stay here. I'm sure they'll be coming for us."

With a shrug, "If they have not caught up to us by now . . ."

"It's not like we've traveled that far, woman. We can't wait here for them to show up."

Elina studied Celyn for a long moment without saying a word.

"What?" he pushed when the silence went on for an uncomfortable amount of time.

"We have been on road for five hours."

As Celyn stumbled back, Elina caught his arm, the only reason he didn't slip in his own vomit.

"*What?*"

"We backtracked a bit, went through river to destroy our scent, then headed long way round until we reached road again. I doubt they will find us."

"I don't remember any of that. I don't remember anything."

Celyn paced around Elina, his hands on his head. "This is bad. Much worse than I thought."

"So what do you want to do? We cannot sit here all day."

"Costentyn."

"I do not know that word."

"It's not a word. It's a dragon. An old dragon. Might no longer be living, but he knows a lot."

"Why would he know anything of what we need?"

"He likes knowledge. From books. From other dragons. Even from people. He loves to wander through towns and villages as human, talking to everyone. When I was younger, my father and I used to go to his cave to chat. My father would ask advice and I would just listen. He always had such interesting information. And, unlike some cranky Riders I know, he was never stingy with the answers when I asked questions."

"It is not that you ask questions, Dolt. It is that you ask so many. Why must you ask so many?"

"Because I'm curious. Imagine if we hadn't gone into that giant penis temple."

"We would not be wanted for murder?"

Celyn winced. "Good point."

"But you are right. Most people find their own way to the gods. This is like . . . they are being trapped. Their mind stopped and wiped clean so someone else's truth and lies can replace everything else the person knows. I do not like that. I do not think it is fair." She walked to her horse. "Come, Dolt. Let us go see your friend who is old. Perhaps he can tell us of the dark times that are coming."

Celyn glanced up at the sky. It was nearing the end of a bright, beautiful early winter's day, but the Rider was right.

Dark times were coming.

Chapter Sixteen

Dagmar Reinholdt studied the parchment handed to her by her assistant Mabsant before signing it with a flourish and affixing her seal.

Many years ago, Annwyl had given Dagmar the power to sign for her just as Dagmar's father had. Except Annwyl had appeared much more relieved to be handing over the tedious day-to-day business to her sister-by-mating. Dagmar's father had handed over the power, but he had done so very grudgingly.

Yet even though Dagmar now had immense power, she never allowed herself to entertain the possibility of abusing it. For two very good reasons. The first, which was new to her, was the intense feeling that to abuse such power would be wrong. Usually, Dagmar didn't bother herself with right and wrong. She left that to men who received their power simply by being born with a penis. Everyone else had to fight for what was theirs.

The second reason was a simple one: Annwyl might hate the day-to-day, but she protected her power as queen the way she protected her children. With a blinding, passionate force of will.

Besides, Dagmar had worked hard all these years to rein in the queen's quirkier tendencies. Not that Dagmar didn't enjoy that side of Annwyl, but she wasn't just some soldier or even some respected general. She was queen. And she needed to represent herself as such. Especially if she hoped to keep control of her lands and her alliances.

But that's what Dagmar was here for. To help Annwyl any way she could.

Mabsant, who'd worked with Dagmar for nearly eight years now, placed another parchment in front of her.

"This is from Baron Neish. He'd like some of Queen Annwyl's troops to help him keep order."

Dagmar squinted up at her assistant. She didn't need her precious spectacles to do close-in work, but she couldn't hope to see anything more than a few feet away without them. "Why can't he maintain his own order?"

"There seems to be some discord among the religious sects in his city."

Dagmar leaned back in the big wood chair. "That's the . . . third?"

"Aye, m'lady."

"Yes. The third time we've heard such complaints from one of the outer cities." The Chramnesind cults were growing bolder—and meaner. Which was interesting since they preached unity and love. But Dagmar was not fooled. The truth was Chramnesind's worshippers believed in hate. Hatred of the ones they called the Abominations. The mixing of human and dragon blood that had created . . .

By all reason, it didn't matter. All that mattered was that the likes of Priestess Abertha were using the fear people had for dragon-human offspring to advance their real agenda of complete domination. For their god, but more importantly, for the Salebiri family.

The Salebiris had always felt they should rule all these lands, from the Northlands to the Desert Lands, from the

Western Provinces to the Eastern Coast. They didn't think much about the Ice Lands, because there was little in those harsh territories to interest them.

But everything else—they wanted. No matter how they had to get it. Something that annoyed Dagmar greatly.

Of course, nothing irritated Dagmar more than when the perfectly ordered kingdom she'd helped to create was being disrupted.

"Let me talk to Queen Annwyl and General Brastias before we do anything." She didn't like that Annwyl's armies were being separated so much. Going off to fight petty skirmishes here, there, and every gods-damn where.

Massaging the fingers of her left hand—they always ached a bit after she did a lot of writing and when it was getting colder, like it was now—Dagmar glanced up and, with a squint, she noticed that her assistant was staring past her.

Dagmar turned her head and came nose to leggings-covered cock with some male.

"By all reason," she squeaked, slapping at the groin that had been right by her face.

"Ow!" she heard her mate snap. "I thought we decided you'd treat my hair and my cock like they were the most important things in your world . . . since they are."

"I never agreed to that, and stop shoving the damn thing in my face."

"You didn't say that last night, my dearest heart."

"*Gwenvael!*"

"Aye, my love?"

Dagmar let out a breath. She knew, after so many years with the gold dragon, that yelling at him would do no good. It merely spurred him on.

"Could you excuse us?" she asked her assistant.

With a nod, Mabsant picked up a few papers and scurried from the room.

"I think I make the lad nervous," Gwenvael said, grinning.

"I'm sure you do."

"Don't you find that odd? Everyone usually adores me."

"Gwenvael," she cut in, "what do you want?"

"You're not being very nice to me."

"Gwenvael, my patience is waning."

"I thought we should talk."

"Talk?" She squinted up at him. "About?"

"Varry."

"Don't call Var that. He hates when you call him that."

"Which is probably why I call him that. He's so bloody uptight. He reminds me of Fearghus in his younger days. Something that wouldn't be a problem except that humans don't do well when they try to live alone in caves."

"Is this what you want to talk about?"

"No."

"Then perhaps you could get to it? I have much to do today. Would you like to see my list?"

"Threatening with those stupid lists only works on my mother."

Damn.

Gwenvael went to his knees beside Dagmar's chair, and using the arms, he turned it so she faced him. When he pulled her closer so that she didn't have to squint so much to see his face, Dagmar announced, "I will not talk about Var leaving."

"Dammit, woman."

"Sending my son away is not a viable option. It will never be a viable option."

"You can't hold him here forever. He wants to go. And now that Uncle Bram's last assistant has finally died of old age—and most likely grave boredom—we have no excuse not to send him."

"No excuse? He's my son."

"And like his mother, he plans to get what he wants. The question is whether we give it to him willingly, or he rips it from our cold, dead hands."

"I ask so little of this world—"

"That's a lie."

"—that I don't think it's unreasonable to insist my only son stay by my side until he's at least eighteen winters so that I may raise him properly."

Gwenvael moved in until Dagmar felt forced to open her legs to allow him closer. He then placed his arms on either side of her and leaned in until their faces were only inches apart.

"Do you really think," he asked, "that I want my son to go?"

"Yes, I do."

"I'll have you know, female, that unlike my father, who has always felt he only loved his sons due to some flaw in his gods-given instincts, I actually love and, more importantly, *like* my son. How could I not? He reminds me of you." He kissed her nose.

"But I do fear," Gwenvael went on, "that he's stagnating here. A mind like his must be constantly occupied or—and I know this from experience—it will only turn to ill."

"I managed."

"Your kin thought so little of you in the beginning, how could you not? Var doesn't have that problem here. Even Briec respects him." Gwenvael lowered his head a bit so that they were looking each other right in the eyes. "*Briec.*"

"But to send him far away—"

"It's not like we're sending him to the Ice Lands, Dagmar. Bram's not even an hour's flight from here. And, even better, my uncle Bram will be able to teach our boy something that neither you nor I can."

"Empathy?"

"I was going to say humility, but now that I think on it . . . both would probably apply."

* * *

Annwyl sat on the outside steps leading into the Great Hall and gulped down more water from the chalice one of the servants had brought her. Her training had not gone well today. She hadn't done her best, leaving herself open to easy hits and sloppy technique. Now her muscles were fairly screaming and she had a few new cuts that hadn't been there this morning. They were also still bleeding, but she knew that Morfyd could tend them. Besides, it wasn't like she was bleeding to death on the steps. Then she would have sent for a healer. Although many didn't believe it, she did have common sense.

Gwenvael's eldest daughter ran out of the Great Hall and down the steps.

"What is it, Arlais?" Annwyl asked the pompous child. Gods, she'd thought her Talwyn had been difficult. She'd take a thousand Talwyns over this one pain-in-the-ass brat.

Arlais didn't answer Annwyl's question, but her gaze was fixed on the sky above. That meant one of two things. Either Rhiannon was coming for a visit or—

"I will not have this argument again!" the red She-dragon snapped as her claws landed hard on the ground, her thick, long hair settling around her in all its shiny, perfect red glory.

"All I'm saying," the purple dragon calmly explained when he landed next to her, his cousin not far behind, "is that you could have handled that better. Now *I* have to fix it."

"Then fix it!" She sat back on her haunches and pointed a sharp black talon at him. "She started this, if you'd bother to remember. And I was kind enough to do nothing more than add a little something to her food that didn't kill her. It merely made her scales fall off. I could have come up with something that would have made her head explode. But I didn't do that, now did I?"

"That was so big of you," the purple dragon replied drily, his eyes rolling back in his head.

"Of course it was." And Keita said those words with so much sincerity that Annwyl had to take a quick moment to close her eyes and bite back her laughter. "I didn't want her dead, my love. I just wanted to make it clear who's in charge."

"In the Northlands, *I'm* in charge, Keita."

The redhead leaned over and patted his forearm. "Of course you are, dear. And you just keep thinking that if it gives you ease."

"Auntie Keita!" Arlais shouted—sounding, for once, like an actual child and not a defiant hell spawn.

"Arlais!" Keita quickly shifted to human just as her young niece threw herself at her.

Hugging the laughing child tight, Keita lifted Arlais up and spun her around while covering her face in kisses. "My dear, dear, niece!"

Keita placed her laughing niece on the ground but held her hand. "Let us go inside and find me a divine gown to put on that will put all these worthless humans to shame with my astounding beauty."

"I have the perfect one for you!" Arlais happily crowed while she dragged Keita toward the stairs.

"Excellent! You have such a fine eye, my dear Arlais."

When Keita was close, Annwyl smiled at her and said, "Hello, sister."

"Good day, dearest Annwyl."

"What brings you all this way?"

"My mother tormented my poor Ragnar about coming home until he couldn't stand it anymore."

"She sings to me inside my head," he complained while getting dressed. "She knows I hate that. She knows!"

"My mother probably just wants information."

"And you are the queen's spy."

"I'm the Protector of the Throne. There's a difference." Keita pointed at Annwyl. "Are you aware you're bleeding onto the steps?"

Annwyl looked down and saw that a small puddle had formed beneath her. "Oh. I didn't think the cuts were that bad." She returned her gaze to Keita. "That explains why I've suddenly begun to feel light-headed."

"You'd best get that stitched up before Fearghus finds you dead where you sit."

Aunt and niece then disappeared into the Great Hall, and Annwyl gave them a wave. "Thank you for your concern," she said after them.

Ragnar of the Northland dragons and his cousin Meinhard, both now in their human forms and in dark grey leggings and black leather boots, stood in front of her.

"Hello, Ragnar," she said.

"Queen Annwyl. Need some help?"

"Normally I'd tell you to piss off, but . . . I probably do." Since she was sure that if she stood, she'd most likely pass out where she was.

The males looked around, and Ragnar asked, "Before I do this, is Fearghus nearby? I don't relish the fight I'll have if he sees me carrying you."

"Oh . . . I don't know." Annwyl studied the purple-haired male and asked, "Aren't you Fearghus?"

"All right then." The dragon quickly came to her and lifted Annwyl up into his arms. "Go find Morfyd or another healer," he ordered his cousin. "I'll get her inside and try to stop the bleeding."

"You're very kind," Annwyl said.

"Thank you."

"For a purple-haired barbarian who was once the sworn enemy of my mate's people."

"We have come a long way."

"And you're very handsome. I see why Keita chose you. She does like her males handsome . . . and kind of stupid."

"Annwyl?"

"Hmm?"

"Perhaps you could stop talking now."

Annwyl nodded. "That's probably a very good idea. You know, you're surprisingly smart for a purple-haired barbarian that Keita actually cares about."

"And unbelievably tolerant."

"I can see that as well."

Atop his stallion, Gaius Lucius Domitus, Iron dragon and the one-eyed Rebel King from the west, stared down into the valley outside Garbhán Isle. His twin sister, Agrippina, rode her horse to his side.

"This is definitely one of your stupider ideas, brother."

"And I love you, too."

Aggie glowered at him. "I'm serious. She's unstable. Drastically so."

"While I'm in the Southlands for the next few weeks, I'll need to know that you're safe if I hope to focus on anything else. Garbhán Isle is the one place I feel I can be assured of that. Besides, I don't see what you still have against Queen Annwyl. She's always helped us when we've needed it before. That human queen is blindingly loyal."

"She's also blindingly mad. She should be chained up in a room in some tower until she finally dies. Not leading a nation. And look—" Aggie pointed. "It seems they're building that tower as we speak."

"Your life's in danger, Aggie."

"So the never-ending rumors say. But you bring me here? To stay with those ridiculously spoiled Southland dragons and that crazed female? That truly seemed like a good idea to you?"

Gaius thought on that a moment, shrugged. "Perhaps I didn't think it through."

"Clearly," she complained, pulling her fur cape tight around her shoulders.

"Are you all right?" he asked.

"I'm fine, Gaius. You know I've always found the winters

in the Southlands unpleasant. That does not mean, however, I'm about to have some sort of emotional breakdown."

"I was just asking. No need to bite my head off."

"I'm sorry. But you know that I hate it here."

"It's not that bad, and I can't honestly think of any place where you'd be safer."

"Well, that doesn't say much for the world we currently live in."

"Times have changed, sister."

"I know. But I still want to go home."

But that wasn't an option. Not when his sister's life was in danger.

Gaius had almost lost Aggie once before. That's how he'd met Annwyl. The Southland queen had needed the help of his army, and he'd needed someone to rescue his sister from the Emperor's Palace and his bitch cousin Vateria Flominia. It was a rescue that had happened years ago, but it was a debt Gaius felt he could never repay, since freeing his sister had been impossible for him. Vateria and her guards had known Gaius and his men on sight and would have killed Aggie before he could have even hoped to track her down. So Annwyl and her friends had gone instead and had given Aggie back to Gaius.

So Gaius wasn't as concerned about bringing his sister to Garbhán Isle as Aggie. Because the one thing he could say about the Mad Queen was that she was loyal to both human and dragon, which meant the queen would make it her business to keep Aggie safe.

There was only one problem with Gaius's plan. The queen tended to forget who he was. Normally, this was something he'd find insulting—something his sister *always* found insulting—except that he couldn't be too upset. Annwyl was an odd woman. Politics bored her. Royal lineage meant little to her. So he didn't think she forgot him to be insulting or as some cold-blooded political maneuver. She forgot him, it seemed, because her poor, beleaguered brain couldn't handle much more. And Gaius simply couldn't hold that against her.

Yet when he looked over at his sister, all Gaius could see was her concern.

No. There'd be no taking her to Garbhán Isle and dropping her off so that he could head to the series of meetings he'd set up through Bram the Merciful. He would need to ease Aggie into this. Thankfully, he did have a little time.

"You know," he finally suggested, "we could go to Lord Bram's castle first." Bram had a wonderful way of easing tensions between all involved. He was a *good* dragon, something that meant a lot to Gaius and his twin since for most of their existence all they'd known was the treachery of their own kin. "If he's there, we can travel with *him* to Garbhán Isle in a day or two." His sister winced a bit. "Or . . . *or* we can spend more time at his castle first, if you'd like."

Aggie nodded. "If that would make you more comfortable, why not?"

They both knew it had nothing to do with Gaius's comfort, but her pride was a bit brittle these days, so Gaius didn't mind her blaming little things like this on him.

"Then let's go."

They turned their horses and met up with the small unit that he'd hand chosen to ride with them to ensure his sister's safety. Although they could fly into this territory, there was still a lot of violent history and bad blood between the Southland and Western dragons. It was better to go as human and blend in to the general throng than it was to risk coming snout to snout with angry Southland dragons who'd lost their kin during the early wars between their kind.

Gaius knew from experience that dragons had very long memories.

Chapter Seventeen

It took two days to make it to a forest outside a medium-sized city.

"There is so much unused space in the Southlands," Elina noted. "Why do these people insist on living in these stone cities and towns . . . unable to move anywhere?"

"Southlanders like permanence. We like to know that when we come home from work, we go to the same place every night. It's comforting."

"Comforting?" Elina shook her head. "Such a strange people."

"You don't like comfort?"

"It leads to weakness and soft hearts."

Celyn reached over and patted her head with his big hand. "You make me sad, little human."

Elina was thinking about stabbing the dragon in his hand so that he'd learn never to do that to her again, but she saw a group of men walking down the road toward them. One of the men led a horse that had a large cart behind it. Elina had no idea what was in that cart because it was covered in cloth. But she did notice the way the men stared at her and the dragon. As if they were waiting for them to do something. Whatever was in that cart was important to them.

As they passed the men, Celyn suddenly slowed his horse to a stop. Elina also stopped and glanced back, watching as the dragon lifted his head and sniffed the air, his entire body growing tense.

Elina rode back to him, circling around his giant travel-cow. "What is it?" she asked softly.

He shook his head and moved on, and Elina fell into place beside him.

Together they passed the city gates and made it down the road another two leagues. That's when Celyn stopped again and looked around. When he saw nothing, he nodded at Elina and turned his horse toward the woods, urging the oversized beast into a gallop. Elina clicked her tongue against her teeth and her horse followed after Celyn's.

They headed back toward the city but stayed in the woods, climbing up and up until they reached the opening of a cave buried deep in the forest.

Celyn quickly dismounted and prepared to call out, but Elina leaned over and slapped her hand over his mouth. When he looked at her, she shook her head and sniffed the air.

Since she'd been a young girl, she'd been taught to track two things: animals, because they were food; and men who were not part of their tribes . . . because, as a whole, men could not be trusted.

And Elina smelled men.

Celyn's heart had raced as they'd made their way up to Costentyn's cave. He'd scented dragon's blood on those men. And their clothes had been singed at the edges as if they'd been touched by a dragon's flame. Since Celyn knew of no other dragons in this region, he feared the worst for his old friend.

And clearly he wasn't alone in that sinking feeling. With her free hand, Elina pointed at her own nose. She scented something, too.

When she seemed confident that Celyn wouldn't call out, she pulled her hand away from his mouth and dismounted from her horse. She took the reins of both horses and led them to nearby trees.

With her curved bow and a quiver full of arrows secured to her back, Elina came to his side and nodded. Once. She was ready.

Celyn removed his fur cloak so that nothing would encumber him should he need to fight as human, and together they entered Costentyn's cave.

As soon as Celyn entered, he became even more worried about his old friend. It didn't smell right. Nothing smelled right.

Celyn moved deeper into the cave and, as he did, he saw books tossed around, some burned. He remembered, quite clearly, Costentyn and Celyn's father arguing about how Bram treated his books. Celyn's father piled those books into the corners of his home. Haphazard with an organizational logic that only Bram and his assistants seemed to understand. Celyn remembered how offended Old Costentyn had been. Books, to him, were to be treated with reverence and placed on shelves in a logical order so that anyone at any time could come in and pick up a book for their reading pleasure. Bram, however, saw books as a means to an end. That end being knowledge.

So finding Costentyn's books lying around . . .

Celyn rushed forward, determined to find his friend. He used his logic to guide him more than his senses. And logic suggested that Costentyn would try to get to an exit. Any exit that would allow him to fly away.

After several long minutes Celyn stopped running. He bowed his head and curled his hands into fists. After a breath, he took a step forward just as Elina ran up behind him. He walked into the alcove, dropped to his human knees, and carefully placed his hand on the head of his murdered friend.

* * *

Elina watched the dragon mourn his friend.

It was obvious this was an old dragon. So old, even his brown scales were mostly grey. She could see bits of brown underneath but it was hard to tell. And, of course, the blood didn't help.

It hadn't been a fair fight. Instead, the old dragon had been pinned down by nets that were then tacked to the ground and, while he probably fought his bindings, he was repeatedly stabbed with long spears and hacked at with axes. It must have taken hours for the dragon to die. Hours while the weak men hacked at his hard scales and stabbed at any weak spots he had.

Finally, Elina turned her head in disgust.

This was why men could not rule. What was the point of killing this dragon? He was old. Probably didn't leave his home much. And based on all the books she saw throughout the cave, she would guess that all he did was read. This was not some great warrior one could defeat with any pride. But Elina knew Southlander men well enough to know they would be crowing about this victory until the end of their time. They would never see the shame in what they'd done.

The dragon suddenly leaned over and picked up two human-sized, bound books. He flipped one open, nodded.

"Costentyn's journals," he said softly, tucking them into his travel bag. "Perhaps they can tell us something."

Elina heard a sound and turned her head, raising one finger to silence the dragon. Her nostrils flared at the smell of human sweat. When she looked back at Celyn, he was watching her.

"Where?" he demanded.

She wasn't sure, so she silently made her way down a long corridor, using her nose and female instincts to lead her.

Eventually she found them. In a place that explained everything.

Elina crouched down and picked up a gold coin. It

wasn't the dragon they had wanted. It was the dragon's hoard. Even now, they were hurriedly taking piles of gold and jewels out through a hole in the cave wall. They were in a line as if trying to take water to a burning building. Buckets of riches being handed off from one male to another while they joked and laughed and bragged about how they'd killed an old being who'd been living his life quiet and alone in his cave.

"Baron Roscommon was right, eh, lads? We'll be rich, all right, when we get our cut."

"And imagine all the pussy we'll get when they find out we slayed a *dragon*."

"But Roscommon told the truth. We couldn't let that dragon live among good people. He was a danger, that one. He had to die."

"And now them dragons will know not to fuck with us or our city."

The men cheered at that while they kept working, nothing deterring them from getting their gold.

Elina stood, the gold coin still in her hand, but as she turned to hand it off to Celyn, she realized that he'd silently shifted to his natural form and was now towering over her. He silently stood in that entryway, nearly filling it.

The weight of her quiver and bow rested against her back, and she felt comfort from them. Because she sensed that she would need them. She wouldn't say that she could read his dragon face. At least not yet. But like most beings of the world, what Celyn's face wouldn't tell you, his energy would.

His black gaze was fixed on the humans, who, so busy bragging, had yet to notice them. The dragon nodded his horned head.

Reaching back, Elina placed one hand on the wood of her bow. She held out her other hand with the gold coin sitting in her palm. Slowly, she turned that hand over, so the coin fell from her palm and made a soft *plunk* sound against all the other gold coins.

There was immediate silence in that cave. All that self-important chatter stopped, human bodies tensing.

Elina was fascinated, but she didn't wait to see any more. She silently and swiftly eased back and found her way to another exit.

Celyn wasn't surprised when Elina made her hasty escape. What human wanted to watch what he was about to do?

Celyn? His father's voice popped into his head after Celyn sent out the call. *What's wrong, son?*

It's Costentyn, Da. He's been killed by humans.

There was a long pause, but his father was merely thinking. He was not a quick reactor. It was why Celyn had contacted him and not his mother. Before he could even have finished a thought, Ghleanna would have been flying to him in a Cadwaladr rage. Although effective, it was not what Celyn thought was needed right now.

Where are you? his father finally asked.

In Costentyn's cave. I've found some humans here. When I walked in, they were talking about how the baron of the nearby city had sent them here. They are stealing Costentyn's gold for this baron. And to send a message.

A message? To whom?

Dragons . . . maybe Annwyl.

I see.

This can't be ignored, Da. I'll be dealing with them, but—

Yes, yes. I know. I think there are Cadwaladr kin nearby you. I will have them join you. But Celyn . . . and this is important, son, keep control of them as best you can. We don't need this spreading outside the walls of that city. Understand me?

I do, Da.

Good.

His father was gone, off to handle this in the best way he could. And since Celyn had utter faith in his father, he thought no more about it, instead focusing all his Cadwaladr rage and hate on these men. These worthless human men.

Finally, after the dragonfear had washed through them and the humans were able to move again, one of the men raised his sword and screamed, "*Kill it!*"

Celyn welcomed them to try. . . .

Miles had just taken another basket filled with gold and jewels when he heard the screams from inside that dragon's cave. He doubted the dragon had come back. The creature had definitely been dead by the time they'd finished with him. Even after they'd known he was dead, they'd kept stabbing him, kept bashing him . . . just to make sure. Them dragons could be tricky. The baron had said they were evil and the one in the cave needed to be killed. Although, truth be told, that dragon hadn't put up much of a fight. Not the kind of fight Miles would have expected. But when they'd walked into that cave filled with gold, he'd understood better what the baron had wanted.

Yeah. Sure. The dragon dead of course. Miles didn't care one way or another about that. But the baron really wanted this gold. He wanted to raise an army, perhaps take on the queen. How people could be okay with that woman ruling their lands when she lay down every night with a dragon— even worse, had its unholy babies—Miles could and would never understand.

But this had nothing to do with any of that. Miles understood that once he saw all that damn gold. For hours now, they'd been working to clean out this cave and yet they weren't even half done.

A few of the men had already shoved some gold and
jewels into their pockets, but Miles wasn't about to risk that.
At least not yet. The baron could be mean when he thought
he was being cheated and Miles had no intention of hanging from any gallows for some bloody gold. So he kept
moving those buckets along.

Until the first body nearly hit him in the head.

It was Terence, landing hard between the two lines of
men. He was still alive, and desperately trying to hold his
guts in. A chore with that large hole in his stomach.

They were about to go to him, to help, when they heard
more screaming, saw more of their friends and family come
flying out of that hole that they'd spent days opening so they
wouldn't have to travel all the way through that big cave
with buckets of coin

Black claws gripped the cave opening and a massive
head covered in black scales suddenly appeared. Lowering
that head, the creature was able to maneuver those bright
white horns past the opening, and then it was there.

Big. Black. Covered in scales. And not nearly as old as
the one they'd found in the cave. Reading a bloody book,
no less, and drinking a giant chalice of wine. Miles remembered thinking, "Well la-de-da," before they'd rushed it.

Maybe this one was its son or something. But whatever
it was, it was bigger, younger, and meaner.

So much meaner.

Old Robert, thank the gods, was the only one not pissing
himself from that dragonfear they'd all heard about but that
they hadn't felt when the old dragon had reared itself up.
And it was Old Robert who rallied the boys.

"What are you doing?" he bellowed. "Kill it! Kill it
now!"

Swords were unsheathed and spears raised.

"Charge!" Old Robert screamed and a group of the lads
ran forward as Miles scrambled for his spear.

This dragon, unlike that other one, didn't panic though.

He just lifted his back claw and slammed it down, and the screams of his friends filled Miles's ears.

Then the dragon opened its maw and flames came flying out. Big, giant flames that burned a group of the lads in seconds, barely giving them time to scream before they were nothing more than ash.

Panicked, terrified, Miles ran behind a big tree. He hid. Like a weak baby. But he was shaking so much, he couldn't raise a sword or spear if he wanted to.

The baron's soldiers, a unit left behind to keep an eye on the men—probably to keep them from stealing—split apart and went at the dragon from opposite sides.

They weren't scared like the rest of them. They were soldiers, after all. Some of them, it was said, had fought *with* dragons before. So they were ready for this dragon.

What they weren't ready for, however, were the arrows.

One arrow after another came raining down from the top of that cave. Miles leaned back and took a look. It was a woman. Pale, she was. With long, white-blond hair that pooled around her as she crouched at the top of the cave opening with a curved bow. And, she never missed a shot. Not one. Each arrow she sent out hit one of the baron's men in the neck or eye or under the arm. Each shot meant to kill . . . and each shot did.

Even the dragon looked surprised—if it were possible for a thing to be surprised—as he glanced back at the woman. He nodded and then focused on the rest of the men. He pulled out the smallest sword. At least small compared to the dragon. But he slammed it against the side of the cave wall and the damn thing grew! Like some kind of evil magicks, it grew! Into a full-sized sword big enough for this dragon. And, with a roar, he began to swing that sword. Cutting the rest of the men into pieces, following up with his flame, stomping on a few for good measure. It was over in seconds.

Bloody seconds.

Slowly, the dragon turned to face the woman. "I thought you'd run to safety," he said.

"Do not assume," she said with some strange accent, "that I live in fear, Dolt. I went to higher ground."

"I see that now. Sorry I questioned you. I should have remembered that you run *toward* death."

"I do not run toward. I merely accept that death will come for me. What is point of fighting when death will have its way? And I will *not* have this argument with you again."

"Who's arguing?"

The woman gave a short hiss between her teeth, then asked, "What about him?"

She didn't point at Miles, but the dragon slowly looked over his shoulder at the tree Miles was standing behind. ". . . I could use a snack."

That's when Miles pushed away from the tree and tried to run.

He tried. . . .

Chapter Eighteen

Elina retrieved as many of her arrows, the ones that hadn't been broken or burned, as she could and returned to the top of the cave opening, where she'd had an excellent view. She sat down, her legs hanging over the side.

While she cleaned the arrowheads off with a cloth and put them back in her quiver, the dragon sat down beside her.

Still in his dragon form, his back legs hanging over the top of the cave just as hers were, his front legs resting on his knees. She barely glanced at him, but it seemed a strange way for a dragon to sit.

Then, suddenly, the dragon burped, the sound of it sending birds flying from nearby trees.

Disgusted, Elina slowly turned her head to glower at him.

He stared back for a few seconds before telling her, "Oh, stop it. I didn't eat him. I just stomped him into the ground. But I did find a sheep over there." He shrugged. "And I was a little hungry."

Deciding to take the dragon at his word, Elina went back to cleaning her arrows. That's when the dragon shocked her more than she'd ever thought possible.

"Thank you, Elina of the Impossibly Long Name."

"Your father managed to remember my impossibly long name with no trouble. As did that boy."

"They're clearly smarter than me."

"My horse is smarter than you." She slipped a clean arrow into her quiver and picked up another. "And you are welcome. I . . . I am sorry about your friend." She glanced at him. "What happened to him was cruel."

"It was. But I know he's happy now. Annwyl told me."

Elina stopped what she was doing and looked over at the dragon. "What do you mean, Annwyl told you?"

"She died once. Ended up in the afterworld among the dragons. She said it was really nice there."

Lowering the arrow she held to her lap, Elina sighed. "Annwyl has seen death, embraced it, and has returned to speak of it. Does she fear nothing?"

"Mice."

"Mice?"

"She's not a fan. She saw a mouse in the Great Hall once and she screamed like someone was stabbing her children. She didn't calm down until Morfyd made everyone go outside.

So she could bring in some cats. But Dagmar's dogs fought with the cats. The cats fought with the dogs. And Gwenvael kept eating the cats. Eventually—"

"Why," Elina cut in, "must you ruin *everything*?"

"I didn't know I had."

"I was imagining the wonder of a strong queen fighting her way back from the embrace of death and you give me stories of mice and cats and Gwenvael."

"You asked a question. I merely answered it."

"Then do not. Do not answer any more questions. Just sit and look pretty. It seems that is what you are best at." Elina glanced off, then back at Celyn before ending with, "Dolt."

The cold winter breeze suddenly turned into a blustery wind that bowed the trees and raised the dirt, until the ground shook as many claws landed hard against it.

The dolt's mouth pulled back in that unnerving dragon's smile, revealing row after row of shiny white fangs.

"Uncle Addolgar!" Celyn called out.

"Nephew!" The silver-scaled dragon looked at the carnage he'd landed in. "Looks like we're too late for any fun."

"Actually . . . no, Uncle. You're just in time."

Addolgar looked down at what was left of the human bodies. He didn't know what his sister had been so worried about. Celyn appeared to be able to handle himself just fine. A message he sent her quickly and then cut off so he didn't have to hear her screaming in his head, *Are you sure? Are you sure he's all right? Do I need to be there? Are you sure?*

It was rare, but when his sister became hysterical, all he wanted to do was hit her in the head with the blunt part of his axe to calm her down. She hated when he did that, but it was quite effective.

And it was true that Addolgar's nephew could be a little chatty for a dragon. The boy did like to talk. Even more annoying, ask questions. But nothing that couldn't be stopped with a, "Shut it, Celyn." Yet, Ghleanna had insisted on babying the dragon as if he were as weak as her Fal. Also one of Addolgar's nephews, but one he liked to pretend wasn't.

Addolgar moved closer as Celyn got to his claws and gestured at the human female beside him. "Uncle Addolgar, this is Elina of the Impossibly Long Name."

"That is not my name, Dolt," the female shot back.

"And Dolt is not mine."

"And yet you continue to act like one!"

"I am Addolgar the Cheerful," Addolgar stepped in before the bickering could start again. "And what is your name?"

"I am Elina Shestakova of the Black Bear Riders of the Midnight Mountains of Despair in the Far Reaches of the Steppes of the Outerplains."

Gods! That *was* a long name. No wonder Celyn refused to use it. He probably couldn't remember it.

"But," the woman went on, "you can call me Elina Shestakova."

"Nice to meet you, Elina Shestakova." Addolgar glanced around. "So what happened here?"

"Costentyn is dead, Uncle. Murdered."

"Old Costentyn? Murdered? By these bastards?" he asked, gesturing around him.

"Baron Roscommon ordered it."

"Did he now?" Addolgar sneered.

"He did," Celyn said. "And I think he should be dealt with quickly and by us."

"Probably a good idea."

Addolgar studied the woman for a bit as she cleaned and sharpened her arrows. Or, at least, what remained of them. Based on the bloody cloth she was using, she'd been helpful while Celyn faced all those men. He liked that. Nothing bothered Addolgar more these days than weak females.

He hadn't always felt that way. At one time he'd just liked them pretty and eager, but things change, don't they?

Addolgar glanced back at the battle unit that had traveled with him, focusing on the young blue-haired She-dragon. "My bag, Elara."

"Here, Daddy," she said when she tossed the bag to him, nearly knocking him off his claws from the power of her throw. He remembered when she couldn't even take him to the ground during training. Now, like the rest of her sisters, she'd grown into a powerful dragoness. Just like her mum, too, favoring the hammer and all. She'd gotten damn good at it.

Addolgar dug into his travel bag and pulled out the cloth-covered stash of arrows that he used in his human-sized bows. He handed them to the human female. "Take these, Elina Shestakova. You look low."

She unwrapped the big stack and grinned. "Thank you so much, Addolgar the Cheerful." She pulled out one of the arrows, examining it closely. As she did, she went on. "Although you do not seem so cheerful. Is that *his* fault?" she asked with a jerk of her head in Celyn's direction.

Addolgar's nephew threw his claws up. "Now you're just attacking me."

"You make it easy!" she snapped back, her focus still on the arrows.

There were many arrows in the stack Addolgar had given her, but they weren't all the same because he'd taken most from the bodies of his fallen enemies. He even had orc arrows in there somewhere.

He watched her test one. Her form was perfect, and she took down a squirrel that he could barely see several hundred yards away.

Addolgar grinned. He liked this woman. He wasn't so sure, though, whether his nephew did.

"Are you done showing off?" Celyn sniffed.

"Are you done being pain in ass?"

"As a matter of fact . . . I'm not!"

"Celyn," Addolgar cut in again, "perhaps we should talk about what we plan to do."

"Of course, Uncle."

"Oh, look," the woman taunted. "You *can* follow orders."

"You don't give me orders, insolent female."

"Do not point talons at me, Dolt!"

"I'll point my talons anywhere I want to. Because I don't take orders from *you.*"

Addolgar glanced back at his daughter and crossed his eyes. And, as it did with her mother, that made her laugh.

Celyn didn't know why Elina was being so mean to him. Before Addolgar had arrived, they'd been getting along. Now, she was sniping at him like some fishmonger's wife.

And he was sniping back; he simply didn't know why. Over the years he'd found not reacting to those yelling at him was infinitely more effective than yelling back. The calmer he remained, the angrier they became, until they snapped. Gods knew, he used to do it with his cousins all the time.

Yet now, this one tiny, pale, ready-for-death female was making him angrier than he'd ever been before. Over nothing. That was the worst part. Angry over the murder of Costentyn? Completely justifiable. Angry over this woman's general rudeness . . . ? A bit absurd.

Addolgar's claw landed on the back of Celyn's neck and he cringed, waiting for Addolgar to slam his head into the nearest tree. Sadly, it wouldn't be the first time his uncle had done this to him . . . or to his brothers. His sisters, including mouthy Brannie, had all managed to avoid the Addolgar Head Tree Slam—as the brothers called it when they woke up a few days later.

Thankfully, though, Addolgar just steered Celyn off, away from the insolent female.

"Everything all right here, lad?" Addolgar asked.

"Aye. Why?"

Addolgar huffed a bit. "*Celyn?*" he pushed.

"She's just being sensitive. You put a girl in jail and forget about her for a few months, and they all take it so bloody personally."

"You forgot about her?"

"She's lucky I did. She'd been sent to kill Rhiannon."

"Then why isn't she dead?"

Celyn sighed. "It was a sad, weak attempt, really. She clearly didn't want to do it. Auntie Rhiannon just felt bad for her."

"Guess you didn't tell me brother about any of this."

"Rhiannon told me not to."

"Don't lie to me, my lad. You wouldn't have told him anyway."

"He tends to overreact. Like a dog that attacks at every new sound." Celyn glanced back toward where he'd left Elina. "She climbed all the way up Devenallt Mountain by herself but didn't even bring her bow. But with her bow, she could have easily put arrows through the closest guards and had an arrow through Rhiannon's eye before the rest of us could have reached either of them . . . yet she didn't."

"What are you doing with her now?"

"Taking her back to the Outerplains. She's going to meet with the tribes' leader to see if we can arrange a meeting between her and Annwyl."

"Good luck with that. That tribes leader ain't a friendly girl." Addolgar shrugged his massive shoulders. "But I don't care much about this political stuff. I leave that to Dagmar and your father." Addolgar suddenly looked around. "If you're taking her back to her people, though, you're taking the long way, ain't ya?"

"We thought getting a little more information about what's been happening around the Southlands and, possibly, the Outerplains, would help our cause once Elina reached her tribe leader."

Addolgar shook his head. "You and your bloody excuses to ask questions."

"What does that mean?"

"It means you ask too many questions." Addolgar made a *tsk-tsk* sound. "Personally, I blame your father. It's his blood that made you like this."

"Made me like what?"

"Always thinking. Don't you ever stop thinking?"

Celyn could only give one answer to that. "*No.*"

"See what I mean? Just like your father."

Celyn moved away from his uncle. "Look, I'll admit, I may ask more questions than most Cadwaladrs, but I don't think there's anything wrong with that. What would you prefer, Uncle . . . that I was more like one of your sons?"

And, as if the gods themselves had willed it, "Hey, Da! Look what I found!" One of Addolgar's younger sons raised his arm. "A bucket of gold!" Then, for some unfathomable reason, the silver dragon laughed hysterically. For a good long while, too.

Addolgar let out a pained sigh. "I want you, lad, to be who you are. But then you need to have the guts to stand behind that."

"What do you mean?"

"Look at me brother. Bercelak. He is a mean, heartless, ruthless bastard of a dragon. He's been loathed for centuries by nearly everyone except his own kin and Rhiannon. But you don't hear him whining about it. He just accepts who he is and goes on about his day . . . being a mean, heartless, ruthless bastard of a dragon. So, you want to ask your questions. Then ask your questions. You want to be nosy and a pain in the ass. Then be nosy and a pain in the ass. But don't whine about it. Just do it. Stop taking everything so damn personally. With that," he said, pointing a talon at him, "you're just like your mum, you know? She used to take everything so damn personally. Let everybody get her so bloody upset because they accused her of being a murdering viper or a whore like our father."

"Well, that does seem a tad rude—"

"See?" Addolgar said, exasperated. "Just like her! You can't let the petty shit stop you from being who you are. And getting what you want." He swept his forearm in a half circle, taking in the carnage around them. "Look at all this, boy. You found there was trouble and you moved. You saw what was happening and you dealt with it. Then you sent for us . . . so we can set these humans straight. You know what that is . . . ?"

"No."

"That's smart, you little bastard. Smart. You *think*. That's good! Just like your dad, you are."

"I thought I was just like me mum."

"Shut it. And there's nothing wrong with being like your dad. Tell ya this . . . your dad was smart enough to get your mum. And she didn't make it easy."

"Cadwaladr females never make it easy."

"They don't. And your dad loved her even after she used two swords to cut off the head of the bastard she used to be with. He deserved it, but still . . . takes a brave dragon willing to risk being the next notch on her pummel."

Addolgar put his forearm around Celyn's shoulders. "All I'm saying is, if your future is being more than just the charming Cadwaladr . . . embrace it. That's the thing about Cadwaladrs. We are who we are. And we don't back down from that. You shouldn't either. Even if who you are is kind of an annoying, never-shuts-up git."

Celyn smiled. "Thanks, Uncle Addolgar."

"Any time. Now . . . let's go wipe that Baron Roscommon and his city from the bloody map, shall we?"

"No, no," Elina heard the dragon saying to his uncle as they walked back toward the rest of the group.

"What do you mean, no?" Addolgar asked.

"We're not going to wipe out the city."

"We're not?"

"*We* would," Elina volunteered.

The dolt turned those dark eyes on her. "No one asked you."

"But—" Elina began, but the dragon turned away from her and then, suddenly, she was battling that damn tail of his. It kept reaching around and slapping her ass while the dragon continued his conversation with his uncle.

Elina grabbed one of the arrows she'd been given and tried to stab at the tail, but it moved too fast. Amazing, since the dragon never stopped his conversation with his uncle. It was as if the tail had a life of its own.

The tail suddenly reared up like a snake, the tip pointing right between her eyes. Now on her knees, Elina tightened her grip on the arrow she held and pulled it back for one last attempt to stop the damn thing.

"Are you done?" the dragon asked her.

"Your tail is trying to kill me. Have you no control over it?"

"Of course I do."

"So you *are* trying to kill me?"

"Don't flatter yourself. I'm not about to disappoint my queen simply to get you to stop bothering me."

"It moves like snake."

"It moves as I tell it to move. It's *my* tail. And you can stop trying to stare it down. Everyone just thinks you're a mad cow at this point."

Elina looked up and realized that the dragon's kin were watching her closely.

Clearing her throat, she lowered the arrow. "I did what I had to," she told them.

The dragons moved away without saying anything, and Celyn leaned his forearms against the rocky ground next to where she sat.

"We're going back to the city to deal with Roscommon. You'll wait here until I come for you."

"No."

"You want to go on ahead?"

"No. I come with."

"That'll be dangerous."

"Again you suggest I am weak," she snapped.

"I did not! But I'm supposed to be protecting you."

"Yet I protect you. My arrows helped, did they not?"

He let out a sigh. "They did."

"Then I come. I want to see how decadent Southlanders handle such a problem."

"Unlike your tribes that would—"

"Attack the city full force, capture the older boys and young men to hold until they were old enough for marriage, and wipe everything else from the land until there was nothing but ashes and the tears of the dying."

The dragon blinked. "And that seems like a good plan to you?"

"No," she answered honestly. "Not at all. That is just what we would do. I never say it was good idea. But I am tragic disappointment to my people."

"Well, then, as your host while in this land, I think it is my responsibility to show you how we handle things, don't you?"

"Yes. Then I can judge you and your corrupt, immoral people wanting."

The dragon grinned, showing all those bright white

fangs again, which sparkled like pretty cave stones. "That sounds like a delightful plan."

"Something told me you would like, dragon."

Chapter Nineteen

Baron Roscommon walked quickly down the third-floor hallway of his castle, his assistant following, his captain of the guard right by his side.

"What do you mean they haven't returned with another shipment from that cave?"

"There's been nothing from them in hours, my lord," his assistant informed him as he worked hard to get his short legs to catch up with them.

"Captain?" the baron asked just as they reached the end of the hall and were nearing the stairs to the next floor down.

"I'll send a unit of my men out there, Baron, and have them report back to me immed—"

The captain's word stopped as soon as they heard the screaming outside.

"What the holy hells?" the baron snarled.

"You two stay here," the captain ordered. "I'll—"

The three men quickly moved as the stone wall beside them shook. The captain pulled his sword and stepped in front of them, pushing the baron and his assistant back.

The stone was torn away, the late-afternoon suns briefly blinding them until an enormous scale-covered snout suddenly appeared, the nostrils flaring as it sniffed the air. It pulled back a bit so that the baron could now see cold, black eyes staring at him.

"Good day to you, Baron Roscommon."

"Move!" the captain ordered, before he charged the dragon with his blade.

The baron only had seconds to see the dragon pull back completely from that hole just as the captain was about to make contact. But the captain didn't have time to change his strategy and he went flying out the opening, falling three stories. His screams of panic brutally cut off when he hit the ground.

"Ooopsie!" the dragon sang out.

Horrified, the baron turned and raced toward the other end of the hall. But a blue-scaled fist rammed through the stained glass, only to be replaced a few seconds later by a blue-scaled dragon head.

"Hello, Baron Roscommon," a female voice said.

Gods! A She-dragon! He'd always heard they were more terrifying than the males.

The baron, in a panic, shoved his assistant toward the female, ignoring her "Oh! That's just wrong, you bastard!" and ran down another hallway to another set of stairs.

Panting from the exertion and fear, he rushed down those stairs until he reached the wooden door. He snatched it open and stumbled outside. His people were screaming and running in all directions, yelling warnings of "Dragons! Run! Dragons!" Words he'd never heard in his time except in stories told by his father and grandfather.

Gods, what had he done?

Roscommon went around the corner of his castle and started to run toward an entrance to tunnels that the queen had ordered built so that the city could have sewers. Something she'd apparently learned from the Desert Land people. Those tunnels would allow the baron to escape out of the city.

But just as he reached the entrance, a silver spike landed in front of him, blocking his exit. And he quickly realized that the spike was actually part of a tail.

And from above, he heard a low voice sneer at him, "Going somewhere, m'lord?"

Elina sat in a tree safe from the action in the city but still close enough that she could see and hear most of it.

She understood why the dragons didn't need to go the route of her people and swoop in like the terrifying horde they were.

Because they were *dragons*. All they had to do was drop their enormous bodies from the skies, and the terror was on without their doing much of anything.

The funny thing was, these "terrifying" dragons were much more thoughtful than any human Elina had ever met. Although a few had talked about going into the city and wiping everyone out, it was mostly just talk. They had considerately listened to other ideas and, in the end, supported Celyn's.

Elina had been rather amazed by it all.

Even more fascinating, they'd all decided it was in their best interest to handle all this themselves rather than get Queen Annwyl involved. Apparently her way of dealing with things was also different from the tribal hordes'. She seemed to have no desire to destroy those she considered innocent. But wiping out the entire army protecting the city? It seemed that was something she would be more than willing to do. All by herself.

What really interested Elina the most about all of this was how protective the dragons were, not only of the people, but of Annwyl and her rule. To be honest, Elina had assumed the dragons didn't take the human queen very seriously. She'd assumed that they tolerated her merely because of her mate. A dragon prince, no less.

Yet it wasn't like that at all. Whatever Annwyl had done over the years, she'd earned the respect of these dragons. They seemed to love *and* fear her. At the very least, they feared her wrath.

Gods, what was that like? To have your own fear you?

Glebovicha had made sure that no one feared Elina. She mocked her to any and all, telling them how weak and stupid and useless Elina was.

And thinking about that reminded Elina how hard it would be to get to the Anne Atli. Glebovicha would not want that. She probably would not allow it. But Elina was becoming more and more determined as time went on. She felt, deep in her bones, that it was necessary for her to help the dragons as much as she could.

No. Nothing would stop her. Not even Glebovicha.

Deciding not to think on it any longer, Elina again focused on what was going on inside the city.

Addolgar had the baron by his leg and was carrying him to the city's gallows. There were no humans out on the streets now. No humans waiting by the gallows to see what would happen to their leader. Instead, they were hiding in their homes or in their gods' temples. All of them praying that the dragons would just kill their leader and go on their way. None of them seemed ready to fight to protect anything. A desire Elina understood but didn't exactly respect. What about their honor? Or the honor of their city? Or simply the honor of protecting their leader? Did none of that mean anything to these Southlander people?

Or was it the Southland people as a whole? Maybe it was just the people of this city who had no honor? Or perhaps they'd realized long ago that their baron wasn't worth fighting for? The remainder of the city guards had not been killed, but none of them came out to help their baron either.

As always, Elina saw many sides to this debate and sadly . . . it was this ability that often got her into the most trouble with her people. Her people loved a good argument but only about silly things. Who made the best beer? Who could drink the most? Who was the best warrior? Who had the prettiest husbands?

Big questions like, "Are *all* Southlanders truly worthless, decadent, imperialist scum?" were answered one way and one way only: "Yes, they are!"

Celyn and his other cousins were already waiting at the gallows. A few dragons perched on the protective gate that surrounded the city. A gate that Elina's people would have had no problem taking down.

Elina was impressed by how quickly Celyn's nearby kin had rallied around him. A call had gone out and so quickly they'd been here, by his side, ready to help him in any way he might need. Elina thought of her own sister, Kachka, and wished she were here by her side. They always worked well together, her sister never pushing Elina to be more than she was.

"Your baron," Celyn was saying to the people of the city, who were still in hiding, "killed one of our own. Not because he was a danger to all of you, because he wasn't. The dragon who was killed was old. He liked nothing more than to sit in his cave, drink his favorite wine, and read. But your baron lied to you. He lied when he said that this old dragon was evil. That this old dragon had to be handled. And using that lie, he sent his guards and people from this city out to kill this old dragon and raid what had become his tomb."

Celyn looked over the empty city, but he knew, as did Elina, that all the people were listening. Cowering and listening. "Now, because of his greed, Baron Roscommon has brought down the wrath of the dragons. Even worse, his betrayal would normally bring the wrath of Annwyl the Bloody. She asks for little from her fellow royals . . . except loyalty. Something Baron Roscommon did not give her. For that, he will be taken to Garbhán Isle to face his fate. Queen Annwyl will have her final say on Baron Roscommon. The dragon nation will not deny her that. As for the rest of you . . . you will suffer enough. Those who were sent to the dragon's cave have experienced the old dragon's fate." And yes, the people *were* listening, because Elina could hear the cries of those who called those men family or friend. "That was their punishment, and their loss is yours. Tomorrow morning you may come and retrieve your dead. There will be no further retaliation, but understand our revenge could have been much worse. And, should something like this happen again, it will be."

Finished with his speech, Celyn nodded at Addolgar and his uncle wrapped his claw around a now-screaming Baron Roscommon. He was ordering his people to kill the dragons. To save him. But no one came forward. No one dared.

Addolgar flew off, with Celyn following behind. The rest of his cousins soon followed, making sure everything was safe before they took to the skies.

Elina was about to climb down from the tree when a black-scaled tail wrapped around her waist and yanked her up.

Suddenly . . . she was flying.

Celyn landed near Costentyn's cave. His uncle already had the threatening and begging and bloody sobbing baron bound and now, thankfully, gagged. As Celyn had promised, Addolgar and the others would be taking the baron back to Garbhán Isle to face Annwyl. No one envied the man that fate.

"Good work, lad," Addolgar said when Celyn landed. "That was a nice speech you gave."

"You sure we shouldn't kill them all?" Addolgar's son asked. There was no malice in his voice. No viciousness. Also, not much logic. Unlike his daughters, Addolgar's sons didn't have much logic.

"I'm sure," Celyn insisted. "I'm sure the baron only picked the best men of the city to help in this crime. Trust me, the people will be feeling the loss of those men for quite some time."

"He's right," Addolgar agreed. "We've made our point. No need to get nasty this early in the game. It's always better to escalate only when necessary." Addolgar faced Celyn. "And you, nephew. Are you coming with us?"

"No. I still have my task." He raised his tail to show that he had Elina wrapped in it. She hadn't complained once. "I have to get this one back to the Outerplains."

"Good, lad. Never forget the job your queen has given you. If you happen to slaughter a few enemies along the way . . . that's just like extra biscuits at tea time, really."

"Also, give these journals to my father. They were Costentyn's. Perhaps they will tell him something useful. Tell him that if he finds anything interesting to let me know." Celyn handed over the journals he'd found in Costentyn's cave.

His uncle dropped the journals into his travel bag.

Good-byes were said and Celyn's kin took to the skies. Once they were gone, he brought his tail around.

"Think our horses are still there?" he asked the woman wrapped in his tail.

"I do not know about your oversized travel-cow, but the Steppes horse will be where I left him."

"Good." Celyn started to place her on the ground.

"What are you doing?" she asked.

"Allowing you to walk."

"Why? What is wrong with flying?"

"You want to fly back to our horses?" he asked, stunned. The only human he'd ever met who'd seemed to love flying right off had been Izzy. To be honest, that's how he got close to her. Letting her ride his back whenever he could. But with Elina, he'd merely been attempting to torture her for a bit of fun. It had never occurred to him she'd enjoy it. "They're not that far away."

"I am very tired, dragon. It has been long morning. Now

you make me walk? Like sheep? Does my well-being mean nothing to you?"

"Why don't you just say that you like to fly and you want to try it again?"

"I could," she admitted grudgingly. "But I am more comfortable with yelling at you."

Celyn shook out his wings, ready to take to the skies again, but first noted, "I swear, She of the Excessively Long Name, it's like you were born and raised among my kin."

Chapter Twenty

They rode hard for the rest of the day, stopping only briefly so Celyn's horse could get water and they could relieve themselves. Other than that, they kept conversation to a minimum and ate while they rode. Something Celyn was sure he now loathed doing.

They finally stopped late after suns-down, when they found a freshwater creek and some wild boar nearby. The pair separated so they could do their own hunting. Elina wanted to test out some of her new arrows while Celyn simply wanted to feed in peace without that look of horror humans often got when they watched dragons eat animals still kicking and screaming.

After washing off the boar's blood in a lake not too far away, Celyn returned to their camp to find that Elina had already taken down three boars. She'd also skinned them, deboned two, put one on a spit over a fire, and stripped the flesh off the other two so that she could dry them out over the fire during the night. That way they'd have fresh dried meat to take with them the next day.

The human had turned out to be quite the hunter.

"Have you tried working with other weapons?" Celyn asked as he sat down by the fire in human form.

"I have. I sadly have no skill with sword or mace. I can use dagger for close-in work but I do not enjoy killing so much that I want to do close-in work. Besides," she went on, surprisingly chatty for this time of evening, "I enjoy bow."

"Because it takes precision, strength, and real skill."

She nodded as she finished with the last of the meat. Walking over to the creek, she crouched down and washed the blood from her hands. Somehow she'd managed not to get any on her clothes, which impressed Celyn even more than the fact she'd taken down three wild boars in a relatively short amount of time.

With her hands clean, she turned and walked back toward their little camp. That's when she proceeded to remove the leather jerkin he'd purchased for her and then the cotton shirt underneath.

Celyn didn't think much of that—until Elina straddled his waist and dropped her pert little ass onto his lap. She still wore her leggings and boots, but the only thing that would be between his hands and her breasts was the material she had binding them.

"What are you doing?" he asked, sounding much more panicked than he'd like to.

"It has been long day," she replied nonchalantly. "Much activity. I am tired but not sleepy. I thought we could fuck and then I would have good night's sleep, making me ready for ride tomorrow."

"You want to fuck me?"

"You are only one here. I could play with myself, but . . . you are here. And sometimes my hands get tired. I do not want them worn out in case we have more murderers to kill tomorrow."

"Uh . . . well . . . um . . ."

"Do you not want to fuck me? Is it because I am weak and pathetic?"

"What? No. No! You're not weak and pathetic. Who keeps telling you these things?"

She crossed her arms over her chest. "If you want to fuck me, then what is problem?"

"Shouldn't I take you out to a pub for dinner? Or write you poems or something?"

Her lip curled while her brows pulled down into a vicious frown, and yet she still managed to look horrified as well. "Poems?"

"You know. I'm charming. I usually *charm* females into bed."

Her eyes crossed. "I do not want any of that. I just want fuck. I am using you."

Now annoyed, Celyn snapped. "Gee . . . thanks."

"It is not like you will get nothing from it."

"That's not the point."

"Then what is point?"

"My point is a simple one," he began. "We are traveling together, relying on each other in case things go bad. We really shouldn't be risking that to . . . what are you doing?"

"I get comfortable while you ramble," she said while removing the bindings on her breasts. "Please. Continue. This *fascinates* me."

"Although I can do without your sarcastic tone, I will continue. As I was saying . . ."

Elina stood and removed her boots, her socks. She tossed them aside.

". . . should we really risk the friendship we are just beginning to build to have a quick romp late at night so that

you can get some sleep? Does that really seem like a good
plan to you? Or would it be wiser . . ."

She untied the leather laces of her leggings and pushed
them down her slim hips. She tossed those aside as well.
Then she placed her feet on either side of his hips and
slowly—gods, so slowly—lowered herself until she sat
naked on his lap again.

Celyn swallowed, which was when he realized he'd
stopped talking.

"Go on," she pushed. "I want to hear more about our
budding friendship."

Clearing his throat, Celyn said, "I just don't want to
end up . . ."

"End up what?" she asked around the two fingers she'd
slowly pushed into her mouth.

"Ruining what could be a very good collaborative relationship. Down the road."

"Uh-huh."

She pulled her fingers out of her mouth and lowered
them down her body while she rose up on her knees.

"Go on," she ordered.

Celyn licked his now incredibly dry lips. "I guess, I think
that we should just wait until . . . until . . ."

"Until what?" she gasped out as her fingers slipped
inside her own pussy.

"Until . . . um . . ." He closed his eyes, licked his lips,
tried again. "Until we know each other better?"

She slapped her free hand on his shoulder to maintain
her balance while she began to slowly ride her fingers. "Is
that question?" she panted out. "Or confusion?"

"Both."

"Do you want to keep talking?"

"I don't think I can."

"Good." She leaned in. "I finally found way to shut
you up."

* * *

Elina kissed the dragon, the heat of his mouth surprising her. Even though it probably shouldn't. He was a dragon, after all. Fire breather and all that.

Yet with a human or not, Elina had never been so aroused before. So ready to take what she wanted without thought to consequences or what others in her tribe would think.

Ever since she'd passed fifteen summers, Elina had been graced with lovers. Men born into the tribes who she thought were attractive enough to bother with. None of them would ever be her husband. Glebovicha had made sure of that, but those not bound to another were usually hers for a night or three. But they had all been human . . . belonging to one of the many Steppes Tribes.

Celyn was none of those things and, more importantly, he was a corrupt, immoral Southlander. Something that, at the moment, didn't bother Elina in the least.

Strong hands slid around her waist and eased up her spine. Celyn leaned forward, while gently pushing Elina back.

She tried to use her hands to stop him, but he growled against her mouth, "Keep those fingers deep in your pussy."

Elina didn't take orders from men—or, in this case, males—in bed. But when she tried to pull her fingers away, his hand caught hers and held it in place . . . until he pushed them deeper.

"Fuck yourself with your fingers," he ordered her. And, when she hesitated, "Do it."

She went ahead and did as he told her to, and was quickly rewarded when he moved out of their kiss and licked his way down her throat, then chest, until he reached her breasts. He curled his tongue around her nipple and enclosed most of her breast inside his mouth. The heat increased against her sensitive skin while his tongue twisted

and tugged. The triple sensations of what he was doing to
her breast, what she was doing with her own fingers, and
him holding her hand in place, leaving her very little choice,
had Elina screaming out into the night as her body shook
from the strength of overwhelming sensations.

The orgasm seemed to last forever, rolling through her
until she was too weak to do much more than whimper.

That's when the dragon roughly flipped her onto her
stomach. She placed her hands against the ground, trying
to push her body up, but a firm hand against her back
shoved her down and pinned her there.

Celyn pressed his free hand against her pelvis and lifted
her hips up. His fingers slid around, searching for and finding her pussy. He slid three fingers in and she heard him
sigh, "Gods, so tight." Then his fingers were gone and she
felt the head of his cock press against her.

That's when she began to put up a fight. Or at least tried
to. The head alone was huge, and she wasn't sure she
wanted all of his cock shoved inside her. Then again, she
wasn't sure she didn't. She actually enjoyed that he gave her
no quarter. That he was as strong in bed as she was.

She tested him, but she knew enough about him never to
say the word "no." That was, she sensed, the one thing that
would stop all of this. She didn't want it to stop. She just
wanted it to be a bit of a challenge.

Fuck that. Who was she kidding? Elina wanted a fight.

When it came to sex, Elina liked to know she was bedding an equal, not some weak-willed male who would take
whatever she gave.

And she was more than pleased when she realized that
Celyn the Charming was not that male.

When he tried to fuck her, suddenly the limp doll Elina
had become turned back into the vicious little spitfire who

had gotten naked in front of him and straddled him like a horse she wanted to break.

She pushed herself up, then swung back with one fist, trying to push him off while attempting to get to her feet.

Celyn caught that fist and held it. But he waited. To hear her say the one word that would stop everything. He waited to hear "no" and he only needed to hear it once. He would never force Elina or any female to do anything she didn't want . . . unless Elina wanted him to.

But that "no" never came. She just tried to pull her arm away while still pushing her body up so that she had some leverage.

Celyn, however, wasn't about to give her that leverage. He caught hold of her one free hand, then reached around and gripped the other. With a good pull, he had control and Elina, still on her knees, had control of nothing. The only thing that kept her face from hitting the ground was him.

She continued to struggle, but he pulled her arms back and then gripped both her slim wrists in one hand. With Elina securely held, Celyn again pressed his cock against her pussy, which, he was happy to note, was wetter and hotter than it had been before. And it had been so very wet and hot before.

He pressed his cock against her and, with a rather undignified grunt, he shoved home.

Elina let out a cry; then she began to curse him. At least, he was guessing she was cursing him since she now spoke the language of the tribes and he didn't understand a bloody word she said.

Yet, there was still absolutely no sign of the one word he needed to hear if he was going to stop this. And he thanked the gods every second as he began to take her with long, powerful, and incredibly hard strokes.

Although Elina still struggled to get her arms free, her hips were slamming back against his as he took her with, even he had to admit, absolutely no charm whatsoever.

It was true. He'd always known it. When it came to sex, no matter how much Celyn might fight it, he was and always would be a Cadwaladr. Which meant one thing . . . he liked a bit of fight from his bed partners. He wanted them to go down swinging. He wanted to wake up in the mornings scratched, scarred, and sore.

And, much to his eternal surprise, Elina was one of those partners. She snarled, she screamed, she threatened, she said things in her own language that he was positive he never wanted to know the meaning of. She, in short, put up one hell of a fight . . . but she never said no. Or stop.

So he fucked her, hard, while she fought. And he kept his own orgasm at bay—as bloody hard as that was—until he ripped that climax from her.

Her screams didn't scare off the birds, but he sensed they now had an audience of animals, watching the superior beings do what they mostly did during mating season.

Celyn continued to fuck her through that orgasm and when he could tell she was fighting off another one, her body too sensitive to go through it again, he pulled back his hand and slapped her ass. Her pussy clenched his cock like a vise and they both exploded, his head back, flames bursting from his throat, a few of the viewing birds singed before they managed to take to the air.

Wrung dry, the pair landed hard on the ground, Celyn now spooning Elina from behind.

Trying to catch their breath, they lay there for so long that Celyn lost track of time. That is, until Elina noted, "You are still hard inside me."

Celyn nodded, then realized she couldn't see that. "Aye," he finally answered.

"How is that possible?"

"I am dragon," he answered honestly. "Anything is possible. We're that amazing."

"Are you?" she asked, seconds before her elbow came back and rammed into his face.

"Ow! You mad cow!"

Suddenly Celyn was flat on his back and Elina was on top of him, his cock inside her again, her small hand trying to wrap itself around his throat.

"Then show me," she ordered him. "Show me how amazing the dragon is."

It was the way she rolled her tongue when she said "dragon" that had Celyn gripping Elina by her shoulders and throwing her to her back. He held her down by pinning her arms above her head and unceremoniously shoved his cock inside her.

"I can show you whatever you want," he told her as he fucked her hard. "I'm just not sure you can take it all."

"I am Daughter of Steppes," she reminded him, seconds before she managed to pull one of her hands away and dragged her nails across his chest, leaving bloody claw marks. "I can take *anything.*"

Celyn really hoped that was true. Because they had hours before the suns would rise and he wasn't the least bit tired . . .

Chapter Twenty-One

"Get up, lazy dragon. We must ride."

"No," Celyn told her flatly, turning onto his side. "Take a turn with your hand and leave me be."

"I mean ride our horses . . . out of here."

Celyn opened his eyes, then quickly closed them again when the rays of the two suns nearly blinded him.

Gods, he felt like he'd been drinking all night. But he hadn't. Although he almost wished he'd been doing that instead. He'd feel less pain . . . and probably less used.

Something hit him in the head, and he opened his eyes again—more carefully this time—to see a pigskin of water and several strips of meat lying near him.

"Thanks," Celyn croaked out, shocked at how rough his voice sounded.

What had this female done to him? She was human. Human! Not a She-dragon. Definitely not a centaur, whose skills in bed were legendary. But a mere, weak-skinned human. And yet she hadn't faltered once. She hadn't told him to stop or told him that was enough. Not once! Even when he was praying she would.

It seemed that riding all day on the Steppes created females that could sustain all sorts of things.

Celyn sat up, wincing as parts of his body snapped and popped back into place. His horse made a little judgmental clucking sound with his teeth, but when Celyn glared at him, he quickly turned his head away and went back to eating the grass by the creek.

Picking up one of the slices of meat, Celyn ate and tried desperately to remember what he'd done with his leggings. He glanced over at Elina and saw her pouring herself something hot from the pit fire.

"What's that?" he asked. Gods, his voice still sounded like a road made of crushed glass.

"Tea."

That sounded perfect right now. "Can I have a bit?"

"It is not for you."

Celyn bit off another piece of meat. "Why not?"

"You cannot have little dragon babies."

Celyn choked, that piece of meat stuck somewhere in his throat.

Elina walked over to him and, while holding her cup of tea in one hand, she pounded his back with the other until the meat dislodged.

"Thanks," he squeaked.

She stepped back, with both hands now around the battered metal teacup. She gently blew on the tea to cool it. "You might forget that things have changed, Dolt, between our kinds. But I have not. And I am much too young for anyone's babies. Especially my own."

Celyn felt a sharp bolt of panic. He'd never asked Elina her age; he'd merely assumed she was of age. At least thirty winters. Right?

He tried to sound nonchalant. Tried desperately. "So how old are you?"

"Such a rude question," she teased. "Southlanders and their rude questions."

"Just . . . answer."

"Fine. I am one hundred and forty-five passing summers."

Confused, Celyn asked, "Do you have several summers a year or something?"

"No."

"Then stop fooling around and answer me."

She sipped her tea and gazed at him over the cup.

"Well?" he pushed.

"I am unsure what you want me to say."

Celyn blinked. "You're one hundred and forty-five years old?"

"I said passing summers."

"Is there a difference?"

"No."

"Then—" Celyn stopped short. He would not argue with

her over wording. Not when he was still hungover from their amazing festival of fucking the night before.

He took a breath and started again. "Summers in the Steppes happen once a year?"

"Yes."

"And you've been alive for one hundred and forty-five of them."

"Yes."

"So . . . you're old. Why don't you look old?"

"Why don't you look old?" she snapped back.

."Because I'm a dragon. We live to be nearly a thousand years old."

"And I am Rider," she snarled. "We live to be nearly twelve hundred years old. Even now," she went on, "the woman who gave birth to my great-great-great-grandmother gets up every morning at suns-rise and hunts down male deer for her breakfast. She used to carry the carcasses on her back, but now that she's so old, she drags them to her hut by their antlers."

Celyn stared at the female for a very long moment before he finally said, "Oh. All right then."

Elina shook her head and finished her tea in one gulp.

And that's when Celyn exploded. "*Are you saying I'm not good enough to be the father of your offspring?*"

Eyes wide, Elina gawked at him. "What are you talking about?"

"*I don't know!*" Desperate, Celyn looked around. "Gods, woman! What have you done to me?"

Elina shrugged. "I do not know, but I think you need to calm fuck down."

For a dragon that never seemed capable of shutting up, Celyn the Charming had very little to say as they made their way through small towns and past farms.

To be honest, Elina didn't know if she should be insulted or complimented by the dragon this morning. She'd never seen him so confused before. Although she did have to admit, she was entertained by it all.

But as morning turned to afternoon, she should have remembered that she was traveling with the chattiest dragon the gods had ever created and even massive confusion would not shut him up forever.

"So how old is your mother?"

"Six hundred and sixty-eight, I think."

"You don't know?"

"We do not talk much."

"Oh. I'm sorry."

"For what? You do not make her not talk to me."

"I know. It just couldn't have been easy for you. Growing up in your tribe."

"Tribe life is not easy for anyone. But at least I was born female. I hate to think what my life would be like if I had not been."

That made the dragon chuckle. "You don't hear that very often from Southlander women."

"I do not know why," Elina answered honestly. "I would never want to be man. That cock hanging between your legs all day. You have no control of emotions. If we leave you to yourselves, you destroy without thought; rage without reason; and attempt to fuck anything that wants you to leave them be."

"We're not *all* like that."

"But most. And your lack of control makes all of you essentially weak, even though your upper bodies have so much strength. It is sad."

"If you think so little of us, why do you bother having us around?"

"We need you to have the babies. And . . ."

"And?"

"That is all I can think of."

The dragon's eyes crossed. "The way you think of males, it's a wonder you fucked me at all."

Elina shrugged. "You were there."

Celyn's horse suddenly reared up when he pulled on the reins. "*I was there?*" he snarled.

"That is how we fucked . . . because you were there."

"So you would have fucked anybody who was with you last night?"

"No. I fucked you because I wanted to fuck you." Elina thought about it, then added. "I will probably fuck you tonight as well. You were quite satisfying."

"Gee, thanks."

"Why does that upset you?"

"I have no idea." He placed the palms of his hands against his eyes. "I think you're making me insane."

"Me? That is first."

He lowered his hands and glowered at her. "You don't have to sound so proud of yourself."

"No . . . but I will." She smiled and the dragon did the same. "Believe it or not, Dolt, I choose my lovers carefully. One is fool not to in these dangerous times. But at end of day, I fuck you because I want to fuck you."

He sighed sadly. "Can't you say making love? Fuck is just so harsh."

Elina reared back in her saddle a bit. "Tell me you joke."

"I do joke," he laughed. "But it was worth it to see the look on your face."

He and his travel-cow started off again and Elina followed, fighting her desire to shoot him in the back with an arrow as the laughter went on and on.

* * *

They continued across the Southlands until they reached the territorial lines between the Outerplains. That's where they halted their horses and sat . . . staring.

"You look worried," Celyn finally stated.

"I always look like this."

"No. You usually just look concerned . . . or a little angry. This expression . . . definitely worried."

"I am fine. And we should go. We should reach the Conchobar Mountains pass by nightfall so that we can head through first thing in the morning."

Celyn blinked. "What are you talking about? The mountain pass is right there."

"There are two passes through Conchobar Mountains."

"That's right. I forgot."

"One here," she went on, "that goes into Annaig Valley. The second is the one that will place us inside Steppes territory. That is one we will take."

"Or," Celyn suggested, "we can take this pass and go into Annaig Valley."

"Why would we do that?"

"Mostly for the hells of it. I call it the sweep-through."

"A sweep-through? What battle tactic is that?"

"It's not a battle tactic. It's what my sister Brannie and I used to do when Mum and Da had parties in Da's house. He had a lot of intellectual friends back then. And let me tell you . . . intellectuals can drink. So we would come downstairs like we were just wandering by to say good night or chat a bit with my da's human friends. And by the time we got back upstairs, we would have eight bottles of wine, two whole turkeys, several loaves of bread, and some sweets."

"You want us to sweep through Annaig Valley so you can steal wine and food?"

"No. Just to get a look. If we do it casually enough, I doubt anyone will notice. We won't even go near the city of Levenez; which, in my estimation, would be the most dangerous place to go."

Elina glanced off, but when she looked back at him, she asked, "How did you steal whole turkey and no one notice?"

"Skills. Very impressive skills."

Var tracked his mother down in the library. It was a dark but vast room, its winding length reaching deep into the castle. His mother often found the farthest spot and settled in to get real work done. The only ones who ever bothered her here were Var, Frederik, or his mother's assistant.

As he'd known he would, Var found his mother sitting on the floor, her back against a wall. Books, scrolls, and unused parchment surrounded her. Her spectacles had been pushed up so that they now rested on her forehead rather than her nose.

He sat down beside her and picked up one of the scrolls. He read through the information quickly and, after a few minutes, his mother asked, "So what do you think?"

"I think that the Salebiri family grows in power. And we should be greatly concerned. But if we can get an alliance in place with the Riders of the Steppes . . . that will be nothing but good for us."

"And?"

Var turned things over in his mind before adding, "But we should never trust the Riders. Not fully. Unlike the Northlanders, their loyalties can be bought with enough gold and jewels. They talk of loyalty and honor, but only to their own people. Outsiders are fair game."

Grinning, his mother put her arms around his shoulders and hugged him tightly, kissing his forehead.

Although Var never said it, he adored his mother. She'd given him the tools necessary to think. To analyze. To treat one's mind like a muscle no different from the ones in his arms or legs. How could he not love her more than any being he'd ever known?

This love of Dagmar Reinholdt was, perhaps, the only thing he and Var's father had in common.

With her arms still around him, his mother asked, "So what brings you looking for me this day?"

"I've come to ask, again, about going to live with Uncle Bram. At least for a little while. Until he finds a new assistant."

"You detest your father that much?"

"I don't detest him. I just can't stand him. And my uncles aren't much better, except Uncle Fearghus, and that's only because we barely speak to each other. They are distractions, Mother. How can I hope to learn more when they're busy causing problems? The constant arguing. The constant fighting. The way their voices carry beyond what I would call acceptable levels of discourse. If only you and my aunts lived here, this wouldn't be a problem. But you don't. You live with them. And my sisters, who seem to make no other sound but high-pitched screeching. I don't know how you tolerate it."

"You forget where I come from. You've met your uncles in the north. They make your sisters seem like whispering willows in the breeze."

"All I ask for is a chance to know what it's like to enjoy civilized dinner discussions. To not have those discussions dissolve into yet another episode of who can slam my father's head the hardest against the table or wall. Of not having to constantly think to myself, 'Well . . . Father did deserve that.' Uncle Bram is more than happy to take me on as his protégé, and I want the chance to work with him. Really work with him. Not just spend five or ten minutes with him when he comes by Garbhán Isle, only to lose him to something else Aunt Annwyl did to piss off another royal that Uncle Bram then has to fix."

Her arms tightened a bit around his shoulders. "I don't want to lose you."

"I'm going to Uncle Bram's, Mum, not off to war."

"You have a point, but—"

His mother's words were abruptly cut off when they heard a crash outside the castle walls. Var quickly got to his feet, then grabbed his mother's hands and helped her to her own. Together, they rushed down the aisle of books until they reached a small window. Var pulled over a chair and stood on it so he could see as well as his mother. Their heads pressed together, they watched Aunt Annwyl yell at the stonemason she'd hired to create the new structure she'd been building behind the castle. It wasn't even connected. It stood alone and rather tall.

"Everyone has been trying to figure out what she's building," Var said. "Do you know?"

"No. She's told no one. Not even your uncle Fearghus. I asked him and he just looked terrified."

"The rumor is that she's creating a tower. For her enemies. When she's not ready to kill them right away. That she plans to torture them there. Do you think that's true, Mum? Do you think this is for the Salebiris?"

"I really don't know."

"You'll need Uncle Bram even more now to help keep the peace where we can. And then, one day, I'll do it."

"I don't want to lose you, Var."

Var faced his mother. "By all reason, Mum, I'm going to Uncle Bram's, not riding into battle. He's not even a half-hour's flight from here if the wind is with whoever is carrying me."

"I don't appreciate your condescending tone, Unnvar."

"Because I sound too much like you?"

"Yes."

"Let's face it, Mum. I need to learn what I can from Uncle Bram because you can't teach me all that *you* know until I'm at least eighteen winters. I mean, you could start now, but that leads to a moral dilemma I'm sure neither of us wants to deal with."

His mother glanced off. "Your grandmother did warn me not to spread my evil to her grandson, which I took rather personally considering how many times my evil has helped that She-dragon."

"At least *talk* to Uncle Bram for me."

"All right. I'll talk to him. But I promise nothing."

"Thank you."

Var hugged his mother, but before either could pull away, another crash outside had them turning back to the small window, where they could see Aunt Annwyl point a finger at the stonemason.

"Don't think for a second I won't have you pull all this down and start again. I'm the queen!" she announced. "I can do that!"

That made Var snort, but his mother quickly admonished, "We shouldn't laugh."

But they did anyway.

Chapter Twenty-Two

As Celyn suggested, they "swept through" the Annaig Valley, cutting through a few of the border towns. And each one had what Elina now termed "Penis Temples," but unlike the Southland cities and towns, there were no other temples. No other gods worshipped in the area. At least not openly.

Elina also noticed the same military presence everywhere. Their armor, shields, and capes bore the benign image of flowers—unlike Annwyl's coat of arms, which had two dragons facing each other and two swords clashing behind them—but the soldiers were well-trained, well-armed, and extremely dangerous.

Celyn tried to ride close to the penis temples so that he could get a closer look without going inside, but Elina held him back. She'd felt right away that standing out, being noticed, would do nothing for them. In fact, before they hit the first town, Elina had changed back into her rugged Outerplains wear and told Celyn to make sure his fur cloak covered everything on him, including his face.

To her surprise, he hadn't debated her demand, simply done as she'd bid. She could only assume that he'd sensed it too. Whatever "it" might be.

They could have gone farther into Annaig Valley and still cut through to Outerplains, but Elina didn't want to do that. She had enough to worry about, knowing she'd be facing Glebovicha soon. She wasn't ready to deal with whatever was going on in this seemingly benign valley with its beautiful rolling hills and explosion of flowers. Flowers that managed to bloom even as winter began to crash down on all of them.

Without any fuss, Celyn followed Elina in a shorter arc through Annaig Valley, and by late evening they'd crossed into Outerplains territory. They kept going until Elina could no longer see the valley they'd left behind. And that was when she suggested setting up camp for the evening.

"You all right?" Celyn asked her before they dismounted from their horses.

"I am better now."

"You felt unsafe in Annaig Valley, didn't you?"

"You did not?"

"I am a dragon, Elina."

"So?"

"So . . . I can't just admit that I feel unsafe. Even when I do."

"Then you blame on me?"

"Aye. That's exactly what I do."

Rolling her eyes, Elina dismounted. "Such a proud race you come from, Dolt."

The dragon grinned. "We like it."

He dismounted and looked around. "So where do we go from here?"

"Now? We sleep."

"Out here? There are barely any trees. It's just empty space and grass."

"It is the Steppes. There is little else."

"There's no town nearby where we can get a hot meal . . . and a warm bed?"

"We have warm bed." She lifted up her bedroll. "See?"

"And the horses?"

"There is creek over there. Can you not hear it? And it is the Steppes. There is more than enough grass for them. Snow has barely touched most of it."

"And if we decide to have sex again?"

Elina shrugged. "We fuck right here."

"In front of everybody?"

"We will be like animals."

"Except that we're not animals." He thought on that a moment. "Well . . . I'm not. I'm a dragon. I like shelter."

"What is different from here than where we fuck before?"

"Trees. Dense, shielding trees."

"You are spoiled."

"Elina—"

"If you want shelter"—she pointed at the mountains far off in the distance—"you can go there and get shelter. Fight for space among the dragons of the Outerplains. I am sure they like company."

"We both know that Outerplains dragons do not like company. They're antisocial miscreants."

"I do not know what that means, but you are probably right."

Elina got a small campfire started first. Once that was done, she set out her bedroll and retrieved fresh water from the creek. Her horse, now back on its own territory, drank from the creek and began to indulge in the grass without any prompting from Elina.

Retrieving dried pork and bread from her saddlebag, she sat down on her bedroll and began to eat. That was when she noticed that Celyn was still on his horse.

Both horse and rider looked so out of place, she couldn't help but smile.

"What are you doing?" she asked.

"Trying to come up with other options."

"There are other options but none that make sense." She shrugged. "You might as well get used to this, Dolt. This will be our life until we reach tribes. A life without big, shielding trees."

"Aren't you worried, though?"

"Worried? About what?"

"An attack."

"Is that what has you looking so fussy?"

"I'm not a human baby."

"Look around you, Celyn."

"I have been. There's no protection for us if we're set upon."

"And we cannot be set upon without seeing them first. And hearing them." She pressed her hand against the ground. "Even their footsteps will come through the ground of the Steppes, and we will feel their approach." She took a bite of her pork. "By the time any warriors get near us, we can be ready to fight or, if necessary, you can fly us away or burn them to embers with your flame."

She again patted the ground beside her. "Now come. Sit beside me. I will play with your cock while we eat."

Elina hadn't even finished chewing the second bite of her food before the dragon suddenly dove into place next to her. A smile on his handsome face, his eyebrows wiggling in anticipation.

He was adorably pathetic.

"Take care of your horse first, Dolt."

"Take care of him?"

"He cannot spend all night wearing saddle and equipment."

"Aye, but—"

"I am not going anywhere. My hands will still be here to play with cock when you get back."

"Promise?"

Elina looked out into the dark night of the thousands of leagues of Steppes lands and asked, "Where in all hells would I go?"

Celyn led his horse to the creek before stripping off his saddle and bridle. He carried the equipment over to where Elina had placed her extremely simple saddle and dumped the whole lot there.

Then he sort of . . . dove at her again.

It wasn't pretty. Or elegant. Just kind of desperate.

When he'd woken up that morning, he honestly hadn't thought he'd have the energy for anything after their long day of riding. But his body had different plans once she'd said the word "cock."

No euphemisms for Elina of the Too Long Name. She was as straightforward and brutal about sex as she was about words. Something he was minding less and less these days. He liked her open honesty. Her strange turn of phrase that had nothing to do with the common language of the Southlander not being her first language.

But what he really liked was how, when he tackled her in his wild dive, she simply rolled with him until she had him on his back. They'd rolled away from their small campsite and their warm bedrolls, but neither seemed to care as they began to wrestle in the dirt and snow.

Nothing violent or angry. But their clothes did manage to go flying until they were both naked and Celyn was buried deep inside her. He had her pinned to the ground, his hands holding her arms over her head.

He leaned down and kissed her, but abruptly pulled back and accused, "You faithless cow, you have ale! And you've shared none with me!"

Elina hiked one leg up high on his hip and then lifted and turned until Celyn was flat on his back, but still buried deep inside her.

"You want my ale," she told him, "you have to give me what I want."

"And what's that?"

"A good ride." She pulled her hands from his grip and slapped them against his chest. She began to rock her hips against him, her pussy squeezing and releasing as she writhed on top of him, her head thrown back, her pale hair blowing wildly around her face from the harsh Steppes winds that she didn't seem to notice one bit.

"Yes, dragon," she growled, "just like that."

Celyn gripped her hips with both hands. "Who's riding who when you're on top, female?"

In reply, she squeezed hard on his cock, using just those muscles of hers, and Celyn's back arched as he fought his desire to come now. Right this moment. Damning her and her own enjoyment. But he knew that's what she wanted. To prove him weaker. And he wasn't about to let that happen. Not when it came to sex.

So first he fought for control of his own body . . . then he fought for control of hers.

It wasn't easy. He might be bigger and, as a dragon, considerably stronger. Even when he was in this weaker human body. But the woman had a knowledge of balance that often gave her a surprising edge. If he wanted to win this round—winning being relative when it came to pleasure—he would have to take away her balance.

Once he had her on her back again, Celyn stood, his arms around her hips so that he brought her with him. She laughed when she had to press her hands against the ground so that her head didn't accidentally slam into it. While she was busy with that, he moved his arms down so that he gripped Elina high on her legs. Once he had her secure, he began to fuck her hard, her laughter turning to moans, her toes curling against his back as he took her.

And, even better, with his long arms, he was able to press his thumb against her clit and rub. Gently at first until he felt her legs tighten around his waist, then a little harder, until her entire body was shuddering and she was screaming out into the night.

See? He'd won this round.

He pulled out of Elina, but only long enough to flip her around and set her down on her stomach. He lifted her ass high in the air and buried himself inside her again. He pounded into her from behind while reaching around and playing with her clit, knowing full well it was still sensitive from the last orgasm.

Elina screamed in rage and tried to push his hand away, but he refused. Then, her pussy tightened around him again as another orgasm—too soon after the last—rolled through her. His own climax exploded around him, and Celyn threw his head back, as flames yet again lit up the dark.

When he was done, when he'd squeezed the last from his body, he dropped them both to the ground, side by side. He on his back, Elina on her stomach. She reached over and slapped his arm.

"Bastard," she complained.

"I know."

Chapter Twenty-Three

Elina awoke the next morning with the two suns rising in the distance and Celyn's head between her thighs.

He took long, lingering licks of her, his tongue ending with a little lash against her clit.

She stretched, briefly thinking she could have someone wake her up like this every day.

"Good morn to you," Celyn said between licks.

"And good morn to you," was what Elina meant to say, but all that actually came out was, "Uh."

Chuckling a bit, Celyn gripped her ankles and pushed them back so that her knees bent. Then he spread her thighs wide, and pinned her down with his shoulders. His languid, easy licks turned into harsher ones until he took her clit gently between his teeth and used his tongue to tease it into a pulsating climax that had Elina writhing beneath the big bastard.

Elina dug her hands into his hair and held on as he took her over once, then again. She was covered in sweat by the time he mounted her, his cock pushing its way past pulsating muscles. They both gasped when he was buried deep, Elina's arms around his body as he rocked into her. He kissed her neck, then bit it, the tip of his tongue then soothing the sting. He did it again and again, her body writhing every time he did so.

He was learning to play her body, and she wasn't sure that she minded, which confused her. She'd been raised to have control of the men she fucked. But this wasn't a man teasing her ear with his lips. This was a dragon. And she'd quickly learned there was no telling dragons anything.

Celyn groaned against her and then his body began to shudder. She knew his climax was seconds away, which for some unknown reason, sent her spiraling into another one that had her screaming into his neck.

They orgasmed, their bodies clenched tightly together until they'd wrung each other dry.

Celyn pulled back a bit, staring down into her face, his dark eyes warm. He looked like he was about to say something when Elina turned her head to the side.

"What is it?" he immediately asked.

She pressed her ear to the ground, nodded. "Someone is coming," she said. "And, at the moment, it is not us, dragon."

Elina had been right. She knew long before the interlopers arrived that they were coming. So by the time the male Riders came into view, they were both dressed and armed, Elina with her bow, Celyn with everything else.

Five horsemen rode up to them, stopping their horses as soon as Elina lifted her bow in the air, raising it so that she could send her arrow high and far. As fellow Riders, they knew this, but they didn't seem to know Elina.

They spoke in a language Celyn didn't understand, and they all sounded angry, the words spitting out. The discussion went on for a few minutes until the Riders nodded at Elina, turned their horses, and rode off.

Celyn lowered his sword. "What just happened?"

"What do you mean?" she asked.

"Why did they ride off? What did you say?"

"I told them who I am. Who my tribe is. And they left. What else was there to say?"

"That several-minutes-long conversation was mostly you giving them your name? And you don't think your name is too long?"

She rolled her eyes and walked around him. "It is my name, who I am, that will keep us safe on the Steppes. Do not forget that."

"Were any of you angry?"

She stopped in midst rolling of her bedding. "No. Why?"

"You looked angry. All of you looked angry."

"That is just way we talk." She finished rolling her bedding and tying it up tight.

"Well, you'll need to let me know specifically if you're in trouble; otherwise, I'll just start killing everyone. And then my father will be very angry at me. He hates when the Cadwaladrs just start killing."

Elina stood, clicked her tongue against her teeth. The horse that did not belong to her trotted to her side and stopped so that she could get him ready. "Is that problem for your people? You all just start killing?"

"Not for all of us. Just my kin." He thought a moment. "And Annwyl. It used to be she was the worst of us. But not lately."

"I do not see the crazed monster that you all think she is."

"We never said she was a crazed monster." Celyn glanced off, winced a bit. "Well, *we* never say it. Others say it, but not us. But normally she is quick to react. Sometimes with a good outcome . . . sometimes not so good."

"But she has many around to help, does she not? Your father. The Reinholdt Beast. That ten-year-old boy with his mother's heartless, cold eyes. Even you."

"Me?"

Elina finished securing her saddle to her horse and

everything else to her saddle. She faced Celyn. "You are helping her now."

"I am?"

"You are here, with me, in the Outerplains. That is helping."

"Is it?"

"I do not understand you, dragon." She mounted her horse and settled in the saddle. "When you help, you do not see it. When you do nothing, you think you save world."

Celyn almost joked about saving the world just by being who he was every day, but no one had ever told him he was helpful before. Like all Cadwaladrs, he was expected to do his job. Nothing more, nothing less. But a little appreciation was kind of a lovely thing.

He walked over to Elina and placed his arms loosely around her hips. Leaning in a bit, he kissed her. A soft, gentle kiss. Not the wild devouring from the night before.

"What was that for?" she asked when he finally—and grudgingly—pulled back.

"Because I felt like it."

"Oh. All right then." And, after a few seconds: "Are you going to keep staring into my eyes like thoughtful oxen or are you going to mount up and ride, so we can meet with the tribes before I die of old age?"

"You're already kind of old—owwww! No need to start punching!"

Gavrilovich Trifonov of the Bear Hunters of the Heartless Clouds in the Far Reaches of the Steppes of the Outerplains rode to the territorial lines between the Outerplains and the Annaig Valley.

He was about to turn the horse and head up the line when his brother stopped him. "I think they come to talk."

Gavrilovich had seen the mounted Annaig Valley Protectors—knights in armor who provided protection to the lands—but he saw them almost every time any of them got a little too close to the territorial lines. Yet they rarely bothered to speak to each other.

The three Protectors stopped right at the line where Outerplains became Annaig Valley. The knight in the middle raised his hand in greeting.

"Good day to you, mighty Riders," he said in the language of Gavrilovich's people, a big smile on his face.

Gavrilovich nodded. "Morn."

"We were wondering if you saw a man and a woman passing this way. Nothing's wrong, of course, but our local priest would like to spend some time with them."

Gavrilovich shrugged. "Sorry. We haven't seen anyone coming this way in days."

"All right," the knight said, his smile never fading. It was so bright, it nearly blinded poor Gavrilovich's eyes. "Well, thank you for your help. Good day to you, mighty Rider. May death find you well."

Gavrilovich watched the Protectors ride off, muttering under his breath, "And may death find you."

"Why did you not tell them about the Black Bear Rider and her oversized slave?" his brother asked.

"We tell them nothing about the people of the Steppes." He turned in his saddle and looked right at his men. "Ever. I never trust anyone who smiles that much."

"It's like looking at the suns," his cousin grumbled.

"Now come," Gavrilovich ordered. "We still have to check the rest of the line and then I have to get back to pick up my girls from battle practice." He glanced at his brother. "The youngest is only ten passing summers and they're already doing well."

"Of course. They have shoulders like their mother—and short tempers like bulls raging in field. How could you not be proud?"

* * *

The farther they traveled through the Outerplains that day, the more Celyn had to admit that he knew nothing about this territory.

Any time he'd cut through the land, whether it was with human armies or dragon, he'd always gone through the narrow eastern part on the other side of the Conchobar Mountains. It was a much shorter trip and had some farms, a few towns, and definitely forests. One of Rhiannon's sisters lived a nice, quiet life in that area. And even when marching as human, it took very little time to get to the Northlands through there.

Yet the farther west they traveled through the Outerplains, the fewer trees—and the ones they saw were more like sturdy bushes—and the more grasslands they rode through. It was, as Elina had said, beautiful country.

But like most truly beautiful things, heartless. Living out here was clearly not for the weak. One could travel for leagues and see nothing but grassy stretches of nothingness. Even the mountains that appeared so close turned out to be far away, almost as if they moved back if anyone came near.

To travel this land, alone or with others, year-round, season after season . . . Celyn couldn't imagine it. Couldn't imagine seeing nothing but miles of grassland; feeling nothing but the brutal Steppes winds rushing by; hearing nothing but the occasional hawk cawing in the distance.

They did pass a few travelers, but other than a head nod, there was little communication.

No. Celyn couldn't do it. He couldn't live out here. He'd thought the Northlands were bad with their snow and so few females to keep him warm, but he'd been wrong. At least there he'd eventually find a town. A town that had a pub. There'd be ale and warmth. There'd be talk. Lots of it, even if it was the guttural, low conversation of a Northlander.

But even that was better than this.

Gods, anything was better than this.

* * *

Celyn's roar echoed out over the Steppes, and the horse Elina rode immediately stopped. The horse didn't panic. At least not like Celyn's horse, which reared up at his master's sudden explosion, almost unseating the dragon.

Elina turned in her saddle. "What?"

"How do you stand this?" the dragon demanded, barely managing to keep control of that panicked travel-cow he rode.

"Stand what?"

"The silence! No people! Nothing! There's been nothing! I feel like we've been traveling in this hell for days!"

"It has been one *hour* since we left camp."

"What has that got to do with anything?"

With a sad shake of her head, Elina turned back around and set off again.

"That is not an answer, woman!"

He'd been forced to travel that hellscape for a whole entire day before they finally set up camp that night. At least then Celyn had been able to talk to Elina until his throat was raw, which was about the time she'd pounced on him, pinning him to the ground with her naked body and begging him to, "Shut up. By all the horse gods in all the worlds, *shut up!*"

That order had led to a lusty bout of more naked wrestling, something he was enjoying more and more each night he spent with her.

Then, finally, sleep. Until he woke up to hear Elina crying out.

When Celyn opened his eyes, he was already standing, his sword clutched in his hand, his human body in the first battle stance he'd ever learned from his mother. Ghleanna would be proud of how well she'd taught him all those years ago when he was still a hatchling, hanging from her tail.

But, when Celyn finally realized where he was and what was going on, he saw that they were alone and safe, but Elina was having one hells of a dream.

Naked, she'd tossed her fur covering off her body and was sweating, despite the wicked cold of the Steppes. Her arms swung and batted, as if she was trying to ward off something terrible.

Celyn dropped his sword and crouched at her side.

"Elina," he said, stroking her shoulder. "Elina! Wake up!"

She did, still screaming. Almost begging. And, when she saw Celyn over her, she did something quite shocking.

She threw herself into his arms, her entire body shaking—which he sensed was *not* from the cold.

Arms around her, Celyn held her tight, assured that he was at least keeping her warm.

"Elina, what is it?"

"Nothing, nothing." She gripped him tighter. "Just bad dream."

Although Celyn wanted to ask what her dream was about, what could be so horrifying as to terrify a woman who spent all day wishing everyone a good meeting with death, he knew the last thing she needed was his questions.

Showing weakness was not something Elina did. Ever. No matter what her tribe might think of her. But she was showing it now, to him, and he would respect her by not being . . . well . . . himself.

It took some time, but eventually her body stopped shaking, and she finally pulled away from him. She stood and walked over to a large boulder. Celyn watched as, naked, she climbed up on it, and sat down. She raised her knees and wrapped her arms around them.

Celyn began to follow her, to slide in behind her, and hold her. But, again, something told him that wasn't what she wanted. So he tried something else.

* * *

Elina sat on the large boulder and stared up at the sky. She worked hard to control her racing heart, her desire to flee.

By the horse gods, how desperately she wanted to flee. Not from Celyn. He was perhaps the only reason she'd gotten this far. His constant questions and chatter had kept her so distracted that she hadn't had time to think about returning to her tribe. To Glebovicha. To that woman's mocking tone, her obvious hatred, her utter disgust at Elina's very presence.

Celyn continually marveled at how strong a hunter Elina was, but hunting and horses had always been Elina's escape. She could track a lone buck through the mountains and take him down with one shot since she'd passed her twelfth summer, ensuring that she could always provide food or live on her own if it was ever necessary. And after she met with Glebovicha about Annwyl's request, something told Elina that would be necessary.

Elina stared up at the sky, allowing the wonderful silence of the Steppes to ease her panicked soul . . . until she heard the breathing.

She turned her head and saw scales.

"Climb on," Celyn said in his deep voice, ten times deeper when in his dragon form.

She liked that.

Without hesitation, Elina climbed onto Celyn's back, her naked body kept warm by his natural heat and all that black hair.

She kept close to his neck, her legs wrapped around it, her hands pressed against the back of it. Elina felt no fear being this close to a being that she knew could eat her whole . . . like a little treat before a larger meal. She felt safe with Celyn the Dolt. Had felt safe with him from the very beginning. From the day he'd found her standing on Devenallt Mountain, trying to decide whether to run—and bring shame upon herself—throw herself at the mercy of the Dragon Queen and most likely get eaten, or simply throw herself off Devenallt Mountain so she wouldn't have to worry about any of her problems, Elina had felt safe with Celyn. She'd instinctually felt he'd never hurt her, even though she had no idea why she felt that way.

So sitting on his dragon back, his scales rubbing against her naked thighs and legs as he breathed or moved the slightest bit, did not scare her. If anything . . . she loved the feel of it.

"Watch this," he quietly ordered. "The queen taught me this. I'm not as good as her, but I'm not bad either."

The dragon took in a breath and then unleashed his flame. It wasn't the big explosion of fire and death that she'd seen when he'd confronted those who'd killed the old dragon. It was just as deadly, but there was an elegance to the flame as it moved across the Steppes, zigging this way and that, cutting down layers of grass. It was fascinating to watch, but Elina assumed he was just showing off his flame to her. Like a man showing her what he could do with a sword or trying to impress her with the accuracy of his bow.

Then Celyn rose into the air. Not too high, just high enough for her to see the ground below in the bright moonlight overhead.

The lines of what he'd burned into the ground were simple and clean. Like a beautiful drawing.

"What is that?" she asked, assuming it was some sort of dragon rune.

"Your name in dragon script."

Elina gasped, surprisingly shocked by his answer. Perhaps because it was so simple and yet so . . . charming.

Damn him! He *was* Celyn the Charming!

"Want to fly for a bit?" he asked.

"I do."

"Then burrow close to my neck and wrap my hair around you. That will keep you warm. And hold on."

She did as Celyn bade as he rose high in the air and began a leisurely loop around the Steppes, giving her another view of the lands she loved so much.

It almost made her forget what had made her wake up screaming in the middle of the night. Not completely . . . but almost.

Honestly, that was more than she could have ever asked for.

Chapter Twenty-Four

Frederik had his shield up while he kneeled beneath it. The battle-axe rammed into the steel over and over again.

Finally, after a few minutes, it stopped, and he let out a breath.

"You going to keep hiding under there?"

"I'm not hiding," Frederik lied. "I'm . . . biding my time. Before launching a brutal counterattack."

The shield was snatched from his hands with more ease than he cared to think about, and Bercelak the Great stared down at him.

"Brutal counterattack? Really?" The dragon held his hand out, and Frederik grasped it, allowing himself to be pulled to his feet.

"You give up too easy, boy."

"I know. I saw the axe and I panicked. But let's try again."

Bercelak nodded. "Aye. We'll try again."

Picking his sword back up, Frederik readjusted his shield and his stance. He nodded at Bercelak.

But before the dragon could make his first swing, Addolgar dropped from the skies into the training ring with them, several Cadwaladr right behind him.

"Brother," Addolgar greeted happily. "And small Northland human."

"What have you got there?" Bercelak asked about the squirming bundle Addolgar held.

"This is the Baron Roscommon."

Bercelak sneered in disgust. "The one who killed old Costentyn?"

"That's the one. Celyn told me to take him to Annwyl since he's one of her subjects."

"Annwyl's in her library. Take him to her."

"I'd suggest," Frederik cut in, "that we not do that."

The brothers looked at each other and back at Frederik.

"Really?" Bercelak asked. "You suggest we not do that? Then what do you suggest that we do?"

"Aunt Dagmar has worked hard to . . . tamp down a few of Queen Annwyl's more endearing . . . qualities."

Addolgar chuckled at that, but his brother just snorted and said, "Get to your point, boy."

"I'm concerned that once she knows what happened with Roscommon and his people, she will react harshly."

"The boy's got a point, brother. Celyn figures the people of that city have already suffered enough with most of the able-bodied men dead. But Annwyl may feel different."

"All right, fine. We'll leave Annwyl out of it."

Frederik smiled. "Thank you, Bercelak."

After grunting at him—something Frederik was sadly

used to from his own kin—Bercelak again motioned to the sack that held Roscommon. "Take him to Rhiannon. She hasn't had a snack that begs in years."

"Will do."

Addolgar and those who'd flown with him took to the air again. After watching him leave, Bercelak turned around.

With a shrug, he asked Frederik, "What? What are you looking at me like that for?"

Bram was busy scanning some information he'd received from Keita's spy network. It was fascinating and disturbing reading.

So fascinating, he didn't realize he wasn't alone until he sat back in his chair to stretch his tired shoulders.

"Ahhh!"

Addolgar raised dark silver eyebrows. "You always were jumpy."

"Don't sneak up on me."

"I didn't. I've been sitting here, eating and drinking, for the last thirty minutes."

"Oh."

He jerked his thumb behind him. "You left those front gates open again. Didn't Ghleanna tell you not to leave those gates open?"

"She has. Just *anyone* can walk in."

"Exactly," Addolgar replied . . . oblivious.

"So . . . why are you here?"

"Celyn wanted me to give this to you. It's Costentyn's journals."

Bram took the two large leather-bound tomes from Addolgar. "Thank you for bringing them to me."

"You're welcome."

Bram flipped one of the books open, and as he scanned the information, he asked Addolgar, "How is Celyn?"

"Good. He handled this well."

Bram smiled, feeling immense pride.

"I heard you have visitors," Addolgar said.

"I do. The Rebel King and his sister are here."

"Why? Why aren't they at Devenallt Mountain . . . or Garbhán Isle?"

Bram glanced up from Costentyn's journal.

Addolgar cleared his throat. "All right. Good point."

Bram went back to scanning the material. "The King has meetings in the Southlands, but he didn't want to leave his sister behind in the Provinces. There have been threats against her life."

"Not surprising."

"He wants her to stay under Annwyl's protection until he's done and they can return to the Provinces together."

"Annwyl? Why not Rhiannon?"

Bram sighed, glanced up at Addolgar. "Do I really have to keep looking up at you?"

Addolgar shrugged. "Sorry."

Returning to the journal, "I'll escort them over to Garbhán Isle soon."

Addolgar chuckled. "Bet you never thought you'd be the one escorting anyone anywhere, huh?"

"Not really." Bram abruptly sat up. "Speaking of death threats . . ."

"What is it?" his brother-by-mating asked.

"Costentyn was worried that plans are being put into place to assassinate someone of great power. Probably one or both of the queens."

"Why did he think that? I mean, other than the obvious?"

"Rumors he was hearing in town. Recent rumors."

Bram sat back in his seat, one hand stroking his chin.

"What do you think we should do?" Addolgar asked.

"Let everyone know, of course. But other than that all we can do is wait."

"Yeah . . . except Bercelak's not good with that. The waiting."

Bram sighed. "Yes. This we all know a little too well."

It took them two days to reach the territory of the Steppes Tribes and then another whole day to reach the Black Bear Riders, Elina's tribe.

In the last hour, as they'd moved closer and closer to her home, Elina had become more and more silent, sullen, and tense. So tense, Celyn hadn't said much to her. Something told him she didn't want to hear anything at the moment and that asking her his usual range of questions about what he saw around him would only upset her.

Dismounting from his horse, Celyn grabbed the reins of Elina's. "Are you all right?" he asked.

"I am fine," she lied and dismounted from her own tiny horse. "Remember, do not talk of what you are here."

"Don't worry. I have no intention."

"And no questions. Just watch. Hopefully, I will be able to send you back to Queen Annwyl with good news."

Shocked by that, Celyn stammered out "You're not coming back with me. . . . I mean, uh, well . . ." He shook his head to get hold of himself. "I mean, to discuss the outcome with Annwyl yourself?"

"I am sure that will not be option."

Celyn should have known that, but he hadn't thought much about it. He'd been too busy riding his horse all day . . . and Elina all night. The last thing he'd worried about was that this could be the last he'd see of her. And the thought that it was did not make him happy.

"I wish I'd known," he attempted to joke. "I would have tried to make last night more special. With flowers or something."

She tried to smile, but it was unsuccessful.

"Elina, talk to me. What is it?"

She let out a breath. "Sorry." The confident, opinionated, curious woman he'd known for days was gone. Now she was tense, terse . . . and afraid. He hadn't seen her this bad since the night he'd awakened her from that dream. Now he was wondering if that had been what she'd been dreaming of. Returning here to meet the commander of her tribe.

That said a lot about the woman she was going to face, because he'd never seen Elina this terrified. Aye, she was terrified. Even when he'd plopped her down in front of the most feared She-dragon in all the worlds, he'd never seen her so.

"Just . . . less talk now. Please," she softly begged.

"Of course." She started to turn away, but Celyn quickly placed his hand on her shoulder. "But . . . if you need me to do anything—anything at all, Elina—you just let me know. Understand? I'm right here."

She nodded but said nothing else.

With a deep breath that Celyn found telling, Elina began walking and Celyn followed.

They passed round homes made of wood frames surrounded by a material Celyn didn't recognize. There was a hole in the middle of each one of the structures and smoke came from most of them. He had to admit that though the structures looked flimsy, the mighty wind blowing across the Steppes didn't seem to affect them. From what Elina had told him during one of their many question-and-answer sessions, these structures were not only incredibly sturdy, they could be disassembled and ready to move in less than an hour. That kind of preparedness was something Celyn had only seen from the military.

As they walked through the camps, people emerged from their huts. Some, mostly men, held babies; all were armed to some degree. Dogs ran between the huts, and horses grazed where they liked.

His father had been right. This was not an easy life, and

the people and dragons of this land probably did consider the Southlanders spoiled and lazy. But that was okay. Celyn would rather be spoiled and lazy than be one of several husbands.

The pair was watched closely as they walked by. No. That wasn't accurate. They weren't watched. . . . *He* was watched as he walked by. Watched closely.

In time, they neared a group of structures occupied by a lot of white-blond, blue-eyed Riders, and Celyn immediately knew this was Elina's family. They all looked like her, just different shapes, sizes, and sexes.

As they continued on, a woman whose head and face were covered by a protective scarf strode up to them. She had a bow and an hourglass quiver attached to her back, a short sword sheathed at her side, and several knives strapped to the belt hanging from her waist.

As the female moved in, she rammed her shoulder into Elina's. Celyn stopped and immediately rested his hand on the hilt of his sword, the instincts he'd honed to protect the Dragon Queen coming into play now with Elina.

Elina shoved the woman back, but what Celyn thought was about to turn into a fight turned into a strong hug.

Finally, the woman stepped back and pulled the scarf from her face. Her nose was a little longer than Elina's and she had quite a few battle scars on her face and neck, but these two females were related. He'd guess sisters.

But once the hug ended . . . the arguing began.

And even though he couldn't understand a word that was said, Celyn knew he'd been right.

Definitely sisters.

"You are the biggest fool I've ever known, Elina Shestakova!" Kachka barked at her.

"I missed you, too, sister." In fact, Kachka had been the only one she'd actually missed. These beautiful Steppes lands and her dear sister, Kachka, who was now yelling at her.

"Do not be so ridiculous, Elina! You know you never should have returned here. Never!"

"You thought I'd not only fail in my quest, but that I'd die."

"I thought you'd *run,* you delusional cow!"

Elina was shocked that her sister, *this* sister, would say such a thing. "Run? Me? You think so little of me? Of my honor?"

"Honor? I thought you were smart. Smart enough to know the truth of that stupid, ridiculous que—"

"Well, well," a voice boomed from behind them, and both sisters turned to face their cousin and Glebovicha's favorite, Ivanova. Even with twenty-five children of her own, Glebovicha had rudely chosen outside her direct line for her next in command. "Look who has returned, the mighty and *brave* Elina Shestakova."

Elina glanced back at Celyn, but, thankfully, they spoke in their own language. He was oblivious to just how much she was mocked by her own.

"Ivanova Shestakova. I see that death has found you well," Elina greeted her cousin. The "unfortunately" in that statement was implied and completely understood by Ivanova.

The much larger woman grinned down at Elina. Ivanova was one of the best warriors among them. Tall, powerfully built, and brilliant with sword and bow, she had her pick of husbands and had already borne eighteen strong children to the twelve husbands she had. And not yet two hundred passing summers.

In other words, she was everything that Elina was not and would never be. Because they all knew that Ivanova would have returned from the Southlands with the Dragon Queen's head dragging behind her horse or died in the attempt.

Ivanova brazenly walked around Elina's horse.

"I see no dragon's head," she announced to all those standing by their huts listening. "No offering to the great Glebovicha as you promised."

"She promised nothing," Kachka snarled. She'd never been afraid of their cousin, and she was always the one who defended Elina, something that Ivanova and Glebovicha had never forgiven her for. "She was forced into this ridiculous quest."

Before a fight could escalate between the two, Elina said, "I need to speak with Glebovicha, Ivanova."

"What for? You come with no dragon's head. Just this"—she gestured at Celyn—"male," Ivanova finished with a sneer. "Our great Glebovicha may consider him for a husband, cousin, with such a pretty face and all, but he will not buy you pity from anyone here. Not after such a great failure."

"Can I see Glebovicha or not?"

"You want to see her, cousin?"

"Elina—"

"Quiet, Kachka." Ivanova waved at Glebovicha's hut. "Go to her, Elina Shestakova. I'm sure she'll be more than happy to see you."

Elina looked back at Celyn. "Wait here," she told him. "Back soon."

He nodded and gave her a small smile.

She forced herself to return that smile, then pushed past her cousin and walked to Glebovicha's tent.

Celyn had no idea what was going on. When Elina had begun to argue with her sister, it hadn't bothered him at all. Sisters fight. Gods knew, his own sisters could clear a path through an ancient forest with their brutal fights—throwing each other headfirst into thousand-year-old trees had the wonderful ability to knock down hundreds of them. But then that other woman had come over, and by the gods, had she been huge. Not like Annwyl or even Izzy—two women who, for humans, were quite large. Tall, big-shouldered, and unafraid to fight to the death. But they were almost petite compared to the female who'd lumbered over to Elina and her sister. Tall, wide, and built for the kill, this woman had brought instant panic to Celyn's system.

And even though he hadn't understood a word being said, Celyn had always understood body language. His parents had taught him about that. His mother had taught Celyn what to look for during battle and his father had taught him what to look for during negotiations. Either way, based solely on her body language, Celyn was quite sure both his parents would have stomped on the human until she was nothing but a sticky red-and-white paste.

Even worse, though, was seeing the resignation in Elina's eyes when she'd looked at him before heading into that tent. That look had devastated him.

But he'd felt a tiny bit of relief when her sister had followed. Before she had, she, too, had looked at Celyn, her gaze moving from his head to his feet and back up again. At first, he'd thought he was being sized up, as he had been by every female in this damn camp, but—after a quick glance—she'd focused on him and lifted her chin a bit. It was slight, and he could have easily construed it for a "Later I will fuck you like you've never been fucked before," but something told him that was not even close to what she was telling him. And she was telling him something.

With a gentle brush against his back, Celyn sent off the horse that Elina had been riding. Not surprisingly, his horse happily followed after his friend.

Even if Celyn never saw either horse again, he wanted to ensure they were both safe no matter what he had to do in the next few minutes.

And based on the expressions of both Elina and her sister, Celyn would have to do something very bad.

* * *

Elina stood near the exit of Glebovicha's hut as the great warrior looked up from her meal, the juice from the roasted lamb on her mouth and hands, pieces of the meat clutched in her fingers. Glebovicha's first and second husbands sat on either side of her, the others probably out tending the horses or helping to train the young ones in battle.

As always, Glebovicha glared at Elina with that particular look of overwhelming disappointment before putting another piece of meat in her mouth.

While chewing, she demanded, "Where is my dragon head, Elina Shestakova?"

As always, Elina didn't bother to attempt to find ways to lessen the impact of what she had to tell the tribal leader. "I failed in my task."

"Shocking," Glebovicha sneered, glancing at her husbands, who snorted in laughter.

"But I have not come empty-handed," Elina continued.

"No, she hasn't," Ivanova cut in. "She's brought you a Southlander man to warm your bed."

The thought of Celyn warming anyone's bed but her own had Elina speaking without thought. "Like hells I have!"

"Sister," Kachka warned.

"Well, I haven't. He's with me," she told Glebovicha plainly.

"Is he now?" Glebovicha asked while pulling more meat off the bone with her hands. "You bring an imperialist dog to my home, but you won't let me play with him? How is that fair, Elina Shestakova?"

Determined to get her off the subject of Celyn as quickly as possible, Elina simply dove in to the true intent of her conversation. "I've been given a task, Glebovicha. One that I think you'll find quite important."

"More important than what *I* have told you to do?"

"Yes. Because it involves the future of the Steppes Tribes as a whole. I know how important that is to you," Elina lied, because everyone in their tribe knew Glebovicha's ultimate goal was to one day be the Anne Atli. It was all she dreamed of, and the safety of the tribes had very little to do with it.

"Oh, really?" When Elina nodded, Glebovicha laughed, her head thrown back in a hysterical cackle that ended in a cough because of the lamb that was caught in the back of her throat.

Elina ignored that dismissive laughter and went on. "And I need to speak to the Anne Atli about it."

The laughter and coughing stopped instantly. Glebovicha's cold eyes locked on Elina. "Do you now, Elina Shestakova?"

"It's important."

"Important? What is so important that you *must* speak to the Anne Atli?"

"I have a message from Queen Annwyl the Bloody. And I promised her I'd deliver it to Anne Atli directly."

Meat hanging from her mouth, Glebovicha snarled, "You fail to bring me my head, you dare show your face after such a failure—"

"Pardon, Glebovicha, but—"

"*Do not interrupt me!*" Glebovicha bellowed.

Elina fell silent, and Glebovicha went on. "You run tasks for some spoiled imperialist dog who lives off her people like a leech, and you dare ask to see our great leader so you can spread your imperialist lies?"

"Queen Annwyl is not a leech."

Next to Elina's ear, Kachka whispered, "Watch your step, sister. *Watch. It.*"

Elina didn't have time to watch her step. Nothing she said or did would ease Glebovicha's disgust at Elina's failure so she might as well get this over with so she could see the Anne Atli and move her mission forward. What was the point of dancing around it when the end would be the same either way?

"Queen Annwyl," Elina went on, "does much for her people. If you'd let me tell you—"

"You defend that monstrous whore to me? *To me?*" Glebovicha exploded.

"It's not that simple, Glebovicha." She took a calming breath. "I understand that I have failed you. I regret it. But I must talk to Anne Atli. I've made a commit—"

"You will do, idiot, what I tell you to do. You have no power here, no say. You are a worm, and like a worm, you will hide yourself from the sight of others until *I* decide that you're allowed to speak to the weakest of my husbands, much less the mighty ruler of our tribes."

Knowing that would mean a solid hundred years if Glebovicha had her way—and she would—Elina did something she'd never done before. She said, "No."

Elina heard Kachka's quick, surprised intake of breath, and saw the grin that spread across Ivanova's face.

And in that moment, she realized she'd gone too far.

Glebovicha got to her feet and stepped over the pit fire in the middle of the hut. As she moved in, Elina tried to step back, but Ivanova grabbed her shoulder and held her in place, which was when Kachka stepped in front of her. Ready to defend Elina as she'd been doing since they were children. But Glebovicha expected that and she backhanded Kachka out of the way with a hand still holding greasy pieces of lamb.

Elina understood fully then. She hadn't simply gone too far here. No. To her horror, she'd given Glebovicha exactly what she'd always wanted. Something that she'd hoped a ridiculous quest to kill the Dragon Queen would eliminate the need for. It hadn't, so now Glebovicha was taking it upon herself . . . and Elina had given her all the reasons she needed to justify whatever she did next.

Understanding that fully, Elina was about to run, to try

to escape her fate. She pulled away from Ivanova, but before
she could turn, Glebovicha kicked Elina in the center of
her chest, sending her flying out of the hut to land hard on
the ground.

Celyn slapped off the fourth hand that had grabbed his
ass in the last ten minutes. He'd never thought he would tire
of female attention, but he had to say, being pawed like
some piece of meat, as if he were being judged at a horse
auction, did get tiring quite quickly. And he was moments
from making that sentiment clear when he heard flesh hit
flesh. He turned and saw Elina fly backward out of the tent
she had disappeared into only minutes before.

She landed hard, the wind knocked out of her, but she
was still trying to get to her feet.

Celyn rushed forward to help, but a rope was wrapped
around his neck from behind, yanking him back.

"Where you go, pretty man?" a female voice said from
behind him. He glanced back and saw what he could only
call a very large female Rider standing there, leering at him.

With his hands grabbing hold of the rope, he looked to
the tent and saw a woman walk out of it. And gods. What
exactly were they feeding these women? This one was unbelievably huge! Celyn came from a family of She-dragons
who were known for their substantial size when human . . .
and he'd guess this female was bigger than any of them. She
was tall and wide, muscles straining her deerskin shirt.

And this behemoth was coming at Elina.

All work stopped, and the Riders stood around staring.
Not helping, just waiting to see what would happen next.

Celyn couldn't do the same. He jumped forward but was
yanked back again by the rope around his throat. The rope
that, in his shock, he'd forgotten about. He was reaching to
remove the damn thing when additional ropes by other

women were looped around both wrists, yanking his arms
away from his body.

Two additional Riders now held onto him. "Leave it,
pretty man," one of the Riders told him. "It is too late for
Elina Shestakova. But not for you. You will make fine husband for one of us. You will give us very fine, large girls to
carry on our names. Perhaps it will be me," she growled at
him. "But do not worry. I will give you fine ride, then pretty
things to make you happy."

Dammit. Celyn had been right all along. He would be
doing very bad things today. . . .

Desperate and terrified, Elina struggled backward, using
her elbows and feet as Glebovicha bore down upon her.

"You fail me!" Glebovicha roared. "You continue to fail
me! *And now you tell me what* you *are going to do? As if
you have a right!"*

"Please," Elina begged, still trying to get away, but
unable to get to her feet fast enough. "Please!"

"You are nothing! *Nothing!* Do you hear me, Elina
Shestakova! Simply a mistake that will now be corrected
so the mighty horse gods can drag your worthless carcass
to the next world—*and out of mine!"*

Elina raised her hand to ward Glebovicha off. "Gods,
don't!"

But it was useless. Completely useless. All the begging,
all the attempts to get away. She knew that as soon as Elina
saw Glebovicha raise her arm, the blade she was holding
glinting bright in the suns, seconds before it slashed down
at an angle and cleaved across Elina's face.

Elina screamed out in pain and shock, one hand slapping
over the left side of her face while her free arm still tried
to drag herself back. Her desire to live overriding her need
to be brave.

Glebovicha came at her again, but Kachka charged out

of the tent and landed on Glebovicha's back with one arm around her throat. Her sister raised a blade but before she could strike it home, Ivanova yanked Kachka off and threw her a few feet away.

Free from Kachka's grasp, Glebovicha came at Elina again. This time, however, Elina scrambled to her feet, even though she was now blinded by the blood pouring down her face. It didn't matter. All she could think about was getting away or at least fighting until her last breath. She knew she should welcome death. She'd never beat Glebovicha in a fight. But she couldn't. She simply wasn't ready for that last horse ride home.

She swung wildly at Glebovicha, punching her in the face. It was a good, solid hit, but it did nothing more than piss the larger woman off. Glebovicha caught hold of Elina's long hair and yanked her around, nearly pulling the locks from the root.

"Elina!" she heard Celyn yell. She'd forgotten about him, but she could barely see where he was through the blood-covered haze.

"Elina!" he yelled again, but this time his voice was lower, more powerful. And there were screams and cries of warning from her tribesmen as the winds of her beloved Steppes increased tenfold and flame surrounded Celyn and all those close to him.

None of this would deter Glebovicha, though. She was too determined to kill Elina. She forced Elina to her knees and pressed her blade against Elina's throat.

"Dragon!" someone screamed out. "Get the defenses! Move!"

"Don't hope, pathetic worm," Glebovicha warned Elina. "This demon you brought will not save you."

Elina already knew that. So she closed her eyes and, finally, waited for death *not* to find her well.

* * *

Kachka Shestakova of the Black Bear Riders of the Midnight Mountains of Despair in the Far Reaches of the Steppes of the Outerplains looked up in time to see the male that Elina had brought with her suddenly surround himself with flames, burning the tribesmen who held him back from protecting her sister.

But as Kachka got to her feet, she saw that the flames were not the work of a warlock of some kind. Instead, the man turned into a dragon, with big wings and a long, thick tail, swiping a clear path around him, tossing off and away the tribesmen who had not been burned.

Yet as he took to the air, she knew he'd never reach her sister. Not fast enough. So Kachka ran at Glebovicha again.

Ivanova stepped in front of their leader, who had Elina on her knees and that blood-covered blade about to open her throat. Still, Kachka ran straight at them both, her own dagger in her hand. But, as she neared, she moved one way and, when Ivanova moved the same way to block her, Kachka quickly jerked in the opposite direction. Her body spun to avoid Ivanova's grasping hands.

Kachka quickly tossed her blade into her other hand and cut her bitch cousin across the gut as she did so.

With Ivanova temporarily out of the way, Kachka was able to ram into Glebovicha before she could draw the blade all the way across Elina's throat. They hit the ground and Kachka punched her leader in the face three times.

With Glebovicha stunned, Kachka looked for the dragon. Of course, he wasn't hard to find, flying low over the camp in all his massive, scaled glory.

"Take her!" Kachka yelled up at the dragon. "Take her and *go*!" she screeched.

Black talons came down and snatched Elina up, his wings sending dirt, dust, and air swirling around them all.

Then his great black wings lifted him and he headed off with Elina.

Kachka watched until she sensed movement behind her.

She jerked to the side and off Glebovicha as Ivanova's blade barely missed her.

"Traitor!" Ivanova accused.

And, as Kachka stood tall, the mare she'd bonded with years ago galloping straight for her, Kachka said the only thing she could think of at the moment: "Fuck you."

Without even needing to look, just using the sound of the mare's hooves, Kachka reached out her hand and, as the horse moved by, grasped her mane.

The power of the mare dragged Kachka until she could use her legs to launch herself up and onto the back of the horse. Using its mane, she turned the mare and urged her off in the direction the dragon was heading.

Because she knew . . . this was not even close to over.

Chapter Twenty-Five

Celyn had no idea what was going on. He just knew that he was removing a bleeding Elina from his talons with his tail so that he could place her on his back.

"Elina?" he called out. "Elina? Can you hear me, luv?"

She groaned and made a gurgling cough but didn't answer.

Celyn briefly thought about setting down so he could get a better look at her wounds, but when he looked at the land beneath him, he saw Elina's sister riding hard across the Steppes. And, behind her, a battalion of Riders coming after them all.

No. He couldn't set down now. So he continued on, trying at the very least to put some distance between him and those Riders.

For the first time, he saw the true benefit of the small horses the Riders used. Their speed and stamina . . . phenomenal. He'd outraced horses before, but he could not shake these bastards. None of them. Even worse, he could feel blood dripping against his scales. Blood from Elina.

Celyn began to panic. Panic so intense that he almost called out to his family. But what would be the point of that? They were thousands of leagues away and would only get there in time to retrieve his body.

No. He was in this alone. He'd have to fight alone. But he was Cadwaladr, and Cadwaladrs never backed down, never gave up.

Celyn felt a tug, his entire body jerking a bit in midair. He glanced around, saw no ropes holding him.

Then he felt another tug. And another. One more.

The last one so powerful, Celyn was yanked off course and pulled in a direction he was unfamiliar with.

Desperate, he tried his best to pull his body back, but something had hold of him.

Celyn looked down and saw that the Riders had turned with him. Elina's sister still rode ahead and he watched in awe as she turned at the waist and unleashed arrow after arrow at the Riders behind her. He counted six shots that she made—and each one took out a fellow Rider.

Watching the last Rider fall, Celyn also saw that several of them had raised their bows in his direction. Normally, that wouldn't worry him much. But this time, he could see, even from this distance, that the arrows they were about to unleash were vastly different from normal ones. The heads larger and made of glinting steel.

"Shit." Celyn again tried to redirect his body, but the power that held him had yet to unleash him.

Three of those arrows rammed into his body, one in the underside of his tail, two on his hips.

Even worse than the pain these arrows caused was the fact that each arrow had a rope attached. The Riders who held the ropes turned and rode toward a small group of short, but sturdy ancient trees, where they wrapped the ropes around the bases of the largest ones.

Celyn kept going until he hit the end of the ropes. One arrow tore out on impact, taking a chunk of flesh and scales with it. But the other two ropes yanked him back. He spun, trying to pull away.

Several of the Riders quickly dismounted and grabbed hold of the ropes—then they began to pull.

Instead of continuing his fight, Celyn decided to wait until he was close enough for his flame to burn all those near.

He was about fifty feet from the ground when he took in a large gulp of air.

The Riders cheered each other on in that language Celyn now regretted not learning, but they were so focused on him that they'd forgotten about Elina's sister. She'd looped around and attacked from behind, unleashing arrows on those holding the ropes.

Six of the Riders went down. Then another six. By then, though, the Riders who were still on horseback charged the woman. Using only her knees, she steered her horse away, again turning in her seat to shoot more arrows behind her.

The distraction allowed Celyn to get in close and unleash his flame. Screaming, the Riders holding the ropes released their grip, trying in vain to stop the fire that now covered their burning bodies.

Using the tip of his tail, Celyn slashed the last two ropes. Suddenly released, his body flipped back toward the ground, his tail managing to catch hold of Elina's unconscious body before she was tossed off.

Celyn crashed into the ground, rolling over and over across the grassy land until he clipped a big boulder and spun around, landing on his belly, his arms and legs spread out so that he was sure he resembled a flat star.

Looking up, Celyn watched Elina's sister ride toward him.

"Get up!" she screeched at him. "Get up now, dragon!"

He placed Elina on the flat top of the boulder just as Riders began to move in close.

Elina's sister jumped off her horse, her hands still holding the bow, her quiver still full of arrows, but how long could they last? Unless they were magickal.

He doubted they were magickal.

Standing in front of the boulder to protect her sister, the woman ordered, "Stand beside me, dragon. We may meet death this day, but we will take many of my comrades with us first."

Panting a bit, Celyn observed, "I see you have as positive an outlook as your sister."

"Positive? We are outnumbered. Trapped. Soon . . . we will be surrounded and hacked to death. But," she added, "death will welcome us, for we will bring him many on this day."

That was great and all . . . but honestly, Celyn would rather he and Elina survived. Surviving was good. Planning for death . . . less good.

The Riders stopped, making sure they were out of range of Kachka's arrows and his flames. One of the older Riders, a male, called out something to Elina's sister.

"What did he say?" Celyn asked her.

"He told me that I have betrayed my tribe for my weak sister and lizard with wings. For that, I will die, too."

"I'm sorry to hear that," Celyn replied. "And I'm not a lizard."

Elina's sister stared at him a moment. She had eyes just like Elina's. "That is what keeps you up at night?"

"Sometimes . . . yeah."

She frowned, shook her head. "I do not understand why

you did not out-fly them. Why did you turn? You could have lost them in the mountains, but stopping here with the mountains at our back . . . ? We are doomed."

"We are not doomed and it's not my fault," Celyn argued. "Something caught hold of me."

"I saw nothing until my fellow Riders took you down with their arrows and rope."

"It wasn't . . . a human thing. It was . . . magickal."

The woman let out a very long sigh. "I see. . . ."

"Really! I swear. It was something—"

"Stop. I can hear no more of your tales of spells."

She focused back on her fellow Riders. "Besides . . . it is time to die."

Unwilling to let that happen, Celyn did the only thing he could think of. "Take her."

"Take . . . what?"

"Take Elina. Take her and go."

"She is dying."

"I don't care if she's dead. Get her and yourself out of here." He focused on the Riders about to charge. "I'll deal with them."

"Riders know how to fight dragons. They are not frightened by you. They will destroy you."

"Stop arguing with me and just go."

"You will die to protect my sister?"

"It is not my ultimate plan, but if it means that, then yes. I will. Now go!"

The woman walked toward the boulder Elina lay upon but stopped short, her eyes narrowing.

Celyn turned his head, expecting to see the Riders charging toward him, but they weren't moving. They, like Elina's sister, were simply staring. At a woman.

Fur covered her from head to foot, but Celyn would guess that she was indescribably, outstandingly beautiful. How did he know all that without seeing her? By the way she moved.

Celyn had no idea where she'd come from, but at this moment, she walked between the two groups without bothering to look at either. When she was right at the center, she slowly turned to face the Riders and pulled her hood back.

Celyn still couldn't see her face, but he knew her. Knew her power. Knew her beauty. Knew exactly what she could do.

"Cover your sister," he ordered the woman, impressed at how she immediately dove onto Elina, using her body to cover her.

Princess Rhianwen, Daughter of Talaith and Briec, raised her delicate hand in the air, moving it in a gentle circle. And Celyn watched, shocked, as dark energies that lurked in the squat trees and bushes, the earth and rocks immediately came to her, pouring into her hand like rainwater until Rhian could take no more.

Then she clenched her hand into a fist.

Celyn faced the boulder that Elina and her sister were on and placed his claws on either side of them. He unfurled his wings, using his entire body to protect them and turned his head so he could see Rhian.

With her fist still in the air, she chanted something, the wind around her picking up, the horses that the Riders were on suddenly, perhaps for the first time, beginning to panic, fighting their riders and each other to back away as quickly as possible.

Rhian went on her toes and then, swinging her arm down, she crouched and rammed her fist against the earth.

Everything around them jerked—the trees, the boulder . . . the ground. The ground jerked hardest of all. Then, from where Rhian's hand had landed, the earth broke away, and the Riders and horses who had not moved quickly enough—at least half the battalion—fell as the ground disappeared beneath them. They vanished into the crater that had been created, their cries of terror echoing in Celyn's ears.

* * *

Kachka had to look up to see what was happening. She knew power when she saw it, and this delicate female had power.

The woman stood, quickly turning away from the devastation she'd caused. And Kachka watched her wipe a tear from her cheek. This had not been something she'd wanted to do, but she'd done it. And, Kachka would guess, she'd do it again.

The remainder of Kachka's fellow tribesmen roared in rage at the loss of their comrades and kin. Then they rode around the gaping crevice, no longer interested in Kachka and Elina, but in the woman who'd done this to them.

Kachka stood, her legs braced on either side of Elina, able to see over the dragon because he was bent low to make sure he protected her sister with everything he had.

She raised her bow and readied her arrow, but before she could let loose her own fury, she saw monks. Two of them came through the trees, covered completely by their cowls and fur capes. But they weren't like other monks who'd traveled through her lands. These two were burly, like small oxen. And like oxen, they battered into a few of her tribesmen, knocking horses and riders into the pit. A spear came at the taller of the two, but he expertly dodged it, caught the shaft with his hand, and yanked it away from the Rider. He turned the weapon and impaled the horse. As the poor animal crashed to the ground, he quickly reached down and touched it, his head lowered. He was chanting. First, the horse stopped moving. It was dead. Then . . . it wasn't. With blood still gushing, it got to its feet and turned on the Rider, stomping and stomping until the Rider was no more than chunky red slime to be slipped in later.

Fascinated, Kachka lowered her weapon, unsure whether she should be terrified or thankful.

Then she heard the one cry that sent panic and fear through the strongest Rider's soul.

"Kyvich! It's the Kyvich!"

There were only three riding their demon beasts through the Riders, but when she was a child, Kachka had seen only two of the warrior witches take down an entire squadron of Quintilian soldiers who were under the delusion they'd found some weak females to amuse themselves with.

The three Kyvich were young, but strong. The one leading the way around the opposite side of the crevice from the monks didn't even unsheathe her sword. She simply gestured to the trees, causing vines and limbs to shoot out, grabbing hold of Kachka's fellow Riders and dragging them from their horses. Some were strangled by the vines, some impaled by the limbs. And some dragged off into who knew what horrors.

"Who are these people?" she finally asked the dragon.

He stood tall now, towering over her like a massive building, and blocking the rest of the destruction of her fellow tribesmen from her sight.

The dragon shrugged and replied, "They're family."

Chapter Twenty-Six

"Are you crying?" Talwyn fairly snarled at her younger cousin.

And, as Celyn expected, Rhian was direct and angry when

she replied, "Do you think I *wanted* to do that? Do you think I get enjoyment from killing others?"

"I see some things have tragically not changed with you, cousin."

Rhian stepped toward her cousin, her hand raised, more dark energy swirling around her. And Talwyn? With a disturbing half grin that reminded Celyn of Annwyl more than he cared to think about, she pointed her hand at the ground and green vines began to burst from the dirt.

Yet before Celyn could tell either of them to stop it, Talan stepped between the pair, his arms wrapping around Rhian.

"How I missed you, Rhi," he said, easing the situation without raising his voice or the dead.

A pat against his thigh had Celyn turning.

"She is still alive," Elina's sister told him. "But blood continues to flow from the wounds."

"Let me see," one of the Kyvich said, barely sparing a glance for Celyn as she moved in.

"I do not want Kyvich near my sister."

"Would you rather she bleed out?" the Kyvich snapped back.

"Please," Celyn said. "Let her try . . . uh . . ."

"Kachka Shestakova of the—"

"Yesssss," Celyn hissed. "Can we just agree on Kachka for now?"

"I'm Gisa," the Kyvich said while she examined Elina's neck. "It looks like her artery was nicked. I can fix this, I think. I just need a few things."

Rhian stepped up next to Celyn, standing on one of the smaller boulders surrounding the one Elina lay upon. She pressed her hand against his side. "I have someplace we can take her. We'll take good care of her, Celyn."

"We should go," Kachka said solemnly. "Those were just the men of the tribes. The women will be coming next, and then it will be bad for all of us."

"I wouldn't worry about that." Rhian glanced over at her cousin. "Right, Talwyn?"

"I take orders from you now?"

Rhian spun around, but Talan again quickly stepped between them. Something told Celyn his cousin would be doing that a lot from now on.

"Just do it," Talan told his sister.

"Fine."

Talwyn walked within a few inches of the gaping hole that had once been a nice piece of land and spread her arms toward the trees on either side. She began chanting, and the cold Steppes winds died abruptly, then rose again to swirl around her.

Celyn watched in fascination as the trees first grew tall and strong, then the limbs began to lengthen and spread out until they met in front of Talwyn. Branches twisted and turned together until they'd created a rather frightening-looking shield.

"Done," Talwyn said as she walked toward them, appearing completely unfazed by the magicks she'd just wielded. "Let's go."

Celyn lowered himself to the ground and motioned to Talan. "Put Elina on my back."

"I've got her," the Kyvich said, carefully picking Elina up in her arms, and then climbing onto the top of the boulder. She stepped onto Celyn's back, placed Elina down, and crouched beside her.

"I need a cloth," she ordered her Kyvich sister.

Once a cloth was handed over, the Kyvich said to Celyn, "All right. Go."

He assumed she was trying to staunch the flow of blood, and he would be eternally grateful for that.

Rhian led the way, heading toward a crop of nearby caves. As they walked, they were silent until Rhian abruptly stopped right outside a cave entrance and snapped at Talwyn, *"Must you be so bloody negative?"*

"It was just a damn question. Stop barking at me!"

"No. That was not a question. You're just being negative! And I don't appreciate it."

"So I can't say anything? Is that it? I shouldn't question anything? I should just let this unfold? Is that what you're saying? Because I'm pretty sure I don't like that! At all!"

"*That is enough!*" Celyn bellowed, beyond fed up with these two. "I can feel Elina's lifeblood against my scales while you two petty bitches bicker like you're still twelve years old. *You're not!*"

Talwyn threw up her hands, seemingly done with it all while Rhian had the grace to at least appear contrite.

"I'm sorry, Celyn. Really. Let's get her inside."

Yet as the group went into the cave and moved through the caverns, their way lit by torches embedded in the walls, Celyn's young cousins didn't seem that sorry about anything, what with Talwyn putting her brother in a headlock and Rhian vowing never to speak to either of them again. Because she was sick of them. Sick, sick, sick of them!

But Celyn could hardly enjoy his cousins' bickering, as he liked to do, with Elina possibly dying. He wanted to ask the Kyvich tending her a thousand questions, but he'd rather she focus on keeping Elina alive instead of trying to calm him down.

Still, as worried as Celyn was, he slowed to a stop when he heard a strange sound coming from deep in the cavern. A *tap-scrape* sound moving closer and closer down the passage.

They all stopped. Kachka immediately raised her bow. Talan and Magnus pulled axes out from under their robes. Talwyn and the other Kyvich pulled their swords. Celyn stepped back and readied his flame while lifting his wings to protect Elina and the third Kyvich on his back.

Only Rhian seemed unconcerned. She did stop, but she didn't prepare herself for battle. She simply waited . . . with a smile.

After several long minutes, while Elina lay motionless against his back, a shadow moved through the passageway toward them. As it came near, Celyn could make out a dark grey cape, the hood pulled over the head, the rough wool material wrapped around the body. He could also see the snout peeking out. Could see the front left claw wrapped tight around the walking staff and the back right claw dragging slowly behind.

But just as the caped being moved in front of them all, a voice from behind Celyn barked, "Took your time bringing them here, didn't ya?"

Celyn looked behind him to see a painfully old She-dragon standing there. This one also had a worn, rough wool cape draped around her body and held onto a walking staff with her left claw. Yet when Celyn looked back to where he'd seen the other dragon . . . well, that dragon was gone.

He also quickly noticed that Talan and Talwyn's friends had instantly moved into combat formation without prompting or confusion. Good. Celyn liked that.

Yet while everyone was tense and ready to fight, Rhian walked past them and up to the old She-dragon.

"There was a bit of a battle, but we're all here now."

The old She-dragon looked right past Celyn—although he was three or four times bigger than her—and focused on Talan and Talwyn.

"You two . . . come here."

The twins looked at each other but didn't move.

"Now," Rhian pushed.

With their weapons still drawn, the twins walked around Celyn until they stood in front of the She-dragon.

With the tip of her right talon, she first lifted Talan's face by the chin. "You're a pretty one, ain't'cha?"

"Yes," Talan said. "I am."

"Can you fight?"

"Well enough."

"And raising the dead. That ain't easy."

"It's easy enough for me."

"That's what worries me, boy. It worries me a lot."

She moved to Talwyn, but when she tried to touch her with her talon, Celyn's cousin batted it out of the way with her sword and snarled, "Keep your fucking claws off me."

Rhian quickly stepped in front of her cousin. "Talwyn doesn't like to be touched."

"She's like her mother." The She-dragon leaned her neck down a bit so she could look Talwyn in the eyes. "But unlike her, knives thrown at *my* head will be returned in kind."

"I look forward to the challenge," Talwyn shot back, which got her a punch to the chest from Rhian.

While Talwyn pushed her cousin, the She-dragon finally focused on Celyn.

"You weren't supposed to be here. Bit of a surprise. But I recognize who you come from. You have your mother's eyes, but your father's temperament. Must be more his people than ours."

Celyn studied the old She-dragon, but it wasn't easy. She was a bit hard to look at. There were a lot of scars from gouges that had cut deep, right through the scales on her face, neck, and snout. Plus one eye was crystal blue, while the other was a milky white and grey. Her hair was bright white, reaching down her body and pooling in a ridiculous pile at her clawed feet. There was nothing remotely familiar about her, yet she seemed to know who he was. Or, at the very least, who his parents were.

Rhian, after pushing her cousin again, stepped over and said, "Celyn, this is our aunt."

Celyn thought of all his mother's kin; the Cadwaladrs were a preposterously large clan of dragons. And although Celyn had met all of them at least once in his lifetime, there

were so many, he wouldn't be surprised to have forgotten
one or two . . . or a thousand. Still . . . he did know his immediate family. All his mother's siblings he knew as well as
he knew his parents. So he was sure this female was no aunt
of his.

"I know all my mother's sisters."

"No, no." Rhian smiled. "She's more our great-great,
possibly *great*-aunt."

"What?"

"She's Brigida the Foul. I'm sure you've heard of her.
Grandmum loves telling stories about her."

Celyn glared down at Talan. "Did you do this?"

"Do what?"

"Bring Brigida the Foul back from the dead?"

"It wasn't me. I haven't worked up to humans yet, much
less dragons."

"The Cadwaladrs may want to believe I was dead," the
old witch said, her voice like metal over the roughest stone,
"but that hasn't happened yet."

"But that's not possible," Celyn argued, even as he
knew the truth of what she was saying. "You should be
dead."

"I should be lots of things, boy. But I ain't." The She-
dragon eyed Elina and the Kyvich on his back. "What do we
have here?"

"It's my friend. She's dying."

The old witch snorted at that. "She ain't dyin'." She
leaned over to get a better look. "Her face got cut up pretty
bad. But, as you can see," she noted, gesturing to her own,
"nothing a body can't survive."

She moved around Celyn. "Come on then, lad. Let's see
what we can do for your human. And best part . . . if she
don't make it, we'll have something to snack on."

Then she cackled at her own joke while Talan quickly

caught hold of Kachka before she could unleash several arrows to the back of Brigida's head.

"Leave it," Talan gently warned. "I think she's just joking. Plus, she can kill you simply by looking in your direction."

Sadly and from the stories Celyn had heard over the years from his kin . . . all that was very true.

Chapter Twenty-Seven

Kachka watched as the strange-looking She-dragon shifted to a horrifying-looking human. She was called Brigida the Foul, and although Kachka could tell that Celyn did not know her personally, she sensed that he'd heard of her. And what he'd heard had not been good.

They both wanted to follow the old witch and the Kyvich Gisa into the alcove where they took Elina, but the She-dragon wouldn't hear of it. And when Celyn tried to insist, the old She-dragon simply chanted a few words and drew a rune in the air with her old, crippled hand, and a rock wall appeared where there had been none.

A solid, immovable rock wall. Kachka was sure that even using this dragon's hard head—something she was sorely tempted to do—would not get them through to the other side.

Keeping tight control of her anger and her fear for her

sister's safety, Kachka said, "May I speak to you, dragon? In private."

Kachka walked away, glancing back when one of the humans called out Celyn's name and tossed him some clothes. When she found an alcove with a long bench, she walked in. Books lined the walls, carefully placed on wood shelves, and scrolls were piled in the corners.

She walked to the books and stared at them, giving herself a moment to calm down. But she knew after a minute or two, nothing would calm her down. She was torn between being angry at Glebovicha for what she'd done to Elina and being angry at the world for what it had done to Elina.

Unfortunately, all that was available for Kachka to take her anger out on was the dragon. So she faced him, ready to unleash that rage . . . but she couldn't.

Not once she saw that he'd already shifted to human, put on his chain-mail shirt, leggings, and leather boots, and sat down on the bench. His elbows rested on his knees, his head buried in both hands.

Kachka understood in that moment that the dragon was as worried about Elina as she was. Perhaps even a little more.

Did her sister have any idea how much this dragon cared for her? Probably not. Elina had listened to Glebovicha far too much, believed herself not worthy . . . of anything. Kachka already knew her sister would blame herself for what had happened today. That was her way. To take the weight of the world on her shoulders.

Foolish female!

Kachka placed her bow and quiver on the ground and sat down beside the dragon on the bench. It was strange to know that his true form was a large thing covered in scales. Especially when his human form was so damn pretty.

"Are you all right?" she asked.

"How could I not have known?" he demanded of himself, making her think he'd been having this conversation in his head the entire time. "How could I not have seen this was too dangerous for her?"

"How would you know that? Elina would tell you nothing about Glebovicha. Not without you asking."

"That's just it." He dropped his hands and lifted his head. "I asked her questions. Constantly. Until I thought her bloody head would explode. But my father would say I didn't ask her the *right* questions. I never should have let her see Glebovicha alone. I should have stopped her."

"Stopped her? How? How would any male stop a woman, any woman, from seeing her mother?"

The dragon's human body froze, his gaze locked across the alcove, staring blankly at nothing. And that's when she understood fully what had happened here.

"She never told you that Glebovicha is her mother. *Our* mother. Did she?"

Celyn shook his head. "That's not possible. A mother . . . a mother would never do that to her child. Never."

"Life on the Steppes is hard. It is not for everyone."

"She wanted her dead," he reasoned. "That's why she sent Elina to Queen Rhiannon. Because she wanted her dead."

"A mother cannot just kill her child. Not anymore. There was a time when weak babies or children were left to die while the tribes moved on, but that was stopped. Now, if you have weak child, you must deal with it. Most do. Glebovicha did not want to."

"Elina's not weak. She's amazingly strong."

"Strong of mind. Strong of spirit. Strong of intellect. But when it comes right down to it . . . she hates to kill unless for food or in defense. Glebovicha saw that as weakness not to be overcome. Or overlooked."

"So then she just kills her?"

"As I said, a Steppes mother cannot just kill her child."

"Then what happened?"

"Glebovicha was not going to let her see the Anne Atli, but my sister had made commitment to that Annwyl the Bloody. She was determined to see it through. And that is exactly what she told Glebovicha. But Glebovicha, she runs our tribe."

"Which means Elina was going against a direct order from her leader."

"Exactly. You Southlanders, you beat those who disobey orders. Maybe put them in your dungeons. We are Daughters of the Steppes. We have no dungeons. And beatings are reserved for when horses and livestock are not protected during battle or stealing gold from raids for yourself. But disobeying orders . . . how that is dealt with is up to tribe leaders."

The dragon took in a quick breath and suddenly asked, "You can't go back . . . can you, Kachka? Back to your people?"

Kachka shook her head. "No. Neither of us can."

The dragon rubbed his hands against his face, like he was desperately trying to rub off dirt.

"Kachka, I'm so sorry."

"Horses of Ramsfor," she laughed, "you sound like Elina. What do you apologize for? You did not swing the knife. You did not cut her throat. You could have flown away, left us both to die. You did not do those things. You stayed and fought. You saved my sister. Do you think I can ever repay you for that? You saved all I have left. So stop crying like child—"

"Well, I'm not actually cry—"

"—because my sister will need strong male now by her side. Even if it is unholy scaled monster from netherworld."

"Actually, dragons aren't—"

"You talk much. Is that normal? How did she put up with you for such a long trip?"

"I actually haven't said that—"

"Och!" Kachka said, swiping her hand near his face. "Talk, talk, talk, that is all you do. Shut up!"

The dragon stared at her, his mouth slightly open. But at least he was quiet.

"Celyn?" They both looked to the alcove opening. One of the Kyvich witches stood there. "The wall's down. In case you want to see your barbarian female."

Celyn stood and rushed out of the alcove. Kachka followed, but stopped by the witch and warned, "Watch who you call barbarian, Kyvich."

The witch leaned in and said, "I'm not Kyvich, Rider." She smiled and it was a frightening thing to be forced to look at. "I'm much worse."

Then she turned and walked off.

The brown witch in the wool dress and fur cape rushed by, her arms filled with herbs and clean bandages. She shook her head at Kachka. "My cousin is actually not that bad. She's just misunderstood."

But Kachka was sure she hadn't misunderstood a damn thing.

Celyn walked into the alcove where they had placed Elina. The Kyvich brushed past him on her way out, but Brigida was still washing her hands.

The alcove had been outfitted with human furniture, including a bed, table, chairs, and a small desk. Not surprising. Most dragons had space for human company. Sometimes they had friends, sometimes they had lovers, and humans didn't seem to enjoy lying on top of piles of riches the way dragons did.

Elina was on the bed, her shirt removed so that they could get to the wounds on her face and neck. She was covered in bandages now and was—thankfully—breathing normally. But she was still unconscious, and that worried him.

He lifted the bandage that covered the left side of her neck and face where she'd been slashed. The scars were already fading, but he froze when he saw Elina's left eye. It had been sewn shut.

Celyn knew from what he'd heard about Brigida the Foul that she was a Dragonwitch with much power. Something he could easily believe . . . what with her still being alive and all. So healing Elina's damaged eye should be no problem for someone of Brigida's experience and skill.

"Why did you sew up her eye?" he demanded.

"You don't want dirt gettin' in there, do ya?" Brigida asked calmly as she shook out her wet human hands before grabbing a cloth to dry them. "That's how you get infection. That's hard to fix."

"But how long before she can see out of that eye again?"

Brigida faced him and simply asked, "What eye?"

"Her left eye. Oh, gods." Celyn leaned away from her. "You didn't take her eye, did you? To use for some . . . ritual?"

She let out a harsh, abrasive sound that grated on Celyn's exhausted nerves, even though he knew deep down that was her laugh. "Don't need no worthless human's eyes, *boy*, to bring me power. I make me own power." She walked to the bed, looking down at Elina. "But she ain't had no eye when you brought her here. If ya want me to guess . . . it's probably around the neck of the one who done this to her. Like a trophy."

Horrified, Celyn stared down at Elina. How could he tell her this when she woke up? How could he tell her what had happened to her?

"But you're powerful. Can't you do . . . something?"

"If the eye was still there, yeah. I could probably fix it. At least make it look like mine. But ain't no eye there to fix, is there?" She patted his arm. "But look. I helped with the scars she was gonna have, didn't I? She had slashes from her neck to over her right eye. Skin hanging off and all. But

I fixed that up real nice. You probably won't even be able to tell . . . much . . . after a while."

"I don't care about her scars."

"Well, humans do. They get real upset about that sort of thing."

"But her eye . . ."

"What do you want me to say? Can't create it out of air, can I?"

"But what do I tell her?"

"What do you tell her? How about she's lucky to be alive?"

Celyn faced his kin—although he really thought of her as his ancestor—and said, "Her mother did this. Her mother. How does a mother do that to her offspring?"

Brigida, unmoved, shrugged. "Don't know. Me mother was known for being pure evil . . . but she liked me. We got along real well. But this girl . . . her mother aimed for the arteries. I think she only missed because your human moved. Tell me this, did the attack stop after this cut or did you have to step in?"

"I stepped in. So did her sister."

"Then what you tell this girl is that she's lucky to be alive."

Assuming he had no choice in the matter, Celyn sat down on the edge of the bed.

Brigida stared at him for a bit before asking, "How old are you?"

"One hundred and fifty-eight."

She snorted. "Then you're too old for this."

"Too old for what?"

She waved at him, her face contorting as if she were searching for the right word. "For all this . . . concern." And she said that last word with utter disgust.

Celyn rolled his eyes. "Really?"

"It's a weakness."

"It is not a we—"

"And your mother's fault."

"How is my mother to bl—"

"Like all the females of me line, they baby their boys. Make them weak. Make them think that the world is filled with sweets and roses."

"Ghleanna the Decimator did *not* baby me. She babied none of her hatchlings."

"Hard on her females, I bet she was. But cuddling and showing affection to her males."

"That's not true. My mother was hard on us all and loving to us all. In equal measure. And I'd ask you not to speak ill of my mother."

"Fine. Your father's fault then."

"What's wrong with my father?"

"Nothing, actually. He's not much with strength, but he's smart. We need more of that in our line. Too many of the Cadwaladr males are big and dumb . . . like oxen."

"That's me and my kin you're speaking of."

"No. You take after your father a bit, I think."

"My poor father wishes. But none of us are like our da."

"You are, more than you realize. I remember him, you know, as a whelp. He couldn't stop staring at your mum, but like most Cadwaladr females, it took her forever to realize it."

Elina stirred beside him, grimacing in her sleep, her fingers reaching for her wounded face.

Celyn took her hand in his and gently held it. With his other hand, he pushed her hair off her face.

The move seemed to calm her and she settled back into deep sleep.

When Celyn suddenly remembered he wasn't alone in the room with Elina, he looked up to find the old witch watching him. And gods, she was so very old, but she still had her mind. Something told Celyn that would be the last of her to go.

"It's not your fault, boy," she abruptly told him, with something akin to kindness in her voice.

"I was supposed to protect her."

"She's alive, ain't she? If it hadn't been for you, I can promise you . . . she wouldn't be."

"Aye, but—"

"Her mother wanted her dead. Long before your little Rider even knew your name."

He knew the witch was right, but still . . .

Brigida shook her head. "Aye. Your father's child, you are. All thoughtful and caring, feeling everything deep." She let out a sound of disgust and turned away from him.

"It's not considered a flaw among our clan to be thoughtful and caring," Celyn argued. "As long as you're good with a sword or hammer, you're bloody golden among the Cadwaladrs."

"So you're telling me my entire line's gone weak?" She made her slow way across the alcove. "You know who's fault that is, don't'cha?"

"Don't say my father again."

"No. It started long before him." She turned and, tightly gripping the arms, slowly placed her human body into a high-back wood chair. "Your grandfather. It was his love of the humans that brought this curse down on all our heads. I'd give up all hope if it weren't for that lot out there."

The old She-dragon grinned, and it would have been the most disturbing thing he'd seen in his life if he hadn't recently witnessed a mother cut out the eye of her own child. "Now that there, boy . . . that's power. The three apart are to be reckoned with, but together . . ." Her grin grew, and Celyn suddenly understood where the lizard comparison came from.

With Elina resting near him and knowing they were safe

from the Riders, at least for the moment, Celyn let his natural curiosity take over.

"What are you doing here, Brigida?"

"Doing here?"

"In the Outerplains? Why aren't you in the Southlands? Why aren't you part of Rhiannon's court?"

"Rhiannon's court," she scoffed. "I remember her, too, when she was no more than a hatchling, hanging onto her daddy's tail. Now that," the old witch said, "was a mother and daughter who had true hate for each other."

"Rhiannon doesn't hate Keita. Her daughter just irritates her."

"No. No. Rhiannon and *her* mother. Adienna. Now that Adienna I liked."

"Because you could easily control someone so insipid and worthless?"

"Aye," she replied eagerly, startling Celyn. "That's exactly why! That Rhiannon is a useless girl, too. But we do have something in common."

"You're both White Dragonwitches that terrorize all those around you?"

"You'd think so, but no." She gestured outside the alcove. "It's them three. So much power and they don't even know it yet."

"They know it." Celyn sighed, his fingers stroking Elina's arm. He'd like to think he was doing it for her benefit, but it was really more for his. "And don't pretend for a second they don't."

That disturbing milky eye in Brigida's head that seemed to have a life of its own locked on him.

"You close to them?" she asked.

"Not particularly. We're cousins, Cadwaladrs, and I'd protect them with me life. But if you're asking if I know all their secrets, I don't even know a one."

"Too bad." She tried to push herself up, but stopped after a second or two. "Over here, boy. Give me a hand."

Celyn did as ordered and went to his ancestor. He gripped her arms and helped her to her feet. Once she was standing, he forced himself to be brave and look down into that horrifying face. "What do you want from them, Brigida? What do you want from Rhian and the twins?"

"What do you think, boy?" She patted his chest and began to move slowly around him. "Everything."

She held out her hand. "Give me my staff."

Celyn saw it resting against the wall and retrieved it. But just touching the damn thing made his skin crawl as nothing ever had before. He couldn't hand it over to the witch fast enough.

She leaned heavily on it and began walking again. "Unfortunately," she went on, "it looks like they're Cadwaladr stubborn. So I'll need to find a different way in, won't I?"

She abruptly stopped and looked back at Celyn. "What can you tell me about their mothers?"

Chapter Twenty-Eight

Elina had no idea if it was day or night when she awoke. Nor did she know where she was. The light from a nearby pit fire and torches on the wall lit the room so that she could see. But her head, face, and neck pained her beyond anything she could remember. She tried to go back to sleep, but her body wouldn't allow it.

She thought maybe some water would help, so she slowly—very slowly—sat up. Even that, though, had her feeling dizzy and off-balance, though she hadn't even put her feet on the floor yet. She instinctively put her hand to her head, and that's when she felt the bandages.

Everything rushed back to her then. Every horrible thing.

Determined to face this all head-on, Elina put her feet on the floor. With care, she pushed herself to a standing position and waited until she felt confident she wouldn't fall over or throw up . . . or both at the same time.

Silently and still very slowly, she made her way to the standing mirror she spied in the corner of the room. As she walked, she glanced around at the walls and ceiling. It reminded her of the Dragon Queen's home, making her think she was in another cave. Although this one had a bed and table and chairs and a standing mirror sized for a human.

She stopped walking. *Do dragons have mirrors sized for them? How big would that be? Does anyone make mirrors that big?*

Realizing she was thinking what Glebovicha always called her "stupid thoughts," Elina continued walking. She was near the mirror, but she must have been off a bit, because she ended up walking into the nearby table. She stared down at it, wondering how it had moved.

Elina sidled over a few feet and continued on. After a few seconds, she reached the mirror but ended up walking into it. Now annoyed, she took a step back, then another, before lifting her head. A large bandage covered the entire left side of her face and the right part of her head, which explained why she kept walking into things.

Determined to see the damage, Elina untied the material

holding the bandage in place. That removed, the bandage fell away and Elina just . . . stared.

The skin had healed. Quite well, in fact. Better than she could have hoped.

But her eye . . .

She brought the fingers of her left hand up and felt the eyelid that had been sewn shut. There was nothing behind it. Nothing behind the skin.

"Elina?"

She looked over at Celyn, who'd been sleeping in a chair beside the bed, but was now wide-awake.

"Hello, dragon." She turned back around, continued to stare at her face in the mirror. "I warned you, did I not? Glebovicha hates me."

"Elina, I'm so sorry."

She waved off his words. "There is nothing to be sorry about. At least now I know where I stand among my people. Where I will always stand. Because no one except Kachka stood up for me. No one."

He moved behind her, gently placing his large hands on her shoulders. "I can't believe your mother did this to you."

Elina let out a deep, long sigh. "Well . . . it could be worse."

Confused, Celyn studied Elina in the mirror. "It could be worse?"

"She could have taken both eyes. At least she only had time to take one. Thank you for that. For your help."

She stepped away from him, replacing the bandage over her damaged eye and tying the material around it that held it in place.

He shook his head. "You don't want—"

"Food?" she asked. "I am a bit hungry."

"*No.* You don't want revenge? Are you at least angry? Sad? Devastated?"

Elina faced him. "Over what?"

"Elina, she took your *eye.*"

"I am aware. It was *my* eye she took."

"But you're . . . you're . . ."

"I am what?"

"Not angry. How can you not be angry?"

"What would anger bring? It will not give me back my eye." Her words were simple, her voice calm but sad. Yet that was all. How could that be all?

"It will not make my mother care that she took it," Elina flatly went on. "To be quite honest with you, I am glad to breathe. I am glad to wake up in bed and find you beside it. Because I knew if you were at my side, I was safe."

Kachka's voice cut in. "Sister?"

Elina turned from him. "Kachka, I am—"

"Do not."

"Do not what?"

"Do not say what you are about to say. What we both know you are about to say. I have no regrets. And neither should you."

Elina took in a large breath and let it out. She nodded.

"Good. Now . . . there is food. Cooked food. Would you like some?"

"I would. I am very hungry."

Celyn, unable to take this anymore, said, "Elina, wait."

"Yes?"

"Is that it?"

"I do not understand."

"How are you not . . . angry or sad or . . . or *something*?"

The sisters looked at each other, then back at Celyn.

"I am sad," Elina said.

"You are?"

"Of course. I had two eyes. Now I have one. If something

happens to that one, then I will be blind. I will need horse to lead me anywhere I need to go. But not your big Southland horses since I am not plow."

The sisters chuckled and again started to walk away.

But Celyn, who had never really been able to let things alone, tried once more. "Elina—"

"We are done with this conversation, Celyn."

"Yes, but—"

Celyn's words were brutally cut off when a chair slammed into the wall a few feet away from him.

"Were you aiming at his head?" Kachka asked Elina.

"I was." She let out a breath. "Guess my life as an archer is over as well. I will need to grub in dirt for berries in order to survive. Like weakest of animals."

"When you are ready, we head back to the Southlands. The decadent fools will give you food that you never worked for on plates of gold while the masses starve. So you have nothing to fear. Now, come. Let us eat."

"You're shirtless," Celyn pointed out.

"I doubt these people will care but here." Kachka went to a chair that hadn't been destroyed and grabbed a blue cotton shirt that someone had put out for Elina earlier.

Kachka helped Elina put the shirt on. "There. You already look like a Southlander."

"If you try to hurt me with words, sister, you do good job."

"Do not be so sensitive, sister. It is not like *I* ripped eye from head."

Celyn listened to their laughter echo against the cave walls as they left the room.

He glanced over at the chair Elina had smashed against the wall. "Well, if anything, she's definitely angry at *me*."

Elina sat down at a big wood table and Kachka pulled out a chair beside her.

In their own language, Kachka said, "You shouldn't be so hard on that dragon."

"I don't know what you mean."

"You threw a chair at his head."

"You mean I *tried* to throw a chair at his head."

"Do not whine, sister. In time, you will adapt to the loss of your eye."

"Of course, I will."

"There it is," Kachka accused.

"There is what? I was agreeing with you."

"No. You were feeling sorry for yourself."

"Am I not allowed? It was *my* eye the bitch took! My own mother tried to kill me!"

"What do you think sending you into the Southlands to kill the Dragon Queen was, you idiot? She was trying to kill you then, too! I thought you would run!"

"Well, I didn't run!"

"And now you're missing an eye!"

"Oy!" They both looked up to see a monk standing on the other side of the table. "Here." He dropped plates heavy with food in front of them. "Perhaps," he said, "you two can take time out from yelling at each other to eat."

"I am no longer hungry," Elina said. And now she heard it. She did sound sorry for herself, because that's how she was feeling. But wasn't that her right? At least for a little while?

Kachka dragged her plate in front of her and picked up a knife to cut pieces of meat while she yelled at Elina.

"Oh, poor you," she said. "You lost an eye. How you suffer so."

"Wow," the monk said, wide eyes gazing at Kachka. "Just . . . wow."

"Do not coddle her, priest!" Kachka snapped. "I am trying to help her!"

"There has to be a better way."

"Do not get superior tone with me. I saw you raise dead, wicked priest."

"I'm not a priest and, if I were to be honest, I'm no monk either. And so what if I raise the dead? It's a skill. Like being a stonemason or blacksmith."

"Is she dead?" Kachka asked him, gesturing at the tall Kyvich walking up behind him. "Is she your puppet, necromancer?"

"No. She's just my sister."

The Kyvich now stood beside him, placing freshly baked loaves of bread on the table. He bent down a bit and placed his face against hers. "Do we not look alike?" he asked.

"You look nothing alike," Kachka replied, her mouth full of food.

"Why am I involved in this conversation?" the Kyvich asked. "Because I don't want to be." She slapped at her brother. "Get off me!"

No. They might not look alike, but they were clearly siblings.

"All I'm saying, sister," Kachka went on, "is that you do not want to end up weak and useless like these Southlanders. Even with your missing eye, you are still worth a hundred of these two-eyed Southlanders."

The Kyvich glowered at Kachka, her arms folded over her chest. "You do know," she asked, "that we helped save this one's life and we're now feeding you both?"

Kachka nodded and reached for the bread. "I do. Thanks for that, imperialist scum."

The Kyvich began to say something, but her brother yanked her back by the scruff of her neck.

"Leave it, Talwyn."

Elina pushed her chair back.

"Where are you going?" Kachka demanded. "You need to eat."

"I will. Later. I need to go outside for a bit."

Elina walked around the table, but she rammed her thigh into it, completely misjudging the distance.

"Damn the horse gods!"

"Don't blame them," her sister chastised.

"You are right. I should blame myself."

Kachka slammed her knife down. "No, you idiot!" she yelled after her. "I meant blame our mother!"

Celyn was still sitting on the bed when he saw the twins walk by.

"Oy," he called out. "You two. Come here."

The pair stopped, looked at each other.

"Stop pissing about and get in here," he snapped.

The twins walked into the alcove. Talan slid onto the small table, the wood creaking ominously from his weight. Those monk robes hid his cousin's true physical strength, but Celyn wasn't fooled.

Talwyn stood by her brother, arms folded over her chest, legs braced apart, her expression typically sour. As if she found the entire world wanting. But she did have her mother's glare.

"Why are you here?" Celyn asked them outright.

"It was time for our return," Talan replied, his fingers drumming against the table. It was as if his natural energy were barely harnessed by his big body.

Celyn glanced down, and Talwyn demanded, "What's so funny?"

With a shrug, Celyn dramatically lowered his voice, and said, "It was time for our return . . . for we are the chosen ones!" Then he laughed outright. "I adore your coming-of-doom tone."

Talan grinned while his sister simply continued to glower.

"Look," Celyn explained, "I have no in-depth under-standing of magicks. I don't follow premonitions. Nor do I care that the entire *world* insists on calling you and your cousin the Abominations. But what I do care about is that you've seemed to create some unholy bond with a She-dragon who should have been dead centuries ago."

The twins glanced at each other, and Celyn rolled his eyes. "Please stop having your own little conversations in your heads while I'm sitting right here."

"We weren't—"

"It's rude, Talan! And you both know it!"

Talwyn raised her hands. "Calm down. No need to get hysterical."

"I don't get hysterical. I'm a Cadwaladr. But I do have my mother's temper when pushed." He lowered his head a bit. "My *mother's* temper."

"She called to us," Talan explained. "Brigida the Foul called to us and said it was time."

"How long have you lot been in contact with her?"

Again, the twins glanced at each other, then back at Celyn. Together they said, "Since birth."

Celyn closed his eyes and fell back against the bed, his arms outstretched.

"Oh . . . fuck."

Elina found her way through a tight crevice that led to a little gods-made balcony on the side of the mountain. As soon as she stepped outside and took in some fresh air, she began to feel a little better.

Then, suddenly, she didn't.

She hurt all over, but the entire left side of her head from where her eye used to be to the back of her skull ached in such a way that she felt nauseous.

But that wasn't what truly bothered her. It was that she'd failed Queen Annwyl and Queen Rhiannon. She'd truly hoped to get *something* right. For once.

Elina felt depression and disappointment weigh down upon her. She'd tried so hard and now here she was . . . standing here . . . feeling worthless and . . . and . . .

Where is that noise coming from?

Elina heard sniffling. It wasn't her. She walked along the

little ridge until she found a brown-skinned female sitting on a boulder in a simple wool sheath dress, a long fur cloak around her shaking shoulders, and tears flowing freely down her beautiful face.

"What is wrong with you?" Elina asked. "Are you hurt?"

The female jumped, surprised to hear another voice.

"Oh. Elina." She sniffed. "It is Elina, yes?"

Elina nodded. "I am Elina."

"I'm glad to see you up and about." She sniffed again. "I am Rhianwen, Daughter of Talaith and Briec the Mighty, Sister of General Iseabail, Princess of the House of Gwalch-mai fab Gwyar, Ninth in Line for—"

"Stop, stop," Elina cut in before this could go on another century or two. Those of the Steppes might live longer than most, but she wouldn't live *that* long. "I need hear no more of your imperialist lineage."

Without any rancor, the girl nodded. "Understood. Did Auntie Brigida take good care of you?"

"I still live. I would count that as taking good care." Elina tried to scratch her face, but found nothing but bandage. She lowered her hand. "Why do you cry so?"

"I just feel . . . horrible."

"You hurt?"

"No. It's nothing like that."

"Then what?"

"It's just . . . what I did to your people . . ."

"What did you do to my people?"

Rhianwen looked up at Elina with strange but beautiful-colored eyes that contrasted strikingly with her silver hair and brown skin. Even the tears that still poured could not detract from the intensity of those eyes.

"Oh, yes," Rhianwen said. "You were unconscious when I arrived." She swallowed and admitted, "I was forced to . . . to . . . kill your kinsmen. The ones who had tracked you and your sister here."

"You? *You* killed them?"

"Yes."

"Well," Elina asked, "what choice did you have?"

Rhianwen blinked in surprise. "Pardon?"

"What choice? If they tracked us here, it was only to kill me and Kachka and turn Celyn into an entertaining pet they could toss our enemies to when they were bored. It was either them or us."

"I know. I know. It's just . . . I wish we could have talked it out instead. I wish I'd had time to reason with—"

"Reason? With *my* people? Do you think I would be standing here, Princess of the Fancy House of Dragons, missing my eye and feeling lost and pathetic, if you had not stopped them?"

Rhianwen frowned. "I can't tell if that's praise or an admonishment."

"It is neither, foolish girl. It is just truth. Because of you, I still have my life. I still have my sister."

The princess sniffed again, fresh tears pouring from her *two* eyes. But she smiled gratefully. "Thank you," she said around this new influx of wetness. "It means so much to me that you would say that."

Elina looked off, out over the lands she could no longer call her home. And she realized quite suddenly that her sister was right.

She needed to stop feeling sorry for herself before she started sounding like this pathetic slip of a girl!

"Don't worry. She's not trying to destroy us or any-thing . . . although she may be trying to destroy everyone else."

Celyn gazed up at the ceiling and nodded. "That's so helpful, Talan. Thank you."

He abruptly sat up, his mind going through all the infor-mation he'd heard over the years about the twins and Rhian, about them going off to join monks and covens and what-ever else for knowledge.

"What did you do to leave?" Celyn asked them.

"What do you mean?" Talan asked.

"You know exactly what I mean. Did the Kyvich and those monks just send you both off with a hearty farewell and tankards of ale raised in your honor? Or are they currently planning their counterattack?"

"I wouldn't call it a counterattack. . . ."

"Gods-dammit!"

"I don't think you understand," Talwyn said, that royal haughtiness she tried to hide coming right to the fore. "My brother and I don't report to you, cousin. What we did or what we plan to do has nothing to do with you."

Celyn slowly stood and walked over to his cousin, staring down into her face. She tried to hide it under all that hair—the same way her mother did—but she was quite beautiful.

"Perhaps," he reminded her, "you forget that you are a Cadwaladr. First. Last. And always. The protection of our Clan is and always will be the most important thing. We protect our queen. We protect our people. But we always, and I mean *always,* protect our kin. Now, I don't know what your worthless, royal father may have taught you. But I do know that your human and most likely insane mother did teach you that. And I know you didn't forget it."

Talwyn's eyes narrowed dangerously, but before this could escalate, Talan stepped in front of her, blocking her and Celyn from each other's sight.

"Now," Talan said calmly, stepping back and forcing his sister to do the same, so that there was space between them and Celyn, "we did make an . . . unauthorized departure from our companions of the last few years."

"And you brought company."

"We did. I brought Magnus, and Talwyn brought Gisa and Fia, but we have our reasons for that. And it had to happen. We had never planned to stay with either the Brotherhood or the Kyvich forever. They knew that as well as we did."

"But the leaving still wasn't easy, was it?"

"No. But I doubt the Brotherhood would ever consider coming for me."

"And the Kyvich?" Whom Celyn had always considered much more of a threat than a bunch of wizard-monks.

"I'll tell you—" Talwyn began.

"Shut up," her brother quickly cut in. "We don't know yet."

"That's just great."

"I understand your concern, Celyn, but this is what we had to do."

"This is what you had to do? Not come back to your family but associate yourself with Brigida the Fucking Foul?"

Talwyn marched around her brother. "Maybe I need to make it clear to you, cousin, that—"

Talan caught his sister by her hair—right at the crown, too—and yanked her back, twisting her around while he kept his focus locked on Celyn.

"What my sister means to say—"

"Get off me, you bastard son of a bitch!"

"—is that we will unfortunately have to wait to see the outcome of our dealings with the Kyvich. But have no doubt, cousin, that the three of us will handle it. We will not let our decisions hurt the family."

"It may be too late for that."

"Ow! Talan, get off me!"

"All I can ask is that you trust us."

"And Brigida the Foul?"

"I will tear the skin from your bones if you don't unhand me!"

"Brigida is kin, Celyn. And like you said," Talan went on, ignoring his sister, "she, too, is a Cadwaladr. First. Last. And always. The protection of our Clan is and always will be the most important thing to her."

So this one was sneaky-smart like Gwenvael, throwing Celyn's own words right back in his face. Impressive little bastard.

"Fine," Celyn said, seeing no point in continuing the argument. "But I'll tell you just as your grandfather Bercelak tells me when the queen threatens to twist an Elder into a scale-covered knot . . . *handle* it. Understand?"

"We do."

"Like hells we—*owwww!* Stop it, you bastard!"

Talan gave that smile that promised nothing but trouble. "We'll take care of everything."

"Good."

Talan watched his cousin walk out of the alcove. Damn. Of all the Cadwaladr kin who could have ended up here, why did it have to be Celyn? Even his sister Brannie would have been better. She was amazing in battle, but when it came to politics, she was wonderfully uncaring.

But Celyn was more like his father than he realized. He could see long-term implications that others among their Clan could not. And that made Celyn . . . an annoyance.

A punch to the upper arm had Talan finally releasing his sister. She rubbed her head where he'd held her and snarled, "What did you do that for?"

"Because when you get angry, not only do you threaten, you bloody talk too much."

"I do not!"

"Talwyn . . ."

"Oh, all right."

"Just . . . calm down. He's got other things to focus on."

"Like what?"

Gods, his sister could be oblivious . . . to everything. Or at least anything that didn't have to do with battle and what they ultimately had to do.

"Like the little Steppes girl with the missing eye. Remember her?"

Talwyn waved her hand dismissively. "Oh, she'll be fine!"

"She lost her eye! At her *mother's* hand!"

"Oh, poor her! She lost her eye. Boo-hoo!" Talwyn blinked. "What's so funny?"

Talan went to his sister, wrapped his arms around her, and hugged her tight while he continued to laugh. "This is what I missed so much. Those monks were no challenge to me. But you, sister, *you* are a challenge."

Using a clean cloth, Dagmar wrapped bread and cheese and placed them into the travel bag. As she organized the bag to her satisfaction, she glanced over at Annwyl the Bloody, who was busy reading a thick book while sitting on her throne, a leg thrown casually over one of the arms, the other tucked up awkwardly next to her thigh.

Dagmar could tell that Annwyl had no other plans for the day but to read and occasionally take breaks to train with her men. Annwyl was an unusual monarch, but Dagmar had been getting better at handling the queen the longer they worked together.

"You wanted to see me, Mum?" Var asked. He'd quietly moved up beside her just as she'd taught him when he was old enough to understand. Which, it turned out, happened to be about day five after his birth.

"Yes. Your aunt Ghleanna is returning to Bram's castle near Bolver Fields—"

"Where the Battle of Fychan took place a few centuries back."

Dagmar stared over at Annwyl until she glanced up from her book. "What are you glaring at me for?" the queen asked. When Dagmar did nothing but continue to stare, Annwyl said, "He asks questions, I answer them. Maybe I told him about a few battles, pointed out a few books he could read for more information . . ."

Dagmar slowly let out air through her nose, a trick she used because it made it sound like she was giving a low, animalistic growl. Quite effective during negotiations and very effective when dealing with Queen Annwyl.

"Anyway," Dagmar went on, "you'll be going with her."

Dagmar pushed her son's travel bag into his arms, and the boy's grey eyes grew wide when he understood what she was saying to him. That he'd be traveling with his great-aunt Ghleanna without his mother going along.

"But," Dagmar quickly cut in, "this is just for tonight. I'm not going to just send you off to live with Bram. We're going to ease into this and—"

Var's arms wrapped around Dagmar's waist, cutting off the rest of her words. She stroked his golden head and kissed the top of it.

"You know I'll miss you, don't you?" she said softly.

"Not going into battle, Mum," her son quickly reminded her. "Just over to Uncle Bram's for a day . . . to read. In quiet."

As if to drive that point home, five of his sisters charged from their room and down the stairs and out the front doors . . . screaming, "Destruction-ho!" all the way. And behind them? Their father. He wasn't screaming, though. He was roaring, teasing his daughters as he loved to do every morning.

Gwenvael stopped by Dagmar and Var. He kissed her, then focused on the way she was hugging her son.

"Everything all right?"

"Everything's fine."

"Good," he said, then charged out the door after his daughters, the screaming amplifying once he caught up with them.

Var rested his chin against his mother's chest and gazed up into her face. "Wonderful, blissful *quiet*."

"I understand. I understand."

"Where's Arlais?" Annwyl asked.

Busy brushing Var's hair off his face, Dagmar asked, "Who?"

"Your eldest *daughter*?"

Dagmar blinked, still confused, then she jerked. "Oh. Yes. She's with Keita."

Var pulled away from her abruptly, gazing at his mother in mute horror. Annwyl slammed her book shut and was staring at her the same way as Var.

Dagmar tossed up her hands. "What? What did I do?"

"You handed off your ridiculously pompous and blood-thirsty child to *Keita*?" Annwyl demanded.

"Keita likes spending time with her. She only has male offspring."

"She's the family poisoner," Annwyl reminded her, and with such a tone, too! So much tone!

Dagmar gave a shrug and admitted, "Arlais will need *some* skills beyond being a royal and beautiful, and the only one who can spend more than five minutes with her and not have an overwhelming desire to smother her with a pillow, is Keita."

Var glanced at the queen and nodded. "Mum is right, Auntie Annwyl. Keita is the only one who can do that."

Chapter Twenty-Nine

Elina sat at the small table in the alcove. She hefted the pitcher of clean water and began to pour into the battered pewter mug.

But she missed the mug and poured onto the wood table.

Snarling a curse in her native tongue, she hauled the pitcher back so she could hurl it at the wall, but Celyn was suddenly there, yanking it from her hands.

"I can pour water for you," he said with a smile while gripping the pitcher as if he were protecting a small child from her wrath.

Elina slammed her hands down on the now-wet table. "I do not need you to pour water for me. I am not invalid." She pushed her chair away and stood. "I can manage fine on my own."

And to prove that, she tried to walk around the table but ended up banging her leg against it. Again.

That's when the table went flying, Elina roaring with rage.

Celyn placed the pitcher on the floor and stepped over to Elina's side. He tugged her over to the bed and forced her to sit.

"I know this is frustrating—"

"You know nothing, Dolt."

"Then I can guess. But taking it out on my should-be-dead aunt's furniture doesn't help anything. Least of all you."

"You should have let Glebovicha finish me."

"Don't be an idiot, Elina."

"So I am stupid?"

"Aye! At this moment, you are! Very fucking stupid!" He took in a breath, let it out, was calm again. "I'm not trying to say this will be an easy transition for you, and I'm sure that you are very hurt right now—"

"Hurt?"

"Aye. Hurt. How could you not be hurt? Glebovicha is your mother."

"I know that. But I am not child. I am not hurt. I am angry that she would go this far. And disappointed in myself for failing yet another task!"

"Maybe you're being too hard on yourself."

"And maybe you should stop being so nice!" she said, using both her hands against his chest to push him.

"Maybe I like being nice to you!" he shot back, pushing her by the shoulders.

"Why?" she demanded, pushing him again. "Out of pity? I do not need your pity!"

"I don't pity you! I . . ."

"You . . . what?"

"I don't know." Celyn pushed her again. *"You're confusing the hell out of me!"*

Celyn didn't know what was happening to him. He was telling Elina the truth. He didn't pity her. At all. But, instead, his heart ached for her. He'd known from the very beginning that no matter how good or bad things might have gone on this excursion into the Outerplains, when he went home, his mother would be there to praise or comfort him. Not attack him. Not come at him with weapons.

Even when his brother Fal continued to disappoint Ghleanna, she still loved him. "Always and forever," she'd told all of them at one time or another. And she'd proved that devotion every day.

And it broke Celyn's dragon heart to know that Elina had never known such love or acceptance from her own gargantuan-sized mother. A woman so big but with the tiniest heart known to gods or dragons.

But that wasn't pity. It was empathy. His father had taught him about that. Taught Celyn and Brannie to have empathy for all living beings, often warning with a laugh, "Your royal cousins will need someone in their lives to have empathy, otherwise this world is lost, my little hatchlings."

So while Elina thought he was just feeling bad for the pathetic human, he was instead understanding how devastated he would be if he ever received that kind of welcome home from his own mother.

But that wasn't all of it. Something else was going on inside him right now. Something he didn't understand or like very much.

Of course he felt protective of Elina. He'd been tasked with that position from the day he'd met her. Yet this was something else. Something stronger and rather unsettling.

Especially when he looked at her and Celyn realized that all he wanted to do was hug her close, stroke her hair, and tell her that everything was going to be all right.

Good gods! What was that? That wasn't how the Cadwaladrs handled problems. They fixed them! Or went back and destroyed everything that had been causing the problem in the first place. What they didn't do was sit around trying to soothe.

But every time Celyn looked into Elina's face and saw that bandage, he immediately felt torn between bitter rage and . . . and . . . something else.

Something else he wasn't about to try to name now. No. He was going to bury whatever that other feeling was. He was going to bury it right now and never let it see the light of day again.

Because whatever that new feeling was . . . he didn't like it. He didn't like it one gods-damn bit.

"Why do you stare at me like that?" Elina asked him, her one eye narrowed in distrust.

"Look at you like what?"

"Like your travel-cow when he sees juicy apple he hopes you will give him for treat."

"I don't know what you're talking about. I . . . I . . ." Celyn jumped to his feet. "I'm going for a walk."

"Fine. Go for walk."

Celyn nodded and turned away from Elina, took several steps . . . but stopped.

He closed his eyes in desperation, trying to get control. But . . . he simply couldn't. He couldn't!

So he turned back around, leaned down so he was eye to eye with Elina, then gently took her face in his hands.

Celyn kissed her. Not rough as they both had seemed to enjoy when they'd been wrestling on their bedrolls at night. But gently. Because that's what he needed right now. To know that she was alive and well and here. Even when she was being mean and angry and taking it all out on him.

When he finally pulled out of their kiss, Elina's hands gripped his wrists, but she hadn't tried to push him away. And she appeared just as confused as he felt.

"I'll be back later," he told her.

She said nothing in return until he'd stepped outside the alcove.

"Be careful," she warned. "There may be some tribe patrols out there looking for us."

"Thanks," Celyn replied, nodding his head at her before he headed outside for a breath of fresh air.

"How could you let my sister ride out alone?" Elina demanded, yet again.

The two Kyvich who'd seen Kachka ride off earlier in the day stared blankly at Elina until Talwyn asked her friends, "Yeah. How could you?"

The pair now focused on the princess and together said, "Shut up."

Ignoring the pain in her head, which had become unrelenting in the last few hours since Celyn had walked out after that confusing kiss and her sister had disappeared, Elina continued to pace around the large dining table.

Celyn finally strode in. "Guess what?" he asked, "I found the horses. They were grazing over in a patch of land not far from here. But I set them up in a nice place in the cave with some hay and a fresh stream of water that flows through the caverns, yet away from those terrifying animals Talwyn and her friends brought with them."

Talwyn shrugged. "We like our terrifying animals."

"I do not care!" Elina snapped. "Where is my sister?"

"I didn't see her," Celyn said. When Elina started to turn away in frustration, Celyn caught her arm. "I'm sure she's fine. Your sister is quite . . . self-sufficient."

But Elina didn't want to hear that at the moment. She wanted to be angry. It helped distract her from the pain in her head.

"I blame you," she said, pointing at the silver-haired brown girl, Rhianwen.

Strange eyes wide, she looked up from the book she had in her lap and asked, "Me? What did I do?"

"If I did not have to listen to you whine about your fears over the unholy powers gifted to you by the gods, I would have seen my sister leave!"

For some reason, that made Talwyn laugh, something her cousin—although they looked *nothing* alike—did not appreciate.

In response to the laughter, Rhianwen grabbed hold of Talwyn's upper arm. She didn't seem to have the strongest grip, but when Talwyn pulled away, the bare skin that had been touched by Rhianwen's hand began to turn grey and green with the decay of death.

Talwyn glared down at the area. It looked like the decay was spreading but soon, Talwyn's body fought back and the area turned healthy once more.

Then Talwyn focused on her cousin and spit out some chant in a language Elina didn't understand. Thick vines burst through the cave floor and grew until they reached Princess Rhianwen's neck and wrapped around her throat. She grabbed at the vines, her breath choked off. The vines dragged her and her chair back until they crashed to the ground.

"That is enough!" Talan barked, abruptly waking from his slumber across the table.

Rhianwen finally managed to grip the vines around her throat and she quickly turned them into decaying dust.

Muttering, Celyn marched around the table and helped his kinswoman up.

"You three are much too old for this," he admonished.

"Three?" Talan demanded. "I wasn't doing anything! I was just bloody sleeping!"

"All you do is sleep! Every time I look at you, you're sleeping!"

"*I'm tired!*"

"I have returned!" Kachka announced as she walked into the alcove. She dragged a large wild boar behind her by a rope and carried a wood box on her shoulder. A wood box Elina immediately recognized.

"Gods," Talan noted to Elina around a large yawn. "Your women are strong."

"Is that what I think it is, sister?" Elina asked Kachka, working hard not to show her sister how relieved she was to see her back.

"It is. I knew we had buried at least one case near these mountains. I just had to find it. And I did!"

She tossed the end of the rope to the monk Magnus. "Here, monk," Kachka ordered him, "cook this. We will feast tonight!"

"What makes you think I know how to cook?" the monk asked.

"Then learn. Quickly. We do not have lifetime to wait."

Kachka placed the large wood box on the table and immediately pried off the top with her dagger.

"You risked leaving this cave for ale?" Celyn asked.

"Ale? Daughters of the Steppes do not drink ale. Ale is for the weak Southlander." She lifted one of the precious bottles of clear liquid made each year with potatoes. "This is much better, comrades."

Kachka removed the sealed cap and the small group moved closer to get a sniff.

"It has no scent," Fia noted.

"It needs nothing like that," Kachka said. "It is an amazing elixir that keeps you warm on cold Steppes nights."

"I'll try it," Talwyn said.

"You will all try," Kachka agreed, grinning. "We will celebrate that none of us is dead. At least not yet."

Brigida made her slow, painful way down the passageway. Her bones ached, whether in her natural form or her human one, but after all these years, she'd gotten used to the pain. Used to always moving at a much slower pace. But her body had ever been the weakest part of her. It was her mind and mystical powers that had always meant the most to her, and those were still sharp as a well-honed sword.

So what was a little pain? Nothing. It was nothing.

As Brigida neared the caverns where she'd put Rhianwen and her cousins, all their friends, and now Ghleanna's boy with his Outerplains females, she could hear . . . singing.

Smirking, she made her way into the cavern, stopping as soon as she saw the two sisters sitting on the dining table, their bodies resting against each other, as they sang a jaunty tune in the language of the Outerplains about death and pain and life on the Steppes.

Because only the Daughters and Sons of the Steppes could happily sing about that.

Each woman held a bottle half-filled with drink, and their voices harmonized beautifully together.

As for the rest, they were passed out amongst a number of empty bottles. Even the two males who'd been trained as monks.

Except for Celyn, who'd learned to drink among the Cadwaladr Clan. He was still awake, but so drunk he couldn't even stand. He just kept nodding to the sound of the singing while his eyes stayed closed and his hand gripped a near-empty bottle.

No, this hadn't been what Brigida had planned. She'd thought the offspring, the Abominations, as many liked to call them, were much more advanced. Much more pointed in their hatred and bloodlust. But, for once, Brigida had been wrong.

The boy seemed more than happy sleeping, drinking, chatting with his thickheaded friend, and sizing up the women who'd accompanied his sister and Celyn. He was, basically, a pleasant fellow.

Brigida didn't need pleasant fellows.

Then there were the two girls.

The pretty brown one either smiled too much or cried too much. She seemed incapable of finding a happy center. And forget hatred. She seemed to have none. Everyone could be redeemed in her foolish eyes.

Then there was Talwyn, the smartest of the three, which meant she didn't trust Brigida worth a damn. There was a lovely simmer of rage there, just waiting to be unleashed on the world, but Brigida couldn't get near her. Talwyn had her rage reined in tight and her smarts kept her from making reckless choices that Brigida could feast on for her own ends.

Who knew such deadly beings would turn out to be so useless to Brigida? Not that she'd given up, but time was slipping away from her. She doubted she had another thousand years or so to do what she needed to do.

But she hadn't given up, Brigida never gave up. She'd learned, ages ago, that there were always other options out there. She just had to be willing to search for them.

"Look, sister," the one called Kachka said when she and her sister stopped singing; her finger pointed at Brigida. "The old hag has returned!"

"Shh," the one-eyed female said loudly. "I think she can hear you!"

"She's old. She cannot hear anything. *Can you, old hag?*" Kachka screamed. "*You cannot hear me!*"

Brigida thought about removing the Rider's mouth,

but what was the point? Brigida was no longer a vicious hatchling, known for tormenting those who even looked at her wrong. She was Brigida the Foul, and she had more important works ahead of her.

Much more important.

But, there was still a small part of that hatchling in Brigida's soul. It would never go away. So she made her long, painful way to the box that held the remaining drink and pulled out four more bottles. She handed two to each female.

"We travel tomorrow," she told them. "So drink hearty, Riders. Drink as much as you want. So you'll be bright and ready to face the day as soon as the crows rise."

The sisters looked at each other and back at Brigida. They each held up their already open bottles. "To friendship between our tribes!" they cheered, then finished off the bottles in several hearty gulps.

As they reached for the others, their drunken grins wide, Brigida turned from them and headed toward her sleeping chamber.

Aye, tomorrow would be interesting. At least for her. For the rest of them?

Nothing but pain.

Chapter Thirty

It was the heaving that woke up Elina first.

A sound she didn't hear often among her tribesmen. She was asleep on the dining table, bottles surrounding her. Horse gods of hell, had she drunk *all* this by herself?

Sitting up, she looked around the alcove. Celyn was asleep in a chair, his head resting on the table. Two of the Kyvich, Fia and Gisa, were sitting on the floor, their backs against the wall, their heads in their hands. They were barely holding on by a thread.

The one heaving into a bucket was the monk, Brother Magnus. Poor thing. He sounded as if he were dying. Or, at the very least, as if he wanted to, what with all the quiet sobbing in between loud heaves.

The girl twin, Talwyn, seemed well enough, able to move around without vomiting. But even in this cave, lit only by torches against the wall, she still squinted as if she'd stumbled from complete darkness to the bright morning suns shining down on her in the middle of summer.

The boy twin walked over to Elina and held out a plate of freshly made meats.

"Hungry?" he asked, his voice booming, his grin wide, which was why Elina slapped the plate of food from his hands and then, after reaching back as far as she could manage, slapped his face as hard as her weakened state would allow her.

The boy's head snapped to one side and, startled, he stepped back and then started laughing. His good humor did nothing but make her want to beat him until he stopped smiling.

"Leave her be, Talwyn," Celyn said from the other end of the table, his head now raised but his eyes still closed.

"I'm Talan, cousin. The male."

"I don't care which one of you it is. . . . Just piss off."

Still chuckling, Talan walked off and went to help his still-heaving friend.

Celyn pressed the palms of his hands against his eyes. "I feel like dried dog shit," he grumbled. "I haven't felt like this since I went drinking with my uncle Addolgar."

He pointed a warning finger at Elina. "Don't go drinking

with my uncle Addolgar or Brannie." He thought a moment, then added, "Or me mum. *Never* with me mum."

"Here," someone said next to her. "Drink this."

Elina looked up into those odd-colored eyes and the beautiful, softly smiling face of Rhianwen. "What is it?"

"Tea that will help your pain and soothe your stomach," Rhianwen said.

"All right, but I can do without the yelling."

"I'm not yelling."

"It sounds like yelling!" Elina yelled, then immediately wished she hadn't. She closed her remaining eye and let out a groan.

"Here. Drink."

Elina looked down at the tea before her. She could easily see herself bringing all that tea right back up, but if this could help, she would try anything.

She took a sip, wasn't completely repulsed by the taste, so she finished the rest in several gulps.

When she placed the cup down Rhianwen asked, "Can I look?"

Elina shrugged. "As you like, as long as you stop yelling."

Rhianwen gently removed the bandages covering half her face before lifting Elina's chin and carefully turning her head one way, then another.

"Good. Excellent. No infection."

"You seem more like a healer than the hag," Elina noted.

"Sadly, it's not in my skills. I can clean wounds and such. But I lack the magicks required to help the healing."

"And that bothers you."

Rhianwen shrugged. "It could always be worse."

That made Elina smirk. "Exactly."

Kachka walked into the alcove. If the drink had bothered her, it didn't show. She sat down beside Elina and patted her on the back.

"Here," she said, handing her a piece of bark from one of the Steppes trees. "Chew this."

Elina placed the bark in her mouth, nodded. "Thank you, sister. That helps."

"Tree bark helps?" Celyn asked.

"The trees of the Steppes, yes. If used in poultice, it can help healing. If chewed, it will help with pain in head."

Celyn held out his hand. "Give me."

Smirking, Kachka stretched across the length of the table to drop a piece of bark into Celyn's outstretched hand.

"Thank you."

Kachka glanced around the cave. "Do all Southlanders live in caves?" she asked Elina in their own language.

"No. Only the dragons. The humans live in grand homes. Made of stone. You can't move them anywhere."

"So they live in the same place . . . forever?"

"Yes."

The sisters looked at each other and shook their heads.

"You know," Kachka said after some time, "that dragon is worried about you."

"I don't know why. He's not doing any better than I am after last night's drinking."

"Not your drinking. He's worried about *you*. What happened to you with Glebovicha."

"It's just pity."

"Perhaps. I don't understand these Southlanders so I wouldn't know." She yawned, scratched the side of her neck. "So have you been fucking him long?"

Elina shook her head. "Not long."

"While he's dragon?"

"Don't be stupid."

She glanced over at Celyn. "When human, he's very pretty."

"He is. But that's over now, isn't it?"

"Why do you say that? He was ready to sacrifice himself for you during the battle. You shouldn't hold against him what happened to you."

"I don't. I never would."

"Then what?"

She shrugged. "Why would he want me now? Look at my face."

Kachka's chin dropped. "Your face? How long have you been in the Southlands, sister, that you think so much of how pretty you are rather than *who* you are?"

"I can live with this. But a Southlander?"

"But remember old Tevkel. Her six husbands loved her even after she lost her arm and part of her hip in that battle. They loved her until she was gored by that bull during the spring rains. Love and desire do not fade away because of a few scars. Even for the Southlanders."

"Tevkel was a mighty warrior who never disgraced herself in battle. Of course her husbands loved her. How could they not?"

"Even with your eye gone and your face and body covered in blood, you fought to live. You fought Glebovicha."

"Not very well."

"You fought Glebovicha," Kachka said again. "No one thought you'd even try. But you did. So, there's no shame in your scars."

"Yes, but—"

"*Why do you argue with me?*" Kachka bellowed.

"*Do not bark so when my head throbs from pain!*"

"*Then do not question me!*"

"*I will question you if I have need to!*"

"*Which is why Glebovicha took your eye!*"

"*That is enough!*" Celyn bellowed, then he quickly buried his face in his hands, the piece of bark he'd been chewing falling to the table. "Gods, the pain. Even this bark isn't helping."

"You have not chewed long enough," Kachka told him.

"Look," he said after a moment, his eyes closed, "I don't know what you two are arguing about, but don't."

"Because we are sisters and love each other?" Kachka

taunted him. Elina grinned around her piece of bark at the insult meant only for Southlanders.

"No. But because I am dying and *I'd like to do it in silence!*"

Celyn didn't appreciate the sisterly giggling he heard after his explosion, but he was too close to death to bother taking it any further.

Of course, he still wasn't as bad off as Talan's friend, Magnus. For such a big, hearty fellow, he seemed to handle his drink worst of all. And Rhian handled it best . . . because she'd been smart enough not to have any. He clearly remembered the way her little nose had crinkled when she'd sniffed the bottle, then handed it back to him with a tight-lipped shake of her head. She was a rarity among the Cadwaladrs, and normally Celyn would assume she simply took after her mother, the lovely Talaith. But he'd seen Talaith at a few family feasts when the abilities to do basic math and modulate her voice had vanished after a few ales.

"Good!" Brigida boomed as she entered the alcove. "You're all awake."

Celyn wanted to snatch that damn walking stick from the old She-dragon and burn it to ash.

Once she made her impossibly slow way to the middle of the alcove, she pointed at Celyn. "You, boy—"

"I have a name."

"—get ready to travel. You, too, Riders. We'll be heading back to Garbhán Isle and that human queen."

Celyn shook his head. "No."

"I wasn't asking."

"I'm not taking Elina back to Annwyl until I've had time to—"

"No," Elina cut in. "I must go and face Queen Annwyl. Let her know how I failed her and Queen Rhiannon." She glanced at her sister. "She may take my head. I heard she likes to take heads."

"Does she hack at the neck or—?" Kachka began.

"No, no. She is quite quick. One swipe of her blade and it is over."

"Well . . . as long as it is quick. Your failure was not so great that you should suffer."

"You are so good to me, sister."

Celyn slammed his hands against the table and stood, knocking his chair over. "What bizarre conversation are you two having?"

"I thought we were speaking in your language . . . were we not?"

"That's not what I mean. I don't understand how you two can sit here and discuss this so casually?"

"I failed. What else is there to say? Now, let us go to face the justifiable wrath of Annwyl the Bloody." Elina slipped off the table, but her legs nearly gave out, so her sister had to stop her from crumpling to the floor. "I am fine," she lied. "I am fine."

"You never could handle your drink, sister."

"I kept up with you."

"It is not what you do while drinking. It is what you do after."

"Get your things and meet me outside the cave entrance," Brigida ordered.

"You're coming with us?" Celyn asked the old She-dragon, the idea of the journey growing more and more horrible.

"I long to see my kin again, Celyn the . . . Celyn the . . . what name have you earned, boy?"

"Celyn the Charming."

The old She-dragon cackled. "Really?"

"I'm growing to loathe you. And I don't usually say that to anyone."

"And it's just beginning," Brigida promised. "Now outside.

And you lot," she said, pointing at the others with her stick. "You've got work to do."

"What work?" Celyn demanded.

"Don't like dragons who ask me too many questions," Brigida announced, walking away.

When Celyn felt Brigida was far enough away, he caught Rhianwen around the waist and moved her off to a corner.

"What's going on between you lot and Brigida?"

"Nothing you have to worry about it."

"And yet I'm worried."

"Don't be. We're fine."

"It's not really you and the twins I'm worried about. It's more the world."

Rhianwen stepped back from him, and Celyn immediately regretted hurting her feelings. He really shouldn't have sensitive conversations with relatives when he was still a little drunk.

"I . . . *we* . . . have no intention of destroying the world. No matter what our enemies say."

"But, Rhianwen—"

She held up her hand, turned her face away, her back ramrod straight. "No, no. I think there's nothing else to be said. You've made your feelings about us quite clear."

"Tell me, cousin," Celyn asked, his head pounding too hard to even think of playing this game, "did you get that little performance from Keita or your mother?"

"Neither," she quipped back, lifting her skirt to flounce off. "Uncle Gwenvael."

Celyn stepped aside to let her get by, then tossed after her, "That's nothing to be proud of, you know."

With her travel pack, bow and quiver on her back, Elina followed Celyn to where he'd left the horses. As soon as she entered the chamber, the Steppes horse trotted over to greet her.

"You have made a bond, sister," Kachka said from behind her, smiling.

"We have been through much, he and I."

Saddling up their mounts, the trio took the long walk to the entrance.

Once outside, Elina took in a deep breath. She was already beginning to feel much better.

Brigida waited for them in her human form, a fur cape covering her from head to feet.

"Do we ride or fly?" Celyn asked her. "And I'm really hoping you say fly, because galloping will not be my friend right now."

"Like your mother, your vision is small."

"What does that mean?"

"I am too old and too impatient to take bloody days to travel to Garbhán Isle."

"Which means . . . what? Exactly."

Staring at Celyn, Brigida raised the hand holding her walking stick. The clouds overhead darkened, lightning suddenly danced across the mountains, and a mighty wind seemed to rise from the ground up.

Kachka gasped as the air in front of them darkened and began to swirl.

With her free hand, Brigida motioned to the swirling air before them. "Go," she said calmly.

Kachka shrugged and said, "All right." Leading her horse, she walked until she disappeared.

Elina started to follow, but Celyn held his arm out, blocking her way.

"We're not getting in that," he yelped, his normally low voice hitting an abrupt high.

"Always a mummy's boy, you are," Brigida mocked.

"I am—ahhhhhhhhhh!" Celyn screamed as Brigida grabbed the scruff of his chain-mail shirt with her free hand and tossed him into the void after Kachka.

It seemed the old hag was not nearly as weak as she liked to pretend.

"You, too, horse."

At first, Elina thought Brigida was talking to her, but then she realized that she was talking to Celyn's travel-cow, which was quietly trying to back away.

Disgusted, Elina grabbed the travel-cow's reins and headed toward the void. The Steppes horse followed without hesitation . . . because that's how it should be.

She stopped right in front of the void, took a big breath, and gripped the travel-cow's reins. Hoping for the best, she stepped in—and then screamed her damn head off.

Chapter Thirty-One

Dagmar rushed into what had unofficially become her study. Bram would be bringing her son back this afternoon, but he'd also have Gaius Domitus. And even though the Rebel King was relatively easygoing, she wanted to be prepared. Next to the Northlanders, Gaius was their most important ally.

But Gaius Domitus really wasn't the problem. It was his sister, Agrippina. She, not surprisingly after what she'd been through, trusted no one. And she especially didn't trust Annwyl. Again, not surprising, considering every time she saw the Southlander queen, Annwyl was acting . . . odd.

Dagmar found the scroll that Bram had sent her. She

lifted her spectacles so they rested against her forehead and quickly scanned the material. Once she'd digested it all, she tossed the scroll back onto her desk and turned toward the door.

She stopped, let out a sigh.

"I thought I told you lot not to play in here."

Dagmar returned her spectacles to her nose and faced the back of her study. Two of her youngest daughters peeked over the chairs she had there, but the other three . . . they just sort of appeared. As if they'd been part of the bookcase that covered the entire back wall.

The first time that had happened, Dagmar had screamed as if she'd uncovered a dead body. But by now, she was used to the . . . uniqueness of her youngest daughters. It was similar to a gift their father had. He was a chameleon, a dragon able to blend into any area he was in so that it would seem he'd disappeared.

"Mum," Seva, the eldest of The Five, asked, "will we have to leave, too? Like Var?"

"Var hasn't left. He's just visiting your uncle Bram for the night."

"Do you want us to leave?"

Shocked, Dagmar stared at her daughter for a long moment. "Of course not. Why would you even ask that?"

"Arlais says—"

"First off," Dagmar immediately cut in, "you know better than to listen to Arlais about anything. She lives to torment all of you."

"But we scare you, don't we?"

Dagmar let out a sigh, and walked to the back of the room. She leaned down, placing her hands on her knees so that she could look all her daughters in the eyes.

"You do not scare me. None of you scare me. I am scared *for* you. Times are changing and . . . well, people always fear that which they do not understand. At one time, you never would have existed as you are. The daughters of a dragon and a human. But here you are. Beautiful and healthy—"

"And different," Seva finished for her.

"And different. And many do not like different."

"Do you want us to change?"

"Not on your lives," she said adamantly. "Do you know why?" The five girls shook their golden heads, eyes just like their father's staring back at Dagmar, waiting for what she was going to say next. "Because I never changed. I refused to. It wasn't easy. Some among my family were quite mean about it. But *I* never changed, and do you know what happened? I met your father and Auntie Annwyl and Auntie Morfyd and all your uncles . . . and everything was wonderful. So how can I ask you to change when I never did?"

"We don't want to go anywhere," Seva told her, as always speaking for all five of them. "We like it here."

"You're not going anywhere. I won't allow it. But, more importantly," Dagmar added, "your *father* will never allow it. As far as that dragon is concerned, the suns rise and set on his girls. So you don't need to hide in my study, worried that we'll be sending you away."

"That's not why we come in here. We come to your study because if you don't notice us, we get to hear all sorts of interesting stuff between you and the generals."

Dagmar stood and pointed at the door.

As her daughters marched by, Dagmar noted, "You five are unbelievably sneaky."

"We are, but Daddy says we get that from you."

Dagmar followed her daughters into the hallway, turned, and locked her study door, but when she looked back, her daughters had already disappeared.

All right. Maybe her five youngest daughters made her a little nervous, but that was natural, wasn't it?

As Dagmar headed down the hall, she saw Annwyl

walking toward her, going out for her daily training, no
doubt. Although she didn't usually come this way.

"Where are you off to?" Dagmar asked.

"To check on the tower before I head to the training
field."

"Huh." Dagmar caught the queen's arm and stopped her.
"Mind explaining to me what that is you're building out
there?"

Annwyl shrugged, her face frowning in confusion. "It's
a tower."

"Yes, but—"

A loud crash from outside cut off Dagmar's next words,
and Annwyl stormed off down the hall while yelling at the
stonemason who might or might not be able to hear her
from this far inside the castle walls.

"I will not be paying for whatever just happened!" she
yelled.

Shaking her head, Dagmar headed off for her first meal
before the Rebel King and his distrustful sister arrived.

Elina landed on her hands and knees, everything she'd
eaten or drunk in the last twenty-four hours pouring out of
her in great bouts of vomit.

A few feet away was Kachka, going through the same
thing. And Celyn was nearly lighting the forest on fire as
his vomit came out like lava, spraying the trees and decimating the spongy undergrowth.

"Oh, dear," Brigida's voice rasped, "I completely forgot
to mention not to drink too much before we travel. The
body just expels it."

Kachka, the first to stop retching, fell back against a tree
stump. She pointed an accusing finger at Brigida. "You
hag," she snarled. "You handed us four more bottles last
night before you went to bed."

"Did I?" Brigida asked. "How the mind fades with old age."

"You did this on purpose!"

"Watch your tone, orphan of the Steppes. I'd hate to tear your tongue out by the root."

Brigida quickly turned her head as the right side of her fur cape was sprayed with vomit-flecked lava.

Celyn stumbled toward the old She-dragon. "Don't you threaten—" His words abruptly ended as he fell face-first onto the ground and stopped moving.

Brigida shook her head. "This is what you get for spending your life under your mummy's tail, boy."

She shook off the lava and began to walk away.

"Wait," Elina called out as she pulled herself to her feet by holding onto the low-lying limb of a nearby tree. "Where do you go, old hag?"

"I long to see my homeland again. It's been much too long. You lot can get back on your own from here. Garbhán Isle is just over that ridge."

Elina tried to go after Brigida, but as soon as she stepped away from the tree, she was forced to drop to her hands and knees again so she could continue vomiting.

Once her system cleared out, she crawled over to her sister, dropping down beside her.

"She is so mean," Elina said to Kachka.

"I know." She nodded at their mounts. "At least the horses are doing well. Even that big cow."

"I call him travel-cow."

"Fitting."

"It is not!" Celyn screamed into the ground, still unable, it seemed, to get up.

"We cannot face the fancy Southland queen like this," Kachka said, ignoring Celyn. "We may not be able to ever go home again, but I will not represent the Steppes as poorly as this."

Elina listened for a bit, then pointed to the west. "There is stream or creek over there. We can wash up and change."

Kachka nodded, and together the sisters slowly got to their feet. Once they were steady, they both walked over to Celyn. Each took an arm and they proceeded to drag the dragon in his human form toward the water.

"He weighs as much as that travel-cow," Kachka complained.

"It could be worse, sister. He could be dragon. Then we would be dragging him for *hours*."

After they finished cleaning up and changing their clothes, the trio mounted their horses and rode to Garbhán Isle.

Once they were in the courtyard, Celyn quickly dismounted and moved to Elina's side. He reached up to help her and she immediately slapped his hands away.

"I am not invalid, Dolt."

"I'm trying to help you."

"I do not need help. I have been dismounting horses since birth. This I can do."

Celyn stepped back as Elina's leg swung over the saddle. He barely missed being kicked in the head. She jumped down and landed just fine, but when she tried to take a step she walked into him. Spatially, she was still a bit off.

He stopped her from falling, but that only got him a little snarl.

"I am fine."

"Are you sure?"

"*Do not question me!*" she bellowed, shoving him back.

"Gods, woman! I am just trying to help!"

"I do not need your help. I am missing eye. Not head."

"Elina—"

"Why must we debate *everything*?" she snapped.

Celyn glanced at Kachka and she gave a little jerk of

her head. He understood. Space. Elina needed space. He understood that. He didn't want to give it, but he understood. Besides, he needed to track down Annwyl before she saw Elina. Around this time of day, she would be training.

"Go inside," he said. "I'll catch up."

"What about old hag?" Kachka asked.

All Celyn could do was shrug. "I'll warn the family she's back and . . . somewhere. That's all we can do."

Kachka nodded and together they watched Elina, who'd already walked off toward the stairs that would lead into the Great Hall, her gait still a little cautious as she moved.

"Give her time," Kachka said to him, her voice low. "You tend to push."

"I know. I try not to, but . . . I'm not good at not pushing. I'm Cadwaladr. . . . We push."

Kachka smiled, patted his shoulder, which sent him stumbling a bit.

"You are good dragon. And my sister will be fine. She is . . . what is word . . . ?" She thought a moment. "Resilient. She will not let this hold her back for long."

He knew Kachka was right.

With a nod, he went off in search of Annwyl, but he found Brannie first.

His sister blinked in surprise. "You're back already?"

"It's a long story. Where's Annwyl?"

"Well—"

"Why are you here?" Briec asked as he came around the corner of a building, with Éibhear and Gwenvael a few hundred feet behind him.

"And good tidings to you as well, cousin."

"I asked you a question."

"Oh, back off, Briec," Brannie snapped. "We don't report to you."

Focusing on his sister, Celyn asked her, "Annwyl? Where is she?"

"Haven't seen her this morning. Problems at that death

tower she's building. But she's probably at the training field by now. You know how cranky she gets when she doesn't get in some kind of workout. Why do you ask?"

"Because we need to track her down before she sees Elina. Maybe we could all split up and look for her."

Brannie frowned in confusion as Briec stiffened. "Why? Celyn, what's going on?"

Celyn sighed. "Like I said . . . it's a long story."

Kachka found her sister standing next to a large table in the middle of a big hall. She had her hands against the wood and was leaning on it.

"You need to get some sleep," she told Elina in their own language, now that they were alone.

"I'm fine."

"After what that old witch did to us? And you're still healing. You need to rest."

"Stop babying me, Kachka."

"Caring for you is babying you? And have you not done the same for me when I was wounded? Why should you be so different?" Her sister didn't answer, so Kachka put her arm around Elina's shoulders and leaned in close. "What is it, Elina? You weren't this worried when we were back at the old hag's cave. But now—"

Before Elina could answer—and it did seem she was about to—a voice coming from the back of the hall boomed, "Elina! You've returned! And so quickly!"

The sisters turned and Kachka watched a woman walk toward them. She was tall like Kachka and wore a sleeve-less chain-mail shirt that revealed big shoulders, lots of scars, and strange markings etched into the skin of her forearms. A warrior, but the likes of which Kachka had never seen before. Perhaps another Cadwaladr like Celyn.

"I'm so glad you're back," the woman went on, her gaze

focused on a leather thong she was attempting to tie around her wrist with only one hand. "How did it go with . . . ?"

The woman's words trailed off and her footsteps slowed when she saw Elina's bandaged face.

"My gods, what happened?"

"Queen Ann—"

"*Don't* call me queen." The woman took a breath. "I don't need titles. Just tell me what happened."

"I have failed you," Elina said flatly.

"Elina—" Kachka started to step in, to protect her as she'd always tried to do, but Elina wouldn't have it.

Elina slashed her hand through the air. "No, Kachka. Let me do this." She faced the woman who, Kachka now realized, was the infamous Annwyl the Bloody. "I have failed you," Elina said again. "I did not get to see the Anne Atli. Glebovicha stopped me."

"Is this bandage because of her?" the royal asked, reaching out to touch the cloth wrapped around Elina's head, but Elina jerked back. When she got like this, she didn't like to be touched by anyone.

"She did do this to you," the queen quickly surmised.

"There was a fight," Kachka explained for her sister. "And Glebovicha took her eye."

The queen lowered her hand and blinked several times. "She . . . she took Elina's eye? Because Elina wanted to talk to Anne Atli?"

"The ways of our people," Kachka tried to explain to the Southland leader, "are complicated."

"Well, what about your people? Did they not try to protect her?"

Kachka shrugged. "Some might have wanted to, but . . . well . . . no one gets between mother and daughter in the Outerplains."

The queen's body jerked as if she'd been struck. "Mo . . . mother? Glebovicha is your *mother*, Elina?"

Elina nodded.

"If you will let me explain—" Kachka began.

"No," the queen said quickly. "I can't. I have to . . ." She pointed, but Kachka felt the gesture was meaningless. "To go. I have to go."

Then the queen stalked off.

Elina's head dropped forward and she again faced the table. "I am pathetic," she snarled in their language.

"Stop it, Elina."

"Did you see her face? I failed her. I failed them all. Me with my grand promises, and instead I come back even more useless than when I left."

"Stop *it*."

A tear rolled down Elina's face from the one eye she had left. "Our mother was right. She's always been right about me."

Arms crossed over her chest, Kachka turned away from her sister, resting her butt against the table. She hated when Elina got like this. Insisting on believing the lies their mother had told them all these years. But Kachka also knew there was no point arguing with her until Elina had gotten it out of her system.

A tall, silver-haired male ran into the hall from the court-yard steps. He stopped, turned in a circle, then looked at Kachka. She assumed he was looking for the queen, so she motioned to the stairs leading up to another floor with a tilt of her chin. He ran off, and Kachka continued to hear her sister going on and on about how pathetic and weak she was and how she'd failed the great Queen Annwyl.

That Annwyl didn't seem so great to Kachka. To blame Elina for any of this was beyond ridiculous. Who would do that?

Kachka looked up to see the queen, now dressed for travel, with a travel pack on her back and weapons around her waist, heading toward the stairs. The silver-haired male was right beside her, and they were clearly arguing.

When the queen reached the top of the stairs, the man

grabbed her arm to halt her, and Kachka wondered if this was the king of these lands. Who else would put their hands on a royal? And something about him screamed haughty.

But then that queen turned and kicked the silver-haired man in the knee. It was a hard kick, meant to shatter, but the male merely hissed in pain and released her. She made it down the stairs, but the man caught up with her again. He grabbed her around the waist and she brought her elbow back, hitting him right in the face. Blood immediately poured from his nose, but this time he kept his grip.

He lifted the queen off the ground and started to take her back toward the steps, but she pulled out a dagger she had sheathed at her side and rammed it into his thigh.

He dropped her then and stumbled back.

Readjusting her travel pack, she started for the hall doors. But two more males rushed in from the courtyard. One was big like a bear and had blue hair. *Wait. Blue hair?* The other was like a golden god, and Kachka knew he would be in great demand among the worthy warriors in need of husbands.

The two men stopped in front of the queen, hands up.

"Annwyl," the golden one warned, "don't make us hurt you."

In reply, the queen cracked her neck, lowered her head, and snarled—like an animal. The golden one immediately stepped back. "Nope. I'm much too pretty for this. You handle her," he told the bear.

"Why do I have to do it?" the enormous man asked, panic in his low voice. "I'm pretty, too!"

"Well, where the hell is Fearghus?"

"Not as close as we'd like."

"*Move!*" the queen bellowed, startling Elina out of her self-pity.

She spun around. "What's happening?" she asked Kachka.

"I have no idea. But it's fascinating."

"Annwyl . . ." the golden one tried. "Be reasonable."

The queen unsheathed the sword at her side, and the golden one immediately turned away, hands up to cover his head. "Not the face!" he begged. "Not the face!"

"I have to agree with him," Kachka said low to her sister. "Not that face. It is *beautiful*."

"He's a dragon, too."

Kachka scratched her head. "By the horse gods, they're *everywhere*."

The bear—another dragon, Kachka would guess—stepped in front of Annwyl, his big hands on her shoulders, his face turned away, his eyes closed tight.

"Please, Annwyl!" the bear begged. "Please just calm down!"

"Look!" the queen yelled, her arm swinging out toward Kachka and Elina. "Look what that bitch did to her!"

The two males and Annwyl looked over at Elina, and Kachka and her sister glanced at each other, then behind them. They didn't see anyone back there so Kachka quickly realized Annwyl was talking about Elina.

"Me?" Elina said, pointing at her chest.

"I will not let this go unanswered!" the queen raged.

"I know you're upset, Annwyl," the bear went on, "but let's wait until Dagmar or Bram gets here. Then we can all sit down and discuss the best course of—"

The queen, clearly not liking what she was hearing, grabbed the bear by his blue hair and yanked him down and around.

"Owwwwwwwwwwwwwww!"

She stepped past the bear and out the doors.

Kachka turned to Elina, about to say something, when she heard the unmistakable sound of flesh hitting flesh. The queen stumbled back into the hall and a tall, brown-skinned woman followed her in. The queen was stunned by the first hit, and before she could take a swing of her own, the brown-skinned woman punched her in the face again, then once more. The third hit landed the queen on her back, and the brown-skinned woman shook out her hand. "Her bloody jaw is like granite!"

Celyn rushed in with another woman who resembled him greatly but who had shorter black hair. He stopped right in the doorway and looked down at the queen.

"Tell me I did that for a good reason," the brown-skinned woman growled.

"You probably prevented a war. So . . . good job, Iz!"

"I think I broke my hand."

"Don't whine," he said, rushing over to Elina and Kachka. "Are you two all right?"

"Are *they* all right?" the silver-haired one demanded as he bled heavily from his leg wound. "What about *me*?"

"Is all this because of me?" Elina asked, pointing at the queen.

Celyn shrugged. "Annwyl has issues with . . . family. She didn't really get along with her father. Or her brother." He glanced back at the silver-haired male but quickly turned away, not appearing interested in that one's plight at all. "I had a feeling she would react this way once she found out Glebovicha was your mother."

"Gods," the bear said loudly, "she's waking up!"

"Don't just stand there, you idiots!" the gold one yelled. "Get some chains!"

"Chains will never hold her," the brown-skinned girl nearly screamed. "Let's make a run for it!"

"Where is Fearghus? Why are *we* dealing with this?"

"Again," the silver-haired one yelled. "I am *bleeding* here! *Are none of you going to help me?*"

"Daddy, please!" the brown one chastised, shocking the silver-haired one.

"I say," the gold one suggested, "that we give Annwyl Briec—since he's bleeding to death anyway—and then burn the whole bloody place down around them."

"Really?" the silver-haired one snapped. "That's your grand plan, idiot?"

"You'd survive the flame!"

"She'd survive the flame as well, only then she'd be more pissed off!"

"Someone find Morfyd," the bear ordered. "She can magickally bind her. That'll hold her until Fearghus gets back."

"Why can't you just contact Morfyd yourself?" the one who resembled Celyn demanded.

"Because she's blocking me, which means she's probably with Brastias doing things I don't want to talk about when it's my sister."

"I know where she is then," the female who resembled Celyn said, charging out of the hall.

"She's moving," the brown-skinned woman said. "Do something!"

"I'm not hitting her," the bear snapped back.

"*I* hit her."

"*You* she'll forgive."

"Well, my hand is broken. Until Morfyd or my mother fixes it, I *can't* hit her."

The males shrugged, each one refusing to do anything, including helping the silver-haired male still bleeding on the floor.

"All of you are weak!" the brown-skinned female snarled before she walked over to the queen, who had pushed her head and shoulders up off the floor with her elbows.

"Sorry, Annwyl," the female said before she kicked the queen in the jaw, knocking her out again.

Celyn grinned at the sisters and gave a courtly bow. "My Lady Elina. My Lady Kachka. Welcome to the Southlands!"

Chapter Thirty-Two

Fearghus walked into the bedroom he shared with Annwyl and went to the desk where he kept personal correspondence. He placed the scrolls he'd received from one of the generals regarding defenses on the outskirts of Southland territories onto the desk and removed his travel bag. He dropped that on the floor and turned to leave.

That's when he saw Annwyl. She was in a sitting position on the bed with her arms stretched out and bound to the headboard with ropes that, he was guessing, had been mystically enhanced. Someone had also gagged her. And he quickly noticed that her eyes were angry over that gag. Very angry.

Which was when he started laughing. He couldn't help himself!

"I swear by all the gods, Annwyl. I leave you alone for five minutes. . . ."

"May I?"

Elina nodded at the She-dragon's polite request. With extremely gentle hands, Morfyd the White carefully removed the bandage over her eye. Then, she placed cool fingers against her jaw and slowly tilted Elina's head back so that she could get a good look at the wound.

They'd moved into the "war room," as it was called, and the group had multiplied. Now Dagmar and Talaith had joined them, along with Morfyd.

"I simply don't understand," Dagmar was saying. "Why would your mother do this to you?"

Elina gave a very small shrug since Morfyd was still examining her. "She hates me. She has always hated me."

"Then why not just kill you?"

"I am still her child. She still bore me. To kill me for no reason would have brought curse on our tribe."

"But asking to see the Anne Atli gave her a reason?"

Elina didn't want to answer that question, so Kachka did it for her. "When Glebovicha told her she could not meet with Anne Atli, my sister insisted she would. When she did that, she was disobeying the leader of our tribe."

"And that made it acceptable for Glebovicha to kill her," Dagmar finished.

"Yes."

Gwenvael, who sat next to Celyn, a few chairs over, shook his head. "Nice job protecting the Rider, Celyn. So glad we sent you instead of our father."

Elina, shocked by such an unfair comment, pulled away from Morfyd's skillful touch in time to see Celyn, his lips now a thin line of anger, reach his arm around his cousin, grab the back of Gwenvael's head and slam him face-first into the hard wood table. Three times.

Then, gripping all that golden hair, Celyn tossed the dragon out of his chair and across the floor.

"Celyn!" Morfyd gasped.

Celyn gave a shrug. "Sorry. Me hand slipped."

For several long seconds, Dagmar stared at her snarling, raging mate bleeding on the floor, her brow pulled far down on her face, before she turned back to Elina and asked, "Why the eye?"

Surprised that it was Gwenvael's sister running to his side to help him and not his mate, Elina opened and closed her mouth a few times before she replied, "What?"

"Why the eye? Why did she take your eye?"

"She tried for neck, but I managed to move fast."

"So it wasn't that she joined the cult of Chramnesind and removed your eye as some sort of sacrifice?"

Elina and Kachka laughed at that.

"*Our* mother?" Elina asked.

"Worshipping anyone but *herself*?" Kachka finished.

Then they both laughed again.

Talaith now moved in to examine the wounds.

"The scarring could have been handled better, but I see no infection at all. And the healing time is amazing. This should have taken weeks, if not months, to heal. Did you do this, Celyn?"

"No," Elina answered while rubbing her suddenly itchy nose. "Celyn saved my life, but Brigida the Foul healed my wounds."

Morfyd, who was crouched on the floor by her bleeding and now whining brother, her hands gently lifting his head into her lap, looked up. "There's another Brigida the Foul?" she asked.

"Gods," Briec said, his nose swollen from where Annwyl had broken it, his wounded leg now bound where she'd stabbed him. "Who'd willingly take that name?"

All dragon eyes turned to Celyn, waiting for an answer. He sighed and Elina realized she'd said too much.

"It wasn't another Brigida the Foul," he told his kin. "It was *the* Brigida the Foul."

Morfyd abruptly stood, poor Gwenvael's head slamming hard against the stone floor.

"Owww!"

Morfyd and Briec exchanged quick and panicked glances.

"That's not possible," Morfyd said. "Brigida the Foul was ancient when our grandparents were young. Now they've gone to the afterlife, but you're saying Brigida still lives?"

"She still lives. And there's something else. . . . The twins and Rhian are with her."

The room was still for a long moment. Until Briec broke the silence first with a bellowed, "*What are you saying about my perfect, perfect daughter?*"

Celyn was sure he'd have to fight the rest of his cousins until Talaith took the bandages from Elina's hand as the Rider tried to rewrap them around her own head.

"No, no," she said. "You can't use those. They're dirty from your travels. I will get you fresh bandages."

She turned to make her escape, but Briec slammed his hand down on the table. "*What do you know, woman?*"

"Don't woman me!" the Nolwenn witch snarled back.

"Talaith!"

She rolled her eyes. "Rhian and the twins are fine."

"I could give a battle-fuck about those twins."

"Daddy!" Izzy admonished her adoptive father.

"What?"

"The twins are kin as much as Rhian is."

"Those two vipers can take care of themselves just fine. But my sweet, perfect daughter—"

"Can handle herself quite well," Talaith cut in. "Leave them be."

"*With Brigida the Foul?*"

"I don't know who that is and *stop yelling at me!*"

"She's one of our great-great-great-aunts," Morfyd replied. "Although at this point, we should probably just call her our ancestor. That's how old she is."

"So?"

"Dragons live for centuries, Talaith. Not eons."

"What about those Immortal dragons?"

"They survive by eating their own. Is that what Brigida is doing?"

"I don't know what she's doing. But knowing my daughter, I doubt she'd align herself with someone who did. She'd find that in poor taste." Talaith blinked. "No pun intended."

"Everyone in the Cadwaladr Clan feared Brigida. Many of them thought she'd aligned herself with the less-balanced gods. And her impossibly long life suggests there's truth to that. What I'm saying, Talaith, is that she's dangerous."

"Well, you two met her," Izzy pointed out. "And have no family members telling you about how terrifying she was since you were born. What did you think of her?"

It took a moment before the Steppes sisters realized that Izzy was talking to them. Celyn glanced at Brannie, and they grinned at each other, already anticipating what direction the discussion was about to take.

Kachka asked Elina, "Why do they stare? Are they planning our death?"

"No," Elina replied after removing more cloth from the pouch tied to the belt around her waist and wrapping a fresh bandage into place. "They ask our opinion."

"Our opinion? Why? Is it trick? So they can plan our death?"

Brannie quickly looked in another direction and Celyn dropped his head.

"I do not know." Elina looked at Talaith. "Do you plan our death?"

"No, no!" Talaith exchanged confused glances with Morfyd and Izzy. "We just want your opinion about this Brigida. As outsiders."

"Oh." The sisters looked at each other, back at everyone else.

Elina spoke first. "Everything about Brigida the Foul drips with disdain and hatred of all living things."

"Yes," Kachka agreed. "Evil seems to come from every pore. She clearly has great plans for the whiney little brown girl and the unholy twins that the horse gods should have destroyed at birth."

They looked at each other again, nodded, and said together, "We like her."

Izzy, as confused as everyone else in the room, threw up her hands and said, "Like her? How could you like her?"

Kachka answered for both of them. "She is straightforward. If she were going to kill us all, she would tell us so that she could bask in our despair and cries of suffering. Do you not think, Elina?" she asked her sister.

"I agree, Kachka."

"That's great," Talaith said. "That's so great." Then she hissed, "You two aren't helping me."

Kachka stared at Talaith for a long moment, then asked, "Who are you?"

That's when Celyn realized he couldn't take any more. Neither could Brannie. They both stood at the same time, and he said, "My parents are near. They may want to be part of this."

He quickly cut across the room and went out the door, Brannie right behind him. Once they were down the hall, they both stopped and laughed. Laughed so hard that Celyn slid down the wall and Brannie just stretched out on the floor, rolling back and forth. They couldn't stop. Even when their cousin Keita walked past them and demanded, "What are you two doing?"

Bram and Ghleanna landed in the courtyard just as Annwyl came stomping down the stairs.

"I'm not apologizing!" she yelled at her mate as poor Fearghus followed her. But he was laughing and having a hard time keeping up.

Bram glanced at Ghleanna and she immediately rolled her eyes. This was why they'd come with Gaius Lucius Domitus. The Rebel King had a strained opinion of Annwyl the Bloody, and Bram had been hoping to get a chance to talk to her in private before reintroducing them. But as luck would have it . . .

"Oh, Bram, good," Annwyl said. "You're here." As usual, whether they were in their dragon form or human, Annwyl seemed to see them all in one way. She simply adjusted her voice so that it could reach their ears if they were dragon.

"My queen, allow me—"

"I want to go to the Outerplains and tear the eye out of one of the tribes' leaders."

Good gods, this female! "Perhaps this is something we could talk about later, Annwyl. I think it's more important that you spend some time with Gaius Lucius Domitus."

The queen frowned. "Who?"

"The Rebel King? Of the Quintilian Provinces?"

"I don't know who that is. Am I *supposed* to know who that is?"

"Annwyl, you *must* remember—"

"Lord Bram," the Rebel King gently cut in. "Don't bother."

Fearghus, now behind his mate, laid his hand on her shoulder. "Annwyl, why don't we go to the training field for a bit?"

"I'm queen!" Annwyl snapped. "I should be able to rip the eye out of anyone's head that I want to!" She glanced over at Gaius Domitus, noticed the eye patch over his right eye, and said with an annoyed sigh, "No offense."

"Of course," his sister shot back.

But, not surprisingly, Annwyl missed the tone and she marched off, Fearghus behind her—still laughing.

"I suggest we get the guests set up quickly," Ghleanna offered.

"I can show them the way," Var said, quickly sliding off Bram's back.

Bram nodded at the suggestion and shifted to human. The others followed suit and they all quickly dressed.

Once that was done, Var led Gaius and his sister to the guest quarters that would conveniently keep them out of the castle and away from Annwyl.

With that taken care of, Bram turned toward the castle stairs and, to his great relief, saw Celyn and Brannie coming toward him. Bram had been worried about his son on this trip, but he was glad to see him back and well. Although he was back much sooner than Bram had expected.

Celyn walked up to his parents and stared at them.

"Celyn?" Ghleanna asked. "What is it?"

Then they were both being hugged. Tightly.

Bram looked over at his mate, frowning in question. But all Ghleanna could do was shrug.

"Is everything all right?" Ghleanna demanded. "Have you been hurt?"

"Nah," Brannie answered for her brother. "He's just glad you never hacked off bits of him because you didn't like him."

Horrified, Bram stared at his daughter. *"What?"*

While the dragons and their human kin continued to argue over Brigida the Foul, Elina walked out with her sister.

"I'm hungry," her sister announced.

"There is always food. And servants to get it for you."

"You enjoy this decadence, don't you?"

"You will, too . . . in time."

Disgusted by such a suggestion, Kachka retrieved her bow and quiver from where she'd left them in the Great Hall and walked out to hunt down her meal. Elina also picked up her bow, but she just held it and walked toward the big table in the middle of the hall. As she walked, she collided with a man she hadn't even seen.

Stumbling back, Elina looked up at him as he looked down. All she saw at first was a patch where his right eye should be. They both stared and, slowly, each moved one way, then the other.

Finally, the man asked, "Just lose it?"

Elina nodded. "Yes. And you?"

"Years ago."

He glanced down at her bow. "You're an archer."

"I was. Now . . . I am not even that."

"When I had both eyes, I still closed one in order to shoot arrows."

"But it was my favored eye that I lost."

"So?" he asked, shrugging massive shoulders. "You will just have to relearn what you already know."

"Really?"

"Of course. Where are you from?"

"The Steppes of the Outerplains."

He gave a little laugh. "Then you'll always be an archer. I've seen your people in action. That's something born in your blood. Plus you still have both arms."

"I cannot hit side of hut, much less moving target on horse."

"That'll take time. But I can show you how to compensate."

"Compensate?"

"Make do with what you have." He nodded toward the Great Hall doors. "Come on. I'll show you."

"Now?"

"I was just looking for a book to read while my sister naps. But I think I'd enjoy helping a fellow one-eyer."

Elina glanced around, suddenly wondering if Celyn would have a problem with this. Then she wondered why she should care if Celyn had a problem with this. Then she wondered what the holy hells was wrong with her.

"Besides," the man said softly, his gaze moving to one of Celyn's royal cousins who was coming through the doors in the back of the hall, "you don't want to stay around here right now."

"I don't?"

The female, Keita was her name, stopped and focused on Elina and the man. At the sight of them, she clasped her hands together and went up on her bare toes. "Oh! I have just the thing for both of you! Don't go anywhere!"

Keita charged up the stairs, and Elina turned toward the man. "Let us go. Now. Her good cheer terrifies me."

"As it should."

They headed toward the Great Hall doors. "I am Gaius Lucius Domitus by the way."

"And I am Elina Shestakova of the Black Bear Riders of the Midnight Mountains of Despair in the Far Reaches of the Steppes of the Outerplains. But you can call me Elina since these weak Southlanders cannot seem to handle much more than that."

Gaius Lucius Domitus laughed. "No, they probably can't."

Celyn had taken his parents into the stables and filled them in on what had happened to Elina at her mother's hands.

"That poor girl," Bram said, shaking his head. "I had no idea we were putting her in such danger."

"That's because she didn't tell us. I had no idea how bad it was until her mother literally kicked her out of her tent and then proceeded to slash at her like she was an attacking wild pig."

"What did you do?" Ghleanna asked.

"What I had to. I had to protect her, Mum."

"Yes," his mother said on a strange sigh. "I'm sensing you did have to."

Brannie snorted and their mother grabbed her daughter's

shoulders and turned her toward the exit. She shoved. "Go, brat! And stop taunting your brother."

"I didn't say anything!"

"You'll need to handle Annwyl, Da," Celyn told his father. "When she saw what happened to Elina—"

"Gods, is that what she was going on about?" Bram scratched his head. "I do adore her, but my gods, that woman is a lot of work."

"And you thought Rhiannon was bad," Ghleanna reminded him.

"Only when she's around your brother. But Annwyl . . . it's like trying to rein in an erupting volcano."

"At least Fearghus is with her."

Celyn and his parents headed toward the exit.

"Where is Dagmar?" Bram asked.

"Probably still in the war room. Oh—" He stopped, faced his parents. "There is one other thing."

Ghleanna frowned. "What?"

"Remember Brigida the Foul?"

"Gods, who could forget her?" Now Bram frowned. "Wait . . . why do you ask about her?"

"Well . . . she's not exactly what you'd call dead. But she is still pretty foul."

Brigida moved around the queen's castle unseen. Those with magickal skills often sensed she'd gone by—even if they didn't know exactly what or whom had drifted so close. Especially the young White Dragonwitch. She bristled every time Brigida passed by her. That one must be Morfyd. Looked just like her mother, she did, especially with those crystal-clear blue eyes.

The girl had much power, but she was no match for Brigida. There were few who were.

The human witch, a Nolwenn by the looks of her, also

had power, but unlike her daughter Rhianwen, she didn't have enough to interest Brigida.

They'd all come out of one room and moved into the big hall, servants bringing them food. All a bunch of proper royals, they were. No real Cadwaladrs. Not like the ones Brigida remembered.

She blamed that fool Ailean the Wicked, the royals' grandfather. He'd been born a Cadwaladr but the loss of his mother at an early age had turned him soft. He worried more about protecting the humans than anything else. Like that sorry lot of soft flesh needed protecting. Brigida had never known a more dangerous group of beings. What they lacked in scales and claws, they more than made up for in evil intent.

She stood in a doorway, leaning against the jamb, and watched the descendants of her people eat and chat and worry. About her.

Her return did nothing but upset them. Brigida liked that. She always had.

That Celyn brought his mother and father into the hall. Ghleanna was the same. Short hair and all. Bit more grey among all the black, but she was still powerfully built and had more weapons than seemed necessary on her person.

Bram also appeared the same. Still pretty for a male, still soft of heart, and still always wanting to keep the peace.

There was no sign of the two Riders, which allowed the others to talk freely about what had happened to the one who'd lost her eye. Such drama over such a little thing. Everyone so horrified that a mother would do this to her own child. Clearly they knew nothing of the Daughters of the Steppes. That lot always tried to weed out the weak girls. What was the point of having them around if they served no purpose? And because the sons and daughters lived so long, the women continued to have offspring well into their fifth or sixth hundredth year. Most of them had more than sixty, if they so desired. So weeding out one or two weak ones was not as big a deal as killing off the only offspring you'd ever have.

Still, try telling this lot all that. Such concern. Such claw wringing.

Perhaps Brigida had stayed away too long. Or would her presence not have changed any of this? She really didn't know. All she did know was that she needed a "champion," and so far she saw none who would live up to that title.

Although she needed no champion for herself. The day she couldn't protect herself was the day she needed to light the funeral pyre and climb up on it.

No, Brigida needed a champion to help her with this end game, as she liked to call it. Darkness had settled over the world, but no one could see it. They tried to deal with one problem at a time, as it arose. Never thinking about the true nightmare coming their way.

But looking at this sorry lot of fishwives, Brigida saw no one who could possibly—

"We can see you."

Slowly, Brigida looked over and down. Way down, to the five golden-headed girls staring up at her.

"You hide," the tallest, and most likely eldest, one said, "but we can see you clear as day."

"You're old," said one of the others. "Really, really old."

"You better be here for nice reasons," the tallest warned. "Or we won't like it."

Brigida was about to respond to that when the girls all looked toward the doors at the front of the hall.

"She's back," one said.

"And she's still in a bad mood," said another.

"Run!"

And they all did, scattering and disappearing into the walls of the castle.

Brigida looked to see who had them so concerned. At first, all she saw was a very young-looking Bercelak. Gods, how did he manage not to age at all? But then Brigida realized that this was the oldest of Bercelak's hatchlings. The future Dragon King, Fearghus. And walking behind him was his human mate. The mother of the first Abominations.

As she walked into the hall, everyone stopped talking, and stared at her.

She stared back for a good minute before announcing, "I'm not apologizing!"

"Of course you're not."

"You shouldn't have grabbed me, Briec!"

"I was trying to prevent you from doing something stupid. And now look at me!"

"Oh, stop your whining," said the golden-haired one. Brigida easily guessed who that one was. The infamous Gwenvael the Slag. Even tucked away in the Outerplains, she'd heard all about his exploits. "Look what Celyn did to my beautiful, beautiful nose! Broke it, he did!"

"You deserved it after what you said to him," snarled a hearty female who looked much like Ghleanna.

"What did he say to Celyn?" Ghleanna demanded. "What did you say, you spoiled brat?"

That's when Gwenvael the Slag burst into tears and sobbed, "Why are you yelling at me, Auntie Ghleanna? I've always been your favorite!"

Good gods, what has happened to my people?

While a few in the room tried to stop the crying and most of the others just rolled their eyes at it, the human queen attempted to slip away. But another human with pieces of glass on her plain face barked out, "Hold it!" When that got her a glare, she gave a forced smile and added, "My queen."

That got her a snarl that Brigida found off-putting . . . and intriguing.

The plain-faced human stood and gestured to her chair. "Sit," she ordered.

"I'm in no mood to—"

"Sit!"

The human queen sat down, and the plain-faced one said, "I know you are angry. And I completely understand why. But you cannot go around digging out the eyes of whoever you want, whenever you want."

"Why not?"

"Because we're trying to create alliances, Annwyl. Not start new wars. Do you not understand that?"

"And do you not understand that I sent Elina back to her people as *my* emissary? How can I ignore what they did to her?"

"It wasn't they. It was her. Her mother. A relationship forged since the womb. We cannot and will not involve ourselves with that."

"But—"

"You've come so far, Annwyl. Don't ruin all this by returning to old habits."

The queen suddenly stood, her chair scraping against the stone floor. Everyone who was standing moved back except the future Dragon King and the plain-faced human.

Dragons moved back from her. Dragons.

Without saying a word, the queen stalked away from the group and went to the stairs. Brigida followed by cutting through the stone walls.

By the time the human queen entered her royal bed-chamber, Brigida was already waiting for her. She watched from the shadows as Annwyl the Bloody walked across the room. She began to take off her weapons. She'd dropped most of them onto a large table, but then she abruptly stopped, stared. And, out of nowhere, exploded.

The weapons went flying as the table was lifted and thrown across the room in a burst of pure rage the likes of which Brigida had never seen before.

The queen pushed open one of the windows as far as it

would go, and took big gulps of air, doing her best to calm herself down.

That's when Brigida moved the shadows so that she could be seen and, instantly, the queen was aware she was no longer alone. She spun around and glowered at Brigida.

"Where the battle-fuck did you come from?" she snarled.

Brigida smiled. "Well, girl, it really depends on who you ask."

Chapter Thirty-Three

Elina lifted her bow, aimed. But when she let the arrow loose, it was inches off. A difference between a clean, quick kill and just pissing her prey off—something that she preferred not to do.

"Pathetic," she sighed.

"Are you always this hard on yourself?" the dragon asked. Yes. The helpful, one-eyed man with hair the color of steel turned out to be *another* dragon. The Southlands seemed to be riddled with them. Like decadence.

Not that Elina minded. The dragons were friendly enough. And this dragon was being more than helpful. Plus, she knew his instruction wasn't offered out of pity. He just understood what she was going through and was trying to help.

"Yes," Elina replied to his question. "I am always hard on myself."

"Don't be. You'll be able to adjust. It'll just take some time."

He stood behind Elina and gently turned her shoulders. "Your dominant eye may be gone, but you can train the eye that you have left to fill that spot. But you'll need to do things a little differently. For instance, you'll need to adjust your sights when you're aiming and—"

"Yoo-hoo!"

"Oh, for shit's sake," the dragon grumbled. "She found us."

"There you two are! I've been looking just everywhere for you!"

The beautiful redhead rushed up to them, her grin wide and eager.

"Princess Keita," the dragon began, "this is Elina Shestakova of the Black Bear Riders of the Midnight Mountains of Despair in the Far Reaches of the Steppes of the Outerplains." He faced Elina and, smiling, said, "And Elina Shestakova of the Black Bear Riders of the Midnight Mountains of Despair in the Far Reaches of the Steppes of the Outerplains, this is Keita the Viper: Princess of the Royal House of Gwalchmai fab Gwyar, Second-Born Daughter and Fifth-Born Offspring to the White Dragon Queen of the Southlands, Protector of The Throne, and Bound Mate to Ragnar, Dragonlord Chief of the Olgeirsson Horde."

Keita narrowed blue eyes at the dragon. "Was *that* really necessary, Curled Horns?"

His grin did not falter. "It *felt* necessary and good. Now, if you don't mind, I'd like to get back to working with Elina Shestakova of the—"

"Do not bore me with that ridiculously long name yet again!" the royal roared. Then, just as quickly, her rage turned into the sweetest smile Elina had ever seen, which did nothing but make Elina reach for another arrow and step back from her.

"In light of your recent tragedy—"

"If it is such tragedy, why do you smile at me like viper you were named for?"

"That's an excellent question," Gaius said. "Why, Keita?"

"Quiet," she snapped at Gaius Domitus, before turning her focus back on Elina. "I smile because I have a wonderful gift for you."

She crouched down in the beautiful gown she wore and spread out a silk cloth. On top of the cloth, she laid down several other pieces of cloth in varying colors and designs.

"Here."

"What is that?" Elina asked.

"An array of eye patches! In festive colors and styles! Perfect for an on-the-go Daughter of the Steppes such as yourself."

Elina looked over at Gaius Domitus and he immediately replied, "Yes. She's quite serious."

"Pick one," the royal urged. "Go on."

Putting the arrow she held back in her quiver, Elina reached down and grabbed hold of a simple black eye patch.

"Not that one," the royal snapped, slapping Elina's hand.

Elina dropped the eye patch and reached for another arrow, but Gaius caught hold of her wrist. "No."

"But—"

"No. Believe it or not, she's favored amongst her dragon kin. Killing her will win you no friends."

The dragon gave the smallest tilt of his head, gesturing to the royal. With a disgusted eye roll and sigh—because she knew exactly what he was suggesting she do—Elina said, "Why do you not pick one for me, Princess."

"Oh!" she trilled like an annoying bird Elina wanted to beat to death with a tiny battering ram. "What a lovely idea! Now, let's see. You know, there are just so many choices with your skin color and hair. You are such a lucky girl!"

"Except for whole losing-eye thing, yes?"

Gaius snorted and quickly glanced away, but if the royal noticed, she didn't mention it. Instead, she finally picked a bright blue patch. "Here! This will go perfectly with the eye you still have in your head!"

The royal stood and quickly removed the bandages that had been around Elina's head. She tsk'd a bit. "Will these scars fade with time? You should talk to Morfyd. I'm sure she can help with that."

"My patience wanes, royal!"

"All right, all right! No need to get snappy!"

She carefully placed the eye patch on Elina, stopping several times to adjust it, before she stood back, her hands clasped together. "That's *perfect!* Absolutely adorable!"

"Yes. Because that is what Daughters of Steppes strive for—adorableness."

Gaius lowered his head and began to scrub his face with his hands, but Elina sensed it was only to hide his laughter.

"Ho, sister!" Elina heard Kachka call out. "Look at what I have gotten us for dinner!"

Elina moved around Gaius and watched her sister dragging the buffalo she'd taken down with one shot, the arrow still buried in its neck, blood still pouring.

Her sister's smile was wide and huge until she saw Elina; then she stopped, frowned. "What is that on your face?"

"Eye patch."

"They didn't have black one?"

"They did, but *she* would not let me wear it."

"Why," the redhead wanted to know, "would you condemn yourself to a black eye patch when I have an *array* of festive colors and styles?"

Elina looked at her sister. "She has an array."

"You look like peacock. It is like annoying jewel. It

makes my eyes hurt to stare at." She studied Gaius. "Who is this?"

"Gaius Domitus from the Western Mountains. Handsome, is he not? And no wife has taken him."

"Really?"

"This is my sister, Kachka. She helped save me before I could lose other eye."

Kachka walked around Gaius Domitus, examining him from all sides. "Very nice. Sturdy thighs. I like his steel-colored hair."

"Sister, he is dragon."

"Gods-dammit!" Kachka snarled. "Is that all they have here?"

"Wait, wait," Gaius cut in, his grin mischievous. "Before we go any further. I must make introductions. Keita, this is Kachka Shestakova of the—"

"*Do not,*" the She-dragon roared, startling the birds from the trees, and the men training nearby, "*again bore me with those ridiculously long names!*"

She picked up her *array* of eye patches. "Keep that on," she ordered Elina. "I will help you choose one for tonight when you have gotten rid of this Iron menace!"

"Why do I need to choose another for tonight?"

She immediately calmed down and grinned. "There's a feast tonight! There'll be dancing."

"A feast?" Kachka asked. "Who are we sacrificing?"

"No one. It's just to celebrate."

"What is there to celebrate?"

"I'm sure something."

"Like what?"

"Stop asking me your ridiculous questions, foolish female!" the She-dragon snapped. "I have no time for this!"

The She-dragon lifted her skirt and stormed away.

"She is royal?" Kachka asked Gaius.

"Yes."

"Where are her shoes? Why does she have no shoes?"

"She doesn't like to wear them."

"She makes me uneasy. Avoid her, sister. Her madness could probably be spread like the sickness that took our cousin a few years back." Kachka grabbed hold of her rope. "I will take my offering to a field and butcher it for this feast these decadent royals will be having."

"Or," Gaius quickly suggested, "you can give your prize buffalo to someone in the kitchens."

"What is kitchens?"

Gaius briefly closed his eye before focusing on a young child running by. "Squire? You there." The child ran to Gaius. "Take Lady Kachka to the kitchens so she can give her buffalo to the head cook."

"Of course, sir. This way, m'lady."

"I am *not* a lady. I am—"

"The boy doesn't care. Just go."

Kachka looked Gaius Domitus over before shaking her head. "Such a waste."

"Thank you," he said good-naturedly. "I think you're adorable, too."

Elina stepped between the pair before Kachka could attempt to remove the dragon's spleen for such an insult. "Sister. We are guests. Do not forget."

"No," she snarled. "I will forget nothing."

"You must not pick on her," Elina warned as they watched Kachka drag her still-bleeding offering up the stone steps of the castle and into the Great Hall. "She is not like me. She has . . . short temper."

"I'll make sure to keep that in mind," Gaius Domitus said, still smiling. "Now, would you like to get back to work?"

Celyn looked up from the discussion he was having with his father to see Kachka being led into the hall by one of the squires. Behind her, she dragged an enormous buffalo. He wondered if Kachka had anything to do with the Keita flounce that had happened just a few minutes before. Keita had been in high dudgeon, and no one had bothered her as she'd flounced her way up the stairs.

Staring at the trail of blood that Kachka's buffalo left behind, he heard his father say, "You have no idea how proud I am of you, son."

Startled, Celyn immediately forgot about the blood and focused on his father. "Proud? She came back missing an eye."

"She came back. From what I know of the Riders, that is a remarkable feat. But it's not only that; I'm also impressed with how you handled the Costentyn tragedy and the information you provided about Brigida. And, gods, Costentyn's journals. I can't thank you enough for grabbing those."

"I'm glad the journals were helpful, but we still don't know where Brigida is."

"Let's not dwell on that right now since I'm sure whatever she's doing would disturb us both greatly." Bram placed his hand on Celyn's forearm. "But what I am saying is that you did a very impressive job."

"Really?"

"If it had been any of your other brothers and sisters or your uncle Bercelak, they would have started a war. If it had been your mother, she would have wiped the Riders from the Steppes and left that area open to Priestess Abertha and the zealots of Annaig Valley. I know now that sending you, Celyn, was the best decision that could have been made."

"So you don't think I ask too many questions?"

"Of course you ask too many questions. You can't help yourself. It's in your blood."

"It is?"

"You take after your grandfather. Ailean constantly asked questions. As if he were shooting one arrow after another.

However, unlike him, you actually expect a response. And wait for one. That's how you make that talent your own."

Brannie came in from the back and sat on the table, her legs immediately beginning to kick Celyn's chair. Something he'd always found annoying.

"Looks like we won't have to deal with Annwyl again if she tries to go off and kill Elina's mum."

"Why not?"

"Éibhear's Mì-runach friends are here. Their whole purpose is to run headlong into inevitable death. They can handle Annwyl."

"You do remember that Éibhear is your *cousin*?" Bram asked.

Brannie grabbed a piece of fruit from a bowl on the table, took a bite, shrugged.

"Gods, this family," Bram sighed.

Kachka walked toward the Great Hall doors, this time without her buffalo. She was covered in blood.

"Oy," Celyn called out to her. "Do you need a bath? One of the servants can get that for you."

Kachka stopped, stared at Celyn, her mouth slightly open. "Lakes and streams all around this property and you make your workers fetch water so you can clean yourselves?"

Celyn and his sister said together, "Yes."

Kachka turned toward the servants busy cleaning up the blood she'd left on the floor. "You do not deserve this treatment," she told them. "Fight your oppressors! Stand up for yourselves!" When the servants only stared at her, Kachka's lip curled in disgust. "Sheep!" she accused. "All of you are sheep!"

"Mmmm," Brannie sighed. "Sheep. I am a bit hungry."

"You'll ruin your dinner," their father warned. "And we're having that feast tonight."

Princess Agrippina entered the Great Hall, and Bram

stood and immediately went to her side. "Princess. I hope
your room is to your liking."

The Iron She-dragon nodded. "It'll do."

Brannie rolled her eyes, always a bit put off by the
Western dragon. But even Celyn had to admit, the female
could be a bit of a snob.

"Excellent. And where is King Gaius?"

"Oh, he's out at the training fields, helping that one-eyed
Rider."

Celyn's back snapped straight at that and his sister
chuckled, so Celyn reached over and shoved her off the
table.

"Ow! You mean bastard!"

Using a ladle, Elina poured from the large cask of water
outside the training ring into the battered pewter mug that
Gaius Domitus was holding. Well . . . she *tried* to pour
water into it. Instead, she ended up pouring water onto
Gaius Domitus's foot.

"Horse gods of hell!"

Gaius Domitus laughed. "It's all right."

"It's not all right. I was looking right at it!"

"Here's a trick." He took her hand and wrapped it around
the mug. "Before you pour anything, you hold the cup in one
hand and then you pour with the other. By touching the cup,
you allow your remaining eye to better gauge distance."

She ladled up more water and tried again. Some went
down the side of the mug but most made it in.

"See? My suggestion is that you practice grasping things.
Cups. A sword. Your bow. Door handles. Anything. The
more you use that ability, the easier it will become. Don't
be surprised in the beginning when you miss things. But
over time—"

"I know, I know. Over time, I will adapt."

"You will. I promise. I won't say it will be easy. And it

can take a bit longer than some think it should, but before you know it, you'll be able to compensate for the loss. Now, I leave in the morning for a meeting in Kerezik while my sister is staying behind for her safety—"

"I will kill anyone that looks at her."

"No, no. That's not necessary." The dragon smiled. "I only mention my trip so that when I get back we can practice more. I promise you, Elina, this will all become easier."

Elina let out a breath. "Thank you, Gaius Domitus. I truly appreciate all you have done for me this day."

"Well, Elina Shestakova of the Black Bear Riders of the Midnight Mountains of Despair in the Far Reaches of the Steppes of the Outerplains, it was my eternal pleasure."

"Pleasure?" Celyn said, suddenly appearing beside them. "What pleasure? Are we having pleasure?"

Gaius Domitus smirked, but Elina had only one question. "What is wrong with you?"

"Nothing. Just checking on you, seeing if everything is okay. You are my guest."

"I am?"

"You are now."

Celyn studied the Iron Dragon King standing before him. He was missing an eye, but Celyn had already heard from most of his female kin that the black patch the dragon wore "only makes him more attractive."

Something that Celyn had never cared about . . . until this moment.

"Everything going all right?" Celyn pushed.

"Everything is fine. Gaius Domitus has been showing me how to handle missing eye."

"Great. Great. I see he also got you an eye patch."

"No. That came from crazed She-dragon with hair like fire and no sense of boundaries."

"That sounds like Keita." Celyn shrugged. "It is a nice color on you, though."

When Elina just stared at him, her brows pulled low behind her new eye patch, Celyn quickly turned to the Rebel King.

"Your sister is in the Great Hall."

"And?"

"Alone. And we have no clue where Annwyl is, which means the queen could be not knowing who your sister is right at this moment. Much to your sister's annoyance."

"I see." With that annoying smirk fixed on his face, the Rebel King nodded at Elina. "I hope to see you at the feast tonight, Elina Shestakova."

"I will need to eat," she replied drily. "So most likely I will be there."

"Captain Celyn."

The royal walked away, and Celyn turned to find Elina gazing at him.

"What?" he asked.

"Captain? I did not know you had rank."

"I'm captain of Her Majesty's Personal Guards."

"Did you get title because queen is your aunt and Southlanders are known for their incessant nepotism?"

"No. I got it because I threw the last captain off Devenallt Mountain after he said something rude about one of my older sisters."

"Why would that make you captain? Dragons can fly."

"Aye. But I threw him in such a way that I broke both his wings against the mountainside and made him cry when he landed on his big, fat head. When my uncle Bercelak saw him crying, he called him weak and made me captain."

"That was cold and unfeeling of you." Elina nodded. "I am impressed."

"The feast will be happening soon. You should get cleaned up."

"All right. I need lake."

"Or we can get you a bath in your room. The servants will bring you warm water."

"Lakes and streams all around this property and you make your workers fetch water so you can clean yourselves?"

Celyn gave a small nod. "Yes."

Elina glanced off, then shrugged. "All right."

They headed back to the hall. "You may want to take a nap as well," he suggested. "Our feasts tend to last until the wee hours."

"The wee hours of what?"

"The morning."

"All right."

"And something else . . ."

"Yes?"

"You are not allowed more than one husband or wife in the Southlands."

Elina stopped at his sudden change of topic and, like a confused bird, turned her head to look at him. "Why would any man want more than one wife? Is that not too much work for him? Especially if both wives are warriors and still of breeding age. The male can barely handle one wife, much less two, and would need several brother-husbands to assist him. Although I guess—"

"The point is," he cut in, "only one mate. You can't have several."

"That is sad for Annwyl. She deserves many husbands."

"What I'm saying is that *you* can't have a lot of husbands."

"Of course I cannot."

"You can't?"

"No."

"Oh. All right."

"Because I am not worthy. I have failed two queens and deserve nothing. So I will live out my life alone and bitter.

Perhaps my sister will allow me to care for her offspring until I die of old age . . . in shame. At least, that is my plan."

Celyn threw up his hands. "I have no response to that, Elina."

"Why would you? It is *my* plan. I am sure you have your own plan. One filled with more dragons tossed off mountainsides and many offspring who will get to positions of power through nepotism and the willingness to break the wings of their enemies." She smiled and patted his chest. "See? There are plans for all of us!"

Elina headed up the stairs to the Great Hall, and Celyn stood there . . . so very confused.

Chapter Thirty-Four

Kachka walked into the Great Hall after bathing in the stream. She heard gasps and turned to the poor, sheeplike servants setting up the dining table.

"What?" she asked.

"My lady—" an older woman began.

"I am no lady. I am Kachka Shestakova of the Black Bear Riders of the—"

"Perhaps," the servant stated over Kachka, "my lady would like some fresh clothes to put on."

"Oh." Kachka looked down at her naked body. "I guess—"

A robe was thrown over her shoulders, her dirty clothes removed from her hands so that her arms could be stuffed into the sleeves, and the robe quickly cinched at her waist by a silk belt.

"There," the servant said, smiling, "don't you look lovely?"

"I do not know. Do I look lovely?"

"Um . . ." The servant pointed at the stairs. "Why don't I take you to your room, my lady?"

"Kachka Shestakova. Not my lady. I have no royal ties to this world or the next."

"Very good. This way."

As they walked up the stairs, Kachka asked, "Do you not long for freedom from these shackles of oppression?"

"Shackles?" The servant glanced at her. "I wear no shackles, and I'm free to come and go as I please. Annwyl is a fair and courteous queen."

"Do you fear if she hears your complaints, she will have you killed?"

The servant snorted. "I complain to the queen whenever necessary, and she simply handles our needs. She's never killed one of us for having a concern or voicing it." The servant stopped and faced Kachka. "Perhaps it is her father you've heard of. He was a most unpleasant ruler by all accounts. But that is not Annwyl. If you are displeased in some way, though, please just let one of us know and we'll be more than happy to—"

Kachka waved off the sheep's concern. "No, no. All is well. But do you know where my sister is?"

"Your sister?"

"Yes. She misses eye where our mother gouged it out in rage."

"Your . . . mother?" The woman nodded. "Suddenly everything makes sense." She walked down several long halls until she reached a door. "Your sister has been placed here. You can have the room next door."

Kachka opened the bedroom door and stepped into a room bigger than anything she'd ever seen before that was not a tent used for an entire tribe of people. Elina was stretched out on a bed, sound asleep, her hair wet from a recent bathing, a robe similar to Kachka's around her naked body.

"I will stay here," Kachka announced.

"But your room is right next door."

"I will not leave my sister all alone in this giant room. She might get lost."

The servant opened her mouth as if to debate, but then, she simply closed it, sighed, and said, "As you like." The servant gestured at Elina. "You may want to take a nap as well. The feast does not begin for another three hours and can go on for quite some time. We can also bring you some clean clothes, if you'd like."

"I have clothes."

Again, the mouth opened and closed, and there was an audible sigh. "As you like."

The servant took her leave, and Kachka entered the room and closed the door. She sneered at the big tub that she was now sure her sister had used and went to the bed. She stretched out on it, and loudly said in their language, "I can't believe you used that gods-damn tub."

"It was offered, I used. Are you going to complain the entire time you're here?"

"You could fit twenty people in this room. Much more if some are willing to sleep on top of others."

"They don't do that here, sister. You might as well get used to it. And stop trying to urge the servants into a revolt."

"They deserve better."

"Than what? The hard life of the Steppes? Scrounging for food?"

"Just because your wonderful Annwyl is fair doesn't mean the next ruler will be."

"I know." Elina turned her head and looked at Kachka through her one sleepy eye. She'd removed her startlingly bright eye patch before going to bed and her scars were an ugly reminder of all that she'd been through. But Kachka pretended she didn't see them. As she'd pretended she hadn't seen the bumps, scrapes, and bruises that her sister had suffered at the hands of Glebovicha's favored offspring during the years they were growing up. "So I suggest, Kachka, that we help these people keep Annwyl as ruler for as long as she draws breath."

"Perhaps you are right."

Kachka reached down to the end of the bed and pulled the fur covering over her and Elina. They snuggled in deep, and Kachka let out a sad sigh.

"What?" Elina asked.

"This is all so very comfortable. I fear we will be weak and broken before the next full moon."

"Perhaps. But a very nice way to go, eh, sister?"

Then they giggled, as they hadn't done since they were very young.

Celyn returned from town with new clothes for Elina and her sister. He didn't want them embarrassed at the feast, but, then again, he wasn't sure if they were ever embarrassed by anything. Just in case, he got them clothes that he didn't think either would mind wearing.

As he walked through the Great Hall, the servants were busy putting out tables and chairs. Everyone else was most likely napping. He'd already seen the majority of his Cadwaladr kin down by the lake, happily snoring away and had passed Éibhear on his way to retrieving his Mì-runach friends from the local jail. Again.

Celyn quietly opened the door to the room he'd had Elina placed in. He dropped the new clothes on a chair and walked over to the bed. He could do with a little nap himself and the thought of curling up beside Elina seemed the perfect way to start his evening.

He started to crawl on the bed when a head popped up from under the fur coverings. A head that was not Elina's.

Startled, Celyn froze as Kachka peered at him. She blinked, then smiled. "Oh, Celyn. Hello." Her voice sounded sleepy and her eyes could barely stay open. She moved over a bit and patted the space between herself and Elina.

"Come. Join us."

Celyn jerked so brutally, he lost his balance and fell backward off the bed. He hit the floor hard, but that didn't stop him from scrambling to his feet.

"You know . . . I . . . yeah . . . no . . . thanks, though . . . but . . . uh . . . yeah . . . no . . . bye now."

He charged out the door, and slammed it shut behind him. He stood there a moment, panting hard, and wondering what the hell had just happened.

Elina lifted her head and looked at her sister. "What happened?"

"I have no idea. I thought Celyn wanted to nap, but when I suggested it, he panicked and ran out of the room like a frightened rabbit."

Elina studied the spot on the bed between her and Kachka, studied Kachka, then studied the door. After a moment, she laughed.

"He thought you were suggesting we share him."

Kachka sat up, her eyes wide. "What? Daughters of the Steppes do not share their men. Ever."

"I know. I know. But when I was traveling here, I often heard Southland men say things that suggested they were more than happy to find themselves caught between two women like so much meat caught between two big hunks of bread. Do not worry," she said, patting her sister's arm. "I will explain to Celyn later."

Elina turned over, but her sister did not relax back into the bed. Instead, she noted, "He ran out of here."

"Yes. I know. I heard the door slam."

"But you said Southland men, or in Celyn's case, Southland *males* like to share themselves with more than one woman."

"Yes. So?"

"But he ran out of here."

Elina looked over her shoulder at her sister, but she couldn't see her now that her eye on that side was gone. Instead of turning over completely, she snapped, "What is your point, sister?"

"My point is he didn't get naked and offer himself up to us like a deer to a witch's sacrificial knife. He ran away. . . ." Then, to Elina's horror, her sister's voice turned singsong like it used to when they were children and Kachka relentlessly teased her. "Because he looooovvvess you."

"What?" Elina tried to flip over, but she got caught in the fur covering and the ridiculous robe. She was so thrown off by her missing eye, she ended up on the floor. "Gods-dammit!"

"And you love him tooo-ooo."

"Shut up, demon female! I do not!"

Dagmar, who never napped before a feast since she enjoyed the wonderful quiet so much, walked down the hall. She would make sure that everything was in place downstairs before King Gaius and his sister arrived for the festivities.

But as she passed a room, she heard something crash inside. Worried it was her girls up to no good again, she stepped back and pushed the door open, freezing after taking only a few steps in.

She watched the two Riders wrestling on the bed. Elina was snarling and barking something in her language, while Kachka was laughing hysterically while fighting her sister off and saying something that Dagmar also didn't understand.

Both women were nearly naked, their robes hanging off them as they tried to get each other in a choke hold.

Dagmar stepped back out of the room and closed the door.

"Perhaps it's time I learn the language of the Outerplains, and their . . . *sisterly* . . . customs."

Elina held up clothes she found sitting on a chair. "I think Celyn left this for us."

"We have clothes."

"Nothing that is fancy."

"Why do we need fancy?" Kachka growled. "Are you ashamed of where you come from?"

"Would you stop? You complain like angry old woman."

The bedroom door opened, and the annoying red-haired She-dragon swept into the room.

"Look what I have for you, Elina," she trilled annoyingly. Then she held up a dark red dress, complete with matching eye patch made of the same material. "Isn't this lovely? And will look absolutely darling on you."

When Elina only stared at her, the She-dragon changed her focus to Kachka. "Don't you agree . . . sister person, since I never bothered to learn your name?"

Kachka moved forward, one hand reaching out to touch the dress. "It is lovely."

"Yes! See? Your sister agrees. So you should put it on."

That's when Kachka reached over to the pile of dirty clothes she'd left on the table and pulled out her dagger. She then cut the dress from bodice to hem.

The She-dragon gasped in outrage. "What have you done, barbarian female!"

"No sister of mine will wear your ridiculous dress! She is a Daughter of the Steppes! Not some weak female who needs male to look out for her." Kachka yanked the eye patch from the dragon. "But she will take this. It will look nice with her skin."

"I should burn you to ashes, foreign trash!"

"You could try." Kachka slammed her bare foot down on the She-dragon's, causing the female's yelp to ring out. Then she caught her by the shoulder, shoved her out into the hallway, and slammed the door closed.

Grinning, Kachka tossed the eye patch to Elina and, by some miracle, Elina caught it.

Éibhear was coming back from town after getting his friends out of the local jail. He didn't know how they always managed to get in trouble, but they always did.

Still, he was glad to see his old friends outside of the work they did as Mì-runach. And, thankfully, his friends got along well with Izzy. Although he was going to suggest that she start letting them win, at least once, when they arm-wrestled. It was really starting to crush their egos that they couldn't beat her. Especially when they remembered that she was only human.

As the oversized group of four made their way back to the castle and the awaiting feast, Aidan suddenly stopped and focused on a nearby lake.

"What?" Éibhear asked.

He pointed. "What's that dragon doing?"

Éibhear glanced over and saw his cousin Celyn slamming his head into a tree. As human. To do it as dragon was just an easy way to take down a tree. Éibhear did it all the time when he had to move trees in the Northlands. But as human . . . it was simply stupid.

Éibhear debated walking away. He did not care about Celyn and his problems. But he could already hear Izzy yelling at him that, "Celyn is your cousin! So what if I fucked him once? Get over it already! He's family and that's what counts!"

Unwilling to have *that* particular conversation yet again, Éibhear motioned to his three friends. "You lot go on ahead. I'll be there in a bit."

They set off and Éibhear went over to his kin. He watched Celyn ram his head against the tree a few more times, allowing himself that moment of enjoyment, before he asked, "What are you doing?"

Celyn stopped. "I'm banging my head into this tree."

Gods, did Fearghus and Briec really think Celyn was *smarter* than the rest of his brothers and sisters? Really?

"I can see that. Why?"

Celyn rested his back against the tree and stared off. He asked, "Do you ever think about sharing Izzy?"

Éibhear took in a deep breath. Let it out. Announced, "I can have you skinned, dismembered, and spread from here to the Western Mountains before suns-up and I promise that no one but my dear aunt Ghleanna would ever miss you."

Celyn rolled his eyes. "I'm not talking about with *me*, you idiot."

"You're ramming your human head into a tree, but *I'm* the idiot?"

"I just mean, if there was ever a beautiful female and she and Izzy were all, 'Come here, big boy,' would you—"

"Stop." Éibhear could see where this was going. Deciding

to put the past he had with Celyn aside, he answered from the heart. "I could never and would never share Izzy with anyone. I would never bring anyone else, beautiful or otherwise, into our bed. She's my mate. She'll always be my mate. It's that simple."

Celyn groaned and buried his head in his hands. And that's when Éibhear realized this had nothing to do with Iseabail and their past together.

"Is this about the Rider woman?"

His groan turning into a bearlike growl, Celyn suddenly grabbed Éibhear's chain-mail shirt and yanked him close. "You could finally get your revenge, cousin, and kill me now."

"I could . . . but I can assure you, *cousin*, this is much more fun."

"You're an evil bastard," Celyn hissed.

"I know!"

Elina finished pulling on her boot and looked over at her sister. "Did you hear that?" she asked.

"I did. It's some kind of . . . tapping."

The sisters went to the far wall and pressed their ears against it.

"Perhaps," Kachka whispered, "someone is in the queen's dungeon and is trying to send us message."

"Perhaps there is reason Queen Annwyl put them in dungeon."

Kachka glanced back at her. "What is happening to you?"

Together they moved along the wall, their ears still pressed to it, until they reached the door.

The knock came again, this time much louder, and they both jumped back.

Kachka pulled the dagger she had tucked into her boot

and pushed Elina back. After a few seconds, the door opened slightly, and Queen Annwyl peered around the corner. She seemed surprised to see them.

"You are here." She stepped inside. "Why didn't you answer the door?"

"Answer the door?" Kachka repeated.

"When I knocked."

"Is that what you were doing?"

Elina moved around her sister, reaching back to slap her hand, which still held the dagger defensively. "You will have to forgive us, Queen Annwyl. We do not have doors on Steppes."

"Oh. I see."

"And the red-haired She-dragon did not knock. She simply walked in."

"Yeah." Annwyl closed the door behind her. "Royal dragons aren't good with the knocking."

"Is something wrong, Queen Annwyl?" Elina asked when the royal simply stood there, saying nothing else.

"First off, don't call me Queen Annwyl. My name is Annwyl. Just call me Annwyl."

"Good," Kachka said. "I do not like titles."

"Neither do I. They make me uncomfortable."

"What is wrong?" Elina asked her. "You look upset."

"I haven't had time to apologize to you for what happened. With"—the queen cleared her throat and cracked her neck—"your mother."

Elina glanced at her sister, but Kachka just shrugged.

"We do not understand. What are *you* apologizing for?"

"For sending you back there."

"I lived there. They were my tribe, my people. What happened between me and my mother had nothing to do with you."

"By asking you to talk to the Anne Atli—"

"My mother has hated me since . . . since when, Kachka?"

"Since you stopped growing."

The queen blinked. "You're nearly as tall as me."

"She'd think you were small, too. But your skills in battle would eventually charm her. That's what worked for Kachka."

"Although she just tolerated me. Like dog that keeps showing up every night for food and shelter."

"What we are saying, Annwyl, is that this was coming for long time."

"She doesn't deserve daughters like you."

"It does not matter. She has twenty-three other children to replace us with."

Eyes wide in horror, the queen took a step back, her hand immediately resting on her stomach. "Twenty-three?"

"Some have more," Elina said with a shrug. "Some have less. Kachka and I are youngest and I am biggest disappointment. But you and your request had nothing to do with that."

"Well—" Annwyl scratched her head, and she seemed more . . . out of sorts than when Elina had first met her. Especially when the simple scratch with one finger turned into both hands digging into her hair and scratching like she was digging for gems. When she stopped, her hair covered her eyes and most of her face, but she didn't bother to move it out of her way. She simply gazed at them through it.

"How do you think I'd look bald?" she abruptly asked.

The question so shocked Elina, she didn't have an answer. But, sadly, her sister did.

"You could not pull off. Your face too full in cheeks."

Elina glared at her sister. "Kachka!"

"What? She asked question."

"I did. And I like honest people. Plus she's right. I can't

pull off bald with this face. Keita can. Then again, she can pull off anything. I hate her for that sometimes. Not even human and she's prettier than any human can even dream of being."

"Annwyl—"

"Are you both coming to the feast?"

"Yes. Of course."

"Good. You should. You deserve a feast after what you've been through."

"Yes," Kachka said. "A good feast always makes up for loss of eye."

Elina stamped her foot. "*Kachka!*"

"What?" her sister asked. "I am serious. The buffalo I killed today, I killed in your name. Like offering to your lost eye."

Elina rubbed her head, trying to avoid the eye patch. "She is serious," she explained to Annwyl.

"I know," the queen said. "That's why I like her. And you." She looked off through all that hair. "But your mother," she said, her voice low. "Your mother . . ."

Then the queen opened the door and walked out.

"Annwyl?" Elina began to go after her, but Kachka called her back.

"Leave her be."

"But—"

"Yes, sister. She is mad. But a good monarch is always a little mad."

"That is your logic? That good monarchs are mad?"

"There are three types of rulers in this world. Mad ones, evil ones, and combination of both. Be glad she is only mad."

Celyn walked into the Great Hall and searched the already packed room until he saw Elina. He immediately went to her side and grabbed her hand, turning to lead her back outside so they could talk. But Kachka was standing there, smiling up at him.

"Celyn," she purred. "I hope death finds you well this evening."

"What? I mean . . . oh, yes. You, too."

"You know, Celyn." Kachka placed her hand on his chest. "You scurried away so fast earlier, we could not talk about—"

"Excuse us!"

Celyn pushed past Kachka and dragged Elina out of the Great Hall and down the steps. When he reached the end of the courtyard, he tried to keep going right through the gates, but Elina dug her heels into the dirt and she managed to stop him in his tracks.

When he faced her, she said, "You need to calm down."

"I will *not* service your sister," he told her flatly, unable to think of anything else to say.

Elina laughed. "She does not want servicing. At least not from you."

"But when I came into your room earlier—"

"It gets cold on Steppes. We share beds. We share food. We do *not* share cocks. There is no cock sharing among the Daughters of the Steppes. That is disgusting."

"So then earlier . . ."

"She was inviting you to nap with us, like our brothers and cousins sometimes do. But not fuck."

"Oh."

"You sound disappointed."

"No. Just depressingly relieved."

"What?"

"Beautiful sisters invite me to bed—I usually dive in headfirst. A little time away with you and suddenly I'm . . . my father."

"I like your father. Now *he* is charming. You are dolt

with ineffective travel-cow and cousin that keeps trying to dress me like doll."

"Is that where you got that eye patch from?"

"Yes."

"It's a nice color on you."

Elina shook her head. "Can we go back to feast now? I have not eaten and naked fight with my sister earlier made me very hungry."

"Um . . . uh . . . naked fight?"

"She started it."

"Yeah, but . . . uh . . ."

"Come," she ordered, pulling him back toward the Great Hall. "There is food and drink to be had. Why would you ever make me live without either?"

Once most of the food was eaten, the tables were moved back, the music began, and the dancing started.

Dagmar had never been one for dancing, so instead, she found a comfortable corner and watched. It was one of her favorite things to do, and a pleasure she didn't have nearly enough time to indulge in these days.

But tonight, she was enjoying her favorite pastime less and less as she watched Annwyl. For years and years, she'd been helping to groom the queen into a sane-appearing monarch. And a few days ago, she'd thought she'd done an admirable job. Then the Rider had returned without her eye, and things had been going downhill ever since.

Even worse, Dagmar was not the only one worried. She knew that when Morfyd and Briec suddenly appeared next to her, each holding chalices of wine.

"That crazy cow is about to snap," Briec softly announced.

Morfyd closed her eyes and shook her head. "*Briec.*"

"What? Tell me I'm wrong."

"I didn't say you were. But there has to be a better way to say something like that."

"And what special way is that?"

"It can't be just the Rider's return, Dagmar."

"Maybe the Rider woman said something to her," Briec suggested. "Cried about how bad she feels."

"Cried? A Steppes Rider?" Dagmar shook her head. "Not likely."

"Besides," Morfyd said, "look at her."

They did, focusing on the outsider. She and her pale-haired sister had eaten and drunk enough for a small army, just between the two of them. Then, when the music began, it was the two of them who immediately got in the middle of the dance floor, clasped hands, and began to show everyone the dances of their people. It wasn't that the moves were especially complicated so much as they were physically challenging. They required incredibly strong legs and stamina. Something that both females seemed to have an abundance of.

Yet there was no sadness between them. No sad sighs that showed the woman or her kin mourned the loss of her eye.

Dagmar, of course, didn't believe she had "gotten over it" as Briec liked to tell people to do when he got tired of them complaining. But Dagmar could also tell this female wasn't faking her enjoyment of the festivities either.

"That eye patch is so cute on her," Morfyd noted.

"Gods," Briec snarled, "you sound like Keita. Can we stop talking about eye patches and focus on the bigger issue—the Mad Queen of Garbhán Isle?"

"Has anyone talked to Fearghus?" Dagmar asked.

"I did." Morfyd sighed. "He does not seem overly concerned."

"How is that possible?"

"You forget, brother, he fell in love with her when she

still had no control over her rage. When she tried to kill our father—while he was in his dragon form. When she cut off her brother's head. When she challenged our mother in front of her entire court. That was the Annwyl he fell in love with. So that Annwyl's sudden return doesn't exactly concern him as it does you and I."

Morfyd turned her body toward them and lowered her voice a little more. "And there's something else we haven't discussed."

"Which is?"

"Where the fuck is Brigida?"

"We have no proof that old hag has returned," Briec scoffed. "Just the word of Celyn."

"Say what you will about our cousin, Briec, but he's never been a liar. He doesn't make up stories. And I doubt even liar Gwenvael would dredge up the name of Brigida the Foul. So if Celyn says she brought him back here, I believe it. But then where is she? Why has she not shown herself to us?"

"What about Mum? Has she seen her?"

"I went to Devenallt Mountain earlier," Morfyd said, "and checked in, but Rhiannon has seen no sign. But just the *mention* of that She-dragon's name had our father insisting that our mother not attend the feast tonight. And he doubled her guard. He almost called Celyn back, but I thought it best to keep him here with the Riders."

"How concerned should we be about this Brigida the Foul?" Dagmar asked.

"Very," the siblings replied in unison.

Brannie cut through her dancing kin—laughing as Gwenvael swirled around her like the big girl he truly was—and tracked down her mother. She was chatting with Keita when Brannie stepped between them.

"Guess what Éibhear just told me?"

"That Celyn has fallen for the one-eyed Rider?"

Brannie pouted at Keita. "Your brother has the biggest mouth."

"He didn't tell me anything. Anyone with two eyes can see . . . hmm. Guess that's a bit of an inappropriate phrase in light of recent events."

Ghleanna patted Keita on the shoulder. "Look at you, realizing that on your own. Guess that Northlander bastard has had a good effect on you."

"What does that mean? I'm a lovely dragoness. Everyone adores me."

Ghleanna snorted. "Uh-huh. Sure they do."

"In fact, I am so helpful and loving, I've been desperately trying to help that barbarian female to enhance her personal style a bit."

Brannie frowned. "Her personal style?"

"I had a lovely gown picked out for her—"

"Gown?"

"—and that She-barbarian sister of hers slashed it to ribbons!"

"You tried to put a Daughter of the Steppes into a bloody dress?" Ghleanna demanded.

"Why wouldn't I? It would have looked darling on her! And the eye patch she's wearing now matched it perfectly."

"Riders don't wear dresses, silly hatchling."

"How sad for them."

"Why? They love their life." Ghleanna combed her hand through her short crop of black hair. "But my baby son with a Rider?"

"Oh, what?" Keita asked lightly. "My idiot brothers can make humans their mates, but not your precious son?"

"All my offspring are better than you House of Gwalch-mai fab Gwyar bastards, because they're not spoiled brats. But that's not what I mean. The women rule in the Steppes and my son is not about to become the first husband of many. He's a Cadwaladr. He's first, best, and most important."

"Do you even remember you have other offspring?" Brannie asked.

"If I'm forced to."

"Mum!"

Chuckling, Ghleanna threw her arm around Brannie's shoulders, pulled her in close, and kissed her forehead while putting her in a minor headlock.

"I adore all my offspring equally. Even you, my love."

Brannie rolled her eyes. "Thanks, Mum."

Ghleanna fingered the ends of Brannie's black hair. "This is getting a bit long, don't you think?"

"No. I like my hair to reach my shoulders."

"Just gives them more to grab for in battle."

Brannie pulled away from her mother. "There's absolutely nothing wrong with me hair."

"If you say so."

"I absolutely *hate* when you get that tone!"

"What tone? A tone that would suggest it wouldn't kill you to make your hair more appropriate for a captain of Her Majesty's Army?"

"Am I supposed to believe that Uncle Bercelak or Auntie Rhiannon give one single fuck about the length of my hair?"

"*I* give a single fuck about the length of your hair. Not as your mother, but as general of Her Majesty's legions!"

"Oh for the sake of the gods, Mother, give it a rest!"

"Don't speak to me in that tone, you spoiled brat!"

"You just told Keita there are no spoiled brats among *your* offspring."

"*I lied!*"

"Excuse me," Keita cut in. "Are you two done with the gossip? Because if you are, I'm going to find Talaith and see if she has anything good."

When Brannie and her mum simply stared at her, Keita

waved her hand, gesturing between them and gleefully noted, "Like twin mirrors of rage, you both are!"

"Human?"

"Dragon."

"Really?" Kachka sighed. She'd had no clue there were so many dragons in the world. Dragons who pretended to be human.

But while sitting on this table with her sister, their long legs hanging over the edge while they ate some ridiculously delicious—and definitely decadent—dessert, they'd been guessing which were the dragons and which weren't. And sadly, Kachka was learning that dragons were *everywhere*.

"What about that one?" she asked. "Human?"

"Dragon."

"No!"

The dessert the sisters had been indulging in was some kind of fried dough covered in powdered sugar. The pieces were bite-sized so the pair had been throwing them up in the air and catching them in their mouths for nearly twenty minutes. Although Kachka didn't have the heart to tell her sister that she now had multiple dots of powdered sugar on her face from when her aim had been off.

But Kachka refused to feel sad about that. She had her sister by her side and she was actually happy, even without her eye. Already they'd had much more time together than they'd had since they were children.

As soon as it had become clear that although Elina excelled as a hunter for food but not a slaughterer of humans, the pair had spent less and less time together. Something Kachka was sure their mother had arranged. Not because she held any great hopes for Kachka either, but because she simply wanted Elina to suffer. To be as alone and separate as she could be without it being too obvious.

It no longer mattered. though. They were still Daughters

of the Steppes, always would be, but they were outcasts now. No longer accepted by their own, they only had each other to turn to. Something that didn't bother Kachka as much as it probably should have.

"What about that one?" she asked, pointing out a tall, broad-shouldered, but young-looking male. "He's not a dragon, is he?"

"No. He's not."

"See?"

"He's a Northlander."

Kachka snarled in disgust and spit on the floor to ward off nearby evil.

"I was trying to pretend I wasn't listening," the one they called Izzy stated from nearby, "but now I must ask, why such a reaction to Northlanders?"

Elina motioned the woman closer, and she practically skipped over in excitement. Did these Southlanders have nothing better to do with their time than have their servants cater to them and involve themselves in gossip?

"Back, many centuries ago," Elina explained, "we used to raid the Northland territories for jewels and husbands—"

"Are you sure you shouldn't just call them slaves?"

"We marry them, do we not?" Kachka asked, not appreciating the brown one's judgmental tone.

"I was just asking."

"But they did not have many jewels and the few pretty men we found tended to die on the way back to the Steppes."

"Why?"

"Because they tried to escape and often tried to take a Daughter or two with them. And the Daughters usually killed them out of annoyance."

"Aaah. I see. But why did Kachka do the dramatic . . . spitting? Which, by the way, the servants will be forced to clean up."

"Keep that tone, Southlander," Kachka warned, "and I will make you lick it up."

Elina placed her sugar-covered hands against each one's chest to stop them from charging each other. Not because she wanted to stop them from fighting, but more likely because she wasn't finished telling the story yet. Elina hated when people interrupted her stories.

"But we continued to raid their lands—"

"Wait," the one called Izzy said. "If there were few jewels and the men kept dying . . . why would you continue to raid their lands?"

"They were there and practice makes the perfect. Anyway, a group of powerful Northland hags finally had had enough and they conjured up some Northland demon to rain vengeance down upon our heads. It wiped out a good chunk of our people at the time. It was very bad."

"What kind of demon was it?"

"You ask many questions, brown one," Kachka accused.

"Because I'm interested in her tale. And if you call me brown one again, I'll rip your arms off."

Kachka, curious to see if the Southlander could, slid off the table. But as they went at each other, Celyn was there, practically diving between them.

"What's happening?" he asked, putting his arms around each woman's shoulders and yanking them close to his sides. "What are we talking about?"

"I was telling them about the time the Northland hags sent a demon to destroy our people." Elina popped another treat into her mouth, chewed, and wagged a finger at Celyn and the brown one. "You know, Celyn, when that red-haired cousin of yours who tries to dress me like doll said that you two used to fuck, I was not sure I believed her. You do not seem to have much in common," she noted casually. "But after talking to this one, and seeing how many questions she asks, I now understand it. Of course, like most women, her questions are pointed and short. Unlike yours, which are rambling and endless."

The one called Izzy pulled away from Celyn, her lips in a tight line of anger. "If you'll excuse me. I have to go find my aunt Keita and beat her to death." She started to walk away, stopped, faced Elina. "But before I go . . . demon?"

"They said it was a league high. A purple-scaled, winged She-demon with white horns and cold silver eyes that shot lightning from its maw."

Celyn and the woman stared at Elina for a long moment, but when the woman opened her mouth to speak, Celyn quickly stopped her.

"No, Izzy."

"But—"

"No."

"But Ragnar—"

"No."

"Are you sure—"

"Positive!" He took the woman by the shoulders and spun her around. "Now I thought you were going to go beat Keita to death. There she is," he said while shoving her away.

Kachka again sat on the table and grabbed the last treat on the plate. "Did that brown one take you like whore, Celyn the Charming? Or did she pretend you were her first?"

Then Kachka and Elina laughed at the memories of how they'd often treated men when they were growing up, but Celyn merely snarled and stalked away.

"You best go to him, sister, and soothe his hurt feelings."

"Why should I?"

"You know how men are. If you treat them nice and buy them gifts, they will suck your pussy like champion."

Elina glanced off. "Well, when you put it like that . . ."

"And if you can, have another plate of these fried dough things sent over. I am still hungry."

* * *

"You have no respect for me at all, do you?" Celyn demanded when Elina caught up with him.

"Of course, I do," she lied while stroking his hair.

"*Elina.*"

She dropped her hand to her side. "I respect you more than most men. And every day I learn to respect you more. Of course, you are dragon, so I guess I still do not respect men at all. Just dragons."

"You do seem to like my father."

"He is smart and humble and very handsome—"

"All right," he cut in. "I get your point."

"You are not jealous of your own father, are you?"

"I am if you're busy lusting after him."

"You forget I have met your mother. I have one eye left, Dolt. I plan to keep it *in* my head. Not around your mother's thick neck like trophy."

"She does have a thick neck, but it works for her." Wrapping his arms around her waist, Celyn pulled Elina around to face him. "I just want to know that even though I'm a male, you don't think less of me."

"Of course I don't. When I think less of you, it is because of you."

"That's all I ask." Celyn grinned and kissed her. His mouth, warm and firm against hers, had Elina wondering if there was some place she could drag him off to for a bit so that he could take care of her needs. But then she heard the cheering and pulled away from Celyn to see that everyone, even Annwyl, was banging their drinking cups on tables and against walls while chanting, "Kiss! Kiss! Kiss!"

Perhaps it was the drink, but they all seemed so happy for them that Elina didn't know what to make of such enthusiasm. So she gave them what they all demanded.

Gripping Celyn with both hands around his thick neck, she yanked him down and kissed him hard. The cheering around her grew intense and for the first time in her life, Elina felt like she was . . . home.

With their lips still locked together, Celyn slid his hands under Elina's ass and lifted her until she had to tilt her head down to keep the kiss going. It was a gesture meant to let every dragon in the hall know . . . she was with him.

Possessive, he knew. But Celyn couldn't help himself. And he wasn't even sure he wanted to help himself.

Elina finally pulled away, her cheeks bright with color, her lips slightly bruised from their kiss; but her grin was wide and she didn't seem to mind the cheering crowd of Celyn's family at all.

In fact, the personalities that made Elina and her sister sometimes off-putting to Southland humans made them fit in perfectly with the Cadwaladrs. And their unwillingness to back down kept them from being pushed around by Rhiannon's royal offspring.

The music picked up again and Kachka grabbed her sister's hand and yanked her free from Celyn's arms. She swung Elina out into the middle of the floor and they clapped their hands as they moved around each other. Kachka gripped Elina's right hand with her left and the pair crouched, then leapt up, using only the power of their legs to keep them moving.

A circle was formed around them as everyone clapped and cheered.

Brannie walked over to him, her mouth opening to say something. But Celyn raised his finger, waved it twice. "Not a word," he told her. "Not one word."

As he asked, she said nothing. But she did hug his upper arm with both her hands and rest her head against his shoulder. They stayed like that for a long while as they watched the sisters dance.

"And then," Var went on, oblivious to the dancing and merriment going on around him, "Uncle Bram had me catalog all the books he had stacked in one corner of his house. It took me ages because there were so many. But some of them were very interesting about the history of dragons from the human perspective and the history of wars of Annwyl's great-grandfather. It was said he was never as happy as when he was right in the middle of battle, which reminds me of Annwyl. Even though I've never seen her in battle."

"So you enjoyed yourself then? At your uncle Bram's house?" Dagmar asked.

"Oh, yes. It was just hours of quiet. Wonderful, wonderful quiet. Then at dinner last night, I was able to talk to King Gaius and his sister, Princess Agrippina. Life in the Sovereigns sounds very interesting. After dinner, Uncle Bram pointed out some books about living there that I could read later."

Var took a brief break from talking when he guzzled back a tall chalice of milk. Dagmar glanced over his head at her nephew, Frederik. He gave her a small smile, but she knew what that smile really said. *Your son will be moving in with Uncle Bram and away from you. Forever.*

Placing his nearly empty glass down, Var took another bite of the cake he'd been eating and said, "I'll be heading back with him tomorrow morning. So I can't be up too late tonight."

"You're going back already? We didn't discuss that, Var."

"I have more books to catalog, and I think Uncle Bram is going to let me help him organize his papers. Auntie

Ghleanna says they're a mess. He can never find anything. You know how good I am at organizing. If *I* organize it, I know it will be done right."

Frederik winced even while he smiled. Why? Because Dagmar had created this judgmental little monster. He was so much her son, it would be horrifying if she didn't like herself as much as she did.

Dagmar took a cloth from the hidden pocket inside her dress and wiped her son's nose where he'd managed to get frosting on it. "I guess I should go up now and get a few more of your things packed."

"Already done." When Dagmar just stared at him, he added, "You know I like my things packed a certain way, Mum."

Frederik snorted, but quickly turned so that she didn't have to experience the betrayal of her favored nephew too closely.

Gwenvael danced by with Keita but stopped and turned, his arms open wide to hug his son. Var immediately raised his hand and said, "No."

"But—"

"No."

"Oh, come—"

"Father, *no.*"

Gwenvael dropped his arms. "Would it kill you to show a little affection to a father who adores you?"

"I think so . . . yes."

"Unnvar Reinholdt of the House of Gwalchmai fab Gwyar, hug your gods-damn father!" Dagmar snapped at her only son.

With a heavy sigh, Var handed his small plate of nearly finished cake over to his mother and grudgingly accepted the hug from Gwenvael. The patting on his father's back was painfully perfunctory.

When the "ordeal"—as Dagmar knew her son would

think of it—was over, Var slipped off the table he'd been sitting on and grabbed the last hunk of cake from the plate.

"I'm going to eavesdrop," Var told her nonchalantly before disappearing into the crowd.

"I don't know why you're glaring at me," Gwenvael stated. "If anyone has taught him the casual ease of gathering information, love of my loins, it was *you*."

Dagmar didn't bother arguing with her mate, since she knew he was right.

She turned and placed the dessert plate on the table. That's when she saw that Elina's sister, Kachka, was standing in front of Frederik. She was eyeing him like a prize cow at the fair.

"What is your name, little boy?"

"Frederik Reinholdt."

"A Northlander, yes?"

"Yes."

"And your age?"

"I turn twenty-four winters in another moon."

"Good." The Rider took his hand. "You will dance with me then."

Before Frederik could answer, she yanked him onto the dance floor.

Dagmar had her eating dagger out of her belt and was about to follow when Gwenvael caught her around the waist and pulled her back.

"No."

"He's just a child!"

"He's a man. Full grown, but with much to learn still." Gwenvael kissed her temple. "And something tells me Kachka Shestakova is just the female to teach him."

Izzy gripped Celyn's arm.

"Ow, woman! Unleash me."

"Look! That Rider has poor Frederik in her grip!"

Celyn lifted his head to watch Kachka drag Frederik up the stairs toward the bedrooms.

Celyn looked at Éibhear over Izzy's head, the pair of them grinning at each other over "poor" Frederik's plight.

"You two disgust me," Izzy growled before stalking off.

After rolling his eyes, Éibhear went after her. "Come on, Iz. We didn't mean it like *that*."

Yes, they did, but he understood Éibhear's desire to not get into a fight on such a lovely night as this.

Celyn picked up his empty chalice and went in search of more wine. But he'd barely passed the back door when a hand clamped down on his arm and dragged him down the hall.

"Elina?"

"I did not know you would spend all night dawdling with your family. You see them all day and night anyway."

"But the feast isn't over."

She grabbed the chalice from his hand and, when they passed the kitchens, she tossed it to one of the servants, who had to dive to catch it since her aim . . . still a little off.

The woman, whose Rider strength continued to surprise him, pulled him out one of the back doors, past the nearly finished and ominous-looking tower, and into the woods until they reached a small creek. That's when Elina caught hold of Celyn by his chain-mail shirt, spun him around, and pushed his back against a tree.

"I have need of you to lick my cunt," she told him as she yanked off her boots and wiggled out of the leather leggings he'd chosen for her to wear this evening. "Think you can manage that, Dolt?"

"If you promise to wrap that sweet mouth around my cock later."

"Daughters of Steppes do not make deals with men."

"I am not a man, so you'll make a deal with me. That is if you want my tongue licking out your pussy until you scream, you will."

Naked from the waist down, Elina nodded. "Fine, but you must never tell."

Chuckling, Celyn switched places with her, pressing her back into the tree. "Just shut up and spread your legs, Rider. I have work to do."

Elina watched the big dragon in his human form drop to his knees in front of her. He lifted her leg and placed it over his shoulder, then eased his hands up until they cupped her ass.

"You'll have to muffle your screams," he warned her. "We don't want to attract a crowd, now do we?"

Elina might have had a witty comeback to that, but it disappeared when Celyn pressed his mouth to her cunt and began to make long, delicious strokes over her with his tongue.

She dropped her head back against the tree and stared up through the branches at the sky above. Her world had changed so much in just a few days, but Elina couldn't say for a second that she was unhappy. That she felt out of place or confused or lonely. How could she say any of that when, at least at this moment, she had Celyn the Charming circling her clit with the tip of his tongue? Slowly, too. Over and over again, while his fingers squeezed the cheeks of her ass.

Her breath shortened, her thigh muscles tightened. She laid her hand on the top of his head. She wanted him to go faster, to finish her off. But he refused. He took his time, moving from her clit to her cunt, sliding his tongue inside like a cock. He was playing with her in a way she wasn't used to but was growing to love.

It felt like hours of torment as he took his time. It was so much that even though the Southland evening was quite cool, she was sweating, her hips moving as Elina tried to catch the elusive orgasm that Celyn kept just out of reach.

Her hand tightened in his hair, and she bit her lip to keep from snarling at him.

Then—finally!—he caught her clit between his lips and slid two fingers inside her cunt. He suckled her, his tongue managing to also tease at the same time. It was magnificent.

She came, like a wave crashing over her, her gasps of pleasure filling the air as her body shuddered and her cunt spasmed around his rough fingers. She managed not to cry out, but it wasn't easy.

Another wave began to crash, but before it could finish, Celyn stopped. Elina was about to order him back to work when he stood, kept her left leg up so that it pressed against his chest, and thrust his cock inside her.

He thankfully kissed her at the same time, so that her scream of pleasure and that little bit of pain was lost inside his mouth.

She tasted herself on his lips and tongue, felt her stickiness as his hand pinned her arms above her head.

He was ruthless, the way he fucked her. Ruthless and hard and unrelenting. What every Daughter of the Steppes demanded of a husband.

Elina's eye opened in shock and some panic. She'd just thought of Celyn as a husband. *Her* husband. The thought frightened her and she tried to pull away, but his grip just tightened and his thrusts became harder still.

The second wave that had started earlier finally crashed over her. The pleasure of what Celyn was doing to her washed away any fear she had.

She had no idea how he felt, and couldn't really care about it at this moment as she gave up temporary control of her body to him.

And he took that control, fucking her hard until he'd

ripped two more orgasms from her. Then, and only then, did he allow himself to come inside her, his entire body shuddering with the release as he held her tight.

When he was done, he gently lowered her left leg and brushed her hair from her face. He kissed her lips, her cheeks, her nose.

Then he removed her eye patch and kissed her scars and the lid that no longer had an eye behind it. They were soft, sweet kisses, and told Elina all she needed to know.

She pushed Celyn back, both of them gasping as his cock slipped out of her. She immediately noticed that, as always, he was still hard. A "dragon thing" he'd called it. A thing that Elina could easily live with.

She took his hand and led him toward the sound of moving water.

"What are we doing?" he asked.

She stopped, smiled up at him. "I have a cock to wash," she said, going up on her toes to kiss his jaw and cheek. Then she whispered against his ear, "With my mouth."

The dragon growled as she led him to the nearby stream.

Chapter Thirty-Five

Elina slid out of the bed they'd only made it back to a few hours before and quickly pulled on her clothes. She grabbed her bow and quiver and left the room silently so as not to wake Celyn.

She gently closed the door and was turning to head down the stairs when her sister's door opened and the Northland boy was shoved into the hall. His clothes were balled up and held by one hand while the other hand managed to keep a blanket in front of his naked cock.

He opened his mouth to say something, but Kachka slammed the door in his face.

Elina watched the poor boy's expression fall into dejected misery, and she worked hard to hide her smile. She walked up to him while he stood there, staring at that door like he expected it to open again. It wouldn't. Not for him, anyway.

Elina placed her hand on his forearm, and the Northlander turned those intense grey eyes toward her. Yes. She could see what had attracted her sister—at least for the moment.

"It hurts now, I know," she explained. "But trust me . . . what my sister just taught you in the last few hours will last you for centuries and have a horde of eager females scratching at your door, looking for good fuck." She grinned and patted his shoulder. "And a good fuck you shall give them."

She winked and headed off down the hall toward the stairs.

When Elina reached the Great Hall, she made her way to the table and grabbed a piece of fresh fruit from a bowl.

"You," she heard behind her and turned to see Dagmar Reinholdt walking toward her, while Gwenvael the oh-so-yummy ran across the landing toward the stairs.

Pointing a finger at her, Dagmar demanded, "What did your Outerplains whore of a sister do to my nephew?"

"She made him man. Something these little Southland girls could not do for him. Fucked him raw based on what I heard through walls."

Dagmar took an awkward, clumsy swing at Elina's face that Elina managed to avoid simply by leaning back slightly.

Before the Northlander could swing again, Gwenvael caught his mate from behind and pinned her arms to her sides.

That's when Elina realized that Dagmar Reinholdt was a damn lucky woman. With only his leggings and boots on, Gwenvael the Handsome was the epitome of male beauty. Especially with all that long, golden hair and those rippling muscles. His face was angular perfection. Honestly, Dagmar was lucky Kachka hadn't dragged *him* off to her bed last night. Elina had no idea whether either Dagmar or Kachka was considered pretty by these vapid Southlanders, but Kachka definitely had more to offer. She was a very good provider and protector; could give a punch as well as take one; and would always put food on the table thanks to her hunting skills.

Could Dagmar Reinholdt, a weak, Northlander female, say the same? Elina doubted it. Not to say this woman didn't have her own particular talents, but only in the Southlands was sneaky plotting considered a useful skill.

Gwenvael pulled his mate away while Elina watched them and ate her delicious fruit.

"You should be happy," Elina informed the foolish woman when she saw that the Northlander's anger wasn't abating. "Yesterday he was boy with only worthless girls that took ride on cock. Today he is man. Now you can get several oxen and quite a few horses for his large Northland shoulders and for what my sister taught him in the bed."

"Keep your sister away from my nephew!" Dagmar snarled.

"My sister got what she wanted from him," Elina calmly explained. "She no longer *wants* your nephew."

Gwenvael shook his head and lifted his mate off the floor, stumbling back a few steps. "You are not making this easy, Elina."

"I am honest. I do not know other way to be."

"Of course you don't," he muttered, carrying his mate away.

"Just remember," the Northlander yelled back at her, "I can have you and that sister of yours executed in the town square. I have that kind of power!"

Elina tossed the core of her fruit to one of the dogs sniffing around under the table and grabbed another from the bowl.

She headed outside and as she went down the stairs, she found Annwyl the Bloody standing there, staring off . . . at what, Elina had no idea.

"May death find you well this morning, Annwyl," Elina greeted her, tucking her fruit into the outside pocket of her quiver.

Annwyl chuckled, her gaze still locked on something past the courtyard. "I hate to say that death has found me many ways over the years, Elina. But I'm not sure it *ever* found me well."

"You still live, so it must have." Elina frowned a little. "Are you all right?"

"I was sleeping. . . ." She closed her eyes, her head tilting up so that the suns shone down upon her face. "Fearghus is always so warm. I love sleeping next to him in the winter. Summers can be hard, though. But I wouldn't give it up for anything. Not anything.

"Are you going to stay here?" the royal abruptly asked, her sudden change of subject startling Elina a bit. Annwyl turned her head to look at Elina, but Elina could barely see the queen's eyes through all that hair. When had she stopped combing it? And why? Daughters of the Steppes might live a hard life, but they prided themselves on always being well groomed.

"I . . . I had not thought of it," Elina said, stumbling over her words a bit. "But everything has happened so quickly. Do you want us to go?" Because Elina would never consider sending her sister away alone. Not when Kachka had given up everything to protect Elina. Everything. And that was a debt Elina would never forget or be able to repay.

"No," the queen replied simply, quietly. Almost as if she were talking to herself. "I like you. I like your sister. Her general lack of emotion has a soothing quality. I want you both to stay. For as long as you both want or need."

"That is kind, but I am not sure Dagmar Reinholdt would agree with you."

"Because Dagmar's sane." Annwyl nodded. "She's sane."

"Queen Annwyl . . . ?"

The royal started walking. "I have to go."

"Let me come with you."

"No. You stay here." Annwyl faced her. She might have smiled under all that damn hair, but who could truly tell? "If anyone asks, just say I'll be back."

She suddenly pushed her hair away from her face and Elina realized just how pretty Annwyl was. Clearly, Talan got his looks from his mother while Talwyn took after her father and grandfather. Not that she'd suffered in any way by taking after the males of her clan. Not like some women did.

Annwyl leaned in and kissed Elina on the forehead. "Your sacrifices will not be forgotten, mighty Rider," she murmured before turning away and taking a few steps.

The queen pulled out something she'd tucked into the top of her leather boot. "Here, before I forget. Keita asked me to give this to you." She tossed the item and Elina caught it.

It was a black eye patch.

"She said you can wear that as part of your everyday collection. I have no idea what that means." Annwyl finally walked off, throwing over her shoulder, "But you don't need to wear anything at all to cover your damaged eye, Elina Shestakova. No one here cares about your scars. Gods know, they don't seem to care about mine."

Elina looked down at the eye patch she now clutched in

her hand. She could tuck it into the top of her boot and forget about it. Annwyl was right. No one here cared about her scars. But then she remembered Celyn taking off her patch the night before. The way his hands had felt against her skin. The way he'd kissed her afterward.

Smiling, Elina tied the patch around her eye and went to the training field to practice.

Celyn reached for Elina, but his hand only touched fur bedding. A barked, "*Get up!*" startled him from wondrous sleep.

"What? What's wrong?" Celyn asked, reaching for his sword.

"I could have killed you twenty times over by now, idiot."

Celyn sighed. "And a good morning to you, Uncle Bercelak."

"Get up and get to work."

"Is there a problem?"

"You are the queen's protector . . . so go protect her."

Celyn frowned. "Wait . . . *is* there a problem?"

Bercelak glanced out the stained-glass window. "The day feels . . . wrong."

"Oh . . . okay, then."

His uncle glowered at him. "Once you get some wear on your scales, *boy*, you'll learn to trust your instincts. Until then . . . you'll trust mine. Or find out that I don't play favorites once you piss me off."

"And the love of an uncle fills the room!"

"Get. Moving."

"I'm up. I'm up." Celyn threw off the covers and stood, taking a moment to stretch his muscles.

"What the hells happened to you?" his uncle demanded.

Celyn looked down at his naked body. "What?"

"You look like you were gnawed on by beavers."

Celyn grinned. "Jealous?"

"Moving! Now!" Bercelak bellowed. "I'll meet you down by the lake. I want the whole Clan involved."

Celyn pulled on his clothes and went in search of Elina, since he couldn't leave without seeing her first. Thankfully, he passed his mum in the hallway.

"Can you get to Devenallt Mountain? I shouldn't be too long."

His mother smiled. "Your oh-so-important queen has more than enough guards surrounding her precious ass."

"I know that. You know that. You know who doesn't know that?"

"Me idiot brother?"

"I should round up a few of my brethren who like to spend their off-duty hours at the human pubs. Plus, I have to find Elina before I go. I don't know how long Uncle Bercelak will have his bad feelings about the day."

"What?"

"That's what he said. That the day felt wrong to him."

"Huh." Ghleanna nodded and patted him on the shoulder. "You go. Take care of what you need to. I'll be by Rhiannon's side until you get there."

"All right. Thanks, Mum. Oh . . . and Mum?"

"Yeah?"

"Do me a favor."

"Another one?"

"Don't fight with Rhiannon over Da. She just does that to make you and Uncle Bercelak crazed."

"What are you talking about?" his mother asked, eyes wide as if she was completely confused by what her son was saying. "Me? Argue with dear, sweet Rhiannon? Celyn . . . don't be foolish."

Celyn let out a sigh. "Uh-huh."

* * *

Annwyl walked deep into the forest, following the screams until she reached the edge of royal farmland.

The screaming came from panicked cows, including the one the old She-dragon had pinned to the ground with the help of a long tree trunk engraved with runes that she held in her left claw. She tore open the animal's midsection and dug her snout deep inside, devouring her fill while the cow held on to life longer than Annwyl was used to. All the dragons she knew, if they craved fresh meat, killed their prey quickly before eating. Usually with a quickly snapped neck.

It seemed that Brigida the Foul enjoyed her meals more when they thrashed about.

When the old She-dragon finished sucking in the cow's entrails like soup noodles, she suddenly turned that hard-to-look-at face toward Annwyl.

"What do you want?" that raw voice asked.

"Are you sure?"

Brigida tore off the cow's leg and proceeded to munch on the hoof the way Annwyl tended to munch on chicken bones during quiet dinners when she was able to spend most of her time reading a book.

It suddenly occurred to her that perhaps she should stop that little habit.

"Sure about what?" Brigida asked around the hoof.

"That you can fix Elina Shestakova's eye?"

"You get me a fresh eye, I can fix it."

"How fresh?"

"Very."

"If I ride to and from the Outerplains . . . ?"

Brigida shook her head, the sound of munching filling the valley. It was making Annwyl queasy.

"Nah. That's too long. By the time you get back, that eye will be dry as a raisin and that hole in her head won't be much better."

"That's disappointing," Annwyl said softly.

"Ain't ya got some prisoners? You can take it from one of them."

"If they're in jail it's because they haven't done anything to warrant getting their heads cut off. I'm not mutilating one person for another."

"You mean . . . unless they deserve it."

"It just seems fair," Annwyl snapped back, already preparing the argument she'd have with Dagmar. "Her mother took her eye for no damn reason, so her mother *owes* her an eye."

Annwyl abruptly scratched her head. Her hair itched. Not her scalp. Her *hair*, which even she knew was kind of a bad sign. But she was getting frustrated by all this.

Very fucking frustrated.

Spitting out some cowhide, the She-dragon asked, "What if I told you I could get you there and back from the Outerplains in a day?"

Annwyl immediately dropped her hands to her sides. "I'm not giving you my soul."

"Don't need your fucked-up soul. Got me own, don't I? If I was going to take a soul, it would be a pure one. And I ain't seen a pure soul around Garbhán Isle in many a century."

"Then what do you want? I know you want something. I'm not stupid. I know how these magicks work."

"Little girl, you know nothing. But that's what I like about you. Your fists are hard. Your brain relatively empty. And your soul . . . mean. You and me? We can do things together."

"Will I have to look at your face a lot?" Annwyl asked, closing her eyes. "Because it's freaking me *out*."

The old She-dragon cackled like she'd just heard the best joke ever. And when Annwyl opened her eyes again, Brigida was walking toward her as a flame-covered human, her walking tree trunk now shrunk down to a six-foot walking *stick*, the runes carved into it glowing.

By the time Brigida stopped in front of Annwyl, the flames were gone, but the blood-covered carcass of a mean old woman remained.

"Come on then, Annwyl the Bloody."

"Come where?"

"First to that stream over there. I need to get this blood washed off. Then me and you . . . we've got somewhere to be."

"I should tell Fearghus I'm leaving."

"You don't need to tell no male nothin'. Just come on. We'll be back before anybody notices."

Annwyl watched Brigida walk off and it suddenly occurred to her that she had no limp today. She was just walking along toward that stream as if she didn't have a care or pain in the world.

Annwyl really didn't know what to make of this old bitch. She really didn't. But she knew that she owed it to Elina to at least try to make things right. And something told her that Brigida was the only one willing to do that.

Glancing around and seeing nothing that changed her mind, Annwyl followed Brigida the Foul.

Celyn came into the Great Hall, hoping to see Elina at one of the dining tables. Instead, he found an exhausted and forlorn-looking Frederik.

"What's wrong?" he asked the Northland male while reaching for the fruit sitting in a bowl on the table.

Frederik sighed, long and loud. "Nothing."

Celyn rested his ass against the table and stared down at the boy. "Did Kachka toss you out of her room when she was done with you this morning?"

"Yes. She did. She used me and tossed me aside."

"She did use you."

"Thank you very much, Celyn."

"But so what? From the sound of it when we passed her

room this morning, you were enjoying every second of that
using."

"That's not the point."

"What is the point? That she gave you the time of your
life? Would you have preferred to have that idiot Gwenvael
hire you a girl to break you in proper? Because trust me, if
you'd kept showing up with those little peasant girls and
prissy royal brats you were trying to woo . . . eventually he
would have offered. And among the Cadwaladrs it's hard
coming back from that shame."

"I didn't know everyone took an interest in who I . . . I . . ."

"Fucked. The word is fucked. If you can't say it, you
won't be able to do it. Look," Celyn went on, "my suggestion is that you just take this experience and enjoy it for
what it was."

"And what was it?"

"An amazing night of fucking with a one-hundred-and
fifty-four-year-old woman."

Frederik froze and slowly looked up at Celyn. "Pardon?"

"She didn't mention that?"

"No. *Her* age never came up."

"Elina's her *younger* sister. She's a hundred and forty-
five."

"I had sex with an old woman?"

"No. You had sex with a Daughter of the Steppes, and
you should be grateful." Celyn grinned, and he knew his
grin was wide. "I know I am." He bit into the fruit, decided
he didn't like the taste, and tossed it back into the bowl.
"Speaking of which, have you seen Elina?"

"I saw her heading toward the training area with her
bow."

"Of course." He patted Frederik's shoulder. "Don't fret.
Kachka won't be considered an old woman by her people
for quite a few more centuries. And in a few days, this will
all be just a glorious memory for you."

Celyn walked out of the Great Hall and down the stairs

into the courtyard. That's where Gwenvael caught his arm and yanked him around.

"You need to keep your Rider females from my lady's sight today."

"First off," Celyn stated calmly, "get your claws off me."

"Listen, Low Born, don't—"

"Second, I *will* cut that pretty face of yours."

Gwenvael gasped and stepped away. "You wouldn't dare!"

"So deep even your sister won't be able to heal the scars."

"Bastard!"

"Now what's the problem?"

"Your whorish Riders—"

"Watch it. I'm a Cadwaladr, raised by Ghleanna the Decimator herself. I always have a blade at the ready."

"Fine then. Kachka Shestakova fucked Frederik Reinholdt."

"And?"

"Dagmar is not happy."

"What does any of this have to do with the Shestakova sisters?"

"While her only son is with your father, Frederik is all Dagmar has. She still sees him as her little orphan nephew."

"His father may be quite the bastard, but Frederik is *not* an orphan. Plus he's past his twenty-third winter, six-four, and well over two hundred pounds."

"*And he's* still *her little orphan nephew!*" the dragon bellowed.

"What exactly do you want me to do?"

"Just get the Riders out of Dagmar's sight. Right now I've got her holed up in her study with her weird little assistant for the next few hours. It would be nice if when she comes out for luncheon, reminders of her nephew's lost innocence were removed."

"He wasn't a virgin."

"I'm guessing that compared to what he'd had *before* Kachka Shestakova . . . he might as well have been."

Celyn was about to argue the point until he shrugged and nodded, realizing his idiot cousin was right.

"Just get them out of here for a day. Maybe two."

"And where, exactly, do you want me to take them?"

"Your father is going back to his house and taking Var. Let the sisters go with them. They can keep an eye on the boy."

"I'm surprised Dagmar's not sending you to watch out for Var yourself."

"She tried, but unlike my mate, I'm confident he'll be just fine under your father's boring care. But your Riders will be great protection with their bows and bad manners."

"I don't know why you're being so mean to them," Celyn chastised. "Kachka herself told me that you'd fetch nearly a kingdom of gold among the tribes for your good looks."

Gwenvael grinned. "Really?" He shrugged. "Well . . . I *am* beautiful."

"And I'll still happily slice that pretty face right open."

"Stop saying that! Bastard. Just get your women out!"

"Only one is my woman," Celyn barked back. Then he grinned, realizing the meaning of his statement. "Aye. One is *my* woman."

"And surprise. She's not Izzy."

Celyn had his blade out, but Gwenvael immediately covered his face with both his arms.

"You cover your face but leave all your major organs exposed?" Celyn demanded, disgusted by his royal cousin. Always so disgusted.

"I'm protecting the most important thing about me besides my hair." Gwenvael peeked around his arms. "According to castle rumor, it is worth a kingdom of gold."

Celyn rolled his eyes, already regretting telling Gwenvael that, and tucked his sword back into its sheath. "You are pathetic. Absolutely pathetic."

"But I am handsome."

* * *

A young squire placed more arrows in Elina's quiver and then brought a bucket filled with even more arrows, which he placed at her feet.

She nodded her thanks and nocked another arrow, waiting as a second squire moved in a new target since the last one was now covered in the arrows she'd already unleashed.

It was hard going, adjusting to the loss of her eye. But she was glad to see her aim getting better with each arrow shot.

"Elina?" Fearghus asked as he moved next to her from her sighted side. "Have you seen Annwyl this morning?"

She nodded at Fearghus's question. "I have. She was standing in the courtyard, staring off toward the trees." She gestured with her bow. "She seemed . . . preoccupied."

"What do you mean?"

"Something vexed her, but she would not tell me what."

The handsome dragon nodded and patted her shoulder as he quickly moved by. "Thank you, Elina."

With a fresh target in place, Elina automatically turned her head far left, then glanced right, to take in her surroundings. But when she turned her head back toward the left she saw someone moving silently up behind her. She had her bow raised and the arrow loosed before her mind could actually make out who that someone was.

Thankfully, her target was fast of hand and the arrow was caught before it made contact.

Holding the arrow, the head pointed right at where his heart was, Celyn calmly explained, "This *is* one of two ways to quickly kill a dragon in human form. So let's avoid doing that to me or anyone in my family."

Elina turned her whole body and snarled at Celyn, "My left side will forever more be my blind side, you dolt! Move toward me from that direction and I will shoot arrow first and mourn your loss second."

Grinning, he leaned in and kissed her. "And a good morning to you, too, ray of suns-shine."

Elina snatched back her arrow. "Foolish dragon! What do you want?"

"I have to return to the queen's side for a bit—"

"It is your job to protect the Dragon Queen, is it not?"

"—and I was wondering," he continued on, "if you and your sister could escort my father and young Var back to Bram's home?"

Elina smirked. "That Northland female wants us gone from Garbhán Isle, yes?"

"Just for a day or two. Until the sting of your sister twisting her nephew like dough around her naked body is more of a faint memory."

Elina rolled her eye. "I do not understand these Northland females at all. It is not like Kachka made him one of her husbands."

"She has husbands?"

"Not yet, but she will. She has much to offer a cadre of handsome men."

"Well . . . she can offer whatever a cadre is to someone who is not related by blood to Dagmar Reinholdt."

"Will we ever be allowed to return here?"

"*Yes*," Celyn said, his voice vehement. "I said a day or two, not a lifetime. And I have no intention of hiding you and your sister away on Devenallt Mountain to live life among those snooty royal dragons."

"Why would we live there?"

"Because I'm there." He kissed her again. "And where I am—" And again. "—I want you to be." And again.

When he pulled away, Elina licked her lips and nodded. "That is acceptable for now."

"For now? Really? And when should I start expecting you to leave?"

"Eh." She shrugged. "I am Daughter of Steppes. I have more time than most, so I am in no rush to make such a decision. But do not become too comfortable, Dolt. I could make change of mind at any time in the next century or two."

"I'll attempt to remember that," he murmured as he leaned in for another kiss.

"Morning, sister and her dragon whore!" Kachka's voice boomed, startling Celyn away from that tantalizing kiss. Much to Elina's annoyance. "I hope death finds both of you well this glorious morning!"

Elina glanced over at her sister. "You have caused problems, Kachka."

"Me? How? I did not start one fight last night, just as I promised you. Nor did I spit again on floor after first time, and I set nothing on fire."

"Fire?" Celyn asked.

"That is what we do when we raid town," Elina explained. "Burn everything to ground as warning to other towns that dare challenge us. We also sometimes do that to individual people . . . when they annoy us enough."

"How lovely."

Elina faced her sister. "You fucked that boy—"

"He is certainly man *now*."

"—and the Northlander female is not happy."

"We should have wiped the Northlanders out and taken their men when we had the chance." She nodded at Celyn. "No offense."

"None taken. I'm a Southlander."

"Well, we did none of those things," Elina went on, "and now the Northland female whines. So we will go with Bram the Merciful to his home. Protect him and the boy."

"The little smart one?" Kachka nodded. "He takes after

father and one day he will be glorious to look upon." She grinned. "And I will still be here, waiting for that day."

"I am begging you," Celyn said, his eyes briefly closing, "never say that again, ever, within a thousand leagues of this place. Not unless you are *hoping* to be executed. Just . . . never."

Kachka reached up and patted Celyn's face with the tips of her fingers. "I see why my sister likes you so. You are so adorable when there is fear in your black, soulless, dragon eyes."

Chapter Thirty-Six

Just as Bram landed in the courtyard of his castle home, the two Riders came through the gate that, once again, he'd forgotten to close.

"Am I that old?" he asked Var. "That I can't out-fly horses now?"

"Those are Steppes horses, Uncle Bram," the boy patiently explained as he slid off Bram's back. "They are known for their speed and endurance." He patted Bram's side. "And you are getting old."

Bram nodded. "Thank you, dear boy. Your honesty is so refreshing in this day and age."

The horses trotted close to Bram, showing no fear. The same way the women on their backs showed no fear.

"How do you live like this, Bram the Merciful?" Kachka asked. "So much unmovable stone. Do you not feel trapped?"

"Dragons normally live in caves. Castles aren't much different."

"I do not like," Kachka sniffed. "I would feel like I could not breathe."

"Do not complain so, sister. It's not like you will be trapped by walls of stone." Elina pointed at Bram. "Just the dragon. So if walls fall on him and crush his sad head, we will be outside under the stars . . . safe."

Bram nodded. "Thank you both for that."

"You are welcome," they said together.

"Uncle Bram," Var said, "I'm hungry."

"Come, little Abomination," Kachka ordered. "We will hunt your food down."

Var, his face twisted in disgust, pointed at Bram's castle. "I'm sure Uncle Bram has food. He always has food. Food I don't need to hunt down and kill."

"Horse gods of death, what have these dragons been teaching you, boy? How to live off others when you are perfectly healthy to go and hunt for yourself?"

"That's exactly what they've taught me, and I find it perfectly acceptable."

"No." Elina rode over to the boy, reaching down and hauling him onto the back of her horse. "You will not turn into lazy Southlander. Not when you have potential to be a perfectly acceptable husband one day."

"I don't want to be an acceptable husband one day."

"You all say that, but then on knees you beg. 'Pleeeeease make me husband. I will do anything to be your husband.' But you are too pretty to beg. The warriors will come to *you* and offer so much to have someone so pretty raise their children."

"Uncle Bram?" the boy begged in a whiney voice Bram had never heard before, making Bram choke back a laugh. It was always nice when his nephews' dragon-human offspring actually acted like children for once.

"Learn to hunt, Var. It'll be good for you."

"We won't be long," Elina told him.

Wondering if he'd remembered to bring those scrolls that Dagmar had given him last night, Bram began to dig into his travel bag. They had to be in here somewhere.

"Bram!"

Bram looked up, quickly realizing the two Riders and Var were staring at him. "Yes?"

"Close gate after us," Elina said. And based on her tone . . . she'd said it more than once.

"Right. Close gate. I will."

"Good."

The sisters rode out with young Var, and Bram walked toward his gate. But by the time he reached it, he was head-first into his bag, trying to find those damn . . .

"Here they are!" he called out triumphantly.

Bram glanced around, quickly realizing he was talking to the air again. That was always awkward.

He turned and walked toward the castle steps, shifting to human as he did so. And the whole time he walked, he sensed he'd forgotten to do something . . . but damned if he could remember what it was.

Izzy finally made it downstairs and into the Great Hall by early afternoon. Éibhear was already at the dining table, but he had his head resting on his folded arms and she might have heard snoring.

Gratefully taking the tea one of the servants handed her—they'd been through enough Cadwaladr family feasts to know how to treat any lingering morning-after effects—Izzy pushed at her mate's shoulder until he sat up and she could settle on his lap.

"We are never drinking like that again," Éibhear promised as all the Cadwaladrs promised.

A promise they never kept.

She leaned in, kissed him. "Drink some of this tea."

"What will tea do?"

"It is Morfyd's recipe. It'll help."

"Morning!" Brannie announced before dropping into a chair next to Izzy and Éibhear. Both of them growled at her, but she only smiled wider.

"I was smart," Brannie noted. "I didn't drink nearly as much as you two."

"Only because you were running around, gossiping, all night," Izzy noted. "I had no idea you could be as bad as Morfyd."

"This is about my brother. How could I not gossip? Our older sisters will definitely want to know what's going on. I have to have all the information."

"Oh, yes, I'm sure that's it."

"Your sarcasm bites, old friend." Brannie reached over and took the tea out of Izzy's hand before Éibhear could take a sip, eliciting another growl from the dragon. But if Brannie noticed . . .

"Do you think Celyn will really take Elina as his mate?"

"Yes," Izzy and Éibhear answered together.

Their quick and confident response surprised Brannie. "Why? Because he feels sorry about what happened to her eye? Because that was her mother's doing. My brother—"

"Brannie, Brannie," Éibhear said in a tone that suggested he was talking to a small child. "This has nothing to do with the loss of her eye. Your brother will choose Elina Shestakova as his mate because she fucks him stupider than he already is."

Izzy laughed at that, but Brannie didn't.

"You're talking about my brother, worthless Mì-runach."

"Don't act like an innocent with me, cousin. I've been on campaign with you, and seen more than one battle-weary soldier tossed from your tent when you were done with him . . . or *them*." Izzy cringed at that, ready to step in if the fight between cousins turned physical. Gods, she hated when it turned physical while she was still recovering from the prior evening's drink. "So don't pretend with me. Ever."

"I'll have you know, Éibhear the Idiotic, that I—"

Brannie's words stopped when Fearghus walked into the hall. "Morning, Izzy. Brannie. Have either of you seen Annwyl?"

"You can't even be bothered to greet me? I'm your brother."

Fearghus looked Éibhear over, said nothing, and focused again on Izzy, his eyebrows raised in question.

Izzy shook her head, trying not to giggle at the torture of her mate. His brothers were so mean to him. Still! After all these years!

"No," she replied. "Haven't seen Annwyl. Why?"

He shrugged. "I haven't been able to find her and—"

"So she's gone?" Izzy asked as she curled her fingers into her hand and dug her short, battered nails into her palm to help keep herself calm.

"I'm sure she's around some—"

"I'm sure she's around somewhere, too. Why don't you go outside and look for her?"

"I should probably go check the library fir—"

"Great idea. Go check the library."

Fearghus frowned at that, but then shrugged and walked off. When he had disappeared deep into the bowels of the house . . .

"Dammit!" Brannie slammed her hand against the table as Izzy jumped off Éibhear's lap and began to pace. "I told you, Izzy. I *told* you she was not going to let that thing with the Rider go. Not in a million years."

"All right, all right." Izzy put her hands to her head. "Let's not panic."

"I don't know why you two are worried," Éibhear calmly reasoned. "I'm sure Annwyl is just—"

"I said not to panic!" Izzy yelled into Éibhear's face.

The dragon leaned away from her, his hands raised. "I wasn't."

"We have to go get her." Brannie stood. "Now. Before anyone realizes she's gone."

"Éibhear, get Gwenvael and Daddy. Have them meet us outside the gates in fifteen minutes. Do *not* tell Dagmar or Mum. Morfyd either. They'll just get upset. We especially don't need for the Iron dragons to hear of this either."

"She couldn't have gotten far," Brannie desperately reasoned. "It takes days to travel to that part of the Steppes. She's on horseback. If we fly, we'll catch up and bring her back before it's even late afternoon."

"Honestly," Éibhear insisted, "I can go by myself and bring her back if she's really on the road to—"

"Are you insane?" Izzy barked. "When she gets like this, she won't stop. Ever."

"Ever," Brannie echoed.

"Just do what we say, Éibhear. Get Daddy and Gwenvael, but keep this from Fearghus. It'll just upset him."

"With good reason," Brannie agreed.

"And meet us outside the gates."

"All right," Éibhear stated as he got out of his chair.

"And remember . . . quiet. Very quiet. We don't need panic."

"Okay, but—"

"No panic!"

Éibhear reared back. "I'll go find Gwenvael and Briec."

"You do that."

Izzy watched Éibhear walk out of the hall, then focused on Brannie. "We should have seen this coming, Bran."

"Don't worry, Iz. We'll find her."

"You better hope so. We all better hope so. . . ."

"Come now. Don't sound so worried. Annwyl's on horseback and she just left. How far do you really think she could get?"

* * *

Andreeva Fyodorov practiced with the new bow one of her daddies had given her. Her mother said that since she wasn't sure which of them was Andreeva Fyodorov's father, Andreeva would call all of her mother's husbands, "Daddy."

It didn't matter to Andreeva. They made her bows. They healed her wounds. They trained her to ride and hunt, but it would be Andreeva's mother and aunts who taught her how to fight. How to be a warrior. What else mattered for the Daughters of the Steppes?

Andreeva raised her bow and pointed it at the back of her little brother's head. But her older sister slapped the bow from her hand.

"Ow! What was that for?"

"You only aim your bow when you plan to shoot. And we don't shoot those born of the Steppes. Ever. Remember, we are the . . . the . . ."

Andreeva's sister looked around, as did the others nearby. The cold, bracing winds of the Steppes had suddenly begun to rise. But not from the north or south, east or west. But from the ground . . . up.

The land beneath their feet pitched and rolled. Andreeva's sister picked her up in her arms and held her close to her chest as the winds whipped their hair and clothes around, their tents shaking as if they might blow away.

Then, just as quickly as all that wind whipping and ground shaking began . . . it stopped.

And they were there.

An old hag with a tall walking stick and a younger woman wearing a sleeveless chain-mail shirt, chain-mail leggings, and leather boots, and with brands on her scarred arms. She had many weapons.

The woman looked around, her gaze briefly falling on Andreeva. Instinctively, Andreeva leaned back, but her sister wasn't having it. She placed Andreeva on the ground and pushed her forward.

"Never show fear to a Southlander," her sister hissed angrily at her. "An imperialistic, corrupt society that is not worthy of our fear or our attention. Never forget that, Andreeva."

Andreeva nodded at her sister's command and, boldly, she walked up to the woman.

"No, no! Andreeva, wait. That's not what I meant!"

But Andreeva ignored her sister this time. She was too close to the woman not to be curious about her. Her weapons were fine, of very high quality. Her chain mail fit her perfectly. As did her boots. But she was very scarred and unkempt otherwise. As for the old hag . . . she was just horrifying to look at, so Andreeva didn't bother.

The woman suddenly looked down at her, her golden-brown hair falling into her face, nearly covering those eyes.

"Glebovicha," the woman said.

Andreeva knew her. She was one of the tribal leaders who reported to the Anne Atli.

So she took the woman's hand and led her to the tent where an all-tribes meeting was taking place.

The tent of her mother.

The tent of the Anne Atli.

So focused were they on Annwyl, none of the Riders noticed Brigida before she blended in with the surroundings so that she could no longer be seen by anyone but Annwyl, and then only because she was *allowing* Annwyl to see her.

Brigida stood at the tent entrance and watched the human queen walk into the center of all the tribal leaders sitting cross-legged on the ground.

Brigida knew all of them. Over time she'd met them or their mothers . . . or their mothers' mothers. Long ago, Brigida had made it her business to know anyone whom she might one day need. Whether it was for trading or food or souls.

The Daughters of the Steppes had a mighty power among them, one that Brigida wasn't afraid to use when necessary. But her question was, would this human queen be able to use their power? Or had she been so tamped down by logic and reason and royal duty that she no longer knew who she was or what she could do?

That's what Brigida needed to know.

She needed the truth.

Anne Atli, the leader of the Daughters of the Steppes, watched the human queen from her raised spot on the tent floor, but she said nothing. Instead it was her sister, Magdalina Fyodorov, who spoke, as Anne Atli's second in command.

"Who are you, Southlander?"

"I am Annwyl the Bloody."

"The Southlander queen? You?" Magdalina frowned. "Really?"

"Yes, really."

"All right." The Rider shrugged. "So I guess you are here to discuss that alliance between our people and—"

"No," Annwyl cut in, her gaze still sweeping over the other tribal leaders.

"Pssst," Brigida called out. "You kind of are."

"I don't care about fucking alliances," Annwyl shot back. "I'm here for Glebovicha Shestakova. Where is she?"

"I am Glebovicha Shestakova," the Shestakova tribal leader called out. "What do you want, imperialist dog?"

Annwyl placed her hands on her hips. "You owe your daughter an eye."

Grinning, Glebovicha slowly got to her feet. And she kept getting to her feet as she surpassed Annwyl to eventually tower over the human queen.

"Then," Glebovicha snarled down at a suddenly pale Annwyl the Bloody, "come and get it for her."

Chapter Thirty-Seven

Celyn tracked down the off-duty Queen's Guards and instructed them to spread out and look for anything unusual. If his uncle was worried about the day, then Celyn would take him seriously. Though to his face, he'd rather mock his uncle a little. There was just something about Bercelak that begged for a bit of mocking.

Once he'd sent the guards on their way, Celyn cut through town, stopping at a few of his favorite places to chat with the owners.

"Everything all right here, Stenam?"

"Quite well. Business is good. I'll have to start getting my youngest son up to speed with his brothers and sisters so he can help with the new workload."

"Where is young Robert?" Celyn asked as he drank water from the jug Stenam kept for that purpose.

"Off with his friends."

Celyn grinned. "Playing spy again?"

"Of course. Although when I was their age, I liked to play soldier. But these little bastards are a sneaky bunch. So they play spy. And with these new people cutting through town the last few days, their interest has been caught, but good."

Celyn, with a mouthful of water, stared at the blacksmith as he pounded a sword blade into submission.

Finally gulping that water down, Celyn asked, "New people? What new people?"

"Don't know. They've been cutting in and out of town for the last few days. I just figured they were more workers that Harold the Stonemason hired. He says the queen has been pushing him a bit to get her tower done before the first snows. So I know he's hired some outside people."

"And they just started arriving?"

Stenam shrugged. "I guess. Maybe in the last week or so."

"Do these new people know each other?"

"Not so's I could tell. Don't see them talking or traveling together."

Celyn put down the water jug. "Thanks, Stenam."

"Everything all right?" Stenam called after him as Celyn strode away.

"Aye. Everything's fine. Thanks."

But Celyn was lying. He didn't think a damn thing was fine.

Briec found Fearghus standing outside the tower in progress staring off into the distance.

"What are you doing?" he asked.

"Annwyl's gone missing."

Briec threw up his hands. "I warned *all* of you she wouldn't—"

"Quiet, quiet," Fearghus said softly before forcing a grin.

Princess Agrippina walked past them. "Prince Fearghus. Prince Briec."

"My lady," the brothers said together.

"Off for a walk?" Briec asked.

"Yes."

"Are you sure you shouldn't have guards?"

"I have no intention of going far." She faced the two dragons. "I promised my brother I'd stay. And stay I will."

"Stop acting like you're doing *us* a bloody favor—ow! Those are my ribs you're banging with your pointy elbow, brother."

"What my brother Briec means to say, Princess, is that all we care about is your safety."

"Of course you do. But I'm sure that . . ." Agrippina's words suddenly faded away and she wrapped her fur cloak tighter around her human shoulders.

"Princess? Are you all right?"

She glanced up at the sky. "Yes. Of course. I just . . ." She shook her head. "I'll be fine."

Fearghus watched the Western royal walk off, wondering what she'd sensed.

"You want to go look for Annwyl?" Briec asked.

"You'll come with me?" Fearghus couldn't help but be surprised by the offer.

"Gods know, you can't drag that woman back here by yourself."

Fearghus laughed. "Good point. Should we tell the others?"

"No. They'll just panic. And we shouldn't be too long. Doubt she got far."

Talaith walked through the Great Hall, stopping to look around. The room was unusually empty and everything was so . . . quiet.

Talaith walked back to the big front doors and stepped out onto the steps. A servant was walking up, smiling and nodding at Talaith.

"My Lady Talaith."

"Hello, Jenna. Is something going on?"

"M'lady?"

Talaith gestured with her hand at the empty courtyard.

"It's so quiet today. No one around. Just wondering if I'd missed news of a street fair in town or something."

"No, m'lady."

"All right. Thank you, Jenna."

"Of course, m'lady."

Crossing her arms over her chest, Talaith shook her head. "Living my life with these dragons and Annwyl has made me paranoid and unreasonably crazy."

She turned to go back inside when . . . wait . . . wait . . .

Talaith spun back, her arms tightening around her body, her gaze searching.

It was like a blanket had settled over her, muting everything around her. She doubted anyone else would notice it. It was magickal and powerful. Extremely powerful.

She couldn't touch it.

Talaith closed her eyes and called out to Rhiannon, but there was nothing.

But . . . but perhaps Rhiannon had noticed on her own.

Of course. She *must* have noticed. What could possibly distract her from something so dangerous?

"You are ridiculous," Rhiannon accused her sister-by-mating as they stood by Rhiannon's throne. "I am not *after* your mate. I adore dear Bram, but it's not like that."

"Then why are you always hugging him? Throwing your scales at him."

"I am doing no such thing!" Rhiannon snapped back as she waved her claws at what felt like bugs or something buzzing around her face.

"That's what it looks like to me!"

"My good ladies," one of the Elders tried to interrupt, but he quickly stepped back when the tips of two tails slashed at him, nearly taking his snout off.

"Keep out of this," Rhiannon ordered before focusing

again on Ghleanna. "And trust me, sister, if I *wanted* your mate, I would have had him a long time ago."

Ghleanna's snout twitched before she growled, "You haughty cow."

Celyn caught up with Stenam's son and the boy's friends about a mile or so outside of town.

"Hello, Robert," Celyn called out with a wave.

"Hello, Lord Celyn!"

The boys ran over to Celyn, and he crouched in front of them, all about ten to twelve years old, and covered in a good amount of dirt from their play.

Celyn leaned in and said in a low voice, "I heard you've been spying a bit. On the search for evil, eh?"

"We have. We don't like the look of these new people coming in and out of town, do we, boys?"

The boys all nodded in agreement.

"So what have you seen? Anything strange?"

"Nothing at first. Some of the new people went right to Queen Annwyl's Tower of Death for work with the stonemason." Celyn didn't even bother to waste time cringing at that, and instead let the boy continue. "But then we started noticing that some of the men . . . they were handing off notes."

"Notes?"

"Little scrolls with red ribbons on them. They'd walk by someone and it was like they'd bumped into each other. But we noticed—"

"*I* noticed," said one of the boys.

"—that they were handing these scrolls off to each other."

Celyn slowly nodded his head as he did his best to remain calm. Then he took a breath and leaned in to whisper to the boys, "You lot didn't happen to get your hands on one of those little scrolls . . . did you?"

When the boys suddenly began staring at their booted feet, Celyn knew he'd been right.

"Lads?"

"The man read it and as he was walking he went to put it in his pouch," Robert rambled, "but it . . . uh . . . it fell out. We didn't steal it or anything."

"Of course you didn't. But I do need to see it. In the name of the queen."

"In the name of Queen Annwyl herself?" Robert asked, his eyes wide.

Sure. Why not? "Absolutely."

Robert jabbed another boy in the ribs. "Give it to him."

The boy handed over the scroll.

The parchment was very high quality. The ribbon hanging from the scroll silk.

Celyn pulled open the curled corners and read it. It bore only a name and a time.

Brannie? Celyn called out. *Brannie? Can you hear me?* When he didn't get an answer, Celyn tried his mother, then his father. Still nothing.

Standing, Celyn motioned the boys back.

"You won't tell me da, will you, Lord Celyn?" Robert asked, tears beginning to fill his eyes.

"I won't tell your da if you lot don't tell what you're about to see."

"Not a word. We all promise."

"Then we have a deal."

Celyn motioned the boys farther back, and when they'd run a good distance away, he shifted to his natural dragon form, unleashed his wings, and lifted into the air. The sound of the young boys cheering the last thing he heard before he shot back toward Garbhán Isle.

* * *

Wearing a dress that Princess Keita had given her "because I can see you need something pretty!" Agrippina walked through a field that, in the summer, was filled with wildflowers. There were a few flowers trying to hold on in the cold, but it was mostly just frozen ground and bare stems.

By great Rhydderch Hael's cock! Agrippina didn't know why she needed to be here with these useless Southlanders and the Mad Queen of Garbhán Isle. She should be by her brother's side, helping him. Not banished to this place.

Why didn't her brother understand? Of *course* there were rumors about people wanting to kill her. There would always be rumors. With the Quintilian Provinces trapped in a power struggle between her brother and their cousins, she and her brother were obvious targets. But Aggie shouldn't be forced to hide, like a child, while her brother secured his throne.

"Princess Agrippina!"

Aggie stopped and looked behind her. Marcellus, of her personal guard, was running toward her.

"What is it, Marcellus?" she asked when he was close.

"You're in danger."

She shrugged. "I thought that's why I was here."

"Assassins are *here*, my lady. I need to get you some-place safe." He grabbed her wrist and pulled.

Aggie went with him, but at the same time she called out to her brother to let him know. When she got no answer back—and her brother *never* blocked her—Aggie immediately stopped, digging her heels into the ground.

Marcellus faced her. "My lady?"

"Where are the others?"

"Attempting to protect you. As I am doing."

Aggie studied the dragon's human face. "You're lying," she said softly.

"Princess—"

"You're lying." This was the same ploy cousin Vateria's people had used to capture her the first time. But Marcellus wouldn't know that. He had been just a soldier in the rebel army then.

The grip on her wrist tightened, and Marcellus said, sadly, "I wanted to make it as painless as possible for you."

Aggie looked up at Marcellus through her lashes. "Yes. I'm sure you did." With her free hand, she stroked his forearm. "I'm sorry I can't do the same for you."

"What do you mean, you can't find Gwenvael or Briec?" Izzy demanded while she nervously readjusted her travel pack for the fifteenth time and continued to walk down the back road they hoped would allow them to cut in front of Annwyl before she got too far.

"I looked for them," Éibhear explained, "but I couldn't find them. But I brought the next best thing."

"Mì-runach?" Brannie asked, pointing at the three dragons in human form. "You brought Mì-runach with you? We're just going to fetch Annwyl. Not kill her."

"Your tone is hurtful, Branwen the Awful."

"Don't think for a second I won't kill you," she shot back at one of the Mì-runach.

Izzy was in no mood to hear this bickering, so she asked Éibhear, "Can't you do that thing . . . with your head?"

Éibhear frowned. "That thing with my head?"

"She means talking to them." Brannie stopped, looking up into the sky. "I think it might snow."

"Then it snows. Come on." Izzy looked back at Éibhear. "Yeah. Talk to them in your head. Can't you do that?"

"I've tried. They must have me blocked out for some reason."

"Just wonderful."

"We'll find her, Iz," Brannie continued to promise.

"Brannie!"

Hearing Celyn calling out to his sister, Izzy stopped and looked up. The dragon landed in front of them, his claws slamming hard into the ground.

Brannie pushed past Izzy and Éibhear. "What is it?"

"Have you seen Princess Agrippina today?"

"No, but—"

"I hear her," Éibhear cut in. He pointed to some nearby trees. "I hear her voice on the other side of—"

Éibhear suddenly dove at Izzy, dropping them both to the ground.

Celyn watched his cousin throw himself and Izzy to the ground just as the hottest flames Celyn had ever experienced torched the trees close to them.

Trying to move out of the way, Celyn gave a painful yelp as flames lashed across his back leg. The fire was so powerful, it cut past his scales and into flesh.

Never. Not once in his existence, had Celyn ever been burned by flame. How could he be? He was made of fire.

Brannie ran to his side once the flame stopped. "Are you all right?"

"I'm fine." Celyn realized he'd forgotten about Agrippina and scrambled to his claws. He ran to the woods, limping a bit because of his wounded leg, while the others followed behind him.

He found Princess Agrippina standing in the middle of a burned-out field, her eyes coldly watching one of her personal guards trying to crawl away from her. Her flame had destroyed half his body, but he wasn't dead yet.

"I don't understand," she said softly as she stared at her

fellow Iron. "Why would they kill *me*? I'm more valuable to them alive."

"Are you sure that's what he wanted to do?" Éibhear asked. "To kill you?"

"He said something about smiting me in the name of his god . . . whatever that means."

"She's right," Celyn said. "She's worth much more alive than dead. That's why Vateria never killed her." He glanced at Agrippina. "She kept control of your brother by keeping you a prisoner."

"But then—"

Celyn held his claw up, and Éibhear immediately fell silent.

"We have a problem," Celyn said as he faced the small group. "This wasn't the only assassin sent out today. Boys in town saw messages given to others. Messages like this one." He held up the scroll that Robert and his friends had given him. "This one had Agrippina's name and a time. I think there are other attempted assassinations taking place at this very moment."

"So what are we waiting for?" Izzy demanded. "Let's go—"

"I don't know who the others are. And I can't reach anyone."

"What do you mean you can't reach anyone?" Brannie asked.

"I've been calling you since I realized what was going on. Did you ever hear me?"

Brannie shook her head.

"Do you hear me now?"

"No."

"Then I can't reach anyone."

"He's right," Agrippina chimed in. "I can't hear my brother. And he *never* blocks me."

Closing his eyes, Celyn started to talk out loud as his brain quickly sorted through the information they had.

"Annwyl said that it felt like Abertha was trying to get her to kill her."

"To turn Abertha into a martyr," Éibhear said.

"Right. Even the guards who challenged Annwyl . . . I don't think they actually tried to kill her. They wanted Annwyl alive. Yet this time they wanted Princess Agrippina dead. Why?"

"That makes absolutely no sense," Izzy said. "Annwyl and Rhiannon are war queens. They should be the first to die, because if something happens to any of their allies or someone close to them—"

"Gods," Celyn breathed. "That's it. They *want* war. They want to cleanse the lands of what they consider the Abominations. Those who don't follow their beliefs. Their god. And they know Annwyl, Rhiannon, and with the death of Agrippina, King Gaius will bring that war even if we're not ready."

And they weren't ready. Not even close.

"But you said there were others," Brannie reminded him. "Other targets besides Agrippina. We need to know who they are."

"The assassins are going after the ones whose deaths will start a war and those . . . who can prevent war." Celyn faced the group again. "Brannie, go to Da's house." Without waiting, Brannie shifted to her dragon form and took to the air. "Izzy and Éibhear . . . you need to get to Dagmar. Now."

As his cousins charged off, Celyn focused on the confused Mì-runach. "You lot, you'll stay with Agrippina. Protect her with your lives."

"And what are you going to do, Queen's Guard?" one of the Mì-runach asked.

"I should go with my sister, but . . . . I feel like I'm missing . . ."

"Are you actually going to *finish* a sentence?"

"The queen."

"Yeah. Our queen. The one you are sworn to protect. Remember her?"

"My mother's with her. No one will be able to . . ."

"You need to finish a bloody thought," the Mì-runach complained.

But Celyn couldn't be bothered as he took to the air once he realized there was one other dragon he needed to protect if he was going to ensure that the Salebiris didn't get their way.

Elina watched the wild boar charge away, her arrow missing the damn thing by a mile.

"I'll get him," Kachka said, running after the animal.

Disappointed in herself, Elina sat down on a tree stump.

"That was pitiful," she told Var.

The young boy was busy reading a book, paying no attention to what Elina and Kachka were trying to teach him.

"It could be worse," he said, turning the page. "Your mother could have taken both eyes."

Elina nodded. "I like you, Var. You are not whiny and constantly sobbing like that brown one."

Var glanced up from his book. "Auntie Talaith?"

"No, no. She is strong like all Nolwenn witches are. I mean her daughter, Rhianwen."

"I haven't met her yet, so I wouldn't be able to agree or disagree on that statement."

"You are strange child. But I still like you."

Elina yawned and scratched the back of her neck. That's when she realized something.

"No birds."

Var looked up from his book. "Pardon?"

"No birds." Elina nocked another arrow in her bow and stood. "They have stopped their singing."

Kachka walked out of the woods. She had no wild boar carcass with her, and Kachka never missed a shot.

Staring at each other, the sisters said together, "No birds."

A twig snapped behind her and Elina spun to her left as she always had, her bow raised, the arrow loosed without thought. It slammed into a man's chest. He stumbled back, eyes wide in disbelief, staring at Elina in shock before he crashed to the ground.

"What have you done?" Var screamed as he jumped up, tossed the book away, and ran to the man's side.

"Shoot first," Kachka said for Elina. "Mourn loss second."

"He came up on my blind side."

"Gods," the boy said. "I know him. He's . . ."

Var suddenly ran at the sisters, his hands out. He pushed them, hard, attempting to shove them back. "Move. Please. Quickly!"

Understanding that *this* particular boy wasn't one for hysterics, Elina and Kachka grabbed Var by his arms, lifted him, and ran until an explosion of flames had them diving for the ground. When they felt safe enough to look, there was a dragon carcass where the man's body had been.

"Everywhere," Kachka complained. "There are dragons *everywhere.*"

Var scrambled up. "That was an Elder Guard."

"Elder Guard?"

"They protect the Elder Dragon Lords just as Celyn protects the queen."

"If that's true, then why is he here?" Kachka asked. "Why is he not protecting his Elder Dragon Lord rather than wandering up behind my sister?"

Var moved close to the dragon, studying him. Then he suddenly dropped to a crouch and began to dig under the body.

"What is he doing?" Kachka asked.

"I have no idea. He is strange boy."

Var stood and he now held a gold blade.

"By all reason," he breathed.

"What is that?" Elina asked.

"A ceremonial dagger." He studied the runes on the side and the hilt. "'In the glory,'" he recited, "'of the one true god.'"

Var looked up at Elina. "Uncle Bram!" he suddenly screamed. "*Uncle Bram!*"

Bram had made it as far as the dining hall before he was forced to dump his bag on one of the tables so that he could sort through all his things.

He didn't know how long he was focused on that task, but he nearly jumped out of his weak human skin when he heard voices behind him.

Bram spun around and let out a sigh of relief. "Oh, Elder Vass, Elder Loran, Elder Reganach. Hello. What brings you here?"

"Important business about the queen." Elder Vass smiled. "You do have some time, though, yes? To talk."

"Of course." Bram invited the dragons into his home with a wave of his hand. "Please come in. Let's talk."

Dagmar was busy in her study, analyzing the bills from the stonemason, hoping to figure out what that tower could possibly be—although she was pretty sure she already knew what it was for . . . much to her great disappointment—when her study door was pushed open.

She glanced up and saw the blurry form of Arlais standing there.

"Yes, Arlais?" Dagmar asked as she leaned back in her chair and put her spectacles on.

"Would you like some tea, my lady?" Mabsant asked.

Dagmar shook her head and waited for her daughter to come close.

"I have a request, Mother," Arlais stated. As she approached Dagmar's desk, Adda came out from under it and pressed her big dog head against the child's neck. It was the only thing that gave Dagmar any comfort. The fact that dogs seemed to love Arlais and, in return, Arlais adored them. If the dogs were terrified of her or aggressive toward her, Dagmar didn't know what she'd do.

A knock at the door had Dagmar rolling her eyes—*Why is it suddenly so busy in here?*—but Mabsant rushed to the door himself.

While he dealt with the message brought by one of the gate guards, Dagmar returned her focus to her eldest daughter.

"So what is it?"

"Auntie Keita has asked me to accompany her and Uncle Ragnar back to the Northlands for a visit."

Dagmar thought on that a second, nodded. "All right. I'll have to talk to your father first, of course, but I doubt he'd say no."

"Good. Thank you."

Arlais turned away, and Dagmar was about to refocus her attention on the bills. But before she could pull off her spectacles, she sensed that Arlais was standing right next to her.

She looked up and . . . she was.

"What is it?"

"You're just going to let me go, aren't you?"

Dagmar blinked, confused. "What?"

"When Var wants to go only a few miles away to Uncle Bram's house you're all, 'Over my dead body' and 'How can my dearest child leave me?' But I say I'm going to go all the way to the bloody Northlands and you're all, 'Bye! Don't let the Garbhán Isle gates hit you on the ass!'"

"Arlais!"

"You don't care about me at all, do you?"

"That's bloody nonsense!"

"Is it? Really, Mother? *Really*?"

"Stop yelling!"

"I bet if it was one of those five little bitch sisters of mine, you wouldn't even *think* of letting them leave!"

"The oldest one is seven!"

"I'm eight!"

"But a very mature eight!"

"Oh! You are the worst mother *ever!*"

"I don't know how that's possible!" Dagmar screamed back. "*You're still alive, aren't you?*"

The boy tried to run past Elina, but she caught him and held him tight. "No!"

"I have to get to Uncle Bram! I have to warn him!"

"I will go!" Kachka whistled for her horse. She started running before it arrived. "Elina, get that boy back to his mother!"

The horse ran past Elina and Var and caught up to Kachka.

Kachka reached out and caught hold of the Steppes horse's mane, launching herself onto its back.

Elina, still holding Var by his shoulders, turned them both and found her horse already standing there. Waiting.

"I love this horse," she told the boy as she walked over and mounted. She reached down and grabbed the boy's arm, hauling him onto the horse with her.

"You will wrap your arms around my waist," she ordered him. "And you will not let go. You will also watch my left side."

"Okay. But don't forget I'm *on* your left side. I don't want you mourning me second."

"Do not worry, little Var. Just hold on and keep your head low."

"Low? Why?"

Elina turned, her bow raised as she heard something rushing up behind them. She shot two arrows, one after another, and the dragon who'd been charging toward them on all fours reared back with a roar, the arrows hitting him in the mouth he'd been opening to unleash flame on both Elina and Var.

"That is why," Elina told the boy before she clicked her tongue against her teeth and the horse sprinted off.

Frederik had been about to go into Aunt Dagmar's study, but he heard her and Arlais getting into it before he even reached the door. In no mood for any of that, he kept walking until he was outside. He briefly gazed up at the tower, but . . . no. He was definitely not in the mood to check on that stupid thing either.

So Frederik kept walking. Past the castle grounds, through the woods, and near a stream. He stopped there and stared at . . . nothing. At least nothing in particular. He just stood there, staring . . . silent.

Good thing, too—otherwise he never would have heard that distinct sound of something cutting through the air, right over his head.

And, as Bercelak had trained him again and again, Frederik dropped into a crouch and rolled to the side. When he jumped to his feet, a sword was buried where he'd just been standing.

At the lake, where his kin stood waiting for orders, Bercelak pointed at three of Addolgar's sons. "You lot, I want you and . . ." He pointed at three of his nieces. ". . . you three, go with them. I want you in the air, watching—"

"Bercelak!"

Bercelak turned to find one of his brothers pointing at him. "Some prissy queen's guard here to see you?"

Bercelak went up on his back claws and recognized the red dragon as Aberthol. One of Rhiannon's guards.

Assuming he had a message from Celyn, Bercelak motioned Aberthol over with a wave of his claw, then focused on his nieces and nephews.

"I want you lot in the air, over Garbhán Isle. Look for anything that seems strange or out of place. I don't care what. If you see something, let your mum or father know and they'll get in touch with me. Understand?"

One of Addolgar's sons raised his claw.

"What?"

"Aren't we *in* Garbhán Isle, Uncle?"

Bercelak gritted his fangs together. Say what you would about his sons, at least none of them were *this* bloody stupid.

Taking a breath—he'd learned long ago that yelling at Addolgar's sons did nothing but make them become absolutely useless; they were so bloody sensitive—Bercelak struggled to keep his temper under control.

"Aye. We are *in* Garbhán Isle. But . . ." Bercelak's words faded off when he noticed that his nephew was no longer listening to him, but busy staring behind him.

That's when he heard someone—it sounded like bloody Celyn—yell out, "Spear!"

Bercelak spun around to see Aberthol running toward him, his sword out, his face a mask of rage as he screamed out, "*In the name of the one true god I smite thee!*"

Bercelak pulled his sword, but as he raised it, Celyn flew in from above, catching the spear that one of his kin threw to him before he spun in midair to give him power, slammed his wings against his sides, his entire body shooting down.

Ramming his back legs into the Red's back, his talons digging past scale and flesh to tear into precious spine, Celyn forced the dragon to the ground and then buried the tip of his spear into the back of Aberthol's neck. He twisted it one way, then another, until the dragon stopped moving.

Bercelak stared down at Aberthol's body.

"You all right?" Celyn asked.

Bercelak nodded. "How did you know?"

"Because you weren't the only one. They already tried to kill Princess Agrippina."

Bercelak shoved his sword back into its sheath. "Rhiannon? You left her?"

"She's with Mum."

Bercelak opened his maw to argue, but they both knew he couldn't. Next to being protected by Celyn or Bercelak himself, the queen couldn't be in better claws.

"But I don't think the assassins will go after Rhiannon or Annwyl. I think they want the deaths that will lead to war."

"What are you talking about?"

"They kill you, there's no stopping Rhiannon from going head to head with the Salebiris and the Cult of Chramnesind. I sent Brannie to my father's, and Izzy and Éibhear to Dagmar. But Brannie will need the most backup, I think. Father has more pull with the dragons than Dagmar."

"Have you talked to your mum?"

"Can't get through to her. Something is blocking the communication between us."

"Keep trying." Bercelak walked through the silent crowd of Cadwaladrs. He pointed at one group. "You lot . . . go to Bram's. Don't waste time. Brannie's on her own." He pointed at another group while the others took to the air. "You lot to Devenallt. And the rest of you back to Annwyl's castle to back up Izzy and Éibhear.

"I'm going back to my mate," he finally told Celyn. "You go to your father. Last I heard, my grandson Var is with him. Make sure he's safe."

Celyn nodded, unleashed his wings, and was gone.

Alone, Bercelak looked down at Aberthol's body. The cult had turned a guard closest to the ruling powers of this land, but they hadn't ordered him to kill Rhiannon. Probably knew they couldn't. As protected as Rhiannon was, she was also bloody dangerous on her own.

But this cult . . . they'd gone after Bercelak instead, not bothering with Rhiannon because they were thinking about long-term and long-lasting damage.

The realization worried Bercelak more than if they'd tried for Rhiannon and Annwyl. Because now he understood what Fearghus had been trying to tell him for years.

That whatever was about to happen with these zealots . . . it might just tear their world apart.

The soldier, a man Frederik didn't recognize, snarled at him.

"Little bastard," he muttered before yanking that blade from the ground and charging him.

Frederik started to jog backward, but then realized he had nowhere to go. He wasn't armed, which would just make him a running target that wasn't nearly as fast as he probably should be with all those days in the library now catching up with him.

So Frederik didn't move. He stood his ground and let the soldier run right at him, the blade held high to impale Frederik in the face.

But as the soldier neared him, Frederik pulled his eating dagger from the belt at his waist, and dropped into a crouch, then brought the dagger in and up, burying it inside the soldier's thigh.

With a scream, the soldier went down and Frederik quickly stood to his full height, the bloody blade in his grip, as he heard someone cutting through the trees toward him. He yanked the blade out of the dying soldier's hand, but he quickly let out a relieved sigh when he saw Izzy and Éibhear.

"Thank all reason," he said, panting.

"Are you all right?" Izzy asked, her hand on his shoulder.

Frederik briefly watched Éibhear continue to run right by him. "He tried to kill me," he said of the soldier bleeding out on the ground.

"I know him," Izzy said, appearing shocked. "He was once in my platoon."

"Where's Éibhear going?" Frederik asked.

Izzy's eyes grew wide. "Fuck. Dagmar."

Arlais pointed her finger in Dagmar's face. "I'm telling Daddy!"

"You do that! In fact, let's go find him right now and I'll tell him myself!"

Dagmar started to push her chair back, but Adda suddenly brought her big dog head over and gripped Dagmar's forearm between her jaws.

Arlais's eyes widened in panic and she yelled out, "Adda, no!"

But the dog ignored Arlais and suddenly scrambled back with Dagmar's arm still caught in her mouth. Afraid the dog would rip it to shreds, Dagmar allowed herself to be dragged out of the chair, across the floor on her knees, and toward the door, where Adda released her, turning her focus on the desk she'd just pulled Dagmar away from.

That's when Dagmar saw that her assistant of the last eight years had buried a ceremonial dagger right where Dagmar had been sitting.

Mabsant looked up, his face an angry snarl. "I should have killed that dog weeks ago," he growled out.

He yanked the knife from the chair as Adda charged him.

"Arlais!" Dagmar screamed. "Run!"

Arlais ran to the door, but it wouldn't open. The key broken off in the lock.

"Help us!" Arlais screamed as she pounded on the door.

"Get us out of here!" Dagmar heard someone trying to get in from the other side, bodies ramming into the thick wood.

Adda wrapped her jaws around Mabsant's throat and bit down, but the bastard managed to ram his blade into the dog's chest and inner thighs.

"No!" Dagmar screamed, getting to her feet.

Arlais ran back to her side, her small arms around Dagmar's waist as Mabsant tossed Adda aside.

The dog had done great damage, but Mabsant was still coming for Dagmar, his bloody dagger raised high.

Dagmar pushed Arlais behind her and yanked her own eating dagger out of the small belt around her waist.

But both of them stopped as they heard a strange hissing noise from the back of the study. They looked over and smoke curled from the bookshelves.

Dagmar assumed it was dragons about to tear down the walls. But then her youngest five girls were standing there, their heads low, their gold eyes locked on Mabsant.

"Abominationsssss," he hissed hysterically. "You all need to—"

They flew at him. Literally. No wings. But their bodies were off the ground and they were on Mabsant in seconds. Fangs tearing into his flesh as they slammed him to the floor.

His ceremonial blade flipped from his hand and landed at Dagmar's feet. She thought nothing of it, until Arlais picked it up.

"Arlais, no!"

Rhiannon swung her forearms wildly.

Ghleanna stepped back. "What are you doing?"

"It's like gnats!" she complained even as she knew Ghleanna, with her very non-magickal self, would never understand. "All that buzzing around me. It's annoying!"

"You're starting to sound as crazy as Annwyl."

"Oh, shut up!"

"Why don't just admit you're wrong. For once in your life, just admit it!"

"I am not wrong about anything! And . . . and . . . och!" Rhiannon swung her forearms again, the feeling of being covered with something magickal becoming overpowering.

Unable to stand even a second more, Rhiannon lowered her claws, called a spell to mind, and spoke it while writing runes in the air with magickal flame.

"There!" she announced triumphantly. "It's gone!"

But before Rhiannon could crow too much, the voices of her offspring railed in her head, most in mid-thought, as if they'd been blocked from her hearing all this time.

Rhiannon looked at Ghleanna. The black She-dragon had her claws to her head, her eyes wide in panic.

"Bram," she said.

"Go," Rhiannon ordered her.

"I can't leave your—"

"It's not me they want. So go! Go save our Bram!"

Brannie was nearing her father's home when they slammed into her from above, and dragged her to the ground.

A squadron of dragons that Brannie had fought with before, as both dragon and human. Dragons she'd once called her comrades, she would now call her enemies.

Brannie brought her head up, slamming it into the dragon who had her pinned facedown.

"Bitch!" he cried out when she heard bone break.

Brannie knew she had only seconds to get to her claws or she'd die on her knees.

She scrambled up, her blade in her hand. She slammed the base against the nearest tree and, as it was designed, it extended to a length and width befitting a She-dragon of her size.

"You will die, blasphemer," a green dragon needlessly warned her.

Brannie grinned. "But first, I will take all of you worthless shits with me."

Kachka rode into the rundown courtyard outside Bram the Merciful's castle. She urged her mare up the stairs and then had the horse rear up on her hindquarters so that when she came down, her hooves smashed the doors open.

She rode inside and across the hall. Bram stood in a circle of men that she now realized were also dragons. Older ones, but still dragons. So Kachka kept moving forward as Bram stared at her with his mouth open, his eyes wide in shock.

Keeping her right foot in one stirrup and pulling the left one out, Kachka leaned over and down. As she hung from the horse's side, she gripped her saddle and held on tight as she swung her free arm out when she neared Bram.

"What the hells are you—*oof!*"

She picked up the dragon—thankfully still in his human form—by his waist. The other dragons dashed out of the way in a panic, giving her room to swing Bram up onto the back of her horse.

"*What are you doing?*" he demanded once she was sitting back in the saddle and had hold of the reins.

"Saving your life, dragon. You are welcome."

"Kachka, what the hells is going on?"

Kachka turned a corner. "You are to be assassinated by the zealots of the one-eyed god."

"Var—"

"Is safe. He is with Elina."

She turned another corner and saw the back door ahead. Thankfully, it was open.

"Hold on, Bram the Merciful," she ordered as the horse reached the doorway. "I will get you—"

Once past the door, the horse reared up again, took several steps back, then turned in circles.

The damn thing really had no choice with all those soldiers outside Bram the Merciful's back door.

Dagmar grabbed her daughter's arm, but Arlais easily pulled away and walked over to her sisters.

Seva pulled back, her face covered in blood. There were so many fangs. So gods-damn many.

"Finish him," Seva told Arlais in a voice that did not sound like hers or anything from this world.

"Arlais . . . don't."

But when Arlais looked over her shoulder at her mother, Dagmar realized that she was no different from her sisters. Not with those gold eyes that were now black with a tinge of dark red around the iris.

"Do it!" Seva ordered in a harsh whisper.

Arlais raised the blade high, but Dagmar shoved Arlais aside and dropped to her knees. Taking her eating dagger in both hands, Dagmar brought it down and buried it to the hilt in Mabsant's chest.

Now, with the threat gone, the fangs and strange eyes disappeared and, suddenly Dagmar was staring at her children. Her babies.

Crying, they ran to her, wrapping their arms around her waist, her legs, the youngest trying to get her to pick her up, which Dagmar did.

That's when she realized that Frederik, Éibhear, and Izzy were in the room. They had been for a bit, the door now sitting against the far wall, its hinges torn away.

They'd seen everything. Dagmar could tell by the look of horror on their faces.

Dagmar faced them. "You will say nothing of what you've

seen here today. Not a word. Do you understand me? This can never get out. This can never be known."

After all three agreed, Dagmar swallowed and held her daughters closer. "Now . . . go get my son."

Chapter Thirty-Eight

Elina turned and shot, her arrow ramming directly into the nostril of the dragon who was chasing them. He fell back with a roar as Elina pulled another arrow and nocked it.

That's when Var yelled out.

"In front of us!"

Elina faced forward in time to see a dragon land directly ahead of them, the ground shaking beneath the horse's hooves.

"Give us the Abomination, female," he ordered as Elina's horse reared up and backward. "And I'll let you live."

"I give you nothing."

"Then you both die."

"Do not let go of me, little Var," she warned him.

"Why? What are you going to do?"

"I—"

Elina's words were cut off by dragon's blood splattering across her face and body. She looked up and saw a dragon-sized sword that had been shoved through the dragon's chest.

When the dragon slumped forward, dead, the sword was yanked out and the body dropped.

At first, Elina saw nothing but trees swaying in the cold

winter wind, but then, born out of nothing, it seemed . . . like a chameleon lizard who'd camouflaged himself against a rock . . . the golden dragon, Gwenvael, appeared.

Var sat up straight in the saddle. "Dad!"

Gwenvael, golden in the sunlight, smiled down at his son. "Thank the gods," he said on a relieved sigh. "I was afraid I'd have to spend my long life listening to your mother complain about how wrong I was to let you go to your uncle Bram's."

The boy laughed, but Elina could hear the tears he was trying to hold back. "And she would have, too. But what are you doing here?"

The dragon rolled his eyes, clearly embarrassed. "What can I say? I lied to your mother."

"Shocking," the boy muttered drily.

"I told her I wouldn't be checking on you while you were at Bram's but . . . well . . ." He shrugged, helpless. "You're too important to me to just let you go off on your own. There, I said it. But if you repeat it, I'll flatly deny I care about anyone that much, especially my own son."

"Take your boy, dragon," Elina said, helping Var dismount from the horse. "Bring him back to his mother."

"Come with us, Elina," Var pleaded.

"I cannot. I have to go to my sister."

"The Cadwaladrs are flying to Bram's as we speak," Gwenvael explained. "I'm sure—"

"No, beautiful golden one—"

"Why, thank you, Elina."

"*Dad!*"

"—but I must get my sister and you must take this boy back to his mother. I would hate to see what she will do to world if he is no longer in it."

Gwenvael picked his son up with his tail and placed the boy on his back. "Thank you for protecting him, Elina."

Elina nodded at his words, turned her horse, and headed back to Bram's castle.

* * *

Celyn saw the battle from above and dove in. He uncurled his fists, making sure his talons were out.

He tackled one of the last remaining dragons, a Gold who was making a wild swing at Brannie's back.

Ramming his claws into the dragon's side, Celyn dug them in deep, then moved them up and down, back and forth, rending valuable organs in the process.

The Gold screamed out in pain, his flames decimating nearby trees.

Celyn yanked his claws from the Gold's body and quickly gripped his head. He turned it one way, then the other, breaking the neck.

He dropped the body and stood. Brannie had gotten some dragon's axe and was chopping away. Someone must have pissed her off.

"I think he's dead enough, sister."

At Celyn's words, Brannie spun around with an angry snarl, the axe raised, her tail taking down a tree in the process.

Blood and brains covered her from head to claw. Her black eyes were wild—the Cadwaladr bloodlust having taken over.

"We have to go," he told his sister.

"Go?"

"We have to help Da."

"What makes you think we're done here?"

Celyn looked over the dragon pieces scattered around his sister. But when he looked up, Brannie was pointing her blood-covered axe at him.

He turned and saw ten dragons standing behind him, their weapons drawn.

"Well then," Celyn said on a sigh, "let's get this over with."

Then he and Brannie charged forward—and killed everything in their way.

Kachka dismounted from her horse and pulled her sword. "Stay behind me, Bram the Merciful," she ordered him.

"I think you need to get behind me now, Kachka Shestakova."

Kachka felt heat on her back and turned to see her horse galloping off and Bram in his dragon form.

His scales were silver, like his hair. And he was large. But, sadly, not as large as the protective unit that had been sent along with these Dragon Elders.

"Run, Kachka."

"I am Daughter of Steppes. I will not run. I will not yield."

"Then you will die," one of the dragons said, laughing.

"Not before you, imperialist scaled scum!" She glanced back at the Southland dragon standing behind her. "No offense to you, Bram the Merciful."

"None taken, considering the circumstances."

"Kill them both," the enemy dragon ordered.

"Wait!" Bram called out, stepping around Kachka.

She winced, worried that the dragon was about to beg for either his or her life.

But, thankfully, he did neither. Instead, he simply asked a question.

"Is this god of yours worth the betrayal of your people?"

"More than worth it," one of the Elder dragons said as they walked out of Bram's castle and casually shifted from human to dragon. "Our god will wash the world of these Abominations created by your godless queen and her brood of despicable offspring."

"But Chramnesind"—and as soon as Bram said the name, the other dragons all closed their eyes, lowered their heads, and wrote a rune in the air with their talons . . . it was stupid—"is not a dragon god. If he comes into full power, you, old friends, will be the first that he wipes from this planet."

"You will never understand, Bram. You've been tainted. And your talking isn't going to extend your life by another second."

"Oh, I know. I was just killing time until the ol' ball and chain got home."

The Elder dragon blinked, then spun around, forcing Kachka to drop into a crouch to avoid his wildly swinging tail.

The She-dragon called Ghleanna had been standing behind him. She grabbed his hair and yanked the old dragon forward while ramming the blade of her sword into his snout.

Bram glanced down at Kachka and smiled. "Isn't she glorious?"

Ghleanna pulled the old dragon off her sword and focused on the soldiers. "*Kill all of them!*" she screamed, and dragons dropped from the skies, landing hard on the soldier dragons.

"The royals always forget," Bram murmured. "Cadwaladrs never fight alone."

Elina was riding hard through the trees, nearing Bram's castle, when her horse suddenly reared back, nearly flipping them both over.

Using her thighs to grip the saddle, Elina managed to keep her seat, but her horse turned in mid-run and bounded forward.

Elina was about to turn him around again when the trees began to shake . . . then fall. Crashing to the ground, they nearly crushed the pair in the process.

Thankfully she was on a Steppes horse and the animal

moved with the grace that eons of good horse breeding managed to create, dancing around falling trees until they reached a clearing.

They'd just leaped to safety when the ground beneath them moved again and the horse jumped to the side several times, allowing two battling dragons to roll past them.

Elina let out a breath and sent a silent prayer of thanks to the horse gods that protected her for gifting her with such an outstanding horse companion. Then she lifted her head and realized that one of the fighting dragons was Celyn.

Another dragon burst onto the clearing, his sword raised. Elina didn't recognize the dragon so she decided not to concern herself with whether it was friend or foe. Instead, she simply nocked an arrow, aimed, and released.

The arrow's route stayed true, ramming right between the seams of his scaled neck. The dragon jerked to the side, his claw immediately going to the arrow and his eyes searching for where it had come from.

He locked on Elina in seconds.

"You."

She nocked another arrow and raised her bow, this time aiming for the eyes, but a speeding burst of black scales slammed into the dragon, taking him to the ground.

Brannie caught hold of the dragon's back leg and dragged him close with one front claw while the other pulled out an axe so large Elina knew it would crush her human body in seconds if it ever landed on her.

Without pause, Brannie hacked at the dragon's spine, splitting it into two, ignoring the screams of pain coming from her victim. She then moved up and hacked at the back of the dragon's head until the screaming stopped altogether. She started toward a still-fighting Celyn when she glanced over and stopped.

"Elina?"

Celyn, who had his opponent pinned to the ground and

his sword about to plunge into the dragon's heart, looked up abruptly.

The relief on his scaled face at seeing her made Elina smile. But that smile quickly turned into a wince when Celyn's opponent was able to toss Celyn off and get back to his claws. He yanked out his own sword and dove toward Celyn.

But Celyn's sister was there, grabbing the dragon by his hair and yanking him back. She used the handle of her axe against his throat to hold the dragon tight while Celyn got up and came at him again. He buried his blade into the dragon's gut, tearing from left to right and back again. The dragon's insides poured out onto the ground and he reached for them, as if he'd be able to tuck them all in again and be fine.

Brannie released the dragon and stepped back, watching as he used his last few seconds of life to scoop up his guts.

Celyn, however, came to Elina.

"Are you all right?"

"My sister?" she immediately asked.

"With my father and mother. She's more than safe. Now answer me. Are you all right?"

"I am fine. My mighty horse of the Steppes did a good job. Unlike your useless travel-cow, which would have been crushed by the weight of two rolling dragons."

"You're really not letting that travel-cow thing go, are you?"

"He is worthless!"

They both jumped when Brannie suddenly lifted her axe and brought it down hard, taking off the head of Celyn's opponent.

When she turned to find both of them staring at her, she shrugged. "He wasn't dying fast enough, and he just kept picking up his guts. . . . It was vile."

Celyn shook his head before smiling at Elina.

"I am glad you are not dead," she told him honestly. "Now I must go and see my sister."

"You're just going to leave me?"

"Yes."

"You care more about your sister than me?"

"Yes."

When Celyn just stared at Elina while his sister rolled on the ground behind him, knocking over trees and gasping between her laughter that, "I love her! I love her so godsdamn much!" Elina turned her horse toward Bram's castle and urged the animal into a gallop.

Ghleanna pressed her snout against her mate's and tangled her tail with his. They stood together for several seconds, just comforted by the presence of each other.

"How did you know?" Bram asked.

"Your son guessed. They even tried to kill Bercelak."

"Bercelak? Are they mad?"

"Not in the slightest. They knew exactly what they were doing. They went after Dagmar, too—but," she quickly put in when he tensed, "she's safe. There are others who may not be so lucky. But I'll worry about all that later."

"This is going to change things."

"I know, but we'll worry about that later, too. Just let me be happy you're here with me."

Over the massacre of zealot soldiers by the Cadwaladr Clan, Ghleanna heard the sound of a galloping horse.

Elina Shestakova rode around the battling dragons toward her sister, who sat mounted on her own horse by Bram's side.

The strange thing was that Ghleanna felt Kachka Shestakova, in her own Rider way, was still standing by Bram to protect him.

This human female was protecting a dragon from other dragons, probably because her sister had asked her to. And that delighted Ghleanna more than she could say.

Elina rode up to Kachka until their horses were right

next to each other, the sisters' knees nearly touching as they sat proud in their saddles.

The pair stared at each other until Elina nodded at her sister. Kachka nodded back. Then Elina led her horse all the way behind Bram until she was positioned at Ghleanna's side. There she sat, her gaze looking out over the lessening battle as the Cadwaladrs did what they always do so well . . . kill things.

Aye. Ghleanna the Decimator and her mate, with their lethal offspring and kin no more than a hundred feet away, were now being protected by the Shestakova sisters.

Ghleanna leaned in and whispered to Bram, "This is the most adorable thing ever."

"Stop."

"*Ever.*"

Celyn finally dragged his sister up by her wings and placed her on her feet. Anything to stop the bloody laughing.

They headed back to their father's castle.

"I don't think she cares about me nearly as much as I care about her," he complained. And the gods knew, he'd only ever have this conversation with Brannie. "It's going to be the Izzy situation all over again."

"Horse shit. You knew what you were getting into with Izzy from the beginning. The only idiot who didn't know how Izzy felt about Éibhear was bloody Éibhear."

"Then why—"

Brannie stopped, held up her claws. "Before I'm forced to beat you because you sound like a pathetic child, I'm just going to say, in the short time I've known those two women, they are not demonstrative females. You want a lovey-dovey female, then get some vapid royal who only knows how to present herself to the queen. But if you want a female with a strong enough vagina to tell you to your face that she's more concerned about her sister than you . . . then you get yourself a Rider."

"You do have a point."

"Of course I do. Now come on. We're missing out on the rest of the killing."

Together, the siblings walked on until Brannie stopped again and gazed off.

"What's wrong?" Celyn asked.

"I feel like we've forgotten something. . . ."

Annwyl's body was flung across the tent, and she hit the ground face-first.

And Brigida had to admit . . . she was disappointed.

True, Annwyl the Bloody had taken her beating like a champion, as Brigida's dear mum used to say. But it seemed as if the edge she'd once had might have been tamped down by that Dagmar Reinholdt and those royal Cadwaladrs— two words that *never* should have gone together—to the point where Annwyl was now nothing more than just a queen. A boring, old queen.

What could Brigida do with that?

The royal was picked up by the waist and lifted over Glebovicha Shestakova's head. Blood poured from Annwyl's nose, mouth, and eyes, and her face was swelling. And Brigida was sure she'd heard the distinctive crush of bone on more than one occasion when Glebovicha's giant, bear-like fists had collided with the queen's body.

Brigida sighed. It was too bad really. She'd had such hope for the human. But that had been her mistake really . . . trusting in a human. Even a female one.

Glebovicha Shestakova slammed the queen down onto the frozen earth beneath the tent, making sure her spine took the brunt of the unyielding Steppes lands.

Annwyl coughed up blood and groaned in abject misery.

"Glebovicha Shestakova," Magdalina Fyodorov called

out in the language of the Steppes. "That is enough. Finish her and let's be done with this. Quickly."

Glebovicha nodded and walked over to one of her kinswomen, who tossed her a flint axe. A weapon that looked crudely made but also was powerful enough to quickly hack thick oxen bone into pieces.

Brigida let out another sigh, so very disappointed. But then she realized that the thought of oxen had made her a bit hungry. And she had seen some oxen on a nearby ridge. . . .

Slowly turning away, Annwyl already forgotten, Brigida heard Glebovicha say in the common tongue—so that Annwyl would be sure to understand it—"You, imperialist dog, think to tell me about being a mother when you brought demon spawn into this world? Well, now you can go to hell and meet your Abominations there when the world wipes those worthless cunt stains from existence. Yes? Then you will *know* what great sin you have committed."

It was true. It would have to be the Abominations Brigida worked with. Young they might be. But there was much potential there and one day they would be powerful enough to . . . to . . .

Pulling back the flap, Brigida stood in the tent opening, waiting to hear the last thud of that axe hitting flesh. But she heard nothing. She waited a few seconds longer. Still . . . nothing.

Swinging around, her hunger forgotten at the moment, she could see Glebovicha desperately trying to lower the axe. But she couldn't finish the swing—because Annwyl's hand now held the weapon as well.

Brigida pushed her way through the crush of lesser leaders whose tribes were too small to allow them to sit on the floor near the Anne Atli. When she reached the outer circle of seated women, Brigida planted her staff and leaned against it. Her leg throbbed horribly from the sudden move, but the blood in her veins sang with hope.

Annwyl, still bleeding profusely, was no longer weak and overwhelmed. No. She was just angry. Unbelievably, blindingly, kill-everyone-in-the-tent angry.

And she used that anger to keep hold of the axe that would have finished her off, and get to her big human feet.

Her body shook, but not from pain. Rage. Even with all that blood on her face, Brigida could see it easily in Annwyl's eyes. Hells, she could *feel* it. Annwyl's rage was a living thing.

No wonder the gods had noticed her. She must have attracted them all, human and dragon, from all the universes that surrounded this world.

Finally, after the two women stared at each other for what seemed an eternity, Annwyl opened her mouth.

Brigida would admit—she expected curses. Threats. A summation of what Annwyl planned to do to Glebovicha.

But, for once, Brigida was thinking too small. Because no words came out of Annwyl the Bloody's mouth. Nothing logical came from her at all.

Instead, the queen opened her mouth . . . and she screamed.

Gods. She screamed with such fury, with such rage, with such insanity that Brigida could see all the powerful Riders of the Steppes recoil in fear and disgust. Because, as Brigida's dear mum used to say, "No one wants to fight a crazy cunt, my love. Absolutely no one."

Even better, that scream seemed to go on for an eternity. This was no tactic. This was no planned assault. To be honest, the girl wasn't that smart.

Instead it was a simple reaction to someone threatening her children. Even now that the children were adults, she was still the mother no one wanted to challenge.

Still screaming, as if the action alone gave her strength and healed her wounds, Annwyl finally yanked that axe from Glebovicha's grasp. She slammed the handle against Glebovicha's face, stunning her, before sweeping her leg under Glebovicha, dropping the bigger woman to the ground like a tree stump.

Annwyl walked around until she stood by Glebovicha's head. Her screaming finally stopped, but rage still came off her in waves.

She planted one foot by the Rider's ear and the other on Glebovicha's chest, pinning her to the ground. It was a strange position for Annwyl to be in and Brigida frowned in confusion, wondering what the royal was up to.

"I have decided, Glebovicha Shestakova of the Black Bear Riders of the Midnight Mountains of Despair in the Far Reaches of the Steppes of the Outerplains," Annwyl panted out, ignoring the big hands that gripped her calf, trying to yank her off, "that you should not be a mother . . . ever again."

Her muscles bulging, her entire body taut with strength and power, Annwyl raised the flint axe high, held it there a moment, then brought it down on Glebovicha's cunt with such force that Annwyl hacked her way straight into the female's belly.

The cries of horror from the tribe leaders—some jumping to their feet, others desperately looking away, almost all of them pulling their weapons and closing their legs— nearly washed out the scream of pain from Glebovicha.

Yet the Anne Atli kept her calm. Then again, one didn't become Leader of All Steppes Tribes without being the strongest dog in the kennel.

Annwyl pulled the axe from a still screaming Glebovicha, stepped away from her, then brought the axe down again— taking the bitch's head.

The Southlander queen reached down, picked up Glebovicha's head—which was still twitching and trying to scream—by its hair and turned toward the tent opening. She didn't run. She was too busy limping from whatever damage Glebovicha had done to her leg.

Abruptly, though, she stopped and looked over the horrified faces of the tribe leaders.

"Don't," she said, suddenly calm, her voice soft, "call my children Abominations." She gave a stiff, awkward shrug. "It bothers me."

With that said, Annwyl continued on, slowly limping her way toward the exit.

"Annwyl the Bloody," the Anne Atli called out as she stood to her own towering height. Her long, blond hair reached down her back in a multitude of braids, and scars ran down her face and hands so that Brigida was sure they must cover her entire body. "Come," she said in the common language, her accent thick. "Sit. We will eat and talk."

Annwyl stopped, slowly turned, and faced her fellow leader. "Can I keep the head?" Annwyl asked, disturbing everyone in the room but Brigida. "I have to keep the head. Because I still need the eye."

"It is your prize. You keep your prize."

"All right."

"And we will have one of our healers tend to you while we talk."

"Why can't she do it?" Annwyl asked, pointing at Brigida.

Anne Atli stared for a moment, then asked, "Why can't . . . who do it?"

"Her." Annwyl pointed again.

Brigida smirked. She still hadn't bothered to reveal herself to the Riders since she'd had no idea how this whole thing would play out. But that was okay, because it made Annwyl appear even *more* insane.

"Uh . . . well . . . perhaps she does not have her healing equipment. But our healers are right here. Sooo . . ."

"Don't touch me. I don't want anyone to touch me," Annwyl suddenly babbled.

"All right," Anne Atli replied. "No one will touch you."

With a nod, Annwyl made her way to Anne Atli's side. There, she was given the second in command's spot. A place of honor among the Daughters of the Steppes. The queen dropped down, carefully set her prized head off to the side, and then as everyone settled in for one of the most important discussions ever to take place between the Southlands and the Outerplains, Annwyl abruptly announced, "I have to pee." She blinked, gazed up at the tent roof. "And I think I lost a back tooth. I hate losing teeth. . . . You need them to eat."

And, as one, all the tribal leaders inched away from the royal. All except the Anne Atli . . . who was the strongest dog in the kennel.

Although Annwyl still held her title as the craziest.

Chapter Thirty-Nine

Dagmar sat on the steps leading into the castle and waited. Her youngest daughter sat on her lap. The others surrounded her, leaned against her, their golden heads pressed against her arm or back or leg. To anyone walking by, the scene probably looked like a concerned mother keeping her daughters close. But Dagmar knew it for what it was . . . her children protecting her.

Seva pointed up at the sky. "Daddy!"

Handing her youngest child off to Izzy, Dagmar ran down the stairs and stood in the middle of the courtyard until Gwenvael landed.

As soon as his talons touched the ground, Dagmar reached for her son, but he slid off his father's back and into her arms. Luckily Gwenvael had quickly lowered his body so that the drop didn't kill them both.

Dagmar held her son close. He was alive.

"Are you all right?" she asked. Well, maybe she actually demanded it.

"I'm fine, Mum."

Rather than take his word for it, she decided to look for herself.

When she began to check his teeth, Gwenvael stepped in. Now in his human form, with brown leggings and boots on, he gently wrapped his arms around Dagmar while pinning her arms to her sides.

"He's fine," Gwenvael soothed. "But, more importantly, he's not a horse that's been brought to market."

"Quiet."

Izzy and Frederik brought the girls over, and Izzy asked, "How is everyone else?"

Gwenvael gazed at her. "How is who?"

Izzy growled in annoyance. "Uncle Bram? The rest of the Cadwaladrs?"

"Oh, them. Well . . . I'm sure they're fine."

"You're sure they're . . . ? Are you telling me you didn't check on them before coming back here?"

"It's not my fault. It was that bossy, one-eyed Rider woman. She ordered me back here."

Dagmar pulled away from Gwenvael and again put her arms around her son and hugged him tight. She did it because she needed to hug him and to prevent a slap fight between him and Arlais. Because that was about to happen. She could see it in their eyes.

"What are you talking about?" Dagmar asked Gwenvael.

"Var wasn't with Bram. I found him with the Rider. She was taking him to safety. Protecting him with her life from what I could see."

Dagmar's eyes narrowed. "That does not change how I feel about her whore sister."

"Completely understandable. But since she did protect our boy, perhaps we could use the term 'whore sister' a little less. Just a suggestion, mind. But still . . . seems in poor taste, considering."

"Elina said I had nothing to fear, Mum. That she'd protect me. And you should have seen the way she rode her horse," Var gushed. "And she still shot her arrows while her horse was moving. She can turn all the way around in mid-gallop so she can shoot whatever's behind her."

"Ooooh," Arlais sang. "Someone's in lo-oo-ve."

Var pushed his sister to the ground and she let out an ear-deafening screech.

"You fool! Auntie Keita gave me this dress! Now there's dirt all over it!"

"Oh, stop whining!" Var shot back. "You already have blood on the front of it." Var stopped. Blinked. "Wait. Why do you already have blood on the front of it?"

"Inside!" Dagmar ordered. "Everyone inside!"

"Mum? What's going on?"

"I'll tell you inside," she whispered to her son. "Now take your sisters and go."

Var helped his still-complaining sister up and dragged her into the Great Hall. Izzy and Frederik followed behind with the rest of the girls.

Once they were gone, Dagmar wrapped her arms around Gwenvael's waist and hugged him.

"Thank you," she said. "Thank you for bringing my son home to me."

Gwenvael hugged her and admitted, "I had little choice. That Rider woman made it very clear she wanted the world to be safe. And the only way to do that was to get your son back to you. I definitely heard fear in her orders."

"You heard nothing of the kind. Not from a death-welcoming Rider." She lifted her chin, resting it against his chest. "But she was right. If you hadn't brought my son back to me alive and well, I would have destroyed everyone and everything."

Gwenvael laughed and kissed her nose. "I'll keep that in mind. Now, I have a question for you."

"Of course."

"Where's your dog, Dagmar? Adda is never far from you."

"She was . . . hurt. Badly. Éibhear was heading to Bram's castle to get Var when communication opened up again. He knew you had Var and that his cousins were protecting Bram, so he came back here and rushed Adda to the kennel master, but I have no idea if she'll survive her injuries. . . ."

Unable to go on, Dagmar held Gwenvael tighter.

"You need to tell me what happened with my daughters."

"I will. I'll tell you everything. When we're alone . . . and absolutely no one in this world can hear a word we say. Ever."

"Well . . . that sounds ominous."

Those sent to Bram's castle had returned and now sat at one table in the Great Hall, mostly silent.

Although Bram and Dagmar had survived the day, Gwenvael and his siblings had heard from Rhiannon that quite a few other peacekeepers—dragon and human—had not. Within the same hour, it seemed, they'd all been assassinated by people or fellow dragons they thought loyal to them or, at the very least, loyal to the queens.

Things had changed in a most sudden and brutal fashion, but none of that would stop Gwenvael's kin. Gods knew, his siblings and the Cadwaladrs loathed change like horse shit caught between one's talons. But that would never stop them from fighting. From defending what belonged to them.

There was just one hindrance to moving forward on any bold plans they could come up with . . . Annwyl.

She was still missing; even Fearghus and Briec, who'd missed all the action while searching, had been unable to track her down.

Even more terrifying, they were all sure that Annwyl had gone off with Brigida the Foul. Once the spell that had blocked communications between kin had been removed by Rhiannon, and Morfyd and Talaith had found out that Annwyl had gone missing, they'd quickly used magick in an attempt to track the errant queen down. They found the last place she'd been in Garbhán Isle just before she'd entered some mystical doorway and disappeared. Opening doorways, they explained, was bloody hard work and often took weeks if not months of preparation. But this doorway had been opened suddenly and with no warning by a great power. A power they could only assume came from Brigida.

And if Annwyl and Brigida *were* together? Well, that was something that could only end badly. And that such a She-dragon might have her talons dug deep into Annwyl the Bloody of all beings . . . ? Gods.

What else did this day hold?

Izzy, sitting on Éibhear's lap, straightened her spine, and looked around the table. "Well I guess the Rebel King won't be asking us to protect his sister again."

"I don't know why he asked us to do it in the first place," Briec grumbled. "Her flame nearly burnt out the valley."

Celyn winced. "What is that flame she has? Me ankle still hurts where her damn flame hit me."

"Your whining sickens me," Elina stated, her gaze locked on the wall behind the table.

And Gwenvael had to know . . . what *was* she always looking at over there?

"I'm a dragon," Celyn shot back. "Flame should never hurt me. I should bathe in it. Like lava. Her flame, though, was unholy."

"King Gaius," Dagmar explained, "is returning to Garbhán Isle as we speak to see his not-even-wounded sister. He is extremely upset about everything that's transpired since he left, so I'd appreciate it if, when he gets here, you lot avoid discussing his sister's unholy flame!"

Keita and Ragnar walked into the hall.

"Hello, family!" his sister greeted. When no one answered, she stopped and stared at them. Then she shrugged and headed up the stairs to her room.

Ragnar frowned. "Keita, shouldn't we ask—"

"I have needs, Northlander! And no sons to interrupt us."

"Good luck to you all," Ragnar announced before following his mate up the stairs.

Morfyd, who'd been tearing tiny pieces off a loaf of bread she held and rolling them into balls, suddenly lifted her head, her eyes blinking wide.

"What is it?" Talaith asked.

"I . . . I think they're back."

And, with that pronouncement, no one moved. No one spoke. They just sat there, terrified at what they might find out.

Finally, it was the two Rider sisters who broke the silent panic.

"Are you all going to sit there like statue?" Kachka asked.

When no one replied, both sisters curled their lips in disgust, slammed their hands against the table, and stood. They were out the front door by the time everyone else got to their feet and ran after them.

As they all came down the stairs, Annwyl and Brigida appeared in the middle of the courtyard. One second they weren't there. . . . The next second, they were.

And while Brigida looked as horrifying as Gwenvael had always heard from his older kin . . . now, so did Annwyl.

The trip by magickal means didn't seem to bother her much, although Gwenvael had always heard those trips could be hard on a body. But perhaps it had not bothered Annwyl because she'd clearly already been beaten within an inch of her life.

Most of her face was swollen, one eye unable to even open—*gods, I hope she didn't lose an eye, too*—she could barely walk on her right leg, instead putting all her weight on her left and using only the toes of her right foot to maintain her balance as she limped forward. There were bruises and cuts all down her arms and across her throat. Blood matted her hair. Actually, blood covered most of her, soaked deep into her clothes and staining her hands and boots.

She looked like a waking nightmare, and yet . . . no one ran to her side. No one offered her assistance. They were simply too afraid to find out what had happened to do anything.

The old witch, moving even more slowly than Annwyl, followed behind the queen. She was smiling, but who the hells knew what that unholy sign meant. But Gwenvael now understood what frightened his mother and aunts and uncles. Even his father. There was just something about this She-dragon that made him feel . . . uncomfortable. An emotion Gwenvael rarely, if ever, had.

Annwyl finally reached the steps of the Great Hall and, with a sigh, she made her slow, painful way up, walking past all of them without a word. Even to Fearghus.

Finally, it was his Dagmar who couldn't stand any more. As she stood by the Great Hall doorway, she asked, "Annwyl, what did you do?"

Annwyl stopped and turned her head to focus on her steward and battle lord.

"I did what I had to do." Annwyl's voice sounded so raw, as if even her throat had been through hell.

Dagmar's sigh was deep, long, and painful. She'd had a very hard day, and all Gwenvael wanted to do was sweep her up in his arms and carry her out of here. But that wouldn't do for now. He'd have to wait until later.

"Annwyl . . ." Dagmar shook her head. "You may have destroyed us. We needed that alliance. More than we may have realized."

Annwyl nodded. "Aye. I know." She reached down and pulled a piece of parchment from her boot. There was blood on that too. She shoved it into Dagmar's hand. Not out of anger, Gwenvael guessed, but because she was too tired to be gentle.

"What's this?" Dagmar asked.

"The alliance. With the Daughters of the Steppes."

Dagmar held the scroll tighter. "Wh . . . what?"

"That's what you wanted, isn't it?"

"Yes, but—"

"Good." Annwyl took another step toward the Great Hall doors but stopped again. "Oh. Here." She pulled a very small bag off her belt and tossed it to Elina. "This is for you."

The bag hit the Rider in the face since it had been aimed more to her left than her right, but her sister caught it and placed it in Elina's hand.

"What is this?" Elina asked.

Annwyl looked back at the Rider. "Your mother's eyes. Do with them as you will. They're yours now."

Shocked into silence, everyone focused on poor Elina as Annwyl finally made her way into the Great Hall.

As for the Riders, for once, they were frozen, unable to speak or move. Not that Gwenvael blamed them. How could he?

Brigida walked slowly up the stairs, but stopped to inform Elina, "If you want, Rider, I can put one of those eyes in your head. But you can't take too long to decide. Them eyes dry up real quick and that eye socket of yours won't be much better in another day or two. Can't promise the new eye will look all that pretty, but it should work. But you're a Rider. Your lot don't care about pretty, do ya?"

Then Brigida cackled at her own joke and followed Annwyl into the Great Hall.

In silence, they all watched as Elina looked down at the small bag in her hands. She glanced at her sister, who replied with nothing but a shrug. A gesture that any sibling would read as, "It's up to you."

That's when Elina tossed the bag—without opening it—to the ground. She pointed at it and said to Celyn, "Burn it."

"Elina," Brannie cut in. "Are you sure? I know it's hard, but . . . if Brigida can fix—"

Her one eye still on Celyn, Elina said again, "Burn. *It.*"

Celyn blasted the small bag with nearly a minute of dragon flame until there was nothing left but ash.

Elina let out a breath, and Gwenvael realized it was not of regret . . . but relief.

Together, they all made their way back into the Great Hall. There they found Annwyl sitting on her throne. Her wounded leg was up on one arm of the throne and her head was bowed.

Celyn looked at Izzy and saw the deep concern on her face. He understood that. How could she not be concerned?

Dagmar slowly moved closer to the queen. "Annwyl?"

"They think I'm insane, you know?" Annwyl suddenly announced. "The Riders. But they have such a low opinion of Southland politics that I don't think it really mattered to them. I'm just one more mad Southland monarch." She took in a deep breath. Let it out. "But better me than zealots who try to turn them away from the life they've always lived on the Steppes."

Dagmar reached out, placing her hand over Annwyl's.

"I lost another tooth," Annwyl felt the need to share. "One of the back ones. I hate that."

"Annwyl?" Dagmar said, her voice very soft.

That's when Annwyl lifted her head and looked right at Dagmar. "I can't be the queen you need me to be," she told her. "I can only be the queen my people need. You do understand that . . . don't you?"

Dagmar gave a small nod. "Yes. I think I do."

"Good." Annwyl patted Dagmar's cheek. "Very good. Because I'd hate to rip the eyes from *your* head."

Then the queen leaned forward, kissed the shocked Dagmar on the forehead, and stood. She headed toward the stairs, where Fearghus caught up to her. He lifted her into his arms and carried her up to their rooms.

"For imperialist dog," Kachka stated, "she makes very good ruler."

Dagmar started to stalk over to the Rider, but Gwenvael quickly caught her around the waist and carried her out of the hall.

"I will hunt for dinner," Kachka said. "So we will not starve like dogs in street."

"I want to nap," Elina stated quietly.

But not quietly enough because her sister yelled from outside, "You are becoming lazy and decadent like these Southlanders!"

Elina shrugged. "I still want nap."

Dagmar wildly swung her arms until Gwenvael placed her on the ground in a small room off the kitchens. She didn't appreciate the laughter.

"How can you laugh about this?" she wanted to know.

"About your less than graceful ways?" Gwenvael asked with a grin. "I laugh about them all the time."

"That's not what I mean." She began to pace around him in a circle. "Do you see what's happening here? That old hag has come in and made Annwyl crazier."

"Dagmar, really. Annwyl has always been crazy. All you've been doing the last few years is muffling it. You've never shut it off. Not completely."

"And did Annwyl just threaten me? *Me*?"

"She threatens me and Briec all the time. I wouldn't take it too personally."

"That, in no way, makes me feel better!" She stopped in

front of him, stamping her foot. "Why are you being so bloody calm about this? Annwyl took out that woman's *eyes*."

"I'm sure she took them only after she took her head. You know Annwyl does her dismembering in a very orderly way."

Beyond frustrated, Dagmar started wildly slapping at Gwenvael's arms and chest.

And again . . . she did not appreciate the laughter.

Fearghus took care when he removed Annwyl's chain mail. He had to. She'd been punched so hard in some places that the metal links were embedded in her skin.

Once he got the shirt and leggings off, he stepped back and into his ancestor.

Considering his back was to the window that overlooked a sheer drop . . . he found her sudden presence a tad off-putting.

"I need you not to creep around my mate's home."

"Is this not your home, too, boy?"

"*Our* home is in Dark Glen. But this is the place my mate was raised, and where her kingdom sits. So I stay."

"To be close to her."

"I love her."

"You do know she's"—Brigida tapped the side of her head—"tetched. In the head, I mean."

"There's nothing I don't know about Annwyl." He stepped up to the old She-dragon, staring right into that somewhat horrifying human face of hers. "But there is much I don't know about you."

"I'm sure you know enough about me not to cross me, boy. Just because you pretend not to be afraid of this human, don't think you can—"

Fearghus chuckled, cutting her off. "Do you think Annwyl and I are ill-matched? That I am merely here to calm her? To soothe her restless heart? That in some way, in *any way*, she frightens me?"

Brigida shook her head, a little disgusted. "I understand now. Just like your father, ain't'cha?"

"Now, now. There's no need to be rude."

"You two unleash your females upon the world, grinning as you do so, and the rest of us need to clean up the nightmare they create." Her eyes narrowed. "But then . . . why did you allow that Northland female to . . . ?"

She snorted and slowly stepped away from Fearghus and the wide grin that had spread across his face. "You are smart, aren't you, future king? Enough in you of your father *and* your mother to make you much more interesting than I first thought. You let the world believe there's a collar on your mad dog so they all get close. Then they find out too late . . . that collar is nothing but an illusion. An illusion you orchestrated so that you can watch the carnage that comes after.

"They were right about you, Fearghus the Destroyer. Them villagers that you wiped from the earth all those years ago to get your name. You are a mean-hearted bastard."

"Oy! Hag!" Annwyl snarled from the bed. "Think this mad dog can get her wounds tended? Sometime this year perhaps?"

Fearghus, happy to see Annwyl awake and alert, grinned again.

That's when Brigida hissed at him like a coiled snake. "*Just* like your father."

After a short nap, Elina walked down to the Great Hall. She stopped on the last step and watched her sister drag two wild boars toward the kitchens.

They nodded at each other as Kachka passed; then Elina walked to the table—stepping over the double lines of boar's blood on the floor—and poured herself a chalice of wine.

"Where's the boy?" a voice asked from behind her.

She glanced over her shoulder and saw Bercelak, decided he wasn't that interesting, and went back to sipping her wine.

"Well?" the dragon in human form pushed.

"I am not his keeper, dragon."

"Aren't you his female now? Heard you two have been defiling the fur coverings together."

Elina faced Bercelak. "*His* female? I am no one's female. I am Daughter of—"

"Yeah, yeah, yeah. Whatever. I just need to know where he is."

"I do not know. And I do not think I like you."

"I let you live, didn't I? After you tried to kill my mate."

Elina thought on that for a moment, then nodded. "What you speak is true, dragon."

"What?"

"You are right. I came here to kill your queen. The fact I failed means nothing. So you letting me live . . . very generous. I will never forget that."

"Oh," he said, his frown suggesting he was confused. "All right."

She motioned to her chalice. "Wine?"

"No. Uh . . . thank you."

They stood in silence for several minutes until Bercelak said, "Tell the boy I'll be back tomorrow."

"Why leave when we can keep staring at each other in awkward silence?"

"Uh . . . I . . ." With a brisk shake of his head, the dragon walked out.

"Who was that?" Kachka asked as she returned to the hall and took the chalice from Elina's hand, finishing off the wine.

"Bercelak, the Dragon Queen's husband."

"What did he want?"

"Celyn. He called me Celyn's female."

"Did you punch him in the face for that?"

"Thought about it."

"Maybe you should get used to it," Kachka said in their own language.

"Why?"

"We are in Southland territories now. They seem to think the females belong to the males here rather than the way the gods truly intended it."

Kachka waved the empty chalice at her and Elina poured her more wine.

"We have to face the fact, Elina, that we can't go back to our lives on the Steppes. Whether Glebovicha has her eyes or not."

"Glebovicha is dead."

"The queen didn't say that."

"From what I've heard of Annwyl the Bloody all these years, she's not one for leaving her enemies alive and blind. More like she took Glebovicha's head and dug the eyes from them afterward."

Kachka shrugged. "Does it matter anymore? Whatever has happened, whatever alliance this queen has in place, means nothing to our situation. We can never go back again. Our people will never trust us now."

Frustrated, Elina tore off her eye patch and rubbed her damaged face with the palm of her hand.

"Are you . . . crying?"

Elina's head snapped up. "Have you become as insane as the queen?"

"Then what are you doing?"

"Sometimes it feels like my eye is still there. But when I close the other one, to kind of test my theory, all I see is darkness. That's when my face, from the scars on my forehead to under my chin, begins to itch like a demon. Sometimes I can't stand it," she snarled, rubbing her face

harder and harder until Kachka caught her hand, held it.
She finally pulled Elina's hand away but still clutched it
in her own.

"Do you know why, sister, I have no husbands?"

"You were waiting for perfect, perfect love, like the
Southlanders do?"

"Do you want to hear this or not?" Kachka barked.

"Sorry."

"With my record in battle, I could have at least ten husbands by now. But I choose none, because I knew that once
I had one husband or a thousand, and the first child was
born—I would be trapped there. In my heart, I've always
felt there was more out here for us. For both of us. And
perhaps, we will find it among these decadent, lazy imperialist dogs."

"I think we may have to stop calling them that. It seems
to bother them."

"Which part?"

Elina thought a moment before replying, "Dogs. I think
the dogs part bothers them more than anything else. Even
they admit they are decadent, lazy, and imperialist."

"Fair enough. Anyway," Kachka went on, "we are now
on this journey together. To see what the horse gods have in
store for us. I do not regret that. Having you by my side.
When Glebovicha sent you off that last time, Elina, when I
thought you would never return—I felt . . . lonely. But now
we can see this through as a team."

"It will be strange. Staying in these lands for good."

"True, but—"

Talaith stormed from the back door leading into the hall,
her dragon husband hot on her heels.

"Piss off, Briec!"

"What else haven't you told me, insolent female? What
other lies are you keeping from me about my perfect,
perfect daughters?"

Talaith stopped and spun around to face Briec, her finger

ramming into his large chest. "You do understand, lizard, that *I'm* the one who bore these perfect daughters of yours? That without me your perfect, *perfect* daughters would not even exist."

"One was lucky enough to sidestep the inherent drawbacks of being terminally human and the other is here because *I* was kind enough to bless your low-born womb with my royal seed, which means you should be grateful to *me*."

"Grate . . . *grateful?*"

"Is the screeching truly necessary?"

Spinning on her heel, Talaith finished storming out of the hall.

"I should have killed you when I had the chance!" she yelled back at him.

"I thought that's what you were trying to do!" the dragon yelled in return. "By *talking* me to death!"

Briec, realizing he wasn't alone, glanced over at Elina and Kachka. A wide grin split his face and he winked at them before going after his wife while yelling, "Don't you dare walk away from me, little witch! We are not—don't you dare throw dog shit at *me*, you crazed, heartless female!"

"But," Kachka continued, "I'm sure we will find much to entertain us."

She stepped away from the table, pulling Elina with her. "Come."

"Where?"

"We need to find potatoes and a blacksmith."

"Why?"

"If we're going to stay in this decadent crazy place, we will need drink. We will need *much* drink."

Elina nodded her head. "As always, sister, you are right . . . but what is the blacksmith for?"

Her sister smiled. "You'll see."

Chapter Forty

Celyn walked into his room and found Elina and Kachka sitting on the bed, several open and finished bottles of his uncle Bercelak's ale surrounding them.

"Good gods, you two didn't drink all that, did you?"

"It was a little weak—" Elina began.

"We use this shit to clean our armor." He snatched the half-empty bottle from Kachka's grasp. "We have a few cousins near the ports who sell it as a barnacle cleaner to the pirates."

"I thought it was smooth," Kachka said.

"I leave you alone for a few hours . . ."

"Speaking of Bercelak"—no, they weren't—"your uncle came by looking for you earlier today."

"What did he want?"

"Do not know. He said he would return tomorrow."

"Just great." That would not be an enjoyable conversation. No matter the outcome of today's events, Celyn had not only disobeyed his uncle's command, but his first priority hadn't been the queen. And he *knew* he'd have to hear about that from Bercelak. Hear about it but good.

Celyn placed the bottle on a small table. He heard one of the Riders get up from the bed and cross the room, but he didn't turn to look. He was too busy worrying about what his uncle wanted.

He felt a tug on his chain-mail shirt and turned to face Elina.

"Give me hand," she ordered.

Celyn did. And she turned it over so that the back of his hand lay in her palm. After pulling the sleeve of his chain-mail shirt up a bit, she gripped his wrist tight, then suddenly pressed a hot iron against his human flesh, searing it.

Celyn let out a surprised roar, almost unleashing a flame that would turn the room and every human in it to ash. But he managed to keep it in. Somehow.

"*What the battle-fuck was that?*" he bellowed.

"Now," Elina said calmly, "you belong to me. Not me to you. You to *me*. Understand?"

Celyn's rage slipped away with the sigh he released. "All right, what did my uncle say to you?"

"He said I was your woman. I am no man's woman. Remember that, Dolt."

Celyn rolled his eyes. "Kachka, can you leave us alone?"

Kachka walked over to him and held out her hand. "Give me bottle."

"Kachka, I don't think that's such a good i—"

"Bottle!"

He returned Bercelak's ale to her.

"Thank you." She walked to the door, but stopped, faced them. "Congratulations on your nuptials. You two make a beautiful, if unnatural, couple."

She walked out and Elina made her shaky, drunken way across the room, dropping onto the bed. She stretched out, fully dressed, and spread her legs. "Come. Service me like whore you are."

"Okay. We need to talk."

"No talk now. Fuck! We must consummate our loving union."

Celyn's mouth twisted as he tried to choose between being angry or laughing. He walked to the bed and sat down next to her. "Branding me like I'm a cow from your farm does not a loving union make. Dragon mates are partners. They work together to get through this long and challenging life." Celyn thought a moment, and added, "Besides, we fear our females too much to try to subjugate them as human males sometimes do to their women. She-dragons have no qualms about tearing our scales off one by one while we sleep, so we have to keep that in mind. Or wake up scale-less."

"I cannot believe you are *still* talking."

Celyn grabbed Elina's arm and hauled her into a sitting position.

"Are we going to talk about this like two beings who, combined, average more than three hundred years old? Or are some of us—*you*—going to be spoiled brats about it all?"

"Spoiled brat?"

"*Elina.*"

"What is there to say?"

"Lots!"

Elina fell back onto the bed. "Why must you talk so much?"

"I don't talk that much. I just like to ask questions."

Celyn stretched out on the bed beside Elina. He rolled onto his stomach, planted his elbows, laced his fingers together, and rested his chin on his raised hands.

"Do you think I'm pretty?" he asked.

Frowning, Elina's gaze shifted to his face. "What?"

"Can I stay home and raise the children while you go work in the fields? Will you tell me you love me and buy me pretty jewelry? Will you promise to be faithful? Forever?"

Elina squeezed her lips together, trying to look stern. It was not working.

"Will you call me lamb chop and brush my hair at night?"

She snorted and rolled away from him.

"Will your sister call me brother and stroke my head like a favored pet?"

Elina rolled back and covered Celyn's mouth with her hand. "I beg you to stop."

Celyn pulled her hand away, kissed the back of it. "At least tell me I'm pretty."

Why, *why* had the horse gods thrown this ridiculous dragon into her life?

She should be mourning the life she'd left behind on the Outerplains. She should be thinking of the kin she'd left behind. She should be thinking of the times she'd seen the suns rise over the Steppes Mountains.

Yet she was doing none of those things. Instead she was listening to a dragon ask her stupid, ridiculous questions.

But then she realized . . . she'd branded the dragon like "a cow from your farm," and yet he didn't seem to mind. He wanted to discuss it, but he hadn't gone for her throat or tossed her out onto the courtyard like so much useless trash. The alliance had been made; none of these people or dragons actually *needed* Elina's help anymore. And yet it seemed they wanted her here. As if they expected her to stay forever. Did they?

Did Celyn?

He was trying to have a rational conversation with a woman who'd imbibed nearly her body weight in ale. Again . . . ridiculous, but now she realized that was because he wanted her to stay . . . with him.

Suddenly, the loss of an eye didn't seem such a high price to pay to end up *here*. With this dolt.

This handsome, ridiculous, unbelievably chatty dolt.

Elina scrambled to her knees and placed her hands on Celyn's shoulders.

"You are right. I should have talked to you first before making your cock my property."

"Actually, that's not quite what I meant."

"You are like most males. Sensitive and moody and desperate to prove you are worthy. I took your chance to *prove* you deserve me away from you. And for that I am sorry."

"Again, I think you're not quite grasping what I've been saying to you."

"But you should not be afraid. You are as worthy as I deserve."

"Well, that doesn't sound very good."

"And I will treat you like treasured king when we are alone, and favored pet when we are in front of others."

"Now wait one bloody sec—"

"But, of course, my sister will be allowed to beat you whenever she feels need. And you will be naked, of course."

"Elina!"

"Just tell her you are sorry that you were bad boy and to please kiss it and make it better. Then it will be over before you know it."

Growling, the dragon shot off the bed and had the door yanked open before he stopped and glanced back at her.

"You're tormenting me, aren't you, Elina?"

"How could I not? *It was so easy!*" she screamed before falling back on the bed, her hysterical laughter echoing out into the hallway.

"Is everything all right with you two?" someone called up from the Great Hall.

"Aye," Celyn replied. "Everything's fine." He closed the door and faced her, shaking his head. "Except that I'm now mated to an idiot."

But, of course, his annoyed tone only made her laugh harder, which did not help the situation at all.

Chapter Forty-One

Elina woke up the next morning mid-orgasm.

Celyn was behind her on the bed with one hand between her thighs, his fingers gently playing with her clit or sliding inside her cunt. His other hand gripped both her wrists, pinning them by the headboard. His tongue danced along her spine, which seemed to only intensify her orgasm. She didn't know why.

But she quickly realized as his tongue moved up and down her spine that along with that astounding orgasm came a large amount of blinding pain.

Elina began to struggle but she didn't know if she was trying to get away from the pain or the orgasm that just kept going . . . and going.

As Celyn's tongue reached the back of her neck, he gripped her clit between two fingers and squeezed and rolled until her legs shook and she had to bury her head into her pillow and scream.

She really thought it was over when Celyn abruptly pulled away, but then he pushed her onto her back, ignoring her yelp of pain when her spine hit the mattress, and he roughly entered her.

He took her with strong, powerful strokes, and she let him, lifting her legs up so that they hung off his hips. She dug her hands into his hair and arched into him as he fucked her harder.

Celyn was merciless, but Elina didn't mind. It was a

beautiful morning. He was wearing her brand. And she'd woken up to an orgasm. What more could a woman want from a relationship?

While he continued to bury himself in her up to the hilt, he sucked on her nipples, which brought another orgasm tearing up on her from, it seemed, out of nowhere.

Writhing beneath him, her fingers now digging into his shoulders until she knew she'd broken the skin, Elina began to scream out again, but his mouth covered hers. They both came like that, gripping each other and screaming into each other's mouths until they collapsed.

Finally, Celyn rolled off her, and for several minutes they lay in the bed, panting and covered in sweat.

When they could speak again, Celyn held up his arm. "A bear?" he demanded. "You branded me with a bear?"

"The local blacksmith made it for me. It is my favorite animal and represents my tribe."

"Dragons eat bears."

"And I hunt them in the winter. I still like them."

He dropped his arm. "Whatever."

Elina started to move, but her back hurt so much, she stopped. "What did you do to me?" she asked.

"What?"

"My back. It hurts."

When the dragon only grinned, Elina ignored the pain and jumped out of bed. She raced across the room to a standing mirror she had assumed she would never have use for. Who needed to look at themselves in the mirror all the time?

But as she turned so that she could see her back, she gasped in horror.

"You son of a—"

"Morning, sister!" Kachka greeted as she threw the bedroom door open. "I thought we could train at the—

horse gods on the field of battle! What happened to your back?"

"He did this to me!" Elina snarled, pointing a damning finger at him.

"Wasn't losing an eye enough? Now you've defiled her body with your . . . your . . ."

"Dragon," Celyn said, pulling the fur covering over his waist. "It's a dragon. And she should be proud. I've officially made her my mate. For eternity."

"You should take him to river and drown him, sister, for such an affront."

Elina let out a sigh. "Wait. It's actually not that bad."

"*What?*"

"Well . . . when you think about it, I did brand him first. And if we are to be . . . what was that ridiculous word you used last night?"

"Partners."

"Yes. If we are to be *partners*, I guess we should both wear each other's mark."

"Especially when mine's a bear."

"He eats bears."

"So do we." Kachka shook her head. "I am disgusted."

"Don't know why," Celyn said. "You're not wearing my mark."

"Shut up, dragon."

"Awww. Is that it? Do you feel sad because you're not wearing my mark? Do you feel a little left out?"

"I am leaving."

"Don't worry," Celyn called after her. "I have some cousins who might find you cute in a pushy, lack-of-empathy way."

Elina shook her head as she went to the door and closed it. "Great. Now I must spend my life protecting you from my sister."

"I went a little far, didn't I?" he asked, chuckling.

"'I have cousins who *might* find you cute?' It is like you *want* arrow in that doltish head of yours."

"Forget your sister," Celyn told her, throwing the fur off to reveal his once-again hard cock. "Just come here and fuck me."

Elina was halfway to the bed when the door was thrown open again.

"Good," Bercelak said, walking into the room. "You're awake."

"*Does no one fucking knock in this house?*" Celyn barked.

"Knock? What are you? Human now?" Bercelak stopped and studied the dragon brand Elina now had down her spine. "Well, that didn't take you long."

"But look," Celyn happily volunteered. "I have a brand now, too!"

Bercelak frowned at his nephew's arm. "A bear? You let this human brand you with a bear?"

"I like bears," Elina told him.

Annoyed but probably unwilling to have this conversation with some human female he barely knew, Bercelak picked Elina up around the waist and carried her out into the hall. The dragon ignored her screamed words since neither of them knew what the hells she was saying. But it showed how mad she was if she'd reverted to her own language.

Bercelak locked the door and walked over to the bed. "You're no longer one of the Queen's Personal Guard."

Celyn shook his head and sat up. "You are such a ridiculous, vindictive bastard, you know that?"

"What?"

"Throwing me off the Queen's Personal Guard because I did what I had to do. She was not in danger. *You* were. But if you want to send me to the bloody salt mines with that idiot brother of mine, fine. Do it. Stupid as I am, I would probably save your bastard ass again. Because you are—much to my great disappointment—still *my uncle!*"

"Are you done?"

"Aye. I'm done."

"Good. You are no longer one of the Queen's Personal Guard because you've been made sergeant major of the Queen's Army. In that position, you'll be working closely with me and your father to maintain alliances, send troops where needed, and battle these zealot fucks coming out of the Annaig Valley."

"Wait . . . what?"

"I'm not repeating all that. You should have gotten it the first time."

"I'm . . . I'm sergeant major? Me?"

"Sadly, yes. Since you'll be forced to work closely with me. Your disappointing uncle."

"I know I owe you an apology for that, but it will have to wait," Celyn told him, pulling on a pair of brown leggings and boots.

"What are you doing?"

"We can talk later. There's something I have to do first. Something much more important."

"Tell your one-eyed female?"

"No. She probably couldn't care less."

Celyn opened the door and ran out into the hallway and to the stairs that led to the Great Hall. There he stopped and, grinning, he yelled out, "Oy! Brannie!"

Brannie, who was eating first meal with Izzy, Éibhear, Kachka, and now a blanket-covered Elina, looked up and smiled. "Congratulations, brother, on Claiming—"

"Guess who's become sergeant major of the Queen's Army?"

Brannie's smile faded and she jumped up from the table. "Not you. It *can't* be you."

"Oh . . . it's me. Me, me *me!*"

"You bastard! *Mum!*"

Celyn strutted back to his room, head held high, grin spread across his face. It was shameless, he knew. But he didn't care.

Not even when his uncle shook his head sadly and asked, "Was that really necessary?"

"To tell my sister that I now outrank her? Yes, Uncle. Yes, it was."

Elina, now wearing leggings, a shirt, and boots provided by the servants, was the only one still sitting at the dining table when the queen entered the hall. She carried with her a wood box that she held in both hands. She placed it on the table and sat catty-corner from Elina.

"Do you like strategy games, Elina Shestakova?" Annwyl asked.

Elina replied with a chuckle.

"What?" the queen asked.

"That was something that bothered Glebovicha greatly. That I was so good at strategy games but had no love of raiding defenseless towns. I was a great disappointment to her."

"A true leader finds what her people are good at and adjusts accordingly. One of the few things my bastard father ever taught me. He knew forcing people into uncomfortable roles would gain him absolutely nothing."

Annwyl opened the box and took out a game board and began to fill it with pieces made of fine marble. "The stonemason gave this to me. I think he was afraid I would take his head."

"Would you?"

"That's what the world would like to think of me. That I go around, cutting off people's heads for my amusement, but one really has to piss me off to get me to go that far."

Annwyl put the box aside and pulled her chair closer to

the table. She made the first move and while she waited for Elina, she said, "I heard you had Celyn burn your mother's eyes to ash."

"I did."

"Sorry if I offended you, Elina." And Elina could tell from her expression, the queen meant those words.

"You did not offend. Instead, you made me feel . . . like I had found home." Elina gazed at Annwyl. "No one but my sister has ever done anything for me before. But then Celyn—"

"He loves you."

"—and you—"

"I don't know you well enough to love you, but I do like you."

"—risk everything for me."

"I sent you as an emissary and you came back missing an eye. It seemed wrong to do nothing about that."

"Most leaders would have sent an assassin to deal with my mother."

"I just wanted to take her eye. Brigida said she could put it in for you but that we were short on time. For me, it was just kind of a tit-for-tat thing. I thought I could challenge her in a fight, get the eye quick, and walk away while still making my point. But your mother wouldn't stop hitting me.

"Then she said something about my children that just . . ." The queen's face briefly contorted in rage, but it was gone just as quickly as it came. ". . . set me off."

"Glebovicha always had way with words . . . and hatred."

"I took her head," Annwyl admitted, shrugging her shoulders like a small child. "But I didn't feel right parading that in front of you. So I left it in the Outerplains, near some sparse-looking woods. By now I'm pretty sure the wolves have got it."

"That's probably for best."

Annwyl nodded. "Probably."

* * *

Dagmar walked into the hall just as Annwyl and Elina were putting away the pieces of the strategy game Annwyl loved so much. She'd spent the morning at the kennels with Adda and was happy that her dog was healing well. It would be some time before she'd be her old self, but Adda had done her job better than Dagmar could have ever asked. And, in a bit, Dagmar was going to have a place made up in her room just for Adda so that she could heal in peace and comfort on a proper bed. Although Dagmar wasn't sure that Gwenvael would be happy about sleeping on the floor until Adda could walk again. But she'd worry about that later.

For now, though, Dagmar was determined to get some answers. So she marched over to the queen and asked, "What are you planning to do with that tower you're building?"

Annwyl frowned. "The tower?"

"The one right outside?" Dagmar practically snarled between clenched teeth. "You really can't miss it."

"Oh! The tower." Annwyl shrugged. "It's going to be a library."

Dagmar jerked a little. "It's going to be a what?"

"A library. Well . . . a library slash new home for Bram."

"A new home for Bram? You mean because of the assassination attempt?"

"No, I was planning all this before the attempt. Because of Var."

Now Dagmar was completely confused. "Var? What does Var have to do with anything?"

"We spend a lot of time in the current library we have. You know, discussing books, battle tactics . . . how not to let his father irritate him so much. He really wanted to go live with Bram, but I knew that would not sit well with you, although you'd probably let him do it anyway. But I need you focused, not worried about your son a few miles away. Especially now. Plus, we needed a new library anyway, since the one we have has already run out of space on the shelves. So I figured Bram could live in the tower rather than where he does and tend the books, since he likes to do that. Add in that Ghleanna and their offspring already spend most of their time here, and it just seemed . . . logical."

Dagmar briefly closed her eyes. "Annwyl . . . why haven't you told any of us this?"

"No one asked."

"Oh, Annwyl, come on! Everyone asked."

"They didn't ask me. Not one of you asked me what the tower was for. You just asked me what I was building . . . which was always a tower."

Dagmar frowned and glanced off. "We didn't ask you what it was for?"

"Nope. The only one who asked was Fearghus. At the very beginning. And he just smiled and nodded and said, 'That's a lovely idea.'"

Dagmar crossed her arms over her chest. "Are you telling me that Fearghus knew what that tower was? He *always* knew?"

"Of course he knew."

Dagmar rubbed her hands over her face. "I am starting to realize that Fearghus is more like his mother than any of us realized."

Annwyl stared at Dagmar with narrowed eyes. "What did you *think* I was building the tower for?"

Dagmar gazed at the queen and then . . . lied her ass off.

"Oh . . . nothing. We . . . didn't have a clue. That's why I was asking. Yes. *That's* why I was asking."

Celyn could only blame himself when he was put into that headlock. And he really didn't help the situation when he kept screaming, "But you report to me! Show me some respect!"

It got so bad that finally their mother yanked them apart.

"Both of you, stop it!"

"I can't believe that Uncle Bercelak put him in charge of anything except the queen's bowel movements!" Brannie screamed.

"Well, someone had to wipe her ass!" Celyn shot back, which got him a slap to the back of the head from his mother.

"I said stop it! You should be congratulating your brother! And you stop egging your sister on! Now apologize!"

"Sorry, Mum," they said together.

"Not to me, you little idiots. To each other!"

"I'd rather have my scales removed!"

"I'd rather be covered in acid!"

Ghleanna grabbed them both by the back of the neck and squeezed. Rather hard. "I. Said. Apologize."

"Sorry, Brannie."

"Sorry, Celyn."

Ghleanna released them. "I have no problem with healthy competition between my offspring. But when one of you does well, the others are supposed to be happy about it. That's what we do! *Do you understand?*" she bellowed.

"Aye."

"*I can't hear you!*"

"*Aye!*"

"Good! Now I'll hear nothing else about it."

"But," Celyn quickly asked, "I'll still get a feast to celebrate my promotion, won't I, Mum?"

Ghleanna gripped her son's face between both her hands and said, "Of course you will, my little hatchling. I am just so proud of you!"

"Thanks, Mum," Celyn said, and he tried not to laugh when he saw his sister making gagging motions behind their mother's back.

"Now I'll go find Annwyl and see when we can have this feast, and you two be nice to each other. Understand?"

"Aye."

"*I can't hear you!*"

"*Aye!*"

"Good."

Elina walked up to them with her bow and quiver. "If you look for Annwyl," she said, "she is gone."

"Gone?" Ghleanna's eyes narrowed. "Gone where?"

"I do not know. But I would not worry; she brought Court of Vipers with her."

Now one of Ghleanna's eyes twitched uncontrollably. "Court of . . . Vipers? And who exactly is that?"

"The Nolwenn, the Northlander, the She-dragon with white hair—the young one, not the queen—and the brown female who is size of hairless bear."

Now Celyn and his sister were standing behind their mother, trying not to let her see their expressions.

"And you call them Annwyl's Court of Vipers?" Ghleanna pushed.

"Yes." Elina gestured to her sister, who was dragging two extremely large buffalo behind her. Gods, the woman was strong. And lethal. There was one arrow each in those buffalo. No more, no less. "Do we not, sister?"

"What?"

"Call the queen's friends her Court of Vipers?"

"That we do."

"And that's a . . . what? Exactly?"

The sisters said together, "Compliment."

"A compliment? Really?"

"Of course," Elina replied.

Kachka explained, "Who would not want a court of plotting, vicious women standing behind them as they face their greatest foe? I know I would."

"As would I," Elina agreed.

"They will help Queen Annwyl to keep her sheeplike

people fat and happy. Who could ask for more in such a decadent, imperialist place as this?"

"I . . ." Ghleanna, her mouth open, looked at her son, then her daughter, then back at the Rider sisters. Eventually, she shook her head and walked away.

With their mother gone, Brannie first hugged Elina, then Kachka, while both women stared closely at the She-dragon.

"Welcome to the family," Brannie said around tears of absolute joy. "Now I must call to my sisters and brothers for the feast, because it's going to be *amazing!*"

The Riders watched Brannie head off.

"Your sister is skipping like child," Kachka noted.

"She is. She is very happy right now. And I owe that to both of you."

"Why?"

"Just because."

"Whatever," Kachka said. "I will get these buffalo to the kitchens."

Elina caught her sister's shoulder. "Annwyl has invited both of us to stay here. On Garbhán Isle. For as long as we want."

"You have to stay," Kachka replied. "You are now bound to this dragon like property, which means I have to stay because I am the sister of such a weak-willed female. How could I hold my head up anywhere with such knowledge?"

Celyn smiled. "And I love you, too, Kachka. Now that we're family."

"Shut up," she said to him. But he saw her grudging smile as she dragged the day's kills across the courtyard.

"You like to poke bear, do you not?" Elina asked the foolish dragon.

"I really do. It brings me such entertainment."

She took his hand. "Then you best come with me. I must show you how to outrun my sister's arrows."

As they headed toward the training field, Elina was forced to stop when Celyn suddenly did. She could tell by the look on his face that something troubled him.

"What is it?" she asked.

"Do you really feel trapped here? I mean, after this ridiculous brand of a bear—"

"I like bears."

"—I thought that you wouldn't mind if I—"

Elina covered his mouth with her hand. "I have accepted the fact that I am a pathetic female who deserves nothing in life. I am sure that Glebovicha's headless corpse is rolling around in her funeral pyre at being proven right about me."

Celyn gazed at her with wide, confused eyes and removed her hand. "I have no idea if that means you are happy or unhappy to be mated with me."

"I am extremely happy that I am mated to you forever—"

"Oh!"

"—which disgusts me."

"Oh."

She gripped him by his chain-mail shirt and pulled him close. "So you must spend the next few centuries, Dolt, making sure that I have no thought in my head but the pleasure you are giving my body. Do you think you can handle that?"

"Well, Elina of the Ridiculously Long Name, I am more than willing to try and try and try until we are nothing more than exhausted, sweaty bodies writhing on the ground to the great embarrassment of everyone around us."

She stepped back and patted his wide chest. "Then I think we will be just fine."

Epilogue

Talan stretched his arms over his head and yawned. He'd grown tired of examining these scrolls although they were filled with a bounty of knowledge. Brigida the Foul had an extensive library of arcane books and scrolls in her Outer-plains cave that would help him expand his skills. But unlike his sister and cousin, he had no need to spend every minute of every day learning. Not when there was a world to explore. A new world.

Through the lines of magick, Talan felt Brigida's return. He waited for her to enter the chamber since he had much to tell her. He heard easy footsteps approaching and said, "I didn't think you needed that damn walking stick. I bet you just use it to beat people over the head with. Anyway, it's a good thing you're back. It's getting a bit unwieldy out there, and you should—"

"Talan?"

Talan looked over his shoulder, his heart stuttering a bit in his chest. "Mum?"

She smiled and Talan bolted out of his chair and ran to his mother, sweeping her up in his arms and hugging her so very tightly that if it were anyone else, he'd fear he'd crush her.

But that was the thing about Annwyl the Bloody. She was so very strong. Amazingly so.

She kissed his face over and over between hugs. "My

son. My handsome son. I was afraid I'd never see you again."

Talan had never wanted to be away from his mother this long, but the Brotherhood had not allowed visits from or to any of his kin. He'd accepted that because he was getting what he wanted from the monks. But gods, how he'd missed his mother.

When he finally set his mother down, a still slow-moving Brigida came around the corner with Talan's aunts and Izzy. Unlike his mother, it seemed that traveling through mystical doorways didn't sit well with them. Even powerful Morfyd looked a tad pale.

Yet his mother . . .

Talan looked deep into her eyes and he saw it there. The rage. It tinged the irises of her eyes. Others called it his mother's insanity, but that was too easy. His mother was far from crazy. Instead, she was a whirlwind of death and destruction. But a whirlwind that loved her kin and, especially, her children.

He hugged Annwyl again before going to his aunts and cousin. He was greeting Morfyd when he heard the squealing and knew that Rhi had walked in. She ran to her mother and sister, hugging them both as if her very life depended on it. That's when the crying started.

Laughing and rolling his eyes, Talan turned to see his sister and mother staring at each other like two wary jungle cats.

Gods, the pair of them.

Talan walked over to his sister and shoved her into their mother's arms.

At first, they both looked horribly uncomfortable, but then Annwyl wrapped her arms around her only daughter and held her so very tightly.

"It's all right, Mum," Talwyn soothed. "I'm fine. I promise."

Brigida, who'd not bothered to watch any of the reunion but had continued to make her slow, painful way across the chamber, ordered, "Come on, you lot. There are much more important things to see."

They followed after Brigida, the only sound in the caves Rhi, Izzy, and Talaith's constant, uninterrupted chatter. The Kyvich that had accompanied Talwyn had gone off hunting and Magnus was asleep somewhere in one of the alcoves.

They walked up and up inside Brigida's home until they reached an opening that led to a stone ledge.

Having already seen this, Talan, Talwyn, and Rhi stepped back so that their mothers, aunts, and Izzy could step out on the ledge and look down over the valley beneath them.

"What am I supposed to see?" Annwyl asked.

"I've been hiding them from prying eyes," Brigida replied, "but the number just keeps growing."

Dagmar frowned. "Them?"

Grinning that frightful grin, Brigida raised her walking stick and slowly swiped it through the air. As she did, like a curtain, the protective illusion was pulled back.

Annwyl took in a startled breath as she moved farther out on the ledge.

Brigida gestured to the thousands of dragon-human offspring who had set up camp in the valley, waiting for their orders while they trained in battle and weapon techniques.

"More have been showing up every day," Talan explained. "Ready to fight. Ready for war."

Brigida smiled and announced, "Welcome to your new army, Queen Annwyl."

ACKNOWLEDGMENTS

Big thanks to Eileen J. Bell, O.D., for taking a few minutes out of the end of my eye exam to answer my eye-related questions for fictional characters that will never come to see her for an appointment. Your patience with me, Dr. Bell, was greatly appreciated.

Continuous, never-ending thanks to Dean M. for his battle and combat expertise on this book and all my others. Your help and willingness to answer all my many questions will always make me the "Squeaky" to your "Charlie." Heh.

If you love the Dragon Kin series by G.A. Aiken,
don't miss the brand-new Call of Crows books
written under her pseudonym,
Shelly Laurenston.
The first one will be available next April!

New York Times **Bestselling Author**
Shelly Laurenston

"Laurenston has a gift with words and humor."
—USA Today

THE UNLEASHING

WINGING IT

Kera Watson never expected to face death behind a Los Angeles coffee shop. Not after surviving two tours lugging an M16 around the Middle East. If it wasn't for her hot Viking customer showing up too late to help, nobody would even see her die.

In uncountable years of service to the Allfather Odin, Ludvig "Vig" Rundstrom has never seen anyone kick ass with quite as much style as Kera. He knows one way to save her life—but she might not like it. Signing up with the Crows will get Kera a new set of battle buddies: cackling, gossiping, squabbling, party-hearty women. With wings. So *not* the Marines.

But Vig can't give up on someone as special as Kera. With a storm of oh-crap magic speeding straight for L.A., survival will depend on combining their strengths: Kera's discipline, Vig's loyalty . . . and the Crows' sheer love of battle. Boy, are they in trouble.

GREAT BOOKS, GREAT SAVINGS!

When You Visit Our Website:
www.kensingtonbooks.com
You Can Save Money Off The Retail Price
Of Any Book You Purchase!

- **All Your Favorite Kensington Authors**
- **New Releases & Timeless Classics**
- **Overnight Shipping Available**
- **eBooks Available For Many Titles**
- **All Major Credit Cards Accepted**

Visit Us Today To Start Saving!
www.kensingtonbooks.com

All Orders Are Subject To Availability.
Shipping and Handling Charges Apply.
Offers and Prices Subject To Change Without Notice.

Romantic Suspense from
Lisa Jackson

Absolute Fear	0-8217-7936-2	$7.99US/$9.99CAN
Afraid to Die	1-4201-1850-1	$7.99US/$9.99CAN
Almost Dead	0-8217-7579-0	$7.99US/$10.99CAN
Born to Die	1-4201-0278-8	$7.99US/$9.99CAN
Chosen to Die	1-4201-0277-X	$7.99US/$10.99CAN
Cold Blooded	1-4201-2581-8	$7.99US/$8.99CAN
Deep Freeze	0-8217-7296-1	$7.99US/$10.99CAN
Devious	1-4201-0275-3	$7.99US/$9.99CAN
Fatal Burn	0-8217-7577-4	$7.99US/$10.99CAN
Final Scream	0-8217-7712-2	$7.99US/$10.99CAN
Hot Blooded	1-4201-0678-3	$7.99US/$9.49CAN
If She Only Knew	1-4201-3241-5	$7.99US/$9.99CAN
Left to Die	1-4201-0276-1	$7.99US/$10.99CAN
Lost Souls	0-8217-7938-9	$7.99US/$10.99CAN
Malice	0-8217-7940-0	$7.99US/$10.99CAN
The Morning After	1-4201-3370-5	$7.99US/$9.99CAN
The Night Before	1-4201-3371-3	$7.99US/$9.99CAN
Ready to Die	1-4201-1851-X	$7.99US/$9.99CAN
Running Scared	1-4201-0182-X	$7.99US/$10.99CAN
See How She Dies	1-4201-2584-2	$7.99US/$8.99CAN
Shiver	0-8217-7578-2	$7.99US/$10.99CAN
Tell Me	1-4201-1854-4	$7.99US/$9.99CAN
Twice Kissed	0-8217-7944-3	$7.99US/$9.99CAN
Unspoken	1-4201-0093-9	$7.99US/$9.99CAN
Whispers	1-4201-5158-4	$7.99US/$9.99CAN
Wicked Game	1-4201-0338-5	$7.99US/$9.99CAN
Wicked Lies	1-4201-0339-3	$7.99US/$9.99CAN
Without Mercy	1-4201-0274-5	$7.99US/$10.99CAN
You Don't Want to Know	1-4201-1853-6	$7.99US/$9.99CAN

Available Wherever Books Are Sold!
Visit our website at **www.kensingtonbooks.com**

Thrilling Suspense from
Beverly Barton

_After Dark	978-1-4201-1893-3	$5.99US/$6.99CAN
_As Good as Dead	978-1-4201-0037-2	$4.99US/$6.99CAN
_Close Enough to Kill	978-0-8217-7688-9	$6.99US/$9.99CAN
_Cold Hearted	978-1-4201-0049-5	$6.99US/$9.99CAN
_Dead by Midnight	978-1-4201-0051-8	$7.99US/$10.99CAN
_Dead by Morning	978-1-4201-1035-7	$7.99US/$10.99CAN
_Dead by Nightfall	978-1-4201-1036 4	$7.99US/$9.99CAN
_Don't Cry	978-1-4201-1034-0	$7.99US/$9.99CAN
_Don't Say a Word	978-1-4201-1037-1	$7.99US/$9.99CAN
_The Dying Game	978-0-8217-7689-6	$6.99US/$9.99CAN
_Every Move She Makes	978-0-8217-8018-3	$4.99US/$6.99CAN
_The Fifth Victim	978-1-4201-0343-4	$4.99US/$6.99CAN
_Killing Her Softly	978-0-8217-7687-2	$6.99US/$9.99CAN
_The Last to Die	978-1-4201-0647-3	$6.99US/$8.49CAN
_Most Likely to Die	978-0-8217-7576-9	$7.99US/$10.99CAN
_The Murder Game	978-0-8217-7690-2	$6.99US/$9.99CAN
_Silent Killer	978-1-4201-0050-1	$6.99US/$9.99CAN
_What She Doesn't Know	978-1-4201-2131-5	$5.99US/$6.99CAN

Available Wherever Books Are Sold!

Visit our website at www.kensingtonbooks.com

Nail-Biting Romantic Suspense from Your Favorite Authors

__Project Eve   0-8217-7632-0 $6.50US/$8.99CAN
  by Lauren Bach

__Klling Her Softly   0-8217-7687-8 $6.99US/$9.99CAN
  by Beverly Barton

__Final Scream   0-8217-7712-2 $7.99US/$10.99CAN
  by Lisa Jackson

__Watching Amanda   0-8217-7890-0 $6.99US/$9.99CAN
  by Janelle Taylor

__Over Her Dead Body   0-8217-7752-1 $5.99US/$7.99CAN
  by E. C. Sheedy

__Fatal Burn   0-8217-7577-4 $7.99US/$10.99CAN
  by Lisa Jackson

__Unspoken Fear   0-8217-7946-X $6.99US/$9.99CAN
  by Hunter Morgan

Available Wherever Books Are Sold!

Visit our Website at **www.kensingtonbooks.com**

Thrilling Suspense From
Wendy Corsi Staub

__All the Way Home   0-7860-1092-4 $6.99US/$8.99CAN

__The Last to Know   0-7860-1196-3 $6.99US/$8.99CAN

__Fade to Black   0-7860-1488-1 $6.99US/$9.99CAN

__In the Blink of an Eye   0-7860-1423-7 $6.99US/$9.99CAN

__She Loves Me Not   0-7860-1768-6 $4.99US/$6.99CAN

__Dearly Beloved   0-7860-1489-X $6.99US/$9.99CAN

__Kiss Her Goodbye   0-7860-1641-8 $6.99US/$9.99CAN

__Lullaby and Goodnight   0-7860-1642-6 $6.99US/$9.99CAN

__The Final Victim   0-8217-7971-0 $6.99US/$9.99CAN

Available Wherever Books Are Sold!

Visit our website at **www.kensingtonbooks.com**

31901055807947